LITTLE SINS

Meredith Rich

June 2006

Dearest Charlotte,

Here's a replacement for the one the dog chewed up. Thank you for being there for me during this last topsy-turvy year. You & Bob are the best, & it's so great to be reunited again.

With love,
Claudia
a.k.a. Meredith Rich

DOUBLEDAY & COMPANY, INC.
GARDEN CITY, NEW YORK
1985

ACKNOWLEDGMENTS

With special thanks to the following people (in alphabetical order), for their help, research, support, and/or editorial advice:

Pascal Aubier, Loretta Barrett, Juanita Brown, Eileen Fallon, Linda Fennimore, Laurie Frank, Barbara Lowenstein, Alan Nebelthau, Sarah Molloy, Fred Muller, Norman Shaw, Abner Stein, Susan Watt, and Belinda Welles.

The publisher thanks the following for permission to quote from the sources listed.

"The Penitent" from *A Few Figs from Thistles* by Edna St. Vincent Millay. Copyright, 1922, 1950 by Edna St. Vincent Millay. Reprinted by permission of the estate of Edna St. Vincent Millay.

"The Great Admissions Sweepstakes . . . How Yale Selected Her First Coeds" by Jonathan Lear. April 13, 1969 (Mag.). Copyright © 1969 by the New York Times Company. Reprinted by permission.

Women at Yale. Copyright © 1971 by Janet Lever and Pepper Schwartz. Used by courtesy of the publisher, The Bobbs-Merrill Company, Inc.

"The Coeducation White Paper: Everything You Need to Know," *Yale Daily News,* November 7, 1968. Copyright © 1968 by *Yale Daily News.*

DESIGNED BY LAURENCE ALEXANDER

Library of Congress Cataloging in Publication Data
Rich, Meredith.
  Little sins.
  I. Title.
PS3568.I3445L5   1985   813'.54   82-45604
ISBN: *0-385-18424-7*
Copyright © Meredith Rich

To Jonathan, with love and thanks

Little Sins

Prologue

I had a little Sorrow,
Born of a little Sin . . .

Edna St. Vincent Millay

Limousines lined both sides of Sixty-second Street, leaving only one lane for the taxis that were trying to get through.

"Jesus, there's the governor's car," the cabbie said. He looked into his rearview mirror at the gorgeous blonde shimmering in the backseat. Gold-flecked stockings, gold sequins, gold body and face glitter, gold sparkles in her hair. "What's goin' on anyway?"

"Where have *you* been? It's an opening. A new club. Night Life, that's the name of it."

"Yeah, just what the city needs. Another goddamned nightclub." The driver leaned on his horn. They had been sitting near the corner of Park Avenue for five minutes, and nothing had moved. He knew his fare would never get out and walk the hundred yards down the block to the twin town houses that were bathed in amber floodlight. Nor would she give him a decent tip. Her kind never did.

"This club's gonna be the best ever. Better than Area or Xenon or Limelight. Haven't you read about it in the columns? It's all they've been talking about for the past six months." The blonde's accent conjured up nights in Queens. "I'll just die if I can't get in," she moaned.

"Hmph," growled the cab driver, hitting his horn again.

The two women kissed each other briefly on the lips, then clinked champagne glasses.

"Tchin-tchin, Juno. Here goes everything." The Countess de La Roche, née Lydia Forrest, struck a dramatic pose in front of the floor-to-ceiling mirrors in the office of Night Life. Her hair was an extraordinary, and natural, coppery gold. Her dress was body-clinging black lace to her hips, with a spiraling Carmen-type skirt of dusty rose taffeta. Around her neck was a gold choker, with a large purple-gray sapphire, the color of her eyes, nesting in the hollow of her throat. Elegant and whimsical, that was her current style. But her clothes changed with her moods, and her moods had always been extreme.

"Not bad for thirty-two," Alex Sage approved, as he came into the room.

"Alex!" Both women ran to him and hugged him.

"It looks great out there. Everybody who's anybody is already elbowing for space. I made a quick check of the other hot spots in town, and they're empty. Danceteria has a black wreath on the door. The Red Parrot is trying to drag in tourists off the street."

Lydia laughed. "Oh, Alex . . . I'm so glad you're here."

"Where else would I be?" He kissed them both. "With my two women, my two loves. On this of all nights."

Juno handed him a glass of champagne. "I can't believe we made it. They were still screwing in light bulbs at quarter of seven."

"Ah . . . at quarter of seven I was creating your opening night present," Alex smiled. "I went all around town trying to find the perfect gift . . . Cartier, Tiffany, Van Cleef, the Mr. Bill Shop, the Ritz Thrift Shop . . . but there was absolutely nothing. So . . . I wrote you a poem."

"Oh, Alex . . . how sweet," Lydia said.

"Please sit, ladies. This is a momentous occasion." He pulled out a sheet of paper from the breast pocket of his dinner jacket and unfolded it ceremoniously. He cleared his throat, and his light blue eyes swept over them. " 'Night Life,' " he said.

> "Night Life cannot possibly fail—
> It was started by women from Yale,
> Name of Juno and Lydia,
> Who are—I don't kid ya—
> Exceptional pieces of tail."

"I want it framed and hung in the office," Juno laughed. "It's wonderful."

"I knew you'd appreciate it," Alex grinned. "And now I'd better go back and warm up the crowd. See you later." He kissed them both again. "I'm really proud of you."

"I'm proud of us, too," Lydia said when he was gone. She lit a Gauloise, took a deep drag, then crushed it out brutally into one of the crystal ashtrays with "Night Life" etched in gold calligraphy. "I'd be even prouder if I could ever give up these damned things. You're lucky you never started. God, I absolutely hate depriving myself . . . of anything," she said, laughing. Lydia's saving grace, given her extremes in mood, was her sense of humor about herself. It did not always surface, which made for some difficult times, but eventually she pulled her life back into perspective. Right now, her perspective was sharp and Lydia was feeling good about herself again. Well, it was about time. Her life, like her moods, had been on a roller coaster in recent years. Lydia believed that she had it all in control now.

"I don't know how you can be so calm. I've never been this nervous in my life," Juno said, refilling their glasses.

"I offered you a Valium," Lydia reminded her. She pointed to a plate of smoked salmon and toast that sat on the polished ebony desk. "Eat something. You should never be nervous on an empty stomach."

"I couldn't eat. Oh, Lydia, I want to apologize for being so snappish these last few weeks. I don't know how you've put up with me."

Lydia hugged her. "There's been so much going on, we've both been touchy. But tonight's our night." She dabbed a bit of a Jean Laporte scent behind her ears and in her cleavage. "Well, I guess I'm as ready as I'll ever be. Shall we make our grand entrance together?"

"Let's stagger ourselves," Juno said. "You go on. I'll monitor things from here for a bit."

"Scaredy-cat!" Lydia laughed affectionately. "Okay, see you when I see you." She went out, leaving the aroma of French cigarettes and perfume to mingle in the geometric-black carpeted room.

Juno Johnson buckled the straps of the Maud Frizon pumps

that lifted her to over six feet and checked out her own image in the mirrors. Her shiny black hair was braided into a chignon instead of hanging loosely around her shoulder blades as it usually did. Her long legs were covered by pencil-slim black crepe de chine pants. Over her rose satin blouse, a multicolored brocaded Ungaro jacket hung loosely around her hips. The jacket had been delivered this afternoon, a gift for the opening from Gustav Pallenberg, Juno's lover. She wondered if he would show up tonight. No chance, she decided. There were too many reasons why he would not be there.

Staring through the smoky two-way mirror, Juno looked down over the main dance floor, jammed with a Who's Who of the international celebrity and café society crowd. Juno smiled. It tickled her to think that they were all there because of her and Lydia. Lydia, of course, took it in stride; she was used to being around money and titles. Juno knew that she *should* be used to it by now, but there was a part of her that would forever be in awe of these people who now called her by her first name and clamored to invite her to their dinner parties and charity balls. What was that saying? You could take the girl out of the West, but you could not take the West out of the girl. That was how she felt.

Juno sat down at the video bank and began pressing buttons. Punch. On the screen in front of her appeared the candlelit sculpture garden, alfresco now, to be glassed in later when the weather grew cold. There was Lydia, making her way among the glittering people and lush vegetation, greeting friends, chatting vivaciously. She did it all with an easy grace that had impressed Juno ever since they had become friends, at Yale, in that extraordinary first year of coeducation.

Hovering near Lydia was Bernard Jullien. Bernard had directed Lydia in her brief but celebrated film career, and had recently made the move from France to Hollywood. They had also had a brief but tempestuous love affair a dozen years ago in Paris. And now Bernard was back in Lydia's life again. With him were his brother and sister-in-law, Michel and Marielle Jullien. They had been close friends with Lydia and her late husband, Count Stefan de La Roche.

Over by the bar, Juno spotted Seth Pratt. Seth's eyes were fixed on Lydia. Lately, wherever Lydia was, one knew that Seth would not be far away. Juno found him to be sullen, spoiled, and aimless. And Juno had another reason to be uncomfortable around Seth and his older sister, Camy. They were Gus Pallenberg's stepchildren. Seth and Camy knew nothing of Juno's relationship with the man who had married their wealthy mother. Juno was not sure whether she disliked the Pratts for themselves, or because, deep down, she disapproved of herself for her affair with Gus.

But, like many of the things that had shaped Juno's life, her affair with Gus Pallenberg had come upon her unplanned. It had evolved with an inevitability that had swept her along before she realized the consequences of what was happening.

Punch. Punch. Punch. Juno flicked through the club, screening the dance floors and eating rooms, surveying the celebrities, and looking for Alex. Punch. There he was, at the piano in the Mirror Bar. Juno lingered on his handsome image, sitting there flanked by a bevy of beautiful and famous women. There was Delia Manners, the star of Alex's first Broadway hit, *Plants*. Next to her was Camy Pratt . . . Seth's sister, Lydia's friend, Night Life's publicist. Damn Camy Pratt! She was having an affair with Alex, and while Alex had indicated to Juno that it was not serious, when she looked at Camy, Juno was not so sure. But she had to admit that Camy had done a hell of a good job with the club's preopening publicity. For a woman who did not have to work a day in her life, Camy worked very hard. Her public relations firm was one of the city's most successful.

Punch. Juno clicked off the monitors and decided to head to the Mirror Bar. A few soothing words from Alex were better than all the Valiums and champagne in the world.

The door to the office swung open. A tall, intense man with high cheekbones and thinning gold-gray hair paused at the entrance. Dressed in a three-piece Italian suit, he stood erect, head back, chin jutting out slightly, blue eyes staring intently at Juno. "You look ravishing," he said finally in soft Scandinavian syllables. He stepped into the room, closing the door behind him, and held out his arms. Juno slipped into them and they hugged silently, without kissing.

"Oh, Gus," Juno said. "I didn't think you'd come."

Gus Pallenberg stepped back, took her hands and kissed them.

"I could not stay away, you know that. I'm pleased you are wearing the jacket. I bought it for you in Paris."

"It's beautiful, Gus. I love it." Juno went over to the bar and poured him a club soda. He had cut down on liquor because of a perforated ulcer.

"Skoal!" he toasted. "The opening looks to be a smashing success."

"Yes, but then everyone comes to openings. It's tomorrow and next week and next month that we have to worry about."

"What's the point in worrying at all? Next week and next month will take care of themselves." Gus smiled, but there was a trace of sadness in the lines around his eyes.

"Oh, good advice, coming from you, the man who worried himself into a duodenal ulcer," Juno teased, pulling him down on the sofa next to her. "But what about Nina? How did you . . ."

Gus kissed Juno in midsentence. "Nina has gone to Switzerland, for another visit to the clinic."

"Again? Already?"

Gus nodded. "It's getting worse." She could hear the strain in his voice and did not pursue it. Nina Carruthers Pallenberg was one of America's richest, and most neurotic, women. Nina was obsessive about staying young. Now in her late forties and ten years older than her husband, Nina looked younger than he in the newspaper pictures Juno had seen of the two of them together.

"I have just come from the airport," Gus said. "That's why I'm not dressed for tonight. But I have to talk to you, darling. Will you have supper with me later?"

"Oh, Gus, why do you do this to me?" Juno turned away, agitated. "I haven't seen you for weeks, and now you show up here, on opening night of the club. I can't possibly get away, you know that."

"But we must talk. It's important." Gus's eyes pleaded with hers.

"No! Not tonight. Oh, Gus . . . I'm grateful to you for everything. But you have to understand, I'm not at your beck and call, whenever it's convenient for *you*." Juno stood. "Now, if you'll excuse me, I have to go down and greet people."

"What does this mean, Juno?" Gus put his hands on her shoulders and pulled her around to face him. Her eyes were not as angry as they had been. It was hard for her to stay mad at Gus.

"It means," Juno said softly, "that it's just not working. I love you, but I don't like living my life this way. Having you turn up every once in a while when you can get away from your wife. Let's just call it quits. It'll be better for both of us. We can still be friends . . ."

"And have lunch every once in a while?" Gus snapped. "You are what keeps me alive. I can't give you up. I *won't* give you up! You owe me . . ."

"I owe you nothing!" Juno shouted. Her olive complexion was flushed.

"You owe me just to listen to what I have to tell you. Please, darling, let us spend some time together. We must talk before you make any decisions. Tomorrow evening? At your place?"

Juno sighed. "All right. But it'll have to be early. I should be here by ten."

Gus smiled. "Until then, my love." He kissed her forehead. "The club will be a spectacular success, I know it."

"Thank you, Gus," Juno said as he was leaving. And when the door was closed and he was gone, she whispered, "I'm sorry."

Juno wiped away tears from her eyes as she walked down the private stairway to the club's main floor.

At six in the morning, the last of the paying guests were gone. A buffet had been laid out in the fourth-floor eating salon, one of five intimate rooms decorated in a variation of the club's predominant eighties Art Nouveau motif. Polished silver chafing dishes warmed chef Jean Raphael's nouvelle American cuisine creations: shirred eggs with morels and watercress, bourbon mousse topped with Washington State caviar, sautéed fiddlehead ferns, barbecued chicken wings, eggshells filled with oysters and bacon in a lemony sauce, home-baked cranberry croissants, California champagne, New Orleans chicoried espresso, and freshly squeezed juice of blood-red oranges.

"What happened to Bernard?" Juno asked Lydia. "I thought he'd stay for breakfast."

"He has a breakfast meeting with Paramount. He went home to shower and change," Lydia said, kicking off her shoes.

Camy Pratt, pale blond hair piled on top of her dainty head, wrapped a crimson shawl around her slim shoulders. "You can stay up for the rest of the day gossiping and gloating over your success, but I have to be at the office in three hours. Trying to convince the president of the Speedy Cola Company that I am his only sane choice to handle the promotion for their speedy entrance into the Northeastern market."

Lydia laughed. "Oh, Camy, you really are amazing. I don't know where you get your energy."

"Speedy Cola, no doubt," Alex Sage said, his long legs stretched along the rose suede banquette. "Or speedy something."

"Negative. You're confusing me with my little brother," Camy replied. "What happened to Seth anyway? He was pretty far gone last time I spotted him. I was terrified that he was going to blow lunch on the baroness," she giggled, high from too much champagne and too long an evening.

"I had Dominick and Sam guide him into a cab. Sometime around four," Juno said. "Dominick caught him slipping a pill into someone's drink."

Camy winced. "Oh *merde*. Lydia, you've got to talk to him. Maybe you can get through. God knows, I've tried. So has Mother, although she's never had any influence over him. She's spoiled him all his life, and he walks all over her."

"I'm working on it," Lydia said. "But tonight I could hardly give him my undivided attention."

"Well, I hope he'll listen to you. All right . . . good night again. Don't bother to see me to my car, Alex darling. You look far too comfortable lounging there." Camy leaned over and kissed Lydia's cheek and Alex's. She looked as if she might kiss Juno but thought better of it. "Good night, Juno," she said instead. "You really did a fabulous job designing this place. The lighting and the special effects are stupendous. Everyone was talking about them. God, isn't it marvelous to have a hit on our hands? *Au revoir, mes amis.*"

After Camy left, Juno poured orange juice into her champagne and raised her glass. "Here's to Night Life, long may it live."

"And to us," Lydia said. "The Yale triumvirate, fifteen years later. Alex, remember all your predictions in that play . . . what was it called?"

"*In a Smoke-Filled Room,*" Juno said.

Lydia nodded. "Right, how could I ever forget it? Well, who'd have ever guessed this is where we'd end up?"

"Certainly no one who knew us then," Alex grinned, raising his glass again. "To my two women, the constant flames of my life. I wish I could go back and do it all again. Except this time I'd break all the rules."

"What do you mean, Alex?" Juno laughed. "We *did* break all the rules."

"Then why hasn't it all worked out?" Alex said, the humor gone from his tone. He leaned his head back against the banquette. His hair was no longer sun-bleached and grazing his shoulders. The hole in his right earlobe that had once sported a gold stud had now grown back.

"I think we're all far too sophisticated for happy endings." Lydia ran her fingers through her hair to undo its sleekness and return it to its natural untamed look.

"But I want a happy ending," Juno sighed. A few moments later she spoke again. "I wish I could figure out at what exact point I lost the control over my life."

"That's easy . . . the day you decided to apply to Yale," Lydia said.

Juno nodded. "Boola, boola."

"No," Alex said quietly, "it was the night the three of us fell in love with each other."

A stillness settled over the room. Each of them, Juno, Alex, and Lydia, lapsed into private thoughts. After fifteen years, nothing had been resolved between them.

Something had to happen, to settle things once and for all. That something was very close, closer than any of them could possibly guess.

And it was going to change their lives.

Part One

Yale, 1969-71

Yale started a lot of fuss cuddling up to a certain women's college on the banks of the Hudson. After Old Eli was snubbed, all hell broke loose. The list is growing constantly—Vassar, Colgate, Hamilton, Wesleyan, Sarah Lawrence, Bennington, Amherst, Smith, Williams, and Lord be praised, even Princeton are getting on the bandwagon. . . .

"The Coeducation White Paper:
Everything You Need to Know,"
Yale Daily News, November 7, 1968.

. . . Yale announced that in 1969 it would at long last throw aside its 268-year-old tradition of undergraduate monasticism and admit girls. Up to a point. . . . For there will be just 240 coeds in next fall's freshman class of 1,265—and 250 girl transfers among some 3,000 students in the upper classes.

"The Great Admissions Sweepstakes . . .
How Yale Selected Her First Coeds,"
by Jonathan Lear,
New York *Times Magazine,* April 13, 1969.

If a woman tried to fill all the demands of the situation she felt like a cross between Scarlett O'Hara and Margaret Mead.

Women at Yale
by Janet Lever and Pepper Schwartz.

Chapter One

Santa Fe High School
Santa Fe, New Mexico
November 11, 1968

Director of Admissions
Yale University
New Haven, Connecticut

Dear Sir:

I have taught Juno Johnson for the past four years and feel that she is one of the most outstanding pupils I have had the pleasure to work with in my twenty years of teaching. She is fluent in Spanish, competent in French, charming in English. She's the most well-rounded young person I have ever had the opportunity to teach—creative, athletic, full of intellectual curiosity. Juno is a school leader and has been class president for the past three years. Her classmates and teachers alike find her intelligent, mature, vivacious . . . a real winner.

Yours truly,

Esther Lujan

Her first impulse was to get back on the train. The anxious ripples that began tensing her stomach in New York when she switched trains at Grand Central had mounted into an inner tidal wave here in New Haven. The station was a hubbub of bodies and suitcases, the majority belonging to fledgling Yalies.

This year, for the first time in the school's history, there was a smattering of female bodies hefting luggage and backpacks. To Juno's eyes, everyone appeared to know everyone else—from various prep schools, she guessed, or summers in Martha's Vineyard or the Hamptons. The platform vibrated with reunion shouts and giggles.

Juno Lightfoot Johnson of Santa Fe, New Mexico, felt a bit dazed as she retrieved her baggage from the porter and tipped him. She had never been east of the Mississippi before and, self-possessed as she generally was, she now felt overwhelmed. Originally, she had not been interested in Yale, but her mother had pushed her to apply. Later, when an alumni recruiter in Albuquerque interviewed her, Juno's interest began to quicken. The balding Albuquerque lawyer's enthusiasm about Yale and the opportunities and prestige it offered had been contagious. *There's nowhere in the world you can get a finer education,* he had said. *Besides, it's a state of being, of connectedness. Your Yale friends will be with you for the rest of your life.* And she had a chance to be a member of Yale's *first* coed class. It was a challenge that Juno could not resist.

By mid-April 1969, when the acceptance letters were being sent out, Juno had convinced herself that Yale was the only place she wanted to spend the next four years. She was terrified she would not make it. The odds were astronomical. She rushed home after school every day to check the mail and took each day of no news to be a bad omen. When the letter finally came, welcoming her to the Class of 1973, she went into a high of delighted shock and did not come back down to earth for at least a week. She was not aware, until later, of how astronomical the odds had actually been: 2,850 applications for 240 places.

"Hey? Want to share a cab? We have room for one more." A stocky girl whom Juno had met on the train was waving to her. Her name was Boo, and she was from Lake Forest. She had spent her summer working on an archaeological dig in British Honduras.

"Sure . . . thanks." Juno pushed her two suitcases and duffel bag over to the waiting driver and he crammed them into the tightly packed trunk. Juno's footlocker, stereo, and two boxes of

books and records had been shipped on ahead to Vanderbilt
Hall.

While Boo and a former classmate of hers from Miss Porter's
animatedly reviewed their summers, Juno tuned out and took in
the New England frame houses with well-tended green lawns
and gardens. It was so different from Santa Fe—the light, the
way the sun cast shadows on the elm-lined streets, the air, moist
and fragrant from a morning shower. She was used to earth-
colored adobe structures, and piñon trees and wild chamiso.
Now it seemed to Juno as if she had landed on a new planet. It
was not only college that she was going to have to adjust to, it
was the altitude, or rather the lack of it. Juno Johnson was accustomed to life at seven thousand feet above sea level.

The taxi turned off Chapel Street and pulled to a stop next to
Vanderbilt Hall, where Yale's freshman women were to be
housed. The building was an imposing Victorian Gothic, designed in 1894 by New York architect Charles C. Haight.

"Oh my God. Can you believe it? Look at all those boys hanging around to check us out." Boo's fingers moved automatically
to push a few straight wisps of hair out of her face. "Should be a
busy year. I figured out the ratio's going to be about eight guys
for each of us."

None of the boys offered to help them, but Juno was aware
that their focuses had scanned the trio and settled on her. She
knew she was attractive, but she had no idea how stunning she
appeared to the gawking cluster. The antithesis of preppy, not
completely hippie, Juno was a mix of Western chic (cowboy
boots, jeans with a silver-and-turquoise concho belt) and antique
eclecticism (a thirties straw hat and a black crushed velvet
jacket). She was used to the way she looked. Standing five feet
ten inches in bare feet, she was used to towering over many of
the boys with whom she had gone to high school. She was used
to her hip-length black-brown hair that had not been cut since
she was seven. And she was used to the mix of her blood—
Anglo, a quarter Navajo, an eighth Spanish. But she could never
adjust to the fact that people considered her beautiful. There
was no vanity in her. At least, at eighteen, none had appeared so
far.

Boo from Shaker Heights and her friend hastily said good-

bye, and Juno hoisted her bags to her assigned room on the
second floor. One of her roommates, a chemistry whiz from
Brooklyn named Marjorie Ginsberg, sized her up with squinting nearsighted eyes. Marjorie was already settled in, and after
greeting Juno with a harsh nasal accent that Juno had never
heard before, she headed off to Sterling Memorial Library. The
other two roommates had not yet arrived, so Juno staked out the
next-best bed. She sat, gazing out the window onto the interior
courtyard of the Old Campus, and for a few moments allowed
herself to give in to exhaustion. Her blood was still jangling
from the two-and-a-half-day train ride across country. A pan-
icky swell of homesickness began to take over her. Raising the
window higher to allow in more of the tepid breeze, Juno wondered how the hell she was going to get through the next four
years. And *if* she was going to get through the next four years.

"Er, hello, excuse me?" A small, slim girl with copper hair
and enormous gray-blue eyes stood in the doorway. "I was wondering if you happened to have a hash pipe?" Her accent was
Eastern well-bred.

Juno smiled. "Sure . . . somewhere. I'm not unpacked yet."

"Well, if you find it we're a couple of doors down. On the
right." The girl slipped out, without further conversation.

Juno heard voices and music wafting down the corridor, and
dug around for her pipe. It had been a going-away gift from one
of her friends and had never been used. She took it down the
hall.

There was no space to move about. Packed with young men
and women sitting on the beds and the floor, the dormitory
room was identical to Juno's, except for Beatles and Jefferson
Airplane posters tacked to the wall. Bass Weejuns, crewneck
sweaters, and Brooks Brothers shirts were the general mode of
attire, although there were a few tie-dyed articles of clothing
and Levi's.

"Hi, I'm Juno Johnson." She held out her pipe, and it was
quickly snatched from her hand by an aristocratic-looking
young man with a straight nose and reddish complexion.

"What timing! I'm Randall. This is Lydia . . . Darcy . . .
David . . . Whitney . . . oh hell, it's too difficult." Randall

opened a box of kitchen matches, removed a chunk of Moroccan
hashish, and lit it, inhaling rapidly to keep the pipe from going
out. Lydia, the girl who had appeared in Juno's doorway, gave
her a vague smile but continued talking to one of the boys.

Juno knelt next to Randall, took a toke, and settled into the
background, observing the group.

"My father was in Saybrook. That's where I'm going to be
next year. What about you, Josh?"

Josh laughed. "I'm merely slumming here. My old man went
to Harvard."

"Yeah," Randall quipped. "It's so convenient to where the
Mayflower docked."

"Oh come on," Darcy drawled. *"Everybody* has ancestors who
came over on the *Mayflower."*

Juno had the feeling that it was probably true, at least of this
assembled group. They were Eastern, had been to top prepara-
tory schools, and seemed to have known each other for a hundred years. Most had fathers or relatives who had been to Yale.
She had nothing in common with any of them.

"It's really going to be bizarre to see what happens this year,"
Randall said. "You know, I haven't been to school with girls
since kindergarten."

"I've *never* been to school with boys," Darcy said.

"Boys? What about all those exotic types from ghettos and
public schools? All that talented brilliance," Lydia said lan-
guidly. "Democracy in action. Inky's children." She was refer-
ring to Yale's admissions officer, R. Inslee "Inky" Clark, Jr., who
had initiated many of the progressive changes in Yale's admissions policy in order to combat Yale's elitist, clubby reputation.

"Well, kid, if it weren't for him, *you*—a mere female—
wouldn't be here," Randall said. "Don't put him down."

"It's about time the school moved into the twentieth century,
don't you think?" Juno spoke up. She had taken an instant dislike to Lydia. Clearly *she* had been accepted only on the merits of
her Yale forefathers.

"I suppose," Lydia shrugged. "But I'm a snob. I refuse to be
hypocritical about it."

"Well, I'm surprised you decided to come here with all the
riffraff," Juno said, standing. "I have to get back to my room.

It'll probably take the rest of the afternoon for me to get it into ghetto shape."

The others laughed, except for Lydia, who took a deep drag of the hashish and lay back against the pillows on her bed.

Back in her room, Juno put things away in a fury. For the first time in her life she felt underprivileged. She was at Yale on a partial scholarship, from a public high school in a small South-western town. She was just what that supercilious Lydia was talking about: one of "Inky's children," a university experiment. She lay down on her unmade bed, indulging in feelings of utter misery. Juno did not now feel a part of an exclusive 240. She felt like a freak.

Alexander Sage opened a bottle of Châteauneuf-du-Pape and put a Crosby, Stills, and Nash album on the stereo while the wine was breathing.

"Come on, Alex. Just give it five minutes. History's first all-Yale mixer. Aren't you curious to see these superwomen?" Bruce Hopkins put on his leather jacket.

Alex shook his head. "Not me. I'm not going to get involved with girls I'm going to have to face the next morning in my first class. Give me the exotic allure of the weekend import . . . Smith, Wellesley, Briarcliff. Who wants to date Yalies? It'd be like kissing your sister."

"What've you got against incest?" Bruce laughed. "See you later."

Alex poured himself a glass of wine and rolled a fresh sheet of paper into the portable typewriter that loomed out of the clutter of books and letters on his desk. He was not going out tonight because he had an idea for a new play, and he wanted to get an outline down before he allowed himself to be distracted. He did not have to worry about meeting women. They always found him.

After a while, Alex became aware that the phone was ringing. He considered ignoring it, but on the ninth ring he picked it up.

"Alex, darling! I'm *so* glad to reach you. I never thought you'd be there on a Saturday evening." It was his mother, currently Cassie Trevillian, currently residing in Dallas. Jack Trevillian, a top financial consultant, was the other half of her third or fourth marriage, depending upon whether you counted the first which was annulled after four months. Numero Uno, Cassie had told Alex, could not cut the mustard in bed. Cassie had been a virgin at the start of the marriage and, had it not been for an obliging friend of the groom, she would have been a virgin at the end as well.

"Hi, Mother, is anything wrong? I'm surprised *you're* in on a Saturday night."

"No, nothing's wrong. Jack's away on business and I decided to stay home and spend a constructive evening organizing my desk. I just felt like talking to you. Didn't Bruce tell you I called several times last week?"

"No," Alex lied. "He's pretty forgetful."

"Well, darling, I wanted to see if I could entice you home next weekend. It's been ages since we've seen you, and Jack could send the plane for you." Cassie paused. Alex could hear her taking a sip of champagne. She never drank anything else, and never more than two glasses per evening. "We're having a small party on Saturday. One of Jack's business associates from France will be there with his wife and daughter who'll be starting Vassar in January."

"Aha! I get the drift. You want me to entertain *la jeune fille.*"

"Well, yes. As long as you'll be home anyway it'd be so nice for her to have someone her own age to talk to."

Alex cleared his throat. "Wait, Mother. Hold on. I haven't said I'm coming. In fact, I can't. Carolina's coming over from Smith next weekend."

"Oh, darling, can't you get out of it?" Alex conjured up the petulant scowl that he was sure was on his mother's face now, with her eyebrows knitted under her curly blond bangs. "You can see Carolina anytime. Besides, I thought you had broken up with her."

"That was Angela."

"Please, darling, as a favor to me? I'm *longing* to see you."

Alex sighed. It was pointless to argue. Cassie would badger and cajole and call back constantly until she got her way. "I'll see what I can do. I'll let you know in a few days."

"Thanks, love. I knew I could count on you. But I must know

by tomorrow. I'm on my way to Palm Beach for a quick visit. I have to get everything organized before I go." Cassie blew a kiss into the phone and rang off.

Alex pressed the button, started to dial Carolina's number, then stopped. It was a familiar routine, one to which he usually succumbed, but why should he change his plans to accommodate Cassie? He loved his mother, in abstract, but he was painfully aware of how selfish she was. Not that many people would agree with him. Cassie was known from coast to coast for her charm, and she certainly manipulated her friends, lovers, and husbands into thinking that she put them first, ahead of herself, every time.

Alex began typing again, although part of his consciousness stayed on his mother. It was only in the last year that he had begun to analyze her and his relationship with her. He had begun to realize that he projected Cassie's egocentricity onto every girl with whom he became involved. And, because of this, he had become increasingly terrified of commitment. His behavior with women had taken on a pattern. He would meet a new girl and throw himself into the relationship until he felt that the young lady assumed he was hers. Then he would begin to withdraw. Being terrified of commitment was part of it, but being taken for granted and used for convenience upset him even more.

Although he had overcome many of the early insecurities that had sprouted out of the uprootedness of his childhood, a few remained. For all of his self-assurance, Alex secretly suffered from an anxiety that was classically female: he was afraid that women wanted him only because he was attractive, not for himself. He tried to work his problems out through his writing. That had kept him from falling apart on many occasions. He had started out writing Hardy Boys-type mystery stories when he was ten, and during high school he had dashed off short stories to *The New Yorker* and the *Atlantic Monthly*. Eventually, with a stack of rejection slips for his stories, he turned to writing plays. And at Yale he had concentrated his creative efforts on writing for the stage. Nothing thus far had been published, aside from pieces in school magazines and papers, but Alex's professors were full of praise, and he himself had confidence that it was only a matter of time until his work was presented on Broadway to critical and popular success.

Of course, that was not what his mother, his father, or his stepfather wanted. Being a playwright was far too flashy and flamboyant for his family. Alex, however, was determined to do what he wanted to do. And so concessions had to be made now to ensure good grace in the future. He reached for the phone and dialed.

"Carolina, babe, I've got some bad news. Next weekend's off. Big family gathering at home and I'm afraid I can't get out of it."

"There was another call for you, Lydia. The guy at Princeton."

Lydia tossed her books on the bed and shrugged. "I really should write him a letter, but I haven't had time. God, he's persistent. You'd think he'd get the hint." She opened her closet door to the blend of pastels that hung there.

"Cece," she told her roommate, "I'm giving you all these clothes."

"What? Don't you want them?"

Lydia Forrest shook her head. "My mother bought them for me. College clothes. We've never exactly agreed on style. Well, at Brearley I kind of had to conform. But not here. From now on I'm going to be me."

"Jesus, Lydia, no one could ever accuse you of being a conformist."

"Cece, you have no idea what nonconformity is all about. You think I'm different because I once waded around the fountains in front of the Seagram Building with my clothes on. But that was dumb and childish. There are parts of me that nobody knows. Nobody."

"I'll bet we'll see them before the year's over," Cece said, going through the garments in Lydia's closet.

Lydia lit a cigarette. "Oh God, Cece. I'm so restless." She put on a newly purchased secondhand denim jacket. "I'm going over to Tim's room. They usually have something to smoke over there. And I need the company of men."

"What's with her?" Lydia's other roommate, who had been reading in bed, looked up after she left.

"To know Lydia is to love her," Cece said. "If you can put up with her. She's in one of her dramatic moods tonight. Probably getting her period."

Chapter Two

"Juno, what do *you* think? I mean, as a woman, how do you feel about the draft?" Randall Fitzpatrick and his friends passed around a joint. Juno was the only woman in the room. The boys craved her company, vied for her attention, were eager to hear her point of view on every subject. It was early December, a few weeks before Christmas vacation, and women were still an exciting novelty at Yale. But during serious debates and verbal word games, Juno felt shut out after she had given her opinion.

"I don't want to kill anybody, or be killed. But it's not fair for you guys to fight either. The whole point is to end war. There shouldn't even be a draft system. But if it has to continue, then it should be coed, with men and women being taught the same things. Anyway, armies should do more than fight. They should teach, like VISTA or the Peace Corps."

"Right on, Juno. But say we were each given a gun and trained to use it. What if you were face-to-face with the enemy?"

"I don't think I could kill anybody, but I do know how to use a gun. I learned when I was eleven. My grandfather used to take me bear hunting."

"Bear hunting. Far out. I love this frontier woman." Randall put his arm around Juno. "Hey, let's go over to Rudy's Bar and continue this discussion over a beer."

"Not me," Juno said. "There's a poetry reading I want to catch."

"*Poetry?*" Randall groaned. "You have *got* to be kidding." But in the end he went with her.

The poetry reading was in a small lecture room at Saybrook College. About twenty-five people showed up to hear three undergraduate poets read their works. The first was forgettable, the second unfathomable.

"Let's get out of here," Randall whispered.

"Wait," Juno said. "This guy looks interesting. Let's give it a few minutes."

"Max Milton? He's an asshole. He was a couple of years ahead of me at Andover."

"Well, go if you want to. I'm staying."

"Oh, all right." Randall settled sulkily down in his seat.

Max Milton stepped up to the podium and laid a sheaf of papers dramatically down. His face was gaunt, but with full, sensual lips that twisted into a slight sneer as he looked at the audience and smiled. Black silky hair flowed down his back. He had on a studied outfit: an ankle-length black cape, a white silk shirt, and buccaneer's pants with high boots.

"My first poem is called 'Diversion with Hennaed Hair.'" Max Milton scanned the audience with dark, intense eyes that fell on Juno and lingered there for a long moment before moving on. As he read, his eyes kept coming back to her and Juno barely heard the words as she felt the electric current that was passing between them.

When the reading was over and she was leaving with Randall, Max Milton approached them.

"Hello, Fitzpatrick," he said, speaking to Randall, but with his eyes on Juno. "I didn't know you were into poetry. Aren't you going to introduce me to your friend?"

Randall grudgingly made the introductions.

"I really liked your poems," Juno smiled.

"I'd like to give you one." He placed a folded sheet of paper in her hand.

"Come on, Juno. We've got to go," Randall said, taking her arm and steering her toward the door.

"Perhaps we'll meet again," Max called after her.

"Boy, what a pretentious asshole," Randall said as they left the building and walked out into the cold, crisp night.

"Well, I don't know . . . it was kind of interesting."

Randall shrugged. "Why don't we go over to Hungry Charlie's and see if anybody's there?"

"I better not. I've got a paper due."

When she got back to her room, Juno looked at the poem Max
had given her. She found that he had scrawled a note across the
bottom inviting her to his room the next afternoon for tea.

Juno could smell incense as she knocked on the door of Max
Milton's room.

"Come in," he said.

He was sitting cross-legged at a low table facing the door. He
was barefoot, wearing black silk pajama pants and an embroidered kimono top. A black silk scarf was tied around his forehead. There was a Japanese teapot with two cups before him,
flanked by tiny incense burners. Strains of Oriental lute music
came from the record player.

"Welcome." He pressed his palms together and bowed his
head. "Take off your shoes and come sit."

Juno smiled and left her boots at the door. She sat opposite
him. Ceremoniously, Max poured a cup of ginseng tea and
handed it to her, then poured one for himself. He raised it to his
forehead, bowing again, in a gesture of respect. He did not speak
while he drank his tea. Juno felt a bit foolish, but she was certainly not going to break the mood. She took her cue from Max
and played along. There was something wonderfully theatrical
about the moment—the exotic music, the heavy fragrance of
myrrh in the air, the eerie pantomime of the tea ceremony. It
was not necessary to take it completely seriously to be caught up
in it.

"I've written a poem for you," Max said finally. He reached
into the breast of his kimono and pulled out a piece of Cor-
rasable Bond on which there were a few typed stanzas. "The
Dark Lady," he began, "crouches like a panther . . . sleek,
loins tensed, glistening like water on a stone . . ."

Juno listened raptly. She had never had a poem written for
her before. Max's eyes kept coming up to hers as he read, and
Juno felt her body beginning to tingle with anticipation. She
tried to decide what she would do, how she would react, when
he made his move.

"Come here," he said. He held out his hand and she took it,
and let herself be drawn around to his side. He kissed her. It was
an expert kiss, slow and deep and exciting, and she closed her

eyes and responded. But when, a moment later, she felt his hand
sliding swiftly up between her thighs, she pushed it away.

"No, Max," she panted. "Please, no."

He stared at her, his dark eyes glittering in the shadows beneath his white patrician brow. "Come here," he said.

"No . . . really." Apologetic and confused, she stood up and
went to the door. Max made no move to stop her. His lips curled
with sardonic patience as he watched her struggle into her
boots. "I'm sorry, Max," she said. "It's just . . . it's just too
fast."

"Then I'll just have to go slower, won't I?"

Juno smiled and closed the door. As she walked across the
campus she felt like an overwound spring. Max was the first boy
she had met at Yale who had really turned her on. But she did
not want him to think that she was some easy hick.

She thought about the poem he had written for her. "The
Dark Lady." Away from the drama of his presentation, Juno
began to suspect that it was not very good. But on the other
hand, she was not sophisticated about poetry. And Max Milton
seemed to her to be the most sophisticated man she had ever
met.

When she got back to her room, Juno found one of her roommates, Clara, trying to fasten the snaps on her bulging suitcase.

"Sit on this for me, will you, Juno?"

Juno sat on the lid while Clara clicked the snaps. "Where are
you going?"

"I'm moving in with Justin."

"Who?"

"*Jus*tin. You know, the guy I met at that SDS rally? He's a
junior."

"Clara . . . that was just last Saturday."

"What difference does that make? He's really cool."

"Well, yeah, but I mean, to move in with him . . . you barely
know him."

Clara smiled. "I'm in love. I'll get to know him." She picked
up her suitcase. "Well . . . see you around."

Juno sat on the bed. She was beginning to wonder if there was
some new boat sailing through New Haven, and she was miss-

ing it. She had always felt that her values were good. She took pride in knowing herself. But maybe that was only in Santa Fe. Here she seemed to be a fish out of water.

It was a self-indulgent time. The Yale experience was dislocating not only for Juno, but for a lot of people as well. There was not much focus on the classroom; no requirements, no grades, only pass-fail. Yet there was an overriding pressure to *do*, to make one's own statement. People acted out their neuroses. Some tried to call as little attention as possible to themselves. A great many more were hell-bent on becoming campus characters.

The atmosphere at Yale was as highly sexual as it was intellectual. No one quite knew how to handle having women at this formerly all-male bastion of education. The coeds would have said the men had an easier time of it, but few of the men would have agreed. It was a difficult time for everyone.

And never again in their lives would the women be so outnumbered by the opposite sex. The coeds were on display and in demand during every waking hour. Sexual promiscuity abounded, yet they still had to walk the line between being easy and being labeled uptight or a cock teaser. The question of sex, whether to do it or not to do it, was with them all the time. As the year went on there were fewer virgins, but those who lost their virginity did not feel any more secure.

Scores of women from Smith, Vassar, Wellesley, Briarcliff, and other colleges were still imported regularly for weekends. Many of the men, used to these weekend relationships, felt it was an easier way to live. It was also an easy structure within which to break off a relationship. But not so with the coeds. There they were, all the time, day in, day out. They could not be got rid of.

Juno went out a lot. With each man she felt as if she were dating all his friends as well. She rapidly got to know men in different cliques and in the various Yale residential colleges, twelve of which made up the undergraduate part of the university. With the preppies she drank daiquiris during football games at the Yale Bowl. She listened to rock music and smoked dope with the druggies, ate tofu and brown rice with the hippies. The politicos enlisted her passionate support for antiwar rallies and the Black Panthers. Juno floated from one world to the next.

But Max Milton did not fit into any of these groups exactly. He seemed, in his Eastern sophisticate sort of way, to be a bit of each. Perhaps that was what attracted Juno to him.

On their third date, just before school broke for Christmas vacation, Max took her out for Chinese food and then to Ingmar Bergman's *The Virgin Spring*. Back at his room he poured two glasses of aquavit.

"Skoal." He looked into her eyes. "You're tense," he said. "Lie down. I'll give you a Swedish massage."

Oh boy, Juno thought; but then, *why not?* It was not the ploy she would have hoped for from the worldly Max Milton, but she had prepared herself that this would be The Night.

"Okay," she said, and stretched out on Max's *futon* on the floor.

Max knelt astride her and slipped his hands up along her back beneath her sweatshirt. He began massaging from the small of her back up to her shoulders, then down again to her shoulder blades, casually squeezing his thumbs together on her bra strap until the clasp came apart.

"Why don't you take off your shirt?"

Well, here goes, Juno thought as she raised up enough to strip the sweatshirt over her head. She lay down again, trying to appear casual. But her heart was pounding. She hoped her inexperience would not show.

"Let's get rid of these, too," he said huskily, and reached beneath her for the button of her jeans.

"No," Juno said, then bit her lip. "Not yet."

"Come on, Juno, for God's sake, you can't stay a virgin all your life."

"What makes you think I'm a virgin?"

Max laughed sardonically. "You're a freshman. You're from New Mexico. And you're acting like one."

Juno unfastened her jeans.

Max opened a teakwood cigarette case and produced a thin

joint. "This is excellent stuff," he said, lighting it and passing it to Juno. "Maui Wowie. You only need a toke or two."

Juno took a deep drag and lay back on the *futon*. The grass hit her like a truck. She raised her hips to allow Max to pull off her jeans and panties.

Max knelt above her, naked, and began massaging her breasts. Juno moaned.

"Dark Lady . . . panther," he gasped, his hands dipping between her thighs. "Loins tensed and glistening . . ." And with a little cry he plunged into her.

"Oh!" she cried out. It was like being struck by lightning. She arched her pelvis and brought her legs up around his back. She seemed to be spinning up through the funnel of a tornado, as Max pounded against her and his hot breath rasped in her ear. She felt her muscles tensing and she rose toward the mystery of orgasm. It was there, just above her, coming closer with every stroke. . . .

And then Max's body stiffened, and he screamed. Juno screamed too. It had been so close. She could almost reach that patch of brilliant blue at the top of the funnel, but even as she writhed and twisted desperately for it, she felt herself drifting back down.

Max slipped out of her and leaned back against the cushion, smiling at her smugly. "You're lucky to have a Yale man for your first time," he said.

Unlike many of the freshmen coeds, Juno Johnson had not arrived at Yale a virgin. She and her high school boyfriend, David Abeyta, had been their class's golden couple. They were well-suited in many ways, but David was considerably more conservative than Juno. He made grand plans for their future together: he would go to law school, then they would marry and have children. Sex, he believed, should wait until then. Juno, however, was not so patient. She was a sensualist. When they made out, it always seemed much harder for her to put on the brakes than for him. And finally, after two years of going steady, she seduced him.

It had been in the waning hours of their postgraduation party when everyone had coupled off into the night. Exhilarated from the long-awaited day, Juno had not wanted the evening to come to an end. She talked David into driving out to Tano Road to watch the sunrise over the Sangre de Cristo Mountains. With the radio blaring Janis Joplin, they sat on the hood of the car and shared a six-pack of Carta Blanca. As the sky grew lighter Juno, bold from too much beer, kicked off her sandals and stripped down to her bikini panties, right before David's disbelieving eyes.

"Come on, David," she said. "This is it. The start of our future together." She danced over to him and slowly began unbuttoning his shirt.

"Juno, you've had too much to drink. I'd better get you home."

"You'll have to deliver me naked. I've made up my mind . . . I'm not getting dressed." Juno began to undo his belt, brushing her hand seductively against the bulge she saw in his pants.

David was breathing more heavily, trying to maintain control. "Juno, come on. We can't. You'll regret it in the morning."

"Davey, it *is* morning. And the only thing I'll regret is if we don't do it. I know you want to marry a virgin, but this is 1969 . . . people don't marry virgins anymore. Take me now, and when we finally get married we can make it retroactive."

David put his arm around her. "I'm trying to be strong enough for both of us."

"I'm strong too, and this is what I want." Juno took off her panties. Then she kissed him, pressing her bare hips into his fully grown erection.

"I love you, Juno. You know I want you more than anything." David dug his fingers into her back and abruptly turned away. He took a deep breath and pounded his fists against the cold blue metal of the car hood. "I'm giving you one last chance to change your mind." His voice was hoarse and he coughed to clear it. "After that, if I start I don't think I'll be able to stop." He paused. "I have a rubber in my wallet. My brother gave it to me for my birthday."

Juno squeezed her arms around David's waist. "I love you. You're the only person I've ever wanted. This is the right time. We've just graduated and we're both going off to college in the fall. It's symbolic."

Spreading out her Mexican peasant dress on the hard ground next to a juniper tree, Juno lay down, looking up at David with dark, loving eyes. Embarrassed and anxious, David took off his clothes as fast as he could.

"Jesus, it's cold!"

"Come here. I'll get you warm."

David inched his slim body close to hers, and tentatively touched her breasts.

"Ohhh . . ." Juno closed her eyes as his hands, growing bolder by her response, began stroking places that had been touched before only in her fantasies.

David's lips rubbed against hers, and his tongue darted wildly around her mouth. It was not the same as their kisses in the past. This time David was more urgent. His hands moved down her torso and he began rubbing Juno's pubic area in a furious, hit-or-miss fashion. She heard an unfamiliarly deep voice gasping at the delights she felt, and realized it was her voice of pleasure, *her* moans.

David paused while he fumbled nervously with the rubber and pulled it on. Then his erection, cool and greasy from the lubricated condom, poked around between her thighs. After a few awkward stabs he guided himself into her. The sudden thrust caused a twinge of pain, not at all as Juno had imagined, but the pain did not last long. As their bodies rocked together Juno, breathing deeply, began to feel she was going someplace she had never been before.

And then it stopped. Within seconds, David choked out her name and his hot body shuddered. Sweating, he lowered himself down next to her. The penis that had been lively and pulsing was now like a candle that had extinguished itself in soft wax.

It—The Big Event—was over, the experience that Juno had daydreamed about since she was fourteen. Afterward, Juno clung to David and pretended that it had been wonderful. She did not know how else to react. She consoled herself with the thought that it was just inexperience, that it would get better.

But it did not get better. She had thought that once the barriers were down their sex life would blossom, but their lovemaking as the summer progressed was infrequent and awkward. By the time she left for Yale, she was secretly questioning whether she would ever marry David Abeyta. She adored him, but there was something missing between them. Either that, or there was something missing within herself.

For as long as she could remember, Juno had loved art. Her father, Hollis Johnson, was a painter and she too had wanted to be an artist when she was younger. Her mother Maria was a cellist. As a young woman she had studied with Pablo Casals and had been an exceptional pupil. Casals had wanted Maria to stay and work with him, but then she met Hollis and fell in love. She thought he was more important than a concert career, and they had married. Juno was born within a year.

Juno's mother seldom regretted her decision. She loved her husband; and in the summers she still played in the orchestra of the Santa Fe Opera. But the boundaries of her world sometimes seemed terribly small to Maria, and she did not want her daughter's horizons to be as limited as hers had become. She was ambitious for Juno and pushed her in little ways to think beyond Santa Fe and the Southwest. It was Maria who had first encouraged Juno to apply to Yale when the university had decided to accept women.

Somewhere in her teens Juno's artistic aspirations began to focus on theater. For the past several summers she had apprenticed to the lighting designer of the Santa Fe Opera. At the same time, during mornings she had worked with the kids at the San Ildefonso Pueblo, teaching them how to draw and paint cardboard sets for the Indian history plays she helped them put on.

But during her first semester in New Haven she was too out of kilter to even think about the theater. She had spent the fall trying to adjust and fit into life in the East, being busily lonely and missing Santa Fe, her parents, her friends, and David, who was at the University of New Mexico.

When Christmas vacation finally arrived, Juno could not wait to see David. But she also felt anxiety about him. She had changed so much during the fall. She was sure he must have changed too.

To her disappointment, he had not. Juno felt infinitely more

worldly and aware than David. He seemed hopelessly provincial
to her.

A couple of nights after Christmas they went to a movie and
then to dinner at a favorite Mexican restaurant.

"I've been doing a lot of thinking," David said as he poured
sangria from a tall glass pitcher. "I don't see any point in your
going back there."

"What do you mean? Where?"

"To Yale. I mean, what the hell, you've experienced Eastern
college life. Now I think you should transfer back to UNM. You
belong here with me, Juno." He put his hand over hers.

Juno was appalled. "UNM? But David, I can't do that. I'm
just finally beginning to feel comfortable. I *love* going to Yale."
She realized suddenly that it was true. The loneliness and disorientation of the fall term had obscured this, but now she saw
how much the experience was beginning to mean to her. Loneliness and disorientation at Yale was much more fulfilling than
placid contentment with David at UNM.

"There're great secretarial courses. And you can take para-
legal courses, too. That way we can work together when I'm a
lawyer." David smiled compassionately. "Look, you can read
philosophy books at home. You don't need to go to Yale for that.
A liberal arts education, what's the point? Your parents are
spending good money to send you to college. You ought to get
something out of it."

Juno shook her head sadly. "Oh no, David, you don't understand." The enormity of trying to explain herself to him overwhelmed her. "You don't understand," she said again.

"Hey, look, I'm not saying you shouldn't go back and finish
out the year, but think about it. It really makes sense. Your life is
here, in New Mexico . . . with me."

"Oh, David, I used to think it was, but now I don't think so."
She looked up at him. "I'm really sorry."

That night in bed, Juno cried miserably. David had been so
much a part of her life she felt as if she had lost a piece of
herself. She had reached one of those moments when life is unal-
terably changed, and it frightened her. But the tears were
cleansing, too. And she felt on the brink of something new.

During second semester, Juno began to adjust to the East and to Yale's intensity. She decided to draw in her fragmented energies and focus them into the theater. Besides the graduate Yale Drama School and the University Dramat, each of the residential colleges had its own dramatic society. Juno found out that she could work wherever she liked, getting credit as well.

One raw midwinter day, Juno walked across campus in the ice-crusted snow to see about working on the set design for a play at Branford College. According to the notice she had seen on a bulletin board, the play was called *In a Smoke-Filled Room, in Some Hotel.* It had been written by an undergraduate who lived in Branford, a junior named Alexander Sage. Juno had heard a lot about him. He was considered the top of the heap of Yale undergraduate talent, and Juno wondered if she was overreaching in starting right off by picking an Alex Sage play to be her first try. But then, if she had not been ambitious, she would not be at Yale in the first place.

A lot of people turned out for the audition. The director was a senior who had changed his name from Bill Rogers to Raoul Rogers after consulting with a clairvoyant in the Ansonia Hotel in New York City. He had a reputation for being talented and gay.

"Er, hello. Have they started yet?" Lydia Forrest, the girl who had lived down the hall from Juno at the beginning of the year, walked in right behind her. No longer preppie-looking, her reddish gold hair was covered by a scarf, Russian peasant-style, and she was wearing a calico granny dress. They had not exchanged anything more than an occasional cool hello since that first day of school.

"I just got here," Juno said. "From the way people are milling around, I'd say it'll be a while before they get started."

Lydia rooted around in her canvas book bag. "God, I'm out of cigarettes. Do you have one?"

"No. Sorry."

Lydia rolled her large gray-blue eyes. "I've been on the weed since I was fourteen. I really should quit, but I guess I'm basically destructive." She drifted off in search of cigarettes but to Juno's surprise, returned when she had one. "There're some chairs over there. Want to sit down?"

"Sure. This'll probably drag on for hours." They made their way across the room.

Lydia set her bag on the floor and pulled her legs up on the chair under her long skirt. "I didn't know you were interested in acting."

"Oh, I'm not. I'd be paralyzed in front of an audience. I want to be a set and lighting designer."

"Set *and* lighting? That's ambitious."

"Well, I don't see why one can't do both," Juno said defensively.

"Lydia, my love! You made it!" A bespectacled young man in jeans came over and planted a kiss in the air next to Lydia's cheek. "I want you to read for the part of Phoebe. We'll get started in a few minutes."

"Raoul . . . I want you to meet . . ." Lydia looked at Juno. "I'm sorry, I can't remember your name."

Juno smiled at Raoul Rogers. "Juno Johnson. I want to work on the set or lighting. Or both, if possible."

"Well, you'll have to talk to Alex. He's over by the piano." He blew a kiss into the air and dashed off.

"Alex . . . do you know him?" Juno asked Lydia.

"Not really. I've seen him around. He's divine-looking. That's him."

Juno looked at the tall young man standing by the piano bench. Alexander Sage had on faded jeans, a pink silk shirt, and a red ascot casually tied around his neck. There was an unlit pipe in his hand, and he was gesturing with it as he talked to a short, plump girl. Several inches over six feet, he was lanky, with shoulder-length blond hair and light blue eyes framed in dark lashes.

"Oh," Juno said. "He's wonderful!"

"Yeah . . . and he's so talented that the Rep's talking about putting on one of his plays. Come on, let's go over and introduce ourselves."

"Wait . . . what's the play about? Do you know?"

"The fifteenth reunion of Yale's first coed class. *Us*, in nineteen eighty-whatsis, if we all live that long. It's a semimusical and has a large cast."

They waited while he finished his conversation with the

plump girl. Then he looked at Juno and Lydia and smiled. His teeth were a bit crooked but very white.

"Hello," he said.

"Hi. I'm Lydia Forrest, and this is Juno Johnson."

"Lydia Forrest, sure. I saw your Portia last semester, and I really liked what you did." He turned to Juno. "And you're an actress too, Juno?"

"No, I want to do set design . . ." She trailed off, feeling absurdly tongue-tied.

"And lighting, too." Lydia prompted.

"A designer? Hey, you're in luck. Or we're in luck. Jules Kline was going to do the set, but he's gone home with hepatitis. Dave Burns was working with Jules and has sort of taken over for him. I'll introduce you." He turned back to Lydia and handed her a script from a stack on the piano. "Here, check out Sharon's part and Phoebe's. I think you'd be good for either role."

Alex touched Juno's elbow. "Come with me." As they walked across the room, Alex put his arm around Juno's waist and lowered his voice conspiratorially. "Jules and Dave have been living together. Dave started doing sets in order to work with Jules . . . but he's a little short on inspiration. Except he doesn't know it, and he's a real prima donna. If you work with him, you'd have to be his assistant, and I don't know how easy that'll be."

"I've worked with difficult people before," Juno said. "I'm certainly willing to give it a try."

"Super. You have a portfolio I can look at?"

Juno fetched her leather case of sketches, and Alex went through them slowly, without comment. Most were of plays she had done at school and at the pueblo, but there were also renderings of sets she had designed for fun . . . her versions of Tennessee Williams's *Cat on a Hot Tin Roof,* Bertolt Brecht's *The Caucasian Chalk Circle,* and Harold Pinter's *The Birthday Party.*

She stood over Alex Sage and waited as he scrutinized her work. She did not know whether it was his reputation or his attractiveness that made her tremble, but Juno hoped he would not notice her knees knocking together. She wished he would say something.

"I've never seen a production on Broadway," she babbled nervously, "but I love to read plays and design them in my mind. For practice."

By the time Alex reached the last page of her book Juno was convinced that her work was hopelessly amateurish. She wished that she had not picked Alex Sage's production as her first at Yale. Suddenly it seemed very important to impress him. "Maybe I . . ." she started to say.

But when Alex looked up she could tell from his eyes that he was pleased. "These are really incredible. Juno, I don't know how I'm going to pull it off, or if I can. . . . But I want you to take a script and work up some ideas. How fast can you get me something?"

"Tomorrow . . . if I have a flash of inspiration."

"Great! Stop by my room, let's see, around seven? Here at Branford. Upstairs."

Juno smiled. "Okay. I'll try to have something for you by then."

And she knew that she damned well would have something for him, even if it meant cutting classes and staying up all night.

Juno picked up a script from the piano top and went to gather her books and parka. The room was quieting down. Lydia was up front, preparing to read, so Juno decided to stay and watch for a few minutes.

Half an hour later Juno walked out of Branford, injected with the first creative excitement she had felt since she arrived in New Haven. What she had heard of Alex's play was terrific. Funny and clever and wistful. And Lydia Forrest was a real surprise. The Park Avenue, private-school girl whom Juno had written off as spoiled and shallow, at Yale because of nepotism, that girl had actually made tears come to her eyes. And it had only been a reading.

And there was something else about both of them, something special and magnetic that energized her even though she hardly knew either of them. As she walked back across campus Juno felt elated. She had the feeling that these two people were going to be very important in her life.

"Oh, Juno, really," Max Milton said with a deprecating sigh as they sat over dinner in Hungry Charlie's. "Sage is adept, but hardly Ionesco or O'Neill. Maybe he'll do something significant, but he has a *long* way to go." He ladled two teaspoonfuls of sugar into his coffee.

"Max, how can you judge something you haven't read? *In a Smoke-Filled Room* is a wonderful play. Besides, Alex is still young. He'll obviously get better and better."

"Or burn out early. Playwrights are a strange, fragile breed."

"What about poets? You have your thing, Alex has his. There's room enough in the world for both of you."

"Ah, some of the homespun New Mexican philosophy that I've been missing all week."

Juno stuck her fork into the uneaten portion of her salad and pushed her chair back. "I'm not in the mood to argue, Max. I have a lot of work to do." She put some money on the table and left the crowded mix of Yalies and townies at Hungry Charlie's.

Max caught up with her on the sidewalk outside.

"Listen, Juno, come back to my room and smoke a joint. I wrote a new poem I want you to hear."

"No, Max. Not tonight, I told you."

"Fifteen minutes. Surely you can spare that." His tone was sarcastic.

Juno was finding Max increasingly annoying. He was an intellectual snob who loved putting down everyone else. But there was an undeniable electricity between them, even though she was afraid that it was strictly physical. David Abeyta had always liked *her*, not just the way she looked. She was not sure what Max thought of her.

"Max," Juno tried to explain, "fifteen minutes would drag into hours. I just can't take the time right now." They were the same height and he was glaring into her eyes. She brushed his cheek quickly with her lips. "Good night. I'll see you tomorrow." As she turned to go, Max grabbed the hood of her parka so roughly she heard the fabric rip at the seams.

"Look, if you're too fucking busy to spend fifteen fucking minutes with me then I don't see any point in trying to continue this relationship." Under the streetlamp, his pale face looked more ghostly than usual. "I don't need to waste my time with bitches."

Juno was furious. She pushed him away from her roughly.

Max stumbled back, then grabbed her shoulders and started shaking her.

"Goddammit, you've driving me mad!" he shouted. "I've never wanted anyone in my life as much as I want you."

"Stop it! Stop shaking me!" Juno tried to get loose, but Max pulled her closer to him. His lips pressed against hers and he squeezed her hard. His grip was so tight that Juno struggled to get a breath. When Max finally let go of her they both stood there heaving with the adrenaline that was surging through them. Juno was aware that some passersby were looking at them and whispering.

"I'm sorry, Juno." Max began stroking her cheek gently. "Please come back to my room with me."

Juno's knees felt as if they were going to give way, and so did all reason. Max had turned into her Svengali. She knew she had to get back and work, but she could not break out of the magnetic plane in which she and Max were caught.

"Only for a while," she said softly.

Chapter Three

Juno was unsettled by what happened between her and Max.

After the fight they had gone up to his room and smoked a joint with his roommate. The situation had appeared calm. Max had read his new poem to them, a detached allusion to Nixon and the Vietnam war. The roommate left to catch a lecture by Buckminster Fuller.

And then Max had made love to Juno, much more ferociously than before. The anger of their scene on the sidewalk seemed to spill over into his lovemaking. And Juno responded. She matched his rhythm and his rage. And for the first time she climbed with him over the crest. She felt an ecstatic explosion of light in the back of her head and in her belly. *Oh my God*, she thought. *This is what it's all about.*

But, just as she was coming, Max slapped her on her face. The look in his eyes was not one of love or desire, but of something more excruciating. She orgasmed with tremendous ferocity, even after the slap, or perhaps because of it. That was part of what scared her, this mixture of passion and cruelty. The other part was the power that Max wielded over her while they were fucking. That was what they were doing; it was not lovemaking. It was savage. He called her filthy names. She hated it, and it was shocking to her, but her body responded to his crudeness and the release of his anger with vehement betrayal of the repulsion her mind felt. Juno had stepped across the line into a dangerous arena, and it was going to take time to analyze and sort out the emotions that she brought back with her.

She had left Max's room soon afterward. Max did not ask her to stay the night, but she would not have anyway. She jogged all the way back to Vanderbilt and spent the next half hour in a near-scalding shower, soaping herself over and over again, trying to deal with the mortification she felt for giving herself to Max that way. It was past three in the morning, and she had not even begun to work up design ideas for Alex Sage's play.

The whole evening disturbed her, starting at the point she had agreed to go to Max's room. She had planned to go home and work; instead she had given in to something she could not control.

Juno had always had respect for herself. Now her self-respect was severely shaken.

Back in her room, propped up in bed with a hurricane candle so she would not wake Marjorie, Juno tried to work on Alex's play. But as she stared down at her sketch pad, her mind kept wandering off to what had happened between her and Max. She wondered what Max thought of her now, and whether he would tell his friends. What if he wrote a poem about it for his creative writing class? If he did, she was sure it would not be flattering. She dreaded ever seeing Max Milton again.

All the next day Juno hated herself. She was exhausted from staying up all night, and emotionally strung out from the re-crimination and replays in her mind of the scene with Max. The sketches she had done for *In a Smoke-Filled Room* were bland. The ideas were flat. She wished she had time to start all over again but it was too late. Alex had called to move up their meeting to five-thirty.

"Well . . . these are nice," Alex said, looking through them quickly. "I like the drawing." He smiled, but the enthusiasm he had shown yesterday for her work was missing. On the way over Juno had rationalized that the designs were not so bad, but she knew she should have canceled the meeting and spent another day on them. *Damn Max Milton*, she thought, knowing the blame was not really his.

Seeing Alex again made her realize how much she wanted to work on his play, both for her artistic self-esteem and because she wanted very much to be around him. But she could tell that he was disappointed. Why had she allowed herself to screw up when she had finally begun to feel that things were going to

come together for her? Never before in her life had she been a
self-destructive or irresponsible person. Now she felt she had
become one.

"Thanks, they really should have been a lot better, but . . ."
she trailed off. There was no point in giving excuses.

"Hey, it's cool. Really. I *like* them . . . it's just . . . Well, the
problem is Dave. I think for Jules's sake I have to go along with
Dave's ideas. Jules is real sick, and I think I'd better not make
waves." Alex pushed his hair away from his face. He had a high
forehead, and a tiny scar over his left eyebrow. "I still want you
to work on the play. Dave needs an assistant."

Juno forced herself to smile. She had been confident yesterday
that she would go home and design a set so brilliant that Alex
would be overwhelmed. Well, she had blown it. "Sure, I'd love
to." Then, probably because of the tiredness and disappointment she felt, the tears that would not come the night before
suddenly welled up in her eyes. She looked down into her lap
and tried to blink them away. The more she blinked, the more
they came. "Oh God," she said, looking up. "This is terrible. I'm
sorry."

Alex handed her a tissue from a box that was sitting under
some papers on his desk. "Hey . . . *I'm* sorry. Are you okay?"

"I feel so . . . ridiculous," Juno managed to say, sniffing. The
tears still would not stop. "This is embarrassing." She blew her
nose.

Alex set the box of tissues on her lap, then got a bottle of wine
out of his closet. It was not jug wine. He used a brass corkscrew
and poured the wine into two crystal goblets. He handed one to
Juno. The glass was thin and the stem felt fragile as Juno
wrapped her long, slender fingers around it.

"This should help," Alex said. "It's a St. Emilion. I just got a
case of this for my birthday. From my old man."

Juno smiled, despite her misery. "I've never known anyone
who got a case of wine for his birthday. It's so . . . I don't
know." Juno bit her lip, feeling like the hick of all time.

Alex laughed, cheered by the sign that her tears were drying
up. His laughter was easy, good-natured, and rather loud, as
though he enjoyed the experience of laughing almost as much as
whatever it was that triggered it.

"Try the wine," he said. "Nineteen sixty-four was a good year
for Bordeaux."

"How do you know so much about wine?"

"Dad's an oenophile. He's a diplomat and does a lot of heavy-
duty entertaining. My parents were divorced when I was a kid,
and I spent every other year with him living all around the
world."

"Oh wow. What was it like? It must've been exciting."

Alex shrugged. "I don't know. I don't have much to compare
it to. I guess I saw a lot of the world, but when you're eight or
nine years old, all you want to do is play Little League baseball
and have a lot of kids to hang out with. I missed out on all the
fads. It seemed like I was always leaving someplace just before
they learned something, and getting to the next place after they
already knew it." He grinned ironically. "The mysteries of
growing up stayed mysteries to me . . . I guess that's why I
started writing. I was always an outsider observing, and I decided to put it to some practical use."

"Gee, I lived in the same house in the same little town all my
life. All I've ever wanted was to see the world and do things."

"I'd have traded places with you in a minute."

Juno laughed. "Then *you'd* be drinking Gallo and I'd be im-
pressing you with my knowledge of wines."

"Oh, the wine . . . I learned pretty quickly that I had to be
up on my vintages if I wanted my father to pay attention to me.
Jesus, we used to have family dinners when Dad kept the wine
in a paper bag and made us guess the year and the vineyard.
Now, discussing wine's about the only level we communicate
on." Alex paused and took a sip. "He wants me to become a
lawyer like my brother, or possibly an investment banker if I
really want to kick up my heels. But I'm going to be a playwright. So . . . we talk about wine."

Juno took a sip of the St. Emilion. It was like liquid red velvet
spreading across her palate. "There's no comparison between
this and the red stuff I've had, except they're both called wine. I
mean, this is incredible! I feel as if I'm drinking a Rembrandt
painting."

Alex filled her glass again. Juno's eyes were puffy but the tears
had stopped. The wine calmed her.

"I rushed the drawings before I conceptualized my ideas for the play as a whole," Juno said. "I shouldn't have shown them to you. But that's not what set me off."

"Thank God. I felt terrible." He put the bottle on the floor between them. "Why were you crying? Do you want to talk about it?"

Juno shook her head. "It's too complicated. Mostly I guess I'm just tired. I . . . I'm not really the sort of girl who goes around breaking down. Especially in front of someone she barely knows."

Alex smiled. "We seem to have that effect on each other. I can't remember when I've bored anybody like this with my poor-little-me story. So I guess we're even."

"Oh no, I wasn't bored at all."

"You mean we're not even?"

Juno giggled. "I don't know what to say."

He pulled his chair closer to hers and leaned forward. "Why don't you tell me all about your nice stable childhood in a small town?"

Lydia Forrest arrived at rehearsal visibly agitated. It annoyed her that things got to her so easily, that she was so thin-skinned. She tried to cover it up, but it was no use. Once rehearsal got under way she forgot lines, blew her staging cues, and even snapped at Raoul Rogers, the director, who was not one to snap at. He told her to get the hell out and not come back until she knew what she was doing.

Juno Johnson was behind the scenes painting flats when Lydia grabbed her coat and books and huffed out noisily. On impulse, Juno rinsed her brush and rushed out to catch up with the star of *In a Smoke-Filled Room*.

"Hey? Are you okay?" Juno called out.

Lydia stopped walking and waited for Juno to catch up. "Not really. I'm in an awful mood. This has been a terrible day, and a *hideous* week. I'm thinking about leaving school."

"What? You can't take off before the play."

"Oh no? Try me." Lydia glared at Juno.

"Hold on. I didn't do anything. Don't take it out on me."

Lydia looked up at Juno, who was a good eight inches taller. "You're right. I'm impossible these days."

"Feel like having a cup of coffee?" Juno asked. She had been up all night working with Dave. There were faint circles under her eyes, and she had lost weight over the past few weeks. Even as far back as Christmas vacation her parents had expressed concern over the pallor of her skin, ordinarily a healthy rose-tinged olive.

"Okay. I guess I have time," Lydia said in the throaty voice that Juno had grown to envy over the last few weeks. It lent Lydia a worldly, sexy aura, in sharp contrast to her slim dancer's body and large waif eyes. "Actually, why don't you come over to my room? At Silliman. If you don't mind instant."

"Fine. Who are you living with over there?"

"Bob Penny. A junior. Do you know him?"

Juno shook her head. "I saw him once. Picking you up after rehearsal."

"He's majoring in philosophy. We have absolutely nothing in common, but he's very sexy. I haven't the vaguest idea what he sees in me." Lydia tossed off the remark with the confidence of a woman who knows exactly what men see in her, Bob Penny in particular.

"Oh, come off it, Lydia."

"I mean it. I think it's just sex. We sort of do our own thing the rest of the time." Lydia opened the door to her entrance at Silliman. "It's just up a flight. We'll have the place to ourselves. Bob's dropping acid with his philosophy T-group this afternoon."

The room was a mess. Clothes, books, and papers were cluttering every surface, including the floor. There were copies of the *East Village Other* and *Screw* on the bed, alongside Carlos Castaneda's *The Teachings of Don Juan* and *The Seth Material* by Jane Roberts. Lydia brushed a deck of tarot cards off a chair so Juno could sit, and put a kettle on the hot plate to boil water for coffee.

Juno felt uncomfortable and began to regret her spontaneous friendly overtures to Lydia. It was unlikely that she and Lydia had much in common either, except for a love of the theater. Lydia was very New York and very rich.

"Your sets are fabulous. Alex told me they're mostly your ideas," Lydia said, searching for the coffee jar.

"Thanks. Needless to say, I think you're terrific in the play."

"Compliment accepted," Lydia smiled. "It's a super play . . . and a great part. And you're right. I wouldn't leave school before we put it on. I owe it to Raoul and Alex." She handed Juno a cup of instant espresso and pointed vaguely to sugar and a jar of instant creamer sitting on top of a coffee-stained copy of the *I Ching*.

"Why are you thinking about leaving Yale?"

"Oh . . . a lot of things. My sister Jackie was in town today. She took me to lunch. God, she's such a bitch. Apparently, Mother expressed concern to her that I'm becoming the black sheep of the family. Whenever I go home there're a lot of heavy dinner table discussions about my clothes, my language, my friends. Now I don't even bother to show up for dinner. So, Jackie hotfoots it up here to try to squeeze me back into the mold. She's on a visit from San Francisco, where she's married to a plastic surgeon. Very materialistic. Very into the whole society bit. I can't stand to be around her for more than two minutes. She makes me want to join a commune somewhere and get away from everything. I mean, I didn't even want to come to Yale in the first place."

"You're kidding." Juno could not believe it. She thought of the agonies she had sweated while waiting for her acceptance letter.

Lydia shrugged. "What am I going to get out of Yale? The Old Boy network? Brandy and cigars at the Yale Club when I'm eighty-five?" Lydia stopped and sighed. Her expression softened, and she looked at Juno intently as if trying to assess something about her. "Can you keep a secret? This is something no one knows."

"Of course," Juno said, concerned. Lydia's voice sounded frail now and she was looking down at her lap, resting her head in her hands. Juno touched her shoulder gently. "What is it?"

Lydia lit a cigarette. "Just that I'm pregnant," she said offhandedly.

"Oh no!"

"Yeah. Can you imagine? Me, who's been doing it since I was

sixteen. God, you'd think I'd have it figured out by now, but I screwed up on the Pill."

Juno was stunned by this intimacy. Surely Lydia had closer friends to confide in. "What are you going to do?"

"I suppose I'll have to get an abortion. I mean, there's no choice really." She sighed. "I made an appointment for Wednesday afternoon. At a clinic in the city." She jumped up nervously and paced over to the window. Then she turned back to Juno. Her chin was raised defiantly, but it trembled. "I feel a bit awkward asking you . . . I mean, we don't know each other very well . . . but I wondered if you'd come with me? For moral support . . . or immoral support, or whatever?" She gestured distractedly with her cigarette. "God, I know it's no big deal. They just do it and you leave . . . But I'm . . . a little scared to go by myself. I asked you because I don't have much in common anymore with my old friends from prep school. I don't feel like I have any real friends at all."

Juno came over to Lydia and took her hand. "I'd like us to be friends. Of course I'll come."

"Oh shit, Juno. I don't know if I really want to do this. I mean, why couldn't I just have the baby and go off and live on an island somewhere?" Her eyes glistened. "I *like* children. To hell with Yale and my parents and appearances and everything. I mean, if you have a baby, you're *complete*. You're never alone. You've given birth to a *person* . . ." She trailed off, choked up with tears.

"Oh, Lydia." Juno did not know what to say, so she hugged her and let Lydia cry against her. After a while Lydia pulled away and reached for a Kleenex.

"Oh well," she sniffed. "There's no way I could deal with a kid now. I've got to have the abortion."

"What about Bob?" Juno asked softly.

"What about him?"

"Well . . . what does he want to do?"

"Bob doesn't know anything about it," she snapped. "Look, if you don't want to come with me, just forget it!"

"Hey, take it easy! I said I did. Really, I understand how you feel. I had a scare myself a few weeks ago. I was four days late

and absolutely terrified. I went through all of the emotions. But
then I got my period."

She told Lydia about her affair with Max Milton. Juno had
avoided seeing him since that night. She did not want to repeat
the experience, but she was afraid she would if she saw him.
Her body still longed for his. Then there was the false alarm
pregnancy scare which she had taken as a sign. She had descended into decadence and emerged unscathed.

"You won't tell anyone about this, will you?" Lydia said.

"Word of honor. And you . . ."

"Not a whisper about your wild poet. I swear on . . . oh, old
Immanuel Kant here." She laid her small hand on a copy of
Critique of Pure Reason. "You, too," she instructed, and Juno
placed hers on top of Lydia's.

"Should we prick our fingers?" Juno giggled.

"If only we'd fingered their pricks. We wouldn't get into this
kind of mess!" Lydia started laughing, a bit hysterically, but
Juno joined in.

"It's celibacy from now on," Juno said.

"Absolutely. We'll let our fingers do the walking." And they
dissolved into an uncontrollable giggling fit.

For a short while after the trip to New York, Juno and Lydia
were very chummy. Lydia liked Juno, and felt a singular rap-
port with the tall, exotic Westerner. But then she began to pull
back, afraid that she had exposed too much to Juno. Unmasking
herself scared Lydia. She had succeeded so well for so long without doing it.

"Hey, Lydia!" Juno caught up to her after rehearsal. "That
scene was dynamite."

Lydia pulled her earmuffs over her ears and wound her scarf
around her throat several times. "Thanks, Juno. I think I'm really getting it."

"Want to go have some coffee? We have to catch up. I haven't
seen much of you the last couple of weeks."

"Oh . . . sorry, Juno. I have a paper due."

Juno looked at her intently. "Are you all right? Is anything
wrong?"

"I'm fine. Nothing's wrong," she said breezily. "I've just been swamped, what with the play this weekend and all."

"I know what you mean. But can't you just take half an hour?"

Lydia smiled distractedly. "Ah no . . . I really can't. See you." She rushed off across the quad.

"See you." Juno sighed, wondering what it was she had done to cause Lydia to cool toward her. She headed back to her room. Friendships used to be so easy, when she was little. And now they were not. Once again, Juno felt the familiar pangs of loneliness.

Chapter Four

Alex Sage rummaged around in the pocket of his vintage raccoon coat and pulled out the roach of a joint of Acapulco gold. He stepped into the doorway to light it, then wandered across the courtyard, away from Branford College. *In a Smoke-Filled Room, in Some Hotel* was being premiered at that moment, but Alex was too nervous to sit down and watch.

He had set out to capture the craziness of Yale's coeducation turnover, placing it fifteen years hence at a class reunion, zeroing in on all the things he had experienced this year and all the people he had observed. It had seemed clever as hell when he wrote it. Now he could not imagine what could have possessed him to actually put it on stage.

He returned to Branford and opened the door. The audience was roaring with laughter in the distance. He was tempted to sneak in and watch from the back, but he resisted. What if the audience was laughing in all the wrong places? What if they were laughing at the hilarity of watching Alex Sage fall on his face?

He looked at his watch. Ten minutes to go. He began to wish he had never invited the cast and their friends up to his suite afterward to celebrate. He had watched the scenario in old movies; everybody standing around looking gloomy and embarrassed while the playwright got drunk and spit out hostile jokes that fell flat.

The remaining ten minutes seemed endless as he paced up and down the hall. When they were up, there was silence. *Oh shit*, he thought. It was even worse than he had anticipated. The audience loathed the play so much they refused to clap. He

craned his ears for the sound of hisses and boos, and looked at
his watch again.

And then it happened. An uproar of applause as the curtain
fell and the actors took their bows, and more applause; it kept
coming. Then there were shouts demanding the author. In a
blur Alex propelled himself to the stage, inhaling the cheers and
accepting the hugs and kisses of the cast. The angst was over.
The audience loved it, and him.

"Hey, man, outta sight!"

"Beautiful, Sage, just beautiful."

"God, it was really fucking clever. I bet Yale Rep'll pick it
up."

Backstage, surrounded by well-wishers, Alex was in his ele-
ment. He felt more together than he had all year. This was his
first play that had really accomplished what he had set out to do.
A sense of achievement and exhilaration was bursting inside
him.

"Broadway in five years. Deal?" Raoul Rogers said, hugging
him.

Alex laughed. "I hear you. Maybe sooner, if we keep getting
lucky."

"Don't be modest, Alex. Talent has something to do with it,
too." Lydia, still wearing her slinky black strapless backless costume, broke away from her own admirers to become one of
Alex's.

"Thanks, Lydia. You may join Raoul and me on Broadway
anytime you like." Alex kissed Lydia's cheek. "In fact, you'll
probably get there before we do. You were incredible."

"How would you know?" Raoul asked. He whispered to
Lydia in mock secrecy. "The man was outside, throwing up out
of sheer nervousness for the entire second act."

"What do you mean?" Alex said. "I merely needed some air.
My nerves are as strong as Fort Knox. Now Raoul here . . ."

"Raoul was shredding the script into confetti backstage,"
Juno said as she joined them.

"Okay, so much for our fearless director. What about our
star?" Alex asked.

Lydia stuck out her tongue at him. "I never claimed to be

nerveless. I'm a total basket case before I go on. Can't eat, can't
sleep, can't anything but worry about screwing up my lines."

"Well, it's not easy being light person either," Juno laughed.
"Keeping the spot on the star here, not blowing the cues when
the actors mess up their lines. Believe me, it's a nerve-racking
experience. I just want to know one thing . . . What's so great
about the theater?"

They all laughed, and shook hands in a solemn pledge to
switch their majors to cellular biology at the first opportunity.

The room Alex shared with Bruce Hopkins in Branford was
packed with hip-looking bodies, as parties given by Alex usually
were. Word got around. Besides the theater and creative writing
set, young men and women showed up from all factions of Yale
life. People knew that at Alex's parties there would always be
good wine, provided by his father, good grass, from a dealer
Alex knew in Woodstock, and boxes and tins of good things to
eat, shipped in from Neiman-Marcus by his mother.

This night, Alex's desk had been cleared to make way for a
side of Alaskan smoked salmon as well as a huge selection of
breads, cheeses, and cold cuts sent by special messenger from
Zabar's in New York, also compliments of Cassie Sage Trevillian. There was a batch of hash brownies, baked for Alex by the
loving hands of Genevieve Saint-Roup, the French Vassar girl
whom he was currently seeing. She was there at the party—
dressed in tight faded jeans, an embroidered shirt, ankle-height
suede boots that laced up the shins, and a silk-screened, limited-
edition Rolling Stones scarf—achieving the perfect thrown-to-
gether look for something in the neighborhood of four hundred
dollars.

Mademoiselle Saint-Roup was getting herself quite drunk,
knocking back scotch to camouflage her *tristesse*, brought on by
the knowledge that Alex no longer loved her. Alex did not know
it yet because he had been too busy with his play to think about
his own life and relationships. But Genevieve knew. She was old
for her age and had a heightened intuition in the ways of male-
female relationships. Alex Sage's mind wandered when he was
around her these days, and Genevieve knew that was the kiss of
death. She staggered over to the tape recorder to change tapes,

then lurched back to the sofa. By the time Doc Sausage and his
Five Cuban Jelly Beans were into the second bar of "The Fat
Fornicator" Genevieve had crashed for the night.

The party built up around her. A group in the bedroom was
enjoying—before zonking off to zombie land—the uproarious
effects of sniffing from a tank of nitrous oxide, laughing gas.
Several SDSers were lying in front of the fireplace discussing
Abbie Hoffman and tripping on mescaline. Joints and pipes of
hashish were being passed around liberally, and a psych major
was taking orders for capsules of powdered organic psilocybin.

Juno arrived at the party late, on the arm of a gay friend from
the art department, Hoppy Johns. She had recently decided to
fixate on him because he was sexually safe and they had a great
time together when none of his boyfriends were around.

"Well, it's about time you showed up," Alex called out. He
was carrying a stack of plastic cups and a bottle of Beaujolais.

"Us working peons had to stay and clean up, unlike the celebrated playwright," Juno said, kissing Alex on the cheek. "Anyway, congratulations. They love you here off off-off-Broadway."
She introduced Hoppy, and Alex poured them some wine.
Hoppy spotted one of his lovers dancing across the room and
dashed off in pursuit.

Alex put his arm around Juno. "Alone at last," he smiled.
"Has your friend made a pass at you lately?"

"Oh, very funny, Alex. I've given up sex for Lent."

"But I thought *we* were going to have an affair," Alex laughed,
but his eyes were serious.

Juno felt a pang in her belly, but told herself that he was
merely being flirtatious. He was high from his success and the
wine. "Is your fiancée from Vassar going to join us, or shall we
run away to Bali alone?"

"She's *not* my fiancée. She *is* the stylish creature you see
wasted on the sofa."

Juno felt a hand on her back and looked around to see Max
Milton. A jolt of panic hit her. For weeks she had been expecting to see Max around every corner, searching the campus
warily to spot him in the distance and avoid him. But here tonight she was caught completely off guard. Max's pupils were

dilated and he was unshaven. As he approached, Alex kissed
Juno's cheek and slid away to greet some more latecomers.

"You're a hard woman to find these days," Max said. His
words ran together. "And I've been looking."

"Oh?" Juno said, her eyes searching the room for friends to
whom she could retreat.

"Yeah," Max said. "You're one hell of a bitch, you know that?"

Juno saw the same hostility in his eyes that had been there
during their last night together. She did not want a scene. "If
you say so, Max. See you." She started off, but he grabbed her.
"Get your act together, Max. Leave me alone. I don't want to
talk to you now."

"Is that so?" Max slurred. "Would you rather fuck? That's
what you specialize in, isn't it? Fuck and run?" Max's face grew
uncharacteristically ruddy, and people started turning around
to look as his voice became shriller. He squinted at the assem-
bling audience. "You want to know about this woman here?
She's a fucking Amazon. She didn't care about me. She used me
. . . to get her rocks off. She . . . ."

"Stop it, Max. It's not true!" Juno, embarrassed and enraged,
clenched her fist and did something she had never dreamed of
doing before. She swung out as hard as she could at Max's jaw.
The wineglass in her other hand tumbled to the floor, spilling
onto her purple suede jumpsuit and the rug. Max fell backward
but was caught by two long-haired young men whom Juno recognized as friends of his. Her eyes remained fixed on Max.
There was a trickle of blood coming out of the side of his mouth.
His eyes were blinking.

"He's okay . . . just stunned," someone said.

"Let's get him home," one of the friends said. He looked at
Juno sympathetically. "He's really stoned. He won't remember
any of it in the morning. I'll tell him he got into a fight at
Mory's." They helped Max, semiconscious, stagger out and
down the stairs.

Juno, who had been frozen to the spot, was breathing quickly
from the adrenaline, and her knees began to shake. She wanted
to become invisible, but people were patting her on the back and
a chorus rang out of "Heavy!" "Right on . . . he had it coming!" "Where'd you learn to punch like that?"

"He made me mad," Juno said, forcing a smile. Then she headed for the bathroom to compose herself.

She locked herself in. Fighting back tears, she splashed cold water on her face and jumpsuit. The wine stains did not come out completely. "Damn! Shit! Fuck!" she swore under her breath.

There was a delicate tap on the door.

"Juno? Are you in there? It's me . . . Lydia. Let me in."

Juno unlocked the door and Lydia slipped in, locking it again. "I just got here. I heard all about it . . . what a bummer. Are you okay?"

Juno sighed. "Humiliated out of my mind. Other than that, fine."

"Oh, don't worry about it. Everybody's gone back to partying. Alex wanted me to check on you." She paused to drag on her cigarette. "You know, I think he quite likes you." The concern had vanished from her voice, and Juno noted a distinct chilliness. She wished she could figure Lydia out: she seemed to blow so hot and cold. Earlier that evening, before the performance, Juno had given her a pencil sketch she had done of her onstage during a rehearsal. Lydia had hugged her and seemed genuinely touched. Now she was checking on her welfare only because Alex had asked her to.

"If, for some reason, you're jealous of me and Alex, don't waste your energy," Juno said. "He has dozens of girls. And I'm not one of them."

Lydia smiled. "Neither am I. I'm sorry. I guess I *was* uptight. I just think Alex is so terrific."

"Welcome to the club . . ."

Someone hit on the door. "Hey, hurry up! There're about fifty of us who have to use the pisser."

"I guess I can't stay in here all night," Juno said. "Although I'd like to."

There was another bang, and Alex's voice. "May I come in?"

Juno unlatched the door. Joe Cocker blasted away in the background. "It's getting a bit cozy, but what the hell."

Alex's white swashbuckler shirt was unbuttoned to midribs. Sweat glistened on the light hairs of his chest. Squeezing into the room, Alex slid his arms around both Juno and Lydia. Juno was about four inches shorter than Alex. Lydia, even wearing high-heeled wedgie boots, barely made it to Alex's shoulder.

"I hope you never get that mad at me," Alex grinned.

"I hope you never make me that mad," Juno grinned back.

"Never. I promise," Alex laughed. "Milton was in one of my English lit classes last year. He's a jerk. He had it coming to him."

"Yeah . . . but I wish *I* hadn't done it."

"Don't worry. He'll believe his friends when they tell him he was KO'd by some guy at Mory's."

"I hope so. You know, I've never hit anyone in my life."

"Then you're a natural," Alex said enthusiastically. "Maybe I should be your trainer. With a little work we might get you a title shot by summer."

Lydia laughed, anxious to be included. "Or you could teach a self-defense course for women. I'd sign up. I've met a lot of men I'd like to punch out."

"Hey," Alex said, looking deeply into Juno's dark eyes. "You want us to lay off, don't you? I'm sorry. It's just that you were so splendid."

"Thanks, but I'd like to crawl into a hole. The word'll be all around campus by tomorrow. Max *will* find out. It'll just egg him on more."

"I doubt if he'll want to confront you again," Alex comforted. "He wouldn't dare. He's the motherfucker, not you. And if he does hassle you, let me know. I'll take him on next time." He kissed her brow. "Now, are you ready to boogie again?"

Juno sighed, nodding. "Sure . . . I feel like dancing the night away."

Alex gazed from Juno to Lydia. "Why is it that I find you two so exciting?"

"Well, we're the most exciting women at Yale," Juno said.

"It's our major," Lydia laughed.

Alex leaned down and pressed his lips to Lydia's, and they melded together into a passionate kiss. Juno, feeling extraneous, tried to pull away but Alex tightened his grip on her. The next moment his lips moved from Lydia's to hers and he slowly penetrated her mouth with his tongue. Juno tried to hold back, with

Lydia standing there, but her response to his kiss was uncontrollable. For the seconds it lasted she felt euphoric.

Alex moved his lips over to Lydia's for a quick reunion, then back to Juno's. "I think I could fall in love with both of you," he said lightly. But his light blue eyes regarded them both passionately.

Now there was nonstop pounding on the door. "Hey, Sage, quit screwin' around with the two best-lookin' chicks at the party," someone called out.

"It's my bathroom, man," Alex shouted back. "But, I suppose," he said to Juno and Lydia, "we'd better vacate before someone blows lunch in the hall."

"Well . . . I do feel better," Juno said to Lydia as Alex returned to his guests.

"Me, too," Lydia giggled as they headed for more wine. "But what do you suppose that was all about?"

Juno shrugged. "Three ships passing during an unusual night."

Lydia poured some wine for her and Juno. "Maybe. Maybe not. Time will tell."

Lydia wandered off to look for her date but Juno stood there, wine in hand, gazing absentmindedly at the packed room, everybody doing their thing. She locked eyes with Hoppy and beckoned him over to her. It was time to start fixating on him again. Sex, Juno concluded, was just too damned complicated.

The rest of the semester was a whirl of seminars, rap sessions, moratoria, and Marx Brothers movies running around the clock at exam time. By early June, only Juno and a smattering of coeds were still residing full-time in Vanderbilt Hall.

Over the last months Juno had seen Max Milton in the distance several times, but he seemed to want to avoid her as much as she wanted to avoid him. She ran into Alex seldom; he spent most of his time holed up in Branford, writing another play. Occasionally, she and Lydia got together for coffee. They had long, pleasant chats but Lydia still held back, as if afraid to totally let go with Juno.

A shift was occurring. The coeds were beginning to realize that they could not exist with men twenty-four hours a day.

They needed to talk with one another, compare notes, share emotional experiences. By the end of the year, a spirit of feminism had invaded the campus. The coeducational turmoil was not yet played out. Juno and Lydia, along with the other coeds, were determined not to be swallowed up by the maleness of the place.

Summer vacation arrived, and with it a break in the madness. The undergraduates fanned out in different directions, to regather their strength and try to sort out the experience of the past year.

Chapter Five

Lydia Forrest had planned to do a film, as she had the previous summer, on her children's theater workshop. It was a project that she had started at fifteen, one of the things, besides her grades, that got her accepted at Yale. She taught playacting in a converted chicken coop (an extremely large chicken coop) on the grounds of her parents' summer residence on Georgica Road in East Hampton, Long Island. She had a Super-8 sound camera and plenty of Kodacolor film. There were sixteen kids enrolled, ranging in age from nine to twelve. And she had already cast the play they would do at the end of the month-long session, her own adaptation of an Oscar Wilde fairy tale called *The Star Child*.

But there was trouble in paradise. The play's lead, Lydia's prize student, contracted mononucleosis and had to drop out. The chicken coop sprang a formidable leak during a late-July storm, dousing the props and costumes which mildewed before the disaster was discovered. Lydia's summer love, a tennis player, suddenly decided to turn professional and took off to try his luck in a pro satellite circuit. An old friend from prep school, with whom she had agreed to share a suite at Branford come fall, was having a nervous breakdown and had dropped out of school. Finally, her sister Jackie, in the midst of marital problems, had descended upon the household with her two outrageously bratty kids.

With Jackie there complaining, day in and day out, about her soon-to-be-ex-husband, and the tennis player somewhere in New Zealand, Lydia lost enthusiasm for filming this summer's play, although she did recast the lead and put it on one hot weekend so as not to disappoint the children and their parents.

Once that was over, it was August and there was nothing to do. Lydia had had as much of the beach as she could take, given her fair skin and proclivity toward freckling. Her sister was driving her crazy. Even New York City was out of the question since her mother was having their Park Avenue duplex painted and reupholstered. As far as people to date, it was the same old monied crowd that hung out at the Maidstone Club every summer. Boring.

After a bit too much champagne at a wedding reception one afternoon, Lydia made up her mind to get herself out of the Hamptons. The West might be fun. Lydia had never been anywhere between the East Coast and California, and she remembered that Juno Johnson lived in Santa Fe. Lydia reached for the phone, got the number from information, and dialed.

Juno met Lydia at the Albuquerque airport in a white pickup truck with three large dogs in back, a German shepherd, a standard poodle, and a golden retriever. The truck had no shocks and Juno drove it at a bumpy seventy-five all the way to Santa Fe, about sixty miles away.

"They closed the Santa Fe airport to large commercial planes a while ago," Juno explained. She was deeply tanned and her long black hair was in braids. "Rather than allow more pollution they just shut it down, except for private planes." She glanced over at Lydia. "So . . . what's your impression of New Mexico?"

Lydia's eyes had adjusted already to the mesas and arroyos, the stark brown cowboy-and-Indian scenery and the cloudless blue sky that went on forever. "I love it! I keep thinking I'll see John Wayne riding over the next hill."

Juno had been bowled over by Lydia's unexpected call and had anticipated the visit with a certain amount of trepidation. Not that she did not welcome the opportunity of getting to know Lydia better, on her own turf. But she guessed that Lydia would want more action than Santa Fe could offer.

Juno turned off the highway and headed for the Old Santa Fe Trail. "Nearly there."

"I can't believe it," Lydia said. She had gotten used to the pickup and was enjoying the image of riding in one. "You live on the Old Santa Fe Trail, the very same one as in the old days?"

"Yep . . . except a lot of it's paved now. Not the part we live
on though." Juno turned onto a rutty dirt drive that wound up a
hill covered with piñon and juniper trees and a carpet of orange
and purple wildflowers. "You'll have to excuse the mess. Dad's
building a solar wing onto the house. It'll be his new studio and
a guest apartment. For now, you'll have to share my room." The
house came into view, a sprawling pueblo-style adobe with a
large glass-sided addition facing south.

Juno screeched to a stop, the dogs leaped out of the back, and
some hippie-looking workmen on the roof waved to them.

Juno waved back. "Hey, Dad," she called out. "This is my
friend Lydia from New York."

A handsome man in his early forties with dark hair curling
around his shoulders called down from the roof. "Glad to meet
you, Lydia. Juno's talked a lot about you. See you at dinner."

Lydia smiled and waved at Hollis Johnson. "Wow, Juno, your
father looks like a movie star. I can't believe it. My father looks
like a paunchy, balding tycoon."

"That's what he is, isn't he . . . a tycoon?" Juno carried
Lydia's bags into the house.

"You got it. But didn't you tell me your father's a painter?"

"Yeah, he adds onto the house when he feels blocked. Right
now he's going through a creative transition."

They walked through the white-walled living room mounted
with vibrant abstracts of the New Mexican landscape. "All the
large canvases are his. The smaller ones have been done mostly
by our friends. Okay . . . here we are."

Juno opened the door to her room. It was split level with a
desk, sofa, chairs, and stereo on the ground floor, and a double
bed and electric piano thirteen steps higher on the loft. The
walls were covered with various paintings by Juno, and por-
traits of her at different ages, done by her father.

"Dad added the loft and skylight when I was in high school."
Juno grinned. "That was just prior to the abstract landscape
phase that he's coming out of now."

"This is super . . . just like an apartment. You even have
your own door leading outside. God, what I wouldn't give for
my own entrance to our place in New York. Think of the things
I could do!" Lydia chuckled throatily.

"Think of the things I've done," Juno said as she sank into a chair. "Or the things I haven't done. My boyfriend spent the night here a couple of times, but he wouldn't do anything because my parents were sleeping under the same roof."

"Boys can be so odd sometimes," Lydia said. Juno had cleared out a couple of drawers and Lydia was putting her stuff into them. "Where's your mother? Is she here?"

"You won't see her till tomorrow probably. She's a cellist with the Santa Fe Opera. She's at rehearsal now and they have a performance tonight. Unless you want to go to it. I told Dad I didn't think you would."

"Actually," Lydia said, "I'd love to."

Over the next week, Juno could not believe the change in Lydia. The Eastern veneer of sophistication gave way to a girlish exuberance for all the new things she was seeing and doing. Lydia fell in love with Santa Fe's charm, its dirt roads and earth-colored adobe houses that looked as if they belonged in old Mexico instead of the U.S.A. She insisted on seeing the touristy places that Juno had not visited since grade school field trips— the Palace of the Governors; the Oldest Church, built in 1610, ten years before the Pilgrims landed on Plymouth Rock; the archaeological excavations at Arroyo Hondo. Armed with an ample supply of sun block for Lydia, they went horseback riding near the Ski Basin, hiking and picking wild raspberries in the Pecos Wilderness, exploring the Indian ruins at Bandelier, and taking in the buffalo dances at the Santa Clara Pueblo.

"Really, I can't tell you how much I'm enjoying this visit. I feel like a different person," Lydia exclaimed in her new Southwestern laid-back accent. Around her neck was her latest purchase, a turquoise and bone *heishi* choker.

It was dinnertime. Maria Johnson had prepared *chiles rellenos, posole, carne adovada,* and *sopaipillas,* fried bread served with honey butter. They were washing it down with Mexican beer garnished with wedges of lime.

Hollis Johnson leaned back. "You girls doing anything after dinner?"

"Some guys asked us to the movies," Juno said, "but we're not wild about them. Why?"

"I felt like doing some sketching, and I wondered if you two'd sit for me a bit."

"Depends on whether you want us naked," Juno said.

"Juno!" Maria admonished. "Let's not give Lydia the impression that you and your father have an incestuous relationship."

Juno laughed. "Heavens no. We wouldn't want the rumor spread all around Yale."

"My lips are sealed," Lydia said. "As long as you give me a lifetime supply of green chiles."

"It's a deal," Hollis said. "Anyway, I don't want you nude. You can have on anything you want. I just have a few preliminary ideas. . . . I'm not sure what'll work."

"What do you want to do?" Juno asked. "The movies or an evening here?"

Lydia looked at Hollis with her large wide-set eyes. She had developed a bit of a crush on Juno's father. "Here. There's no choice, really."

"This is a girl," Juno said to her parents, "who probably hasn't spent an evening at home in the past five years."

"Yes, I have," Lydia insisted with a mischievous glint in her eye. "When my parents went to Japan over Christmas and left me the entire place to myself."

The phone rang and Juno dashed into the kitchen to get it. When she came back she said to Lydia, "You won't guess in a thousand years who that was."

"Hmmm." Lydia leaned her head back. "Let's see . . . Max Milton? No? My sister? Kate Millett? James Taylor? Oh, I give up."

"Alex."

"Alex Sage? You're kidding!"

"He's here. He couldn't believe you were, too. We're going to pick him up at the Phillips 66 station on Old Pecos Trail." Juno turned to her parents. "Alex is the one I told you about from school . . . the playwright."

Hollis Johnson nodded. "What's he doing at the Phillips 66 station?"

"Who knows?" Juno pulled the pickup keys out of her jeans pocket. "We'll find out soon."

Maria Johnson had retired from the group to practice her cello. The others were assembled in Hollis's studio. Alex was wolfing down a plate of leftovers. He had lost weight and his high cheekbones were more chiseled than ever.

"Dallas was a horror show. My stepfather kept talking about law schools. My mother kept trying to get me to cut my hair and escort debutantes to balls. Finally, after a couple of weeks I couldn't take it. I decided I had to get back in touch with myself. . . ." Alex paused for a swig of the tequila he had produced from his backpack.

"Anyway," he continued, passing the tequila to Juno and Lydia, "I'd had this idea for a play about a hitchhiker. So I decided to take off and thumb around and see if I flashed on something."

"And did you?" Hollis asked. His fingers were flying across his sketch pad.

"Oh yeah. I've just been going where the rides take me. No destination. I've met some of the most amazing people. Some Jehovah's Witnesses in Colorado who gave birth to a kid on a mountaintop. I mean, I was *there* with them. I even got to hold the baby when it was about five minutes old. It was mystical. And I met an old Indian in Oklahoma who taught me about herbal healing. And I stayed on a commune in Wyoming where everyone has taken the vow of silence . . ."

"That must've been fun," Lydia said skeptically.

"It was an experience, that's the whole point," Alex said, stretching his long legs out in front of him. "Then there was this woman named Nadia who picked me up in Fordyce, Arkansas. She let me take the wheel and told me to drive to St. Louis. She conked out on the backseat and didn't come to till we got there, about six or seven hours later. The only sound out of her that whole time was a loud 'ouch!' somewhere around Poplar Bluff. Then the second we hit the St. Louis city limits she sat bolt upright and started giving me directions to this motel . . . the Golden Slumber, if you can believe it. She invited me in for a drink before I took off. She was real good-looking. Older, maybe early thirties, but she had shiny brown hair and a sensational body . . ."

"Oh, spare us the boring details, Alex," Lydia interrupted.

"Hell no, I'm interested," Hollis said.

"So we open a bottle of wine and she starts asking me if I'm into astral projection. She tells me she takes off regularly in her sleep and visits people she knows all over the world."

"I wonder if the airlines know about this," Juno said. "She might be required to meet FAA regulations."

"I'm not bullshitting you," Alex said. "She was on the level. She told me that while I was driving she was dropping in on her ex-husband in Ottawa." Alex paused. His listeners were all wearing amused expressions. "Believe me . . . she was dead serious. Nadia said her old man was cooking dinner for his girlfriend and it pissed Nadia off so much she knocked the girlfriend's drink off the table and into her lap. The girlfriend blamed the guy and got into a big fight with him, and the ex-husband stepped on Nadia's foot in the scuffle. That's when she said 'ouch!' from the backseat of the car. Isn't that far out?"

"No," Lydia said. "Farfetched."

Hollis Johnson set a large, primed canvas on his easel and started sketching on it in charcoal. "So . . . what happened? You and Nadia at the Golden Slumber?"

Alex took some more tequila and passed the bottle again. "Well . . . it got later and later and she asked me to spend the night with her."

"Aha! The plot moves along predictably," Juno said. She was feeling fuzzy and happy, from the liquor and Alex's unexpected arrival.

"No . . . wait," Alex threw up his hands, laughing. "There's a twist, I swear. There were two big beds in this room. Nadia emerges from the bathroom in a T-shirt that just barely covers her ass and says, 'Okay, I'll take this one, you sleep there.' I wasn't sure what was expected of me. Was I supposed to remain in my assigned bed, or . . ." Alex rubbed his palms together, "move over?"

"I think I can guess what you decided to do," Lydia said, helping herself to more tequila. She was aware that she was getting quite smashed.

"Right on. But it turns out Nadia had other ideas. You see, she had figured out that the beds ran from north to south . . ."

"An interesting observation," Hollis said. "Not run-of-the-mill."

"So," Alex continued, "she turns off the lights and tells me to lie on my back. She leans over, kisses my forehead, and says, 'I'm taking away your pillow. I want you completely flat.' So I'm wondering what sort of kinky scene I'm getting myself into. The next thing I know, she's in her own bed on her back and her pillow's on the floor."

"Sounds *very* kinky to me," Juno giggled.

"She tells me to relax, starting with my toes and working up my body. And then to concentrate real hard on levitating out of my body and up to the astral plane. She says she'll be there waiting for me, to take me on the carnal and spiritual adventure of a lifetime."

"I wonder if you can get pregnant if you do it on the astral plane," Lydia speculated. "It'd be a lot safer than the Pill. But would it be as much fun?"

"I don't know," Alex laughed. "I got so relaxed I fell asleep. I woke up about half an hour later. Nadia was sitting next to me, rubbing my . . . uh . . . chest."

"Ha!" Juno and Lydia said at the same time.

"She admitted it takes a lot of practice before you can soar astrally. She gave me some exercises to work on. Then we spent the rest of the night concentrating on the here and now," Alex said.

"An in-the-body experience, instead of an out-of-the-body one," Hollis said. "Oh, to be young and on the road again."

"Again?" Juno asked. "When were you on the road, Dad?"

"Before you . . . before your mother. In the pre-hippie, pre-beatnik, bohemian days. Stories I'll tell you when you come of age."

"What do you mean by that?"

"When you come of age, you'll know," Hollis chuckled. "Now, I want you and Lydia to sit on the sofa next to Alex, so I can get you all together." He had covered the sofa with some Navajo blankets before Alex started on the *chiles rellenos*.

On into the night they sipped tequila while Alex recounted

the stories of his travels. He had ended up in Santa Fe by chance
and had been calling all the Johnsons in the phone book, one by
one, until he found the right one. He was going to leave the next
morning, as his master plan stipulated that he spend every night
in a different place. School was starting again soon and he still
had not made it to California.

"This has been a weird and enlightening summer," Alex said.
"Believe me, this is the best night I've spent in I can't remember
when."

"Maybe ever," Juno suggested.

"Maybe since St. Louis," Lydia said.

Laughing heartily, Alex put his arms around Juno and Lydia.
They were laughing, too. Juno's long legs were pulled up in
front of her. Lydia's were tucked up under her so she could sit
taller. Both of them were cuddled in close to Alex. The bottle of
tequila was nearly empty, and Hollis Johnson had switched
from charcoal to oils.

They stayed up all night, drinking and laughing and talking.
That solved the problem of where Alex was to sleep, and with
whom.

Chapter Six

"Your parents are so in touch with one another," Lydia said, handing Juno a Diet Pepsi. They were roommates now, along with a third woman who spent all her time at Morse College with her boyfriend. They shared a two-bedroom suite in the neo-Gothic college, Branford, where Alex lived. The painting that Hollis Johnson had done of Lydia, Alex, and Juno hung over the fireplace in the living room.

Lydia walked over to the stained-glass window and gazed out into the courtyard. The wisteria that climbed the sides of the stone buildings was gone now. "I mean, they relate to each other, and they're still in love. I walked in on them one night in Santa Fe. They were listening to music and holding hands. God, my parents never connect, and yet they stay together . . . I can't figure out why. I don't think either of them has *ever* had any fun."

"But that's what life's all about . . . ," Juno said, nibbling at a handful of sunflower seeds. "Sharing experiences, looking for the humor in things. Trying to enjoy yourself in spite of the odds."

"Exactly. Life's too short to waste it on being unhappy." Lydia laughed wryly. "Of course, I'm a hell of a one to talk. I'm unhappy most of the time."

"You?" Juno grinned. "Come on, Lydia, I thought you were the girl who has everything."

"Yeah . . . what do I really have?" Lydia lit a cigarette. "A nicotine habit. A lot of money and a family who's totally out of touch. I'm smart, but I have to play it down with the men I date. I want to be an actress, which my parents equate with jumping off a diving board into hell. I've slept with eight men and never had an orgasm. And I'm terrified to show my true feelings to people." Lydia leaned her head back and sighed. "And then I look at you. You're the most together person I ever met. You don't *need* things. God, we're so different. If I don't have a date almost every night I go bonkers. You get fidgety if you can't stay *in* two or three times a week."

Juno laughed. "Well, the grass is always greener. If I had somebody I liked I'd want to be with him as much as possible. I guess I'm hard to please. Most guys don't turn me on. And you're wrong," Juno said emphatically. "I *do* need things. You have money, so you take it all for granted. Like, when Alex was telling us about his brother's wedding reception at the River Club. You and he were putting it all down . . . the thousands of dollars' worth of gardenias, the Dom Perignon squirting out of the fountain, the boatloads of lobster and caviar. But I thought it sounded great. I'm tired of being poor but happy. I want to be rich but happy."

"Well, marry somebody rich. There're dozens of wealthy scions in New York I could introduce you to." Lydia slipped out of her jeans and into a Betsey Johnson miniskirt.

"But that's just it. You always think in terms of who you're going to marry, and how that'll affect your life. I want to have a career and make it on my own. I want to be able to go out and buy a Porsche because *I* earned the money. I'm ambitious for myself."

"That's all well and good," Lydia said. "You go and hear Betty Friedan lecture and join the Yale Sisterhood. I like society fine just the way it is. And don't tell me I'm oppressed."

"But you just told me you have to camouflage your intelligence when you're around men . . ."

"Well, making it with the opposite sex is one hell of an important part of life," Lydia snapped. "I can do that and still be an actress if I want to."

"Right . . . that's what I'm saying. Like in that interview in the Yale *Daily News,* Elga Wasserman said a woman has a *right* to be a person and have a career and use her mind . . . the same as a man. I'm not suggesting that you're not supposed to get along with men. But you should do it on your own terms. What's the point of a Yale education if you spend your life raising kids and doing volunteer work?"

"Okay . . . okay. You have a point. But I have to go meet Kirk at The Exit. You want to come along?"

Juno shook her head. "I'm working on my lighting chart for the Yale Cabaret."

Lydia put on a quilted patchwork jacket and paused in the doorway. "You know, I truly think it's frightening to spend an evening by myself."

"Come off it, Lydia," Juno chuckled. "When was the last time you tried it?"

After Lydia had gone, Juno sat in the darkening room thinking about her friend. They had both changed a lot since their first encounter. But there was a major difference between them. Lydia expected life to take her by the hand and lead her where she wanted to go. Juno was quite positive that you had to direct yourself and not rely on anyone else.

They both had a lot to learn.

The school year sped by in a live-and-let-live, do-your-own-thing fashion.

For many students, dope and sex were a continuing relief from the tensions of coeducating. The women worked hard to expand the spirit of female camaraderie on campus, and there was constant exploration, by both sexes, of male and female roles. Open and honest discussions on sex became common. Privacy and monogamy were practically nonexistent. During extended vacations, large groups of people took off together for Aspen or the Caribbean or the Mayan ruins in Mexico.

Like other campuses, Yale was boiling over with antiwar protests and antiestablishment reaction. The SDS was active. Juno got involved with Black Panther Bobby Seale's New Haven trial for conspiracy-to-murder charges. Lydia was tear-gassed and hauled off to jail during the huge student May Day demonstration. Even Alex, normally apolitical, wrote and distributed a satirical pamphlet attacking the careless handling of nuclear waste. There were many local causes of uproar as well, including a week-long picket of Mory's, the all-male, private eating club, and condemnation of a Russ Meyer film festival by coeds who felt that it exploited women.

Lydia, Juno, and Alex talked about simplifying their lives and intensifying their awareness. They and all their friends were involved in psychodramas, encounter groups, or sensitivity training—verbal and nonverbal group experiences encouraging honesty and openness. Charles Reich, a professor of law at Yale, wrote *The Greening of America*, first excerpted in *The New Yorker*, extolling a new sensibility in the country, one "comfortable with long hair, funky dress, rock music, psychedelics, and personal growth." Happenings, speed, rainbows, unicorns, Kurt Vonnegut, black light, Zero Population Growth, *The Whole Earth Catalog*, Tom Wolfe's radical chic, alternate life-styles, Alan Watts, bodypainting, Janis Joplin's death by OD, the underground, Abbie Hoffman, metaphysics, Ralph Nader, India and gurus, groupies, primal therapy, Herbert Marcuse's *One Dimensional Man*, Ray Mungo's Total Loss Farm commune, Andy Warhol's Factory and Max's Kansas City, Joe Chaikin's Open Theater, yoga and tai chi, psychic healing, aphrodisiacs, whole grains and vitamins, jazz, video, rock, geodesic domes, Hunter Thompson's gonzo journalism, *Rolling Stone*—all of it was being experienced, read, or talked about.

Yale, in the early seventies, was caught up in a special moment of time. The experience was dizzying and exciting and exhausting. As the year wore on, many women began to talk of taking a year off from the Yale intensity. One of Juno's and Lydia's friends decided to head for Switzerland to study Jungian philosophy. Another wanted to go to Peru to become a revolutionary. Still others made plans to travel to Africa to live with tribes or work with Leakey in his museum, or to meditate and trek in Nepal, or to homestead in Oregon, or to study Buddhist texts in Japan. Even Lydia was planning to leave Juno behind. She had applied to an experimental actor's workshop in Paris, headed by the famous British stage director Noel Potter.

Alex and Juno and Lydia saw a good deal of each other that year, living in the same college and working on various Yale Dramat productions. There was a closeness between them that was charged with sexual tension, but after the kiss they had shared in the bathroom at the *In a Smoke-Filled Room* party, Alex had kept both of them at a sexual arm's length. To Lydia's and Juno's frustration, he spent most weekends with a soul-searching beauty from Radcliffe named Hope Jennings. Lydia had a string of men with whom she fell in and out of love. Juno had a few short affairs, but for the most part she was content with celibacy and the safety of her nonsexual relationship with Hoppy Johns.

Lydia took a box down from her closet shelf. "Guess what came today? Another care package from home."

Juno tossed aside her book. "With Cordelia's orange cupcakes?"

Lydia nodded. "And pineapple turnovers."

"Oh, I can't stand it. Okay, hips, make room for another inch." She grabbed a cupcake.

"Er . . . something else came today," Lydia said. She held out a letter for Juno to read.

Juno scanned it quickly. "Oh . . . you've been accepted to Noel Potter's workshop." She felt a sudden lump in her throat and tried not to let it show. "Oh, Lydia, that's wonderful!" Then the tears came to her eyes. "I'm going to miss you so much."

Lydia hugged her friend. "I know. Me too. But it's something I've just got to do. And I'll be back for senior year."

"How am I going to get through a whole year without having you to talk to? And Alex and Hoppy are graduating . . . God, there'll be nobody left!"

"There'll be plenty of people," Lydia said consolingly, helping herself to a pineapple turnover and passing Juno the box. She tried to move the conversation to more comfortable ground. "What's Alex going to do? Has he told you?"

"Just that he's going somewhere to write a play."

"I can't stand the fact that *neither* of us ever got anywhere with him," Lydia sighed.

"I know. He's so super. Too good to waste on all those Smithies and Cliffies . . . like Hope Jennings."

Lydia giggled. "Maybe we should've taken our sophomore year at Radcliffe."

"I just can't figure him out. I know he likes *you.*"

"He likes you too. Maybe that's the problem . . . he can't make up his mind. Besides, he makes such a big deal about not getting involved with coeds."

Juno laughed. "How many times have we had this conversation? And it always comes down to the same thing."

Lydia grinned. "Yeah . . . there's always Hope."

Alex Sage sat up in bed and lit a joint. The red and green of the neon sign over Al's Grinder Shop across the street from the Windsor Lodge Motel just outside of Cambridge flashed through the gauzy curtains. The colors fell on Alex's chest, and on the smooth back and shoulders of Hope Jennings, asleep beside him.

It was over between him and Hope. He had known it for a while now. But there never seemed to be a time to talk about it. He had sent out signals. He had been moody and difficult, but Hope did not seem to mind. Or to notice.

It was the sort of relationship he fell into with women. He was easygoing, and soon they took over. It was their parties and their events. Part of it had to do with his writer's penchant for observing. And it was easy. These women took over his life, and he did not have to make any decisions. He did what they liked, and it left him free to work.

But eventually he had to take his life back. Tomorrow he was going to tell Hope that it was over. She would be shocked. And he would feel guilty and miserable. But it had to be done.

Why? Hope was intelligent. And beautiful. She looked a lot like Candice Bergen. She was the sort of girl his mother approved of. She was the sort of date his friends envied. But, once again, he had fallen into a pattern. He had allowed himself to become involved because *she* wanted *him*. It was flattering to his ego, but things happened too fast. He did not feel that he knew her very well. He never felt that he knew any woman very well.

No, there were two exceptions—Juno Johnson and Lydia Forrest. He had made a rule, that he would not date any of the women at Yale. And he had stuck to it, although it had been difficult. But because of it, over this past year he had been able to get to know Juno and Lydia—to know them maybe better than he had ever known anyone.

He was tremendously attracted to both of them. He wanted both of them. But how could he pick one over the other, even if he were to break his rule? They were best friends. And he *liked* them both. It did not seem as if there was any solution.

And then one began to form in his head . . .

That spring, Juno designed provocative black-and-white sets for Alex's new play, *Chiaroscuro,* in which he had written a *tour de force* part for Lydia. It turned out to be another triumph for all of them. On opening night Alex insisted that Juno and Lydia come to the cast party alone, and while the party was still going strong he stole them away to their suite on the floor below, leaving his guests to fend for themselves.

"This is a special night," Alex said. "My last play at Yale. Almost graduation. You know, I've been thinking a lot about the last four years. Really more about the last two, since coeducation. So many of the guys were against it. I was sort of middle-of-the-road. Now, I can't remember what Yale was like *without* women." Alex pulled a corkscrew out of his jeans pocket and opened a bottle of 1962 Château d'Yquem. "And I can't imagine what my life would be like without you two. Let's always stay good friends." He poured three glasses and produced a jar of imported foie gras from a basket.

"To us!" Lydia said. She was already high from a giant Chicago Bomber joint that had been passed around upstairs.

They clinked glasses and drank.

"Hmmm, Alex," Juno said, "there's something wrong with this wine. It's awfully sweet."

"Just be patient." Alex spread crackers with the foie gras and handed them to Juno and Lydia. "Now . . . take a bite, then a sip of wine."

Juno followed orders and broke out into a wide grin. "Oh God, this is one of the great tastes of all time. I should have known better than to doubt you. What is it anyway?"

"A French Sauternes. My father turned me on to this, sweet wine and pâté. I pilfered this bottle from his wine cellar during my last visit. He, of course, discovered the crime immediately but let me have the bottle anyway. As long as I promised to keep it for a special occasion."

"I'm flattered," Lydia said, lighting a candle and turning off the overhead light. "That you consider us special enough."

"Tonight is a night I've fantasized about for a long time." Alex opened the window. The evening was humid and fragrant. He took off his black silk shirt and tossed it in the direction of a chair. His light hair grazed his shoulders and he was wearing a beaded headband he had bought in New Mexico. His face and body were tan from crew, and the darkness of his skin accentuated the light blueness of his eyes.

"Oh?" said Lydia. "Just what have you fantasized?"

"The three of us . . . together," he said, smiling at both of them. "Making love."

Juno was stunned. She looked at Lydia, then back at Alex. "I don't know what to say . . ."

"Don't say anything," Alex whispered. "Let's just improvise."

"I'll try anything once," Lydia purred, seductively unbuttoning her camisole until it fell away from her small breasts.

Panic swelled up in Juno. What should she do? Lydia and Alex. Her closest friend, and the man she was secretly in love with. How could she share Alex with Lydia? But how could she not? It was as far from anything she had ever imagined as it possibly could be. But maybe it was inevitable. And this was what the seventies were all about. Everybody was experimenting, trying new things. The experience was what was important. After all, this was what she had come to Yale for—an education.

Lydia had stripped to her bikini panties and was looking at Juno, smiling encouragement. Her heart was racing, but she was high, and tremendously turned on. She had wanted Alex for more than a year now. But she was also curious to know what it would be like to make love to a woman. It was something people talked about a lot these days, but Lydia would never have had the nerve to try it alone. With Alex, though . . . and it *was* Juno, her best friend . . .

Alex waited, watching them both. Juno felt a shudder run through her body and to her surprise she recognized it as pleasurable anticipation. She took hold of the bottom of her T-shirt and pulled it over her head. Her breasts, olive and smooth, gleamed in the flickering light.

Alex hugged them both tightly and guided them over onto the bed. He felt Juno trembling, and kissed her gently on the forehead. "Hey, it's okay. This is going to be beautiful. Just go with it . . . let it happen."

Lydia ran her hand across Alex's chest and down his arm, then over to Juno's arm, up, and across her chest. Then she dipped down and cupped Juno's breast. "Oh my God," she said, almost shyly. "It's so . . . different! The textures. You're so smooth, Juno . . . so . . . incredible . . ." Suddenly she laughed. "There's such a *difference* between men and women!"

Alex and Juno laughed too, and the awkward unsureness was gone. Their mouths came together in a shared kiss, three tongues exploring at random. Juno stopped thinking and allowed instinct to take over. She let herself touch Lydia's body and Alex's, freely, and the newness of it all delighted her as they touched her, too. It was momentous, amazing, and whether it was an experience that was ever repeated or not, it had opened up vast new territories of sensuality that would leave her never the same again.

They made love to each other uninhibitedly and passionately, and it was not Juno and Alex, or Lydia and Alex, but three people who desired and loved each other equally. They soared and filled the room and left it, exploding into new planes of sensation. It was the freedom, the extraordinary erotic softness of another woman's body; and for Alex the multiplicity and variety of breasts and lips and thighs, and the electric current of being at the center of this tiny passionate universe. He made love to Lydia, and Juno caressed them both; then it was Juno's turn, with Lydia's lips and hands busily sharing the pleasure. And over all the passion was a profound caring between the three of them.

When it was finally over they lay there, tangled in one another, their bodies damp with perspiration.

Alex kissed Juno. "Are you sorry?"

She smiled. "Not a bit. It's so strange . . . it all felt so right. I don't regret it for a minute."

"Oh, neither do I," Lydia said huskily. "It was wonderful. Because it was us . . . the three of us. I wouldn't ever want to do it with anyone but you two. I think this was the greatest night of my whole life . . ."

"I've never been any happier," Alex said, giving them each a kiss. "I wish we could stay like this forever. I love you both so much."

Juno hugged him. "I . . . we both love you, too."

"You know, tonight was the first time that I ever came," Lydia said with wonder. "And I did it . . . with both of you . . ."

There were tears in Juno's eyes. "It was so beautiful." She had learned a great many things tonight. And one thing she had learned was that she could make love and feel love at the same time, that she could be fulfilled without the ugliness that Max Milton had brought to it. Alex had made it possible. So had Lydia.

But where did they go from here?

They were all quiet for a long time. All at once, the situation seemed both simple and complicated. Finally Lydia got up to take a shower. Juno remained in bed with Alex for a few minutes longer, but she began to feel awkward with Lydia not there. She put on her robe and went to make coffee on the hot plate in the living room. Alex followed her.

"I have a great idea," he said. "Let's all spend the summer together. In Paris. Lydia'll be there studying acting. And I was planning to go somewhere out of the country to write. So if you come, we could get a place together. It would be great."

Lydia joined them. "Oh, it would! I was dreading being in Paris all by myself."

"I've never been to Europe," Juno said excitedly. "I've been saving up for years to take a trip. God, it'd be wonderful."

"Okay . . . we'll do it!" Alex rolled a joint, lit it, and passed it around. They chattered and made plans, but after a while Alex noticed that Juno had become quiet.

"Hey . . . is anything the matter?"

Juno was fiddling with a piece of thread that she had pulled loose from her robe, winding and unwinding it around her finger. "I'm beginning to have second thoughts . . . about living together. Tonight was special, but I don't know . . . Ultimately, I'm afraid of what might happen. That we'll ruin the most important thing we have together . . . our friendship."

"No," Lydia disagreed. "Living together will only strengthen our love for each other. One for all, and all for one."

"But it's not that easy," Juno protested. "I really care a lot for both of you. And there is the old saying, two's company. I just don't know how long the three of us could manage. What if two of us pair off and leave the other out in the cold? It could happen, you know."

"Well, it's a risk," Lydia agreed. "But why worry about it? It's like saying 'I don't want to fall in love because I might get hurt.' "

Alex spoke up. "Juno has a point. You both do. I'd like us to live together and have sex morning, noon, and night. But I suppose it could lead to problems."

They sat there for a few moments in silence.

"Well," Lydia sighed. "What are we going to do?"

Suddenly Alex grinned. "Did you ever see that old Noël Coward movie, *Design for Living?* Gary Cooper and Fredric March and Miriam Hopkins had our problem."

"What did they do about it?" Juno asked.

"They made a gentlemen's agreement," Alex said. "No sex."

"How boring," Lydia groaned. After a moment, she shrugged. "Still, it might be the only solution."

Juno nodded. "That way we could all live together without jealousy rearing its head."

"I don't know." Alex shook his head. "I don't know if I'll be able to keep my hands off you."

"Now, Alex, remember . . . gentlemen's agreement," Juno said.

"Okay, I guess that's the way it's got to be."

They shook hands. Then Lydia's face lit up with a mischievous grin. "Before the ban goes into effect," she suggested, "what about one for the road?"

Part Two

Paris, 1971

Chapter Seven

They spent the summer in a fourth-floor walk-up above a court-yard off the Rue Bonaparte, near St.-Germain-des-Prés. It belonged to Jean Pascal, a friend of Alex's who was off in Brazil producing a film. The apartment was light and airy, convenient to the Métro, Le Drugstore, the cafés Flore and Deux Magots, and the Brasserie Lipp; but most important, it contained a bedroom, a maid's room, and an office with a daybed. In the beginning, Alex was awarded the bedroom because Jean Pascal was his friend, but it soon became clear that Lydia and her vast wardrobe could not exist in the tiny maid's quarters.

In any case, sleeping arrangements were fluid. It was a time of much coming and going, all-night parties, and a stream of friends from the States crashing for a few nights en route to other places. As a general rule, the bedroom was reserved for whoever needed it most on any given night. But though many different combinations shared the bed, it was never Lydia, Alex, and Juno together. Their pact of celibacy had held up despite more than occasional outbursts of lust, temperament, and frustration.

But frustration aside, it was a wonderful summer, passed in the exhilaration of total freedom an ocean away from families and responsibilities. Lydia attended her drama workshop, Juno sketched all over the city and took a French course at the Alliance Française. Alex whiled away long afternoons in cafés, drinking Ricard and writing drafts of plays in French schoolboy's notebooks. They moved in a crowd of film and theater people, queens and transvestites, painters, and rock stars. They watched four movies in a row at the Cinémathèque, dined at midnight at La Coupole, discoed at Castel's, dropped acid and danced in the streets like Gene Kelly and Leslie Caron in *An American in Paris*. They hopped in cars and drove all night to drink champagne on the beach at dawn in Deauville. On weekend mornings, they rummaged around the *marchés aux puces* for cheap chic and old records, then ate inexpensive Moroccan couscous, or splurged at Fauchon, Hédiard, Maison de la Truffe, and the other gourmet shops around the Place de la Madeleine.

One Saturday, after a visit to the flea market *d'Aligre*, Alex treated Lydia and Juno to an extravagant lunch of caviar and blini at Caviar Kaspia. In the upstairs room, a faded tribute to czarist Russia, they noshed on payasnaya, sevruga, oscietra, beluga, and the coral eggs of Norwegian salmon.

"This is an incredible treat, Alex," Juno said, spreading her blini with payasnaya, "for a girl who never even had lumpfish till a year ago. But then this whole summer has been incredible. I can't believe that in a couple of weeks I'll be back in New Haven."

"Oh God, don't even say it. I'm going to miss you so much," Lydia moaned.

"Me, too. It's not going to seem like Paris without you here," Alex said.

"What are we going to do without you?"

"Well . . . I've been doing a lot of thinking about that. I mean, with me gone, the pact is rather ridiculous. It's hard enough for three people to live together and keep their hands off each other, but for two it would be just plain unnatural."

"Look, Juno," Lydia said, "I've thought about it, too. Our friendship is the most important thing. There's plenty of sex to be had in this town without jeopardizing that. God, look at all the men I've had already this summer, and I'm still working on Noel Potter."

"I'm sure he'll come around. But I just want you guys to know that I'll understand if you get it together. I might not like it, but I'll understand." She forced a smile. "After all, you're young, you're in the most romantic city in the world . . ."

Alex put his hand over Juno's. "Your spirit would be with us all the time. I don't think it could work with just two of us. It would be empty." He paused. "Besides, there's something I was going to tell you both today. Please understand, this in no way affects our friendship . . . nothing could ever do that. But I've been seeing Lorraine Gilbert, and I'm really hung up on her . . ."

"Lorraine Gilbert?" Lydia croaked. "Oh, Alex, you're not star-struck, are you? She's a terrible actress, and she's at least thirty. Besides, she has someone. She's always with that fat Paul what's-his-name."

"He's her agent," Alex explained. "Anyway . . . she's leaving for Malta on Tuesday. To start a new film. And she wants me to come with her."

"And of course you've said yes." Juno looked at Lydia and then back at Alex. "How could you do that without discussing it with us first?"

"You're deserting us," Lydia snapped, "for that *cow*. I can't believe it!"

"Hey . . . hold on a minute! You don't have any right to be jealous. This has nothing to do with the three of us. It's just that Lorraine is fabulous. I want to be with her. You know this had to happen sooner or later . . . that one of us might fall in love. As it turns out, it's probably the best thing for all of us."

"That's easy for you to say," Lydia grumbled. "You take off for Malta, Juno heads back to Yale, then where am I?"

"With Jean's flat all to yourself. Taking a drama course you really love. And probably getting it on with Noel Potter." Alex frowned. "And I'd appreciate it if you wouldn't put down Lorraine. You hardly know her."

There were tears in Lydia's eyes. "Okay, okay. I just thought everything was so perfect between us."

"It has been," Juno said. "But we can't rule each other's emotions. Alex can't help it if he's fallen in love with Lorraine . . ."

"I don't know if I'm in love with her. She's sexy. I like her. I'm just going to Malta to be with her. Who knows what'll happen?" Alex finished off his wine. "Look, I don't want to hurt either of you. But I can't keep living with you two without making love. This summer has been a constant hard-on for me. It's driving me crazy. I have to get away."

"Then *go*, damn it! Juno and I don't need you." Lydia grabbed her handbag and ran downstairs.

"Oh shit," Alex said, signaling for the waiter. "I didn't want this to happen."

"I know," Juno said. "I'll go catch up with her."

Lydia was standing by a flower kiosk down the street. The flower vendor was jabbering at her in French. Lydia ignored him and was staring at the wild orchids.

"Lydia, don't be angry," Juno said, catching up. "It's not Alex's fault."

"That damned femme fatale," Lydia fumed. "Never in my life have I seen anyone so obvious. 'Ohhh, Aleex, you ahr so clayver to write ze plays.' She even bats her false eyelashes at him. I can't believe Alex can't see through it. Really!"

Lydia started across the Place de La Madeleine against the traffic light.

Juno grabbed her arm and pulled her back to the sidewalk. "Take it easy. Look, Alex is right. We don't know Lorraine very well. Besides, we can't really keep him from falling in love with someone else."

"Oh yes, we could have! If only *you* hadn't decided that we shouldn't make love."

"Me? I thought it was a mutual decision." Juno was annoyed by the accusation. "And you went along with it. Besides, even if we had been sleeping together all summer, Alex might still have gotten involved with Lorraine."

"No, he wouldn't have!" Lydia shrieked. "He wouldn't have wanted to, *or* needed to."

"Okay, have it your way! I'm not going to keep arguing about what might have been. And I'd like not to spoil what we have left." Juno walked away. "I'll see you later."

"Wait . . . please!" Lydia called out. Juno stopped and turned around. Her eyes were still angry. "I'm sorry, Juno. It's just that I can't bear it. You and Alex are both leaving . . ." Tears spilled out of her eyes and ran down her cheeks. "I love you both so much . . . and I'm so scared of being left alone. You have *no* idea how hard it's going to be for me. I fall apart when I'm by myself. I've tried it before. It's going to be hell!"

Juno threw her arms around her friend and they hugged each other tightly. "I know . . . I know. Oh, Lydia, I don't want to go back to school either without you there. It's been such a terrific summer, and now it's turning so awful." Juno began to cry, too.

After several blocks of walking and crying, Lydia stopped in a pharmacy and bought a packet of tissue. They blew their noses and dried their eyes, then stopped at a sidewalk café and ordered tea. They drank in silence, each lost in thought. Finally, Juno spoke.

"I've never been jealous before. I know I might have been if I had left and you and Alex had fallen in love." Juno brushed her dark hair away from her face. "But I must say, I am jealous of Lorraine. She's a celebrity, and she's very sophisticated. I agree she's not entirely beautiful, but she does have great personal style." Juno laughed. "And I hate her!"

Lydia giggled huskily. "Maybe we can get rid of her. We could tell her Alex has VD."

"I'm sure it wouldn't matter to her . . . she probably already has it."

"Well, what if we tell her that Alex is impotent. No . . . ," Lydia said, "she must already know he isn't."

"You know, it's probably fine that Alex is going away with her. He'll get bored faster."

"Do you think so?"

Juno nodded. "Or she'll tire of him. I give it a month."

"You're right. They have nothing in common. It's just an infatuation that'll run its course. I was ridiculous to blow my cool . . . I feel really awful." But her eyes lit up. "I know . . . let's throw a going-away party for Alex."

"That's a great idea. It'll show him we have no hard feelings . . . and that we still care for him, no matter what."

"But we won't invite *her* to the party," Lydia said.

"Lydia! We *have* to invite her," Juno laughed. "So we can slip poison in her Perrier."

As it turned out, Lorraine Gilbert was too busy packing for Malta to come to the party. Nearly everyone else showed up though, including quite a few who were not invited. Even Noel Potter was there, which went a long way toward distracting Lydia from her funk over Alex's leaving.

Lydia looked fabulous in an American fifties prom dress she

had picked up for thirty francs at a flea market. It was pink taffeta, widely crinolined, with a tight-fitting bodice exposing plenty of cleavage. There was a black sash around the middle, dotted with rhinestones. The skirt was accented with campy black bows. She had found a pair of elbow-length red gloves, and she wore a white orchid above one ear.

Juno had put together an equally outrageous outfit, black bikini-cut chiffon trousers, the legs of which she had shredded in strips to the thigh with scissors. The waistband dipped low at her hips to reveal a tiny cluster of stars that she had had tattooed by a man named Bruno in Pigalle. Her breasts were barely covered by a jeweled halter hung from a narrow chain around her neck and clasped in back below her shoulder blades. Her hair was pulled high and to the side into a long ponytail entwined with gold and sequined rope. She was barefoot, a habit she had fallen into to minimize her height among the diminutive French, but she had painted a design on her feet with different colors of acrylic paint.

"Juno, come here!" Lydia called. "I want you to meet Noel Potter. You've heard me mention him, haven't you?"

Noel Potter was drinking straight scotch, and probably had been for some time from what Juno could see. He was a man of medium height with thinning salt-and-pepper hair that bushed in sideburns around his ears and curled below his collar. His cheeks were veined. One eye was covered by a black leather patch. The other, a deep, watery blue, was fixed on Juno's skimpily covered breasts. His thin lips curved in a greeting as he held out a hand to Juno.

"I'm afraid I've heard nothing about you, but I hope Lydia will remedy that."

"Forget it, Noel. She's engaged to three of the richest oilmen in Texas and they all carry guns."

"My, my. You Americans are all so amusing."

"Oh, there's one of my fiancés now. Excuse me. Nice to meet you," Juno said. She slipped adroitly away just as Noel Potter's hand was reaching out in the direction of her breasts.

She found Alex in the kitchen uncorking more wine. "Have you met the great Noel Potter yet?"

"Great with drink. I think Lydia's got herself a handful of trouble there."

"Well, he almost got a handful of *me,*" Juno said. "I'm steering clear of him. I suspect he's not a one-woman man."

"He certainly has an eye for the ladies," Alex said, covering one eye with a pot holder.

"Oh, Alex, you're terrible," she said, laughing.

"Is this a private party, or may anyone throw darts at that legendary British lecher?" A young Frenchman wearing a black leather jacket and camouflage infantry pants walked into the kitchen.

"Bernard! When the hell did you get back?" Alex greeted the new arrival with a Gallic hug. "Juno, this is Bernard Jullien, one of the next great French filmmakers."

"If I can ever get the money to make a film," said Bernard with an ironic shrug. "I've been working as assistant director in Brussels with one of the greatest fools of the French cinema. He makes one successful film twenty years ago and they keep giving him money, but me . . ." He shrugged again and looked at Juno.

"Oh, sorry, Bernard. This is Juno Johnson. She's one of my roommates."

"You are a very fortunate man. Are they all as beautiful as this, your roommates?"

"More," Juno said. "The other is the one who's currently infatuated with Noel Potter."

"Ah," Bernard said with a low whistle. "The redhead in the pink gown . . . *pas mal, mon ami.* How do you do it, Alex?"

Alex exchanged a glance with Juno, and they both laughed. "I don't," he said.

By three o'clock the last of the guests had left. Alex broke open a bottle of Dom Perignon. "I've been saving this, for just the three of us." He poured it into three glasses and passed them around. "To us," he toasted, "the Three Musketeers."

"All for one, and one for all." Lydia raised her glass.

"Now and forever," Juno said. She burst into tears.

Lydia hugged her. "Oh, Juno, darling, don't cry," she said, and started crying herself.

"Hey," said Alex miserably, "we're supposed to be having a good time."

"But it's over," Juno sobbed.

"Nothing's over," Alex reassured her. Then he smiled. "Well, I guess something is. The pact." He held out his arms. "What the hell . . . it was only to get us through the summer."

Juno looked up and blotted her tears on a napkin. "Well," she said, "fall *is* in the air."

It was not like the first time. Then, it had been a rushing together of bodies and passions, all joyous discovery. This was slow and savoring, pleasure that also ached with sadness.

They undressed each other by the yellow streetlight that cut across the bed, dividing it into triangles of light and darkness. They knelt, facing each other, touching with tender fingers that moved over the skin as much to remember as to caress. Lydia ran her hand down Juno's cheek, and Juno turned her head to press her lips against the soft palm. Alex stroked their backs, and the different swells of their buttocks. The women's hands met at his groin and traveled together the length of his hard and trembling penis. Juno kissed Lydia's breast and pulled the nipple into her mouth, and felt a hand—Lydia's or Alex's, she could not be sure—slip between her thighs. They lay back on the bed, half in light and half in shadow, and made love.

It was not like the first time. Then it had been Yale, and the beginning of something. Now it was Paris, the City of Light, the city of lovers. And though it might not be the end of everything, it felt like the end of something.

Chapter Eight

Alex waited until Lydia and Juno were asleep. He kissed them each gently, and quietly slipped out of bed. His flight for Malta was at eight and he had to pack. He was to pick up Lorraine beforehand.

Juno awoke at the touch of Alex's lips on her cheek, but she kept her eyes closed. She lay still and listened to the sounds of his emptying drawers and filling his suitcase in the next room. Lydia moaned heavily beside her and turned over in her sleep. Juno stared at the sky out the window. It appeared as if the day was going to be overcast. Well, she thought, that would match her mood.

She heard Alex carry his bag to the front door, and felt utterly miserable. Then his footsteps came back down the hall. He stood in the doorway of the bedroom. Their eyes locked, and he blew her a kiss. She smiled at him, and he smiled back. Then he closed the door and was gone.

For a long time she lay there, not really thinking about anything, just feeling sad. Suddenly the sound of the front door opening startled her out of her trance. Her first thought was that Alex had forgotten something. *Maybe he's changed his mind* was her second.

But the footsteps that came into the apartment did not sound like Alex's, and a third terrifying thought crossed her mind: that Alex had not locked the door, that somebody was breaking in. The unfamiliar footsteps were heading for the bedroom.

Juno panicked. She snatched the sheet up to cover her breasts and looked frantically around for some sort of a weapon. As the

door handle turned, she grabbed a transistor radio from the bedside table and held it threateningly over her head.

A scruffy, unshaven man appeared in the doorway. "Oh my
God, *excusez moi*," he said, stepping back with his hands raised.
"Je suis un ami de Jean." He put his hand in his pocket and pro-
duced a key. *"J'ai la clef.* Okay?" His English was British, his
French was awkward.

Juno, her heart pounding, lowered the radio. "Okay. Wait in
the living room," she whispered. "Let me get something on. I'll
be out in a minute."

She threw on Lydia's robe, which was too small, and slipped
into the bathroom to brush her teeth. When she came out he was
flopped down on the sofa, rummaging through a duffel bag. He
stood up with a sheepish smile.

"Jesus, I'm sorry," he said. "Jean's an old friend. I always stay
here when I'm in town. I knew he was away, but I had no idea
anybody was using the place. Oh, my name's Tony Silver."

"I'm Juno Johnson. You scared the shit out of me."

"I'm sorry. I've been on a plane for the last twenty-four
hours. All I need is a place to catch some sleep. Then I'll find a
hotel."

"Where are you coming from?" she asked.

"Australia," he said. "Do you think I could trouble you for
something to eat?"

"I'm afraid there's only leftover bread and cheese. We had a
party last night."

"That sounds super." He followed Juno into the kitchen.
While she made coffee he attacked some runny Brie and the
remnants of a salami. Between mouthfuls he told her that he
was the road manager for a rock group, Scrap Metal. They were
in Paris for a concert, then off to the other European capitals.
His sentences were punctuated by yawns, and after a few minutes Juno steered him toward the daybed in the office. Alex's
things were gone, and the room looked strangely empty.

She set about clearing up the remains of the party mess. After
a while Lydia emerged from the bedroom, nude and rubbing
her eyes.

"Oh, *there's* my robe," she said. "A bit small for you, Juno,
don't you think? Have you made any coffee?"

Juno nodded toward the kitchen. "There's a fresh pot."

Lydia poured herself a cup and came out to sit on the sofa. "Gee, I can't believe Alex is gone. The place seems so empty."

"Well, not as empty as you might think."

"Alex?" Her face lit up.

"No. Somebody new arrived. A friend of Jean's, a guy named Tony something. He manages a rock group, and he's crashing here for a few hours."

"Hmm, maybe you'd better give me back my robe."

Juno laughed. "Don't worry. He's out like a light. He'd been on a plane for twenty-four hours."

Lydia sipped her coffee. "I miss Alex."

"Me too." Juno came and sat next to Lydia and put her arm around her. "It was good last night, wasn't it?" She sighed. "I kept thinking while we were making love that maybe he'd change his mind, and not go."

Lydia hugged her. "I know, so was I. It *was* good. But I've been thinking. I'm sorry for what I said on the street the other day. You *were* right. I know we couldn't have made it through the summer with that kind of intensity together. As much as I love you, I honestly wonder if I wouldn't have started trying to cut you out and get Alex for myself."

"I know what you mean. It's great with the three of us, but . . . but there's a natural tendency to want to pair off. Maybe the pact was a pretty good idea after all. I mean, our friendship is more important than sex."

It occurred to Lydia that she was still naked and hugging Juno. She began to feel self-conscious, but then that seemed silly after the way they had been last night. "Juno . . . when we all make love together, how do you feel about it? I mean, with me? Do you think we'd ever . . . ?"

"Well, I'm not sure. I really love it while it's happening, but it all has to do with Alex being there. Somehow that makes it right. But without him . . . I don't think . . . I mean I'm attracted to you, but I don't think I'd want to do it just with another woman."

Lydia nodded. "Yes . . . that's the way I feel, too." She gave a little laugh. "Well, that clears the air, doesn't it? I mean I wasn't quite sure what we were supposed to do, with Alex gone."

Past midnight, Tony Silver was still asleep. Lydia was out with Noel Potter, and Juno had turned down a party invitation. She was still upset about Alex's departure and did not feel like seeing anybody. She was stretched out on the sofa reading Edith Wharton when Tony Silver emerged, rubbing his eyes.

"Good God," he said. "Have I actually slept all day?"

"And a good part of the night. How do you feel?"

"Starving. Have you had dinner?"

"About six hours ago."

"Want to come along and watch me eat? I'll buy you a drink."

"No, thanks."

"Oh come on. I know a great brasserie in Les Halles that's open all night. My shrink says it's bad for me to eat alone."

Juno smiled. "Well . . ."

"Great! Just give me five minutes to shower and change out of these rotting clothes."

Clean and shaven, Tony Silver looked a good deal better than Juno had expected. He was a bit taller than she, and thin, with an almost handsome face. His dark hair was pulled back in a short ponytail, and he wore a fringed leather jacket over a tie-dyed T-shirt. At Au Pied du Cochon she munched on a crisp baguette and drank Beaujolais while Tony hungrily downed an *entrecôte* of beef, grilled rare and served with fresh shallots and *pommes frites.*

Tony, pumped up from all the sleep, talked nonstop about the tour, Australia, the groupies, and the guys in the band. Juno could not help but be impressed. Although Scrap Metal was not yet big in the States, she had heard their first album and liked it. They were one of the most promising of the new generation of Liverpool rock groups.

After the meal they decided to walk back to the flat, across the Pont Neuf and down the Boulevard St.-Germain. Juno was enjoying herself. Tony was funny and interesting, and was helping to ease her out of her depression.

Back at the flat, Tony started putting his things back in his duffel bag.

"I won't impose on you any longer," he said. "Thanks for everything."

"Where are you going?"

"Hotel."

"At this time of night? Don't be silly. We've got an extra room and you're only going to be here a few days. I'm sure Lydia won't mind."

"Well, if you're sure . . . thanks. I'll take you both to the concert to show my appreciation."

"That'd be great." Juno yawned. "Since I didn't sleep all day I'm afraid I'm going to have to leave you. I'm exhausted."

"Okay, good night. Thanks for watching me have dinner." He shook her hand. "See you in the morning, or whenever we get on the same schedule."

Over the next few days, Juno saw a great deal of Tony. She liked him and she could tell he liked her, although he made no overt pass. The two nights before the concert she went with him to the Palais des Sports where Scrap Metal would be performing. He introduced her to the members of the band. The lead singer, Garth Meacham, started to come on to Juno. Then a bit later she saw Tony take him aside and talk to him. Garth looked over at Juno and nodded. After that he left her pretty much alone.

"We've just got to run through some light cues," Tony said around one o'clock. "Then we can go get something to eat, if you feel like it."

"Sure. But, I warn you, I'm not such a cheap date when I'm this hungry."

Juno watched fascinated as the lighting director, a Dutchman named Leo, went through his paces. Afterward, she asked him all sorts of questions. He was patient and seemed impressed with her knowledge of lighting technique.

"Where'd you find this woman?" Leo asked when Tony came to get Juno. "She knows damned near as much as I do."

Afterward, they ate mussels and scallops at Le Vaudeville, a lively brasserie built in the twenties across from the Bourse on Rue Vivienne.

"Where did you learn so much about lighting? You never told me anything about that."

"I haven't told you much about anything, Tony." Juno laughed. "You've been doing most of the talking."

Tony sat back with a grin. "Well, now I'm listening."

"There's not much to tell. I'm studying at Yale. I've been over here with some friends for the summer, but I'm going back next week."

"What about your friend, Lydia? Will she be going back, too?"

"No. She's studying acting with Noel Potter. She's also completely hung up on the guy and having a mad affair with him. I don't think wild horses could drag her back across the Atlantic at this point."

"And how do you feel about that?" Tony asked, looking at her strangely.

Juno shrugged. "I think he's a creep. But it's her own life. I'm no one to judge. I've been involved with some pretty strange types myself."

"Types? You mean guys?"

"Of course." Juno laughed in bafflement at the expression on his face. "What did you think I meant? Horses?"

Tony started laughing, and kept on until his face turned a deep red. Juno sat watching him, not quite understanding why what she had said was so funny. Finally, wiping his eyes with his napkin, he took a large gulp of wine and calmed down.

"I . . . you have no idea why this is so funny," he said. "But this has been the most incredible mistake of my life."

Juno was starting to get annoyed. "What has? Mind letting me in on the joke?"

"You may not find it such a terrific joke. But you see I thought you were . . . that is, when I walked in on you that morning and saw you and Lydia in bed together . . ."

"Oh shit. You mean you thought I was a lesbian?"

He threw up his hands in defense. "Well, wouldn't *you* have?"

Juno sat for a moment looking at him. Suddenly she began to giggle. "And that's why you haven't tried anything with me?"

Tony nodded. "I figured you were out of bounds. Immune to the silver-tongued charm." He paused for a moment. "Are you?"

"Not at all," Juno smiled. "I was beginning to lose all my confidence."

Tony signaled for the waiter. "*Garçon, l'addition, s'il vous plaît. Vite! Vite!*"

The evening was hot and languid, a last gasp of the Parisian summer. The smell of marijuana filled the air, like the incense of a religious ritual. The Scrap Metal concert was sold out and the fans were a kaleidoscope of color as they moved through the stands and aisles of the Palais des Sports. Juno and Lydia, clinging to Tony Silver, were waved past the police barricade and down to the dressing rooms. Dozens of people were milling around backstage, technicians, groupies, girlfriends, even a few small children with a dog.

"I feel as if I should have a T-shirt with Not a Dyke printed on it," Juno said.

Tony laughed. "Don't worry. Your reputation as a heterosexual woman is intact. The guys know. Okay . . . I have a hundred things to take care of. See you later."

"Who's that over there?" Lydia asked, indicating a young man with wild, curly hair. He was drinking beer and smoking a Thai stick. "I like his looks."

"Kenny Thomas, the drummer," Juno said. "Come on, I'll introduce you."

Lydia had taken an evening off from Noel Potter to attend the concert. Actually, she had needed some time away from him. Noel was charismatic, but his legendary drinking was beginning to get on her nerves. The later the evening got, the sharper Noel's humor became, and his manner turned more belligerent. He often ended the night slumped in his chair, snoring. Lydia usually went home before that happened. Late afternoons after the workshop, before he had drunk much scotch, were the only times he could get it up to make love. Still, he was a famous director, and his mind, when clear, was innovative and brilliant. She had learned more about acting from him in the last few weeks than in all her previous experience. Lydia could not quite believe that he was as interested in her as he appeared. But Noel was emphatic in his praise of her talent, and it was easy to assume the same sincerity in his declarations of affection.

Juno and Lydia were sharing Kenny the drummer's beer when Garth Meacham, the lead guitarist and singer, came over.

"Hey, girl, Tony wants you. Over there," he said in his North Country accent.

"Thanks." Juno always felt vibrations between herself and Garth. He acted as though he felt them, too. But she was with Tony now, and Garth always had swarms of smashing-looking hopefuls waiting for him everywhere he went.

Juno had no trouble finding Tony. She just followed the sound of his voice. He was shaking his fist at one of the sound men, yelling. "Shit, bloody fucking shit! How could you bloody *let* him get hold of that stuff? He's been cool for three weeks now." He looked at his watch. "We're already running half a fucking hour late. *Shit!*"

Juno waited silently. The sound man looked at her and back at Tony. It was obvious that he was squirming inside from Tony's wrath, but he made no attempt to either interrupt or defend himself. Juno could tell that someone had flaked out because of drugs, but could not figure out who. She had seen most everyone in the crew Tony had been introducing her to over the past few days.

Except Leo, she suddenly realized. Leo, the lighting guy, was nowhere around. Panic began to tug at her stomach. Before Tony calmed down enough to talk to her she knew what he was going to say.

"Juno . . . Leo's completely out of it. So's his assistant. They had a party this afternoon, and this jerk gave them some STP. They're gone for the night. Now, think hard . . . how much of the lighting run-through can you remember?"

"Well, I only sat in on it twice. I can remember pretty much, but . . ."

"Then improvise the rest. D'you think you can?" Tony asked.

"No," she said, frightened. "There are thousands of people out there. This isn't just flipping a switch. It's complicated, it's . . ."

"Juno, by the time I track down someone in Paris and get them here, it'll be an hour. At the very least. And they won't know as much as you about how the band works. Meanwhile, the bloody fans'll be tearing this place apart. Come on . . ." He shoved several heavily marked sheets of paper into her hand. "Follow the cues as best you can and make up the rest. What d'you say?"

"I'll go out there an unknown . . . and I'll come back a basket case." But she felt adrenaline begin to pump through her body. "Yeah . . . I guess I can try."

"You can't do any worse than Leo in his condition." Tony kissed her. "I'll find someone to help you." He pushed her in the direction of the lighting board. "Five minutes," he said, giving her a stick of gum.

Juno was staring at the smudged cue sheets, trying to decipher them, when Lydia found her. "Far out," she said. "Are you really going to do it? You realize it's every ingenue's dream."

"Or nightmare," Juno said. "Oh, Lydia, what am I going to do? I can't make out these cues and pull the switches and do everything at once. Tony was going to find someone to help me, but . . ."

"It's cool," Lydia said. "I'll read the cues, you pull the switches. If you know what all this stuff means."

A voice rasped through the headset into Juno's ear. "Okay, hit it." Juno handed Lydia the sheets.

Juno pushed a lever. A spotlight circled the center mike.

"Fantastic!" Lydia whispered.

Tony Silver ran out to the spotlight. The audience roared. *"Et maintenant, mes amis, le meilleur* band *de* rock and roll *dans le monde,"* he shrieked, "Scrap Metal!"

The audience went wild with clapping, shouting, foot stomping, and whistling.

Juno slid a couple of levers and the lights came up as the band launched into their newest song, "Give It All to Me."

Lydia called out a cue. Juno pushed a switch, and the entire stage plunged into darkness.

"Give it *all* to me," Garth Meacham wailed out of the blackness.

"Merde," said Juno. "Did you say five or nine?"

"Five."

"Oh." Juno flipped another switch and the lights were back to normal.

"Sorry," Lydia said. "So much for three years of elocution lessons."

From then on it went more or less smoothly, Juno's confidence growing as she gained familiarity with the board. Often she improvised, sometimes without complete success, but somehow or other it all worked.

At the end of the concert, after four standing ovations and encores, the band left the stage for the final time. Juno brought up all the lights and slumped in her chair, soaked in perspiration.

"We did it!" Lydia croaked, pride and amazement in her voice. "Oh, Juno, you were brilliant."

Tony Silver rushed up the stairs and hugged her. "You were bloody fabulous," he said. "I knew you'd do it."

"Did you really?" Juno asked, wiping her head with a towel.

"No . . ." He laughed. "But we didn't have much bloody choice, did we? Anyway, girl, you pulled it off."

The waiter wove through the crowded packed tables of La Coupole with many bottles of wine and beer, and set them down on the long table where Scrap Metal and its entourage were celebrating.

Garth Meacham was laughing. "I bloody nearly crapped my pants when the lights went out. There I was, 'Give it *all* to me,' and then *pow!* Black as ink!"

"You should've saved it for 'Heart of Darkness.' 'Twould have been quite effective there," Kenny Thomas said to Juno.

"Oh God, don't remind me. I could've crawled through a hole in the floor." Juno put her head in her hands.

"No, you were super," Garth said. "I really dug that orange spot at the end of 'Blow My Mind.'"

"Yeah . . . that was rather lovely," Kenny said. "You know, come to think of it, this lady here fucked up far less than our beloved Leo."

Tony looked at him. "Christ, you're right. Remember that night in Melbourne . . ."

On until dawn, when they had all filtered out in different directions, Juno basked with the pride of having saved the day.

Back on Rue Bonaparte, as she wolfed down scrambled eggs

with Lydia, Kenny, and Tony she still felt high from the exhilaration of accomplishment. Even after she and Tony had gone to
bed, too exhausted to make love, she still could not calm her
nerve endings enough to sleep.

When she did succumb, finally, it was to a deep, comfortable
sleep, full of dreams of well-being.

Juno awoke in late afternoon to the smell of black *café filtre*.
She opened her eyes. Tony was holding a mug several inches
from her nose. "Hmmm . . ." she murmured. "That's nice, but
later . . . I want to sleep more." She closed her eyes and snug-
gled back into the pillow.

"You can't, love. We have to talk. There isn't a hell of a lot of
time."

Opening her eyes again, she looked at him. He was shaved
and dressed, and he held the cup for her to sip. She lifted her
head and took a swallow of the nondiluted caffeine. "Ohhh . . .
I don't know if I really needed that." She smiled at Tony, but
the expression on his face was serious.

"Come on, Juno. Hold the cup yourself and drink it down. I
want you clear enough to hear what I'm saying."

Juno rearranged the pillows and sat up. The afternoon shadows gave a surreal cast to the room. "What's wrong, Tony? You
look so stern."

He smiled, his brown eyes softening. "I'm sorry. It's just that
I've been up and out since noon. Attending to things. As you
know, we have to be in Amsterdam tomorrow. I had a talk with
Leo. He's going to do the gig there, and then he's out. I'm
bloody sick of dealing with his flakiness."

"What'll you do after that?" Juno asked, draining the cup. She
was wide-awake now.

"That's what we have to talk about. There're a couple of
things going on." Tony sat on the bed and leaned back against
the pillows with her. He rubbed her jaw with the back of his
hand as he talked. "These last few days . . . being with you
. . . have been so real to me. You have no idea what it's like
being on the road, surrounded by strangers all the time. Eating
and drinking with them, going to bed with them, leaving them
behind. They're only interested in what you are, or do, not *who*
you are. After a while, you begin to feel like a chameleon. You

show your different colors to different people . . . but not all your colors to one person. But, I don't know . . . since that morning I walked in on you it's all been different. Even Paris has been different. I really care about you, Juno. I don't want us to end just like that." He blew an imaginary puffball out of his hand.

"Oh, Tony, I've had a wonderful time with you, too. I don't want it to end either. Right now, the last thing in the world I want to do is go back to Yale."

Tony kissed her sweetly, with more caring than passion. "I'm glad you feel that way, because I have a proposition . . ."

"You already propositioned me, Tony," Juno teased, "and, as I recall, you were successful."

"Well, let's hope I am again. After Amsterdam, we go to Copenhagen, Stockholm, Helsinki, Vienna, Hamburg, Munich . . ." He ticked them off on his fingers. "Oh bloody hell, I can't remember them all now. The point is, I can get you a working card . . . and an assistant. Will you come on the road with us? You can do the lighting and we can be together."

"Oh wow . . ." Juno closed her eyes and thought for a few moments. "You know more than anything I'd like to say yes."

"Then say it."

"No . . . I can't quit school. All my life I've thought a college education was the most important thing in the world to get. It'd kill my parents if . . ."

"Love," Tony interrupted. "I was talking about it with Lydia. She's taking a year off. So can you. You could probably get credit for life experience, or something. Working in the real world, for real money, is a lot better than discussing lighting theories with some bloody old professor. Come with me now. I'll get you back to Yale later. Jesus! You can't afford *not* to do it. Think of all the bread you'll make."

Juno shook her head. "This is crazy. I can't!"

"But you want to."

"Oh yes . . . I do."

"Then do it, that's all."

"That's all?" Juno laughed giddily.

"See how easy life can be when you do what you want?" Tony laughed with her.

The next day Juno packed, telephoned her parents, cabled Yale, had a farewell-for-now lunch with Lydia, and rushed to the airport to board an Air France flight for Holland with Tony Silver and Scrap Metal.

Yale had been there for a long time. It could wait.

Chapter Nine

The sun dipped low, and hung at the tops of the swaying masts of the fishing fleet by the quay. Its reddening rays streamed horizontally onto the notebook that Alex balanced in his lap where he sat on the tiny balcony of the hotel room. The Phoenicia Hotel, just outside the gates of Valletta, gave a magnificent view of the Sliema harbor and the sparkling azure-clear water beyond it. The voices of the Maltese fishermen rose up to Alex's balcony in a lively, cheerful cacophony. From closer by came the subdued undertone of softly clinking glassware and the murmur of conversation from cocktail hour on the hotel terrace.

Alex sipped his gin and tonic and frowned in concentration at the notebook. The scene was almost there. He could feel it. But it stayed just beyond his reach.

(Howard is at the kitchen table. The radio, reduced to a baffling litter of components, is strewn across the entire surface. Howard works over it with a screwdriver and a pair of needle-nosed pliers. Outside the snow continues to fall, whipped by the tireless wind.)

HOWARD: Damn!
(The door from the living room swings open as Janet comes in and heads for the refrigerator. It continues to swing back and forth as she extracts a Dr. Pepper.)

JANET: Why don't you just give it up, Howard?

HOWARD: *(Annoyed.)* Give up? What are you talking about? This thing's our goddamn lifeline to the outside world!

JANET: *(Popping the tab on her soda.)* A lifeline to the Top 40 . . . zapped by a faulty transistor.
(She exits to the living room. Again the door swings endlessly, jerkily.)

HOWARD: *(More to himself than calling after her.)* Top 40 my ass. To the world! To the goddamn weather reports. Phone's out, TV's out, and we're trapped here like penguins on a fucking ice floe . . .
(From the living room come the first notes of a Chopin concerto played on a spinet. The music continues as Howard reassembles the radio. Suddenly there is loud static squawking.)

RADIO VOICE: . . . of the continuing snowstorm today to affect a daring escape from the Springfield Women's Detention Facility. Lyons, a member of the Women's Army of Radicals (WAR), was serving . . .
(At this moment the kitchen door blows open. Howard, startled, drops the radio. It smashes to the floor.)

HOWARD: Shit!
(As he drops to his knees to pick up the shattered radio, a young blond woman in gray, loose-fitting pants and jacket, slips through the door and conceals herself, shivering in the pantry. Janet comes in, rushing to close the door.)

JANET: Jesus, Howard!

Alex scratched his lower lip with the end of his pencil. Jesus, Howard what? The scene needed a punch here. A laugh, something that would put into sharp perspective Howard's obsession with the radio, his claustrophobia, his desperate need to stay in touch with the world beyond the blizzard . . . and at the same time, an ironic counterpoint to the unsuspected danger of the escaped radical feminist lurking in the pantry.

A line began to form:

JANET: Jesus, Howard! Isn't there enough snow outside without inviting it in here? By the time you . . .

From the canopied wicker bed came Lorraine Gilbert's sleepy, husky voice.

"Alex? *Mon cher* . . . *viens ici.* Come back to bed."

"Hmmm . . . just a second."

"Ohhh *non.* You are always writing. I want your beautiful body beside me. Inside me. Now."

Alex grinned. "Let me just get this down."

Lorraine climbed out of bed and walked across the room to the balcony. She was naked. Her full tanned breasts swayed gently from side to side. She stood over him, pressed her golden thatch of pubic hair against his arm, and reached into his lap beneath his notebook. "Don't you want to play with me?" she purred.

Alex sighed. The line was gone. He slipped a hand around to caress her buttocks, and licked the nipple she was dangling before his face. "Maybe we ought to continue this inside," he suggested. "No sense performing for the public if we're not getting paid for it."

Smiling, she ran inside and leaped on the bed.

When they dined on the hotel terrace, people watched and envied him. All the hotel guests knew who she was, even if they had never actually seen her on screen. Though she was not as well-known as her leading man, Gianino Toncarlo, the worldly, sexy-eyed Italian, Lorraine's flamboyance easily identified her as a star. When the three of them sat together Alex knew that people assumed it was Gianino who was her lover. When the actor rose and excused himself and Alex remained, he enjoyed the ill-concealed shifting of assumptions that showed in the buzzing and pointing from the other tables.

Alex bought Lorraine a parrot at the market in Valletta. It was a showy bird with red and green and yellow plumage. It was said by the merchant to be a wonderful talker, and that it spoke English and French. Alex did not care for birds, but Lorraine made a great fuss over it in the market, so he bought it for her. She named it Bogart, after the star of *The Maltese Falcon.* They brought it back to the Phoenicia and installed it in their room, to the discomfort of the hotel's management. Bogart was tethered by a leather manacle around his ankle to a T-shaped stand, where he littered the marble floor below him with a viscous carpet of guano. But although Lorraine spent hours with him, nose to beak, murmuring *"Je t'aime,"* Bogart never spoke a word.

One late afternoon as Lorraine lay between Alex's legs, trying to coax another performance out of him before dinner, Bogart succeeded in gnawing away his leather confinement and rose, flapping and squawking, to the ceiling.

"Alex!" Lorrained screamed. "Bogart! *Vite! Ferme les fenêtres!"*

Alex scrambled from the bed. As he dashed to close the doors to the balcony his bare foot slipped on the slimy green-and-white droppings beneath Bogart's perch, and he sprawled head-long into the wall, bloodying his nose and momentarily stunning himself. Bogart, flapping around the room, found his voice.

"Enculé!" he squawked. *"Je t'aime! Enculé! Enculé.* I want gin! Up yours! *Je t'aime!"*

"Les fenêtres!" Lorraine shouted.

Alex struggled to his feet and closed the French windows. Then with a towel from the bathroom he stalked Bogart who for a quarter of an hour eluded him, shrilling *"Je t'aime!"* and "Up yours!" in an ecstatic song of freedom. Finally, his hands and forearms bloodied, Alex succeeded in returning Bogart to his perch. Lorraine gave him a gold chain with which he fastened the bird's leg. Back in captivity, the bird sullenly clammed up.

"Oh, Alex, you were wonderful!" Lorraine kissed him.

After he had showered, she nursed him tenderly, dabbing alcohol on his arms with cotton and kissing each wound.

"Jesus, I hate birds." But the excitement had revived him. Lorraine welcomed his renewed ardor with a squeeze and a kiss. She pulled him down on the bathroom floor.

"What does *enculé* mean?" he asked her.

She smiled. "I will show you," she said. Turning on her stomach, she raised her buttocks and guided him between them.

Lorraine adored him. She pouted when he left for five minutes to buy postcards and a newspaper. She cajoled him into accompanying her on shopping excursions. And when principal shooting began she was not happy until he agreed to accompany her to the set.

While Lorraine was shooting her scenes, Alex watched from

nearby. They lunched together on picnic food that they spread on a low bluff overlooking the Mediterranean.

Lorraine had been shooting a love scene; and flushed with the excitement of the make-believe passion with Gianino on the set, she would grab Alex's hand the moment the director called for a break, and pull him back to her trailer, past the knowing, envious leers of the crew. There she would shed her robe and claw off Alex's shirt and jeans, and the trailer would rock to her moans.

He was writing very little. But for a while, that did not seem important. He was immersed in a fantasy. He was making love with a French movie star till his body and mind were as limp as cotton. When they walked down the streets of Valletta together, holding hands, they passed her face, three times life-size, on a poster by a movie theater. The eyes were wide and liquid with love, and the flowing script of the title read *Je Ne Veux Que Toi.*

"*Je ne veux que toi,*" she murmured, gazing up and into his eyes with a melting look.

Back in the States was a life that was being prepared for Alex by his family, to be ready when his adventure as a playwright had failed. His mother had agreed to subsidize him for a year. After that, if there were not a finished play and an agent or producer on the scene, he would be expected to come to his senses. He could see the tracks stretched out before him, straight and inescapable: job, marriage, family, social responsibilities. With Lorraine he could avoid all that. They would travel to locations in the far corners of the world. He would write the fantasies. She would act them. Together they would live them.

Except that after a while, even Alex's infatuation with Lorraine could not sustain that kind of romantic syrup. Lorraine was wonderful in bed, but—he had to admit—woefully bad on screen. And the sort of stories she played in were not the ones he wanted to write. He began to grow restless, but Lorraine would not let him get back to his play. She resented his attention to anything but her. She teased, sulked, seduced, until he put aside his notebook.

When they were in bed together, nothing else seemed important. Her body was a miracle, and her technique was something that could hardly have been learned in a single lifetime. She could make him forget his own name.

When he was in bed with her, at least, she could make him forget Juno and Lydia.

Lorraine had been his escape hatch. He had seen the end of the summer coming, and did not know how to deal with it. So he had fallen back into his old pattern. He had allowed himself to be taken up by a woman who was determined to have him. And God knew he had needed a release, after the sexual frustration of the summer. Until that last night . . . He had almost changed his mind about leaving. Except that he knew that it could not have continued. He knew himself. Sooner or later he would have had to make a decision between the two of them.

About a month after they had arrived in Malta, Alex began to realize that Lorraine was giving him more time to write. And he found that he did not like it at all.

"Oh no, *chéri*," she said, stroking his bare torso. "Do not bother to come today. Is boring, boring, boring. Retakes. Lie there, my beauty. Sleep. Write your little plays. I see you later."

He had coffee on the terrace, then walked out and sat on a rock over the water and tried to write his little plays. Nothing came. He kept thinking about Lorraine. Last night she had left him to dine alone. "A dinner meeting with Jerome and Duncan," she told him. "Boring, boring." Jerome was the director, Duncan, the producer. They were undeniably boring. But she had not returned to the room until quarter of one.

Alex gave up on the scene he was trying to coax out of a distracted brain. He walked into Valletta, up the narrow, winding medieval streets. He thought about Lydia and Juno, and decided to buy them each a present. He found a handmade lace shawl for Juno that would look wonderful against her dark hair and olive skin. For Lydia, he bought a colorful peasant skirt.

He left the packages at the room in the Phoenicia, ate lunch, and tried to write for another half hour. Then he took a taxi to the film set.

"They're on a break," one of the girls on the director's staff told him. She bit her lip and looked harried.

"Where's Lorraine? In her trailer?"

"She's resting."

"I'll just look in and let her know I'm here."

"I don't think . . . well . . ." The girl shrugged as if to say it was none of her concern. Alex knew what he was likely to find.

He did not quite believe it still, as he walked to the trailer. He imagined everyone was watching him, but when he looked around there were no eyes turned in his direction. *Imagination*, he thought. *That's the trouble with being a writer.*

But the sight when he opened the trailer door owed nothing to the imagination, and left nothing to it either. Lorraine was naked on all fours, head cradled in her arms, ass pointed toward the aluminum ceiling. Slamming into her with the frantic, jerky rhythms of a steam engine about to explode was the handsome, hairy body of Gianino Toncarlo.

"Alex—get out!" Lorraine hissed. "Close the door!"

He got out, but he did not close the door.

Alex went back to the Phoenicia and packed his bag. Before he left, he opened the doors to the balcony and freed Bogart from his chain. He watched with satisfaction as the parrot flew clumsily up into the skies over Valletta.

Two hours later, Alex was on an Air Malta flight for Paris. As the plane lifted high above the crystalline Mediterranean, he ordered a Bloody Mary. Then he opened his notebook and tried, once again, to write.

Chapter Ten

Twenty bodies were lying in a heap on the floor. Lydia lay in the middle. She could feel the weight of arms and legs and torsos pressing her down into other arms and legs and torsos. She felt like the meat spread in a sandwich.

Noel Potter spoke. "All right . . . Lydia. Disengage yourself . . . but with a simple, motivating purpose. Let us see . . . let us feel . . . let us *know* what you're doing from this one simple act."

Lydia stretched out her left arm and then her right, hunched her hips, and started to rise slowly, then with more urgency, out of the pile. Finally, she freed herself from the other bodies. Stiffly, thighs pressed together, she walked determinedly across the floor to an imaginary exit.

Noel's voice, dry and sarcastic, stopped her. "Lydia, love, did you really have a thought in your head?"

"Of course I did."

"Did you really? And what was it?"

"I had to go the bathroom."

Reggie Tooms, Potter's assistant, smiled.

Noel Potter lit a cigarette, then sat back and stared at her, shaking his head. "I didn't believe it. What have you been trying to do here these last months? To get rid of this bloody *acting* you've brought here with you. We don't act, we *are*. Acting is artificial . . . onstage *being* is everything. All right, get back into the pile." He tapped his cigarette lighter against the arm of his chair. "Elsbeth," he said, "let's see what you can do. Remember, a simple . . . motivating . . . force."

In the café where they always went after class to wind down,

Reggie Tooms sat next to Lydia. "Don't let it get to you," he told her. "I thought you were marvelous. By now you should know how Noel works."

"Oh boy, do I ever," Lydia said. "Short, fast, and brutal."

Reggie smiled. "I know it's tough," he said. "If it's any comfort, he only picks out the beautiful, talented ones. The best first. But believe me, you're better off as an actress now that the affair is over. Now he'll pick on you and shred you down until he's tapped the innermost stuff. Because the truth is, Noel Potter may be an absolute shit as a human being but he's an incredible acting teacher."

Lydia came out of the Métro at St.-Germain-des-Prés and bought a *Herald Tribune* from the kiosk near the exit. Next she stopped at the stall where she had often bought flowers in the summer. Then it had been a tableau of color and fragrance. Now, in October, the selection was skimpy.

"*Une rose jaune,*" she said.

The *vendeuse* wrapped a single yellow rose with a sprig of fern in a sheet of newspaper. "*Merci, mademoiselle.*"

On the way home, she went into the *pâtisserie* for a *ficelle,* a long, narrow, crusty French bread. In Félix Potin, she bought a bottle of *vin ordinaire,* some *gruyère,* and a couple of apples.

Everywhere she went the tradespeople knew her. They greeted her warmly instead of with the perfunctory French *politesse* that she had encountered during the first months of her stay in Paris. It made her feel at home, but there was still the empty flat waiting for her as she walked through the heavy doors into the courtyard off Rue Bonaparte.

"*Mademoiselle* Forrest," the plump concierge called out through her window. "*Il y a une carte postale pour vous.*"

Lydia smiled and took the postcard. It was from Juno, in Berlin. The black-and-white picture was of three rundown-looking whores standing by a front stoop. Lydia grinned and turned over the card to read the tiny writing as she climbed the stairs.

Meine liebe Lydia,
   Ich bin ein Berliner, or at least I think that's where we are now. The fans here love us . . . Germany's R & R heaven. (See over for pic of me with a couple of the groupies.) How's Paris in October?

Heard anything from Alex? How's the great romance with N. P.? I miss you terribly. *Things are up & down with Tony & me, but mostly I'm too busy to tell which is which. See you sometime in Dec.*
                                                                    XXXOOO Juno

Lydia reached the top landing as she finished the card. When she unlocked the door the emptiness of the apartment hit her like a cold draft. She went to the kitchen and put down her bundles. Retrieving an empty wine bottle from the trash, she filled it with water and stuck the rose in it. Suddenly her shoulders started shaking and tears spilled down her cheeks. She sat down at the kitchen table and cried.

It was beginning to get dark but she did not feel like turning on a light. She wiped her eyes with a dish towel and took the rose into the living room. There were other flowers that she had bought on every table, so she carried it into the study.

As she walked toward the desk something moved. In the near darkness she could see a man's form stretched out on the daybed. She screamed, dropping the bottle which shattered on the floor. The sleeping form stirred. Lydia turned in terror and ran for the front door.

Her hand was on the knob when she heard a familiar voice behind her.

"Lydia! Wait!"

"Alex!" She turned around and fell into his arms.

The bottle of wine was nearly empty and the bread and cheese were long gone.

"Oh, Alex, what a miserable time you must've had," Lydia commiserated.

"Well, it was fun for a while," Alex said. "And I don't know how much longer my body could've kept up that pace. Anyway, I know you're dying to say 'I told you so.'"

"No." Lydia shook her head. "Not me. I'd be the last one to do that."

He looked at her. "Noel Potter?"

She nodded. "I feel like a nerd. Throwing myself at him like that. I've never done that with a man before. At least, not unless I was with a guy who could catch . . ." She smiled wryly and curled her feet up under her. "No . . . things were great for a while . . . but a while is all you get with Noel."

"His reputation is well earned then. What about classes? You haven't quit the workshop, have you?"

"Hell no," Lydia snapped. "I came here to learn to act and I'm damned well going to. I was warned about Noel. I walked into it with my eyes open."

"Good girl," Alex smiled. "That's what us artists need to tap the old creative impulse."

"Right," she laughed. "Tragic life experience. Where'd we be without it?"

"Happy . . . and boring." He poured the rest of the wine into their glasses. "So . . . Juno's on the road with Scrap Metal. And all this time I've been picturing her back in the sacred halls of ivy. What's her friend Tony Silver like?"

"Okay, I guess . . . a bit frenetic. Well, she couldn't have picked any worse than we did." Lydia paused. "You know, suddenly I'm beginning to feel self-conscious with you here. I mean, do you realize we've never actually been alone together like this?"

Alex stared into his wineglass. "Yeah," he said, "I know. What are we going to do about it?"

"Well, Juno's on the road with Tony," Lydia said. "At least *she's* being physically and emotionally taken care of."

"And the pact is no longer in effect. Even if it were, there's really nothing to stop us."

"That's true."

"So . . ." He held out his hand. Lydia took it, but as she stood up her skirt brushed against Juno's postcard on the coffee table, and it fluttered to the floor. For a moment they both stared at the card as if it had spoken. Then Alex shook his head with a laugh that broke the tension.

"Do you suppose that's a sign?"

"Of course. What a bitch I am. Juno's my best friend."

Alex nodded. "Mine, too." He picked up the postcard and set it back on the table. "Okay, Juno, you win."

When Lydia came home the next afternoon, Alex held up a cable.

"Guess what? We're evicted. Jean's coming back on Saturday."

"Oh shit," Lydia said. "Just when things were going so smoothly."

Alex laughed. "Don't worry. I ran into Bernard Jullien today at the Deux Magots. He was all pissed because his girlfriend's taking off for China for six months. Maybe we could get her place."

"Alex, you're incredible. You always come up with a solution for everything. Call him right now!"

The apartment was on Rue Vergniaud in the Thirteenth Arrondissement, still on the Left Bank but far from the fabled cafés of Montparnasse, St.-Michel, and St.-Germain. It was on the *rez-de-chaussée*, the ground floor, in the back. The Chinese red walls were cracking in places. The floor was covered by an Oriental rug whose pile was so worn away that more fiber than pattern remained. The corners of the living room were adrift with dust, and the dirt-streaked windows offered only a dim idea of the courtyard outside. On one wall was a poster of an American GI with a baby speared on his bayonet. Mao Tse-tung glowered serenely from over the bed, which was actually a hard and rumpled mattress on the living room floor. There was a bathtub in the kitchen with a piece of plywood over it to serve as a counter. On it were boxes of Lapsang souchong and brown rice. Dirty dishes were piled in the sink. Cockroach powder had been sprinkled along the floorboards by the walls. The light was a bare bulb dangling by a wire from the ceiling. Off the kitchen was a cramped room with a desk, a bookcase, and a small cot.

"Jesus," Lydia muttered, "no wonder she took off for China."

"I don't know," said Alex. "I kind of like it."

"Nelsia is a pig," Bernard stated flatly. "I cannot stand to come here."

"I'm not crazy about this part of town," Lydia said. "It's so bourgeois . . . and so far from everything."

"Well, the rent's cheap, and we don't have to walk up those four fucking flights of stairs. Besides, it's available."

Bernard shrugged. "Do what you like. I don't care."

Alex looked at Lydia. "What do you think? We can keep looking."

"Oh hell," Lydia said, rolling up her sleeves, "let's see if we
can get this place cleaned up before the seven dwarfs get home."

The place on Rue Vergniaud never came to seem as much like
home as the old one had. Alex spent most of his time at his old
haunts—Le Dôme, the Deux Magots, the Café Flore, Le Clown
Bar, La Rotonde—writing, or trying to write. But somebody
was always turning up and sitting down for a drink. Alex rationalized that he was absorbing good material; he would come
away from Paris with enough for five plays. But meanwhile the
one he was writing was bogged down somewhere in the first act.

"Here's to all the dead turkeys," said Sid Bernstein, a reporter
for the *Herald Tribune*, as he raised his *sérieux* of beer to clink
with Alex's. They were at the Café Flore. "Happy Thanksgiving."

"What is this Thanksgiving?" Bernard Jullien asked. "This is
the holiday in *Giant* where they eat the children's pet turkey
named Pedro?"

Alex laughed. "You got it. Except most of the turkeys come
from the freezer section of the supermarket now, and they have
names like Butterball."

"The point of the holiday," Sid explained, "is to give thanks
for our blessings. What are you giving thanks for on this great
American holiday, Alex?"

"Not being in America, for one thing."

Sid nodded. "Me, I'm thankful for not being in Saigon where
I almost got sent. And for finding out what I've got isn't the
clap. What about it, Bernard? Even a Frenchman must have
something to be thankful for."

"*Oui*, I have nearly all the financing for my film."

"Yeah? That's great!" Alex said. "Who's the angel?"

"Count Stefan de La Roche."

"I know him," Sid put in. "I did a story on the great châteaux
of the Loire wine district. A very wealthy guy."

"He was at Oxford with my older brother Michel." Bernard
grinned. "He took quite a fancy to me in my beautiful adoles-
cence."

"He's gay?" Sid asked. "I wouldn't have guessed."

"You Americans," Bernard said. "Everything is so black-and-white with you. We Europeans are not afraid to experiment in our youth. It does not affect our manhood. It is all part of growing up."

"Well, when you're growing up with five hundred million francs, I guess anything's possible," Sid said. "So he's parting with a little of it to back your film, that's great. Happy Thanksgiving."

"No it's not." Lydia stormed in, throwing her canvas bag on the floor, and flopped into an empty chair. "I can think of one turkey I'd like to kill . . . Noel Potter. Do you know what that bastard did? He recommended Elsbeth Langford for a part in Schlesinger's new film. Can you believe it? That simp, I'm ten times better than she is. And he knows it, too! Or at least he did till he started screwing her." She sat back, steaming.

"So what?" Bernard said. "Schlesinger's a pig."

"I don't care what he is. He makes movies, and I wanted that part. Goddamn, I'm tired of Noel Potter and his endless whining improvisations and group gropes. 'Get in touch with your soul,' " she said with a sweep of her hand and a mocking of Noel's British accent. "Jesus, I want to *act*. I want a real part!" She slammed her hand down on the table, rattling the glasses, then leaped to her feet. "Order me a Kir," she said, "I'm going to the loo." She strode across the room and up the stairs.

"*Elle est formidable,*" Bernard said. "What a woman!"

"I'll drink to that," Sid said.

Alex raised his glass. "And she's right. She's a hell of an actress."

A few minutes later Lydia returned to the table. "Okay, I've decided to be nice for the rest of the day . . . Happy Thanksgiving."

"Wait a minute," Alex said. "I just remembered something to be thankful for." From an airmail envelope he extracted a money order. "Three hundred bucks. A birthday present from my mother. Let's blow it on a spectacular dinner, all of us."

"Terrific," Lydia said.

"Ah . . ." Bernard said, smiling. "Now I see what you meant

by Thanksgiving. But I am having dinner with my benefactor tonight."

"And I'll be eating on the train to Lyon," Sid said.

"Well, that leaves us," Alex said to Lydia. "Let's go home and change."

Alex and Lydia sat in an intimate corner of the sixteen-table Le Grand Véfour, one of Michelin's three-star wonders, next to the Palais-Royal garden. The bistro had been a favorite of famous Parisians for two centuries. The menu cover was by Jean Cocteau, and plaques on the tables commemorated where famous patrons such as Victor Hugo, Colette, and other writers, artists, and politicians had sat over the years.

Alex and Lydia passed back and forth tastes of *soufflé de grenouilles, feuilleté d'huitres,* and *côtes d'agneau Albarine,* and with these they drank a succession of half bottles of vintage Bordeaux and Burgundies.

"My God," Lydia said, finishing her salad with artichoke bottoms, "now I'm beginning to understand what food is all about. This meal has been like a light bulb going on over my taste buds."

Alex smiled. "It is incredible, isn't it? The first time I ate at a three-star restaurant I was about ten. I was with my father and thought the whole meal was a waste of time. All I ate in those days were hot dogs and green peas . . . for *every* meal."

"That's more than I know how to make. This dinner really inspires me. One of these days I want to learn how to cook like this. Actually it's beyond cooking. It's more like great theater."

"Yeah, I wish I could write a great bouillabaisse," Alex grinned.

Afterward they went to Castel's where they drank champagne and danced. Then they walked to the Closerie des Lilas on Montparnasse and listened to the piano player, sipping cognac and holding hands. In the taxi back to Rue Vergniaud, Lydia nestled into the crook of Alex's arm. "I don't think I've ever had so much to drink, and yet I don't feel wasted at all. I just feel wonderful." She kissed Alex's cheek. "Happy Thanksgiving. Thank you for helping me over my bad mood."

Alex pulled her closer to him. "Thank *you*. I feel a lot better, too."

"Oh, Alex . . . I didn't know anything was wrong. What is it?"

The taxi pulled to a stop and Alex handed the driver twenty-five francs. "It's my play," he said, unlocking the door to the apartment. "I haven't got much down, and what I have is pure shit."

"Oh, Alex, it's not! What I've read is really good. You're so talented . . ." She tossed her coat on the chair. "Don't ever get down on yourself."

"I know I can write," Alex sighed. "I just don't seem to have much discipline lately. I don't know . . . Hemingway wrote in cafés. I keep thinking I should be able to, but I don't seem to be getting anything done."

"Maybe I should stand over you with a whip."

Alex grinned. "Sounds like fun." He poured himself a cognac. "Do you want one?"

"No thanks . . . I couldn't feel more perfect than I do now." She flung her arms around him. "Oh, Alex, you're going to write wonderful plays, and I'm going to star in them!"

He pulled her to him and kissed her deeply. Lydia responded with her whole body. Within moments they were naked together on the hard rumpled mattress, and all the frustration of the past six weeks dissolved into passion.

As the first rays of morning light broke through the window, Lydia lit a Gitanes. Her body glistened from the shower she had just taken. She lay back down next to Alex. He leaned over and patted her coppery patch of pubic hair.

"How do you feel?" he asked.

"Like I've just been over the rainbow . . . wonderful. Except . . ." She inhaled deeply.

Alex looked at her. "Yeah . . . except. Look, Lydia, we have to come to terms with this. We can't deny how we feel about each other. And I don't think Juno would expect us to keep hands off. I just made love to *you*. Juno's shadow wasn't in bed with us," he said emphatically. "Do you think it was?"

Lydia put out her cigarette and rolled over on top of him. "No
. . . Juno's in Spain with Tony Silver. She's not here."

They made love again, and fell asleep afterward, as the day
was getting under way for the rest of Paris.

They both dreamed about Juno, though neither said anything
about it later.

Four days before Christmas, the Gare de Lyon was abuzz with
travelers. Old people and young, families with small children,
all hoisted luggage and shopping baskets filled with brightly
wrapped presents.

Juno, tall and striking, with a pink cashmere coat over her
jeans, strode down the platform as if the three large suitcases
and two gift-wrapped boxes she carried contained nothing
heavier than feathers. She looked around. She had sent a wire to
Lydia announcing her return, and although she did not really
expect to be met, a part of her hoped enormously that she would
be.

And then she saw Alex rushing toward her, blond and towering above nearly everyone else. As he came nearer she set down
her bags and threw open her arms.

"Juno! You look fabulous!" They hugged and kissed as people
bumped against them.

"Alex . . . I feel like it's about a hundred years since I've
seen you. But you look the same. No . . . better."

Alex picked up the suitcases, and Juno carried her boxes.
"That coat looks great on you," he said as they walked inside the
station.

"Thanks. It was a gift from Tony."

"He gives an excellent Christmas present."

Juno smiled. "Actually, he gives an excellent good-bye present."

"Oh."

"It had been coming on for a long time. Anyway, I'll tell you
about it later. Where's Lydia?"

"She . . . had a class. Before we go back I thought . . .
would you like to have a drink? There's a nice place upstairs."

In Le Train Bleu, Juno and Alex were seated by a window
that looked down on the bustle of the terminal and the tracks

that stretched under huge vaulted glass and metal ceilings out to the yard and the city beyond.

"What a beautiful place!" Juno exclaimed, looking around at the elaborate Belle Epoque decor. "It's great to be back in Paris again."

Juno ordered tea and selected a *mille-feuille* from the *chariot de pâtisseries*. Alex had a whiskey and soda. As the waiter brought the tea and Alex's drink, Juno chattered on about the tour and her problems with Tony.

"It was pretty much a mutual thing," she said. "Tony's sweet, but he was a bit too hyper and self-centered for me. We could have kept going for a while longer, but I wasn't really in love with him, and there was no point, really. I *was* getting some signals from Garth, which was sort of tempting, but that would have been an escape too."

"Escape?"

"You know . . . this summer. It was a lot more complicated emotionally than I thought it would be."

Alex smiled. "I know. That's why I took off with Lorraine."

She offered Alex the last bite of her pastry. "What about you and Lorraine? Are you still with her?"

For the next few minutes Alex told her about his trip to Malta, which he had polished into a very amusing anecdote. But as he brought the story back to Paris, his tone became less facile, and she could tell he was uncomfortable.

"So—are you seeing anybody now?"

"Well . . ."

Suddenly it came to her in an intuitive flash. "Oh. Lydia."

Alex nodded. "I'm sorry. It didn't happen right away. It didn't happen for a long time. Neither of us wanted it to happen at all. But . . ."

"But it did."

"Lydia feels awful. That's why she didn't come to meet you. She couldn't face it."

Juno sipped her tea thoughtfully. Alex stirred his drink with his finger and watched her. Finally she looked up and smiled.

"Well . . . it's nothing to get hassled over. We all knew that this was a real possibility. If *I* had been here with you, and

Lydia had been away, I don't know how long I could have held out either."

"Oh, Juno . . . I'd hoped you'd be understanding. But now that you are, I feel even worse. I almost wish you'd fling your tea at me."

"I can, if it'd make you feel better," Juno said, "but really—I guess we're growing up. We can't expect things to stay frozen in time."

Alex put his hand over hers. "Let's get the check."

As he paid, she stood looking down at the tracks. A train was pulling out.

"This is a far cry from Rue Bonaparte."

"Well . . . you'll see how we've come down in the world," Alex said, putting down her bags and turning the key in the door.

The door swung open on an unfamiliar place. Somehow against all logic, Juno had expected something she would recognize, something like the apartment they had shared. The smell of sautéed onions and garlic filled the air. And then Lydia came out of the kitchen, wiping her hands on her jeans. The feeling of apprehension that had been building up in Juno since the railroad station gripped her hard. Lydia looked different to Juno, as if she were seeing her through the wrong end of a telescope. In Lydia's face she could see the same uneasiness and uncertainty she felt herself—and something more, a kind of nervous defiance. It was territorial, Juno realized: this was Lydia's and Alex's place. For a moment she wished she had never come here, that she had gotten back on a train and gone anywhere rather than here.

"Juno!" Lydia said, and then they were in each other's arms hugging and kissing, and the tension, for the time being, was broken.

"My God, you look great," Juno said.

"Oh, I'm a mess. I'm cooking. Can you believe it? I wanted to fix something special for your homecoming."

"It smells incredible. It smells like . . ."

"Like something's burning!" Lydia dashed back into the kitchen.

"Well, let me take your coat," Alex said. "What can I get you to drink?"

As Alex bustled around being host, Juno could not help feeling like a guest. The strangeness of the situation was something she could not shake.

They ate burned *lapin à la moutarde* and drank a '66 Château Pétrus that Alex had bought for the occasion. Over dinner and coffee, Juno regaled them with anecdotes about the Scrap Metal tour.

"Groupies," she said. "You can't believe what they're like. There are the hard-core ones who traipse along from city to city, and then there're the locals. They all have one purpose—to fuck the stars. Different ones have their specialities. Some give great head, some can go all night, and then there are the plaster casters, who preserve their favorite cocks in plaster and take them home as trophies."

"God," Alex shuddered, "I'm glad I'm not a rock star."

"So, now that you and Tony have split . . . are you going out on tour with them again?" Lydia asked.

Juno shook her head. "I did a lot of thinking on the train. I'm heading back to Yale after Christmas for the second semester."

"Oh, I wish you'd stay in Paris," Lydia said. Still, Juno thought she saw a look of relief come over Lydia's face.

"I'm determined to get that degree. Not that I know what I'll do with it. I sure don't need it for doing rock and roll lighting." Juno laughed. "Anyway, you'll be back at Yale next September."

"Oh sure," Lydia said. "Absolutely. Try to get our old room for us, will you?"

Alex went out to buy cigarettes for Lydia, and Juno pitched in on the kitchen cleanup.

"Oh, Juno, it's so good to have you here. But I feel so rotten about all this."

"Well." Juno made herself smile. "You leave town, you take your chances."

Lydia burst into tears. Juno put down a wet plate and went to comfort her. "Don't," she said, "it's not important. So much has gone down in the last six months. We've all changed."

"But I don't think I know who I am anymore," Lydia sobbed. "You know, that night back at the end of school was the most wonderful night of my life. I wanted Alex, but I wanted you just as much. I had this idea we'd always be together, the three of us. And then when you both took off . . . I can't tell you how I fell apart. I knew I was kidding myself about Noel Potter. It wasn't him, really. I was just snowed by the great acting teacher. And when that ended, I felt like such a jerk. Then Alex came back when I was absolutely in the pits. He was going through a hard time, too . . . withdrawal from Lorraine. We were a great comfort to each other. But it wasn't sexual." Lydia wiped her eyes. "And then one day it was. We didn't plan it . . . it just happened."

"I know," Juno said. "It's all right." And yet in the back of her head it was beginning to annoy her that she should have to comfort Alex and Lydia. After all, *she* was the betrayed one. It hurt like hell, and she could not show it.

Alex came back and tossed the Gitanes on the kitchen table. "I'm tired of feeding your habit," he said as Lydia was tearing open the pack. "This is absolutely the last time."

Juno stretched. "It's been a long day. And an emotionally exhausting one. It started out with Tony's and my good-bye breakfast and went downhill from there. I think I'll go to sleep for a few days."

Alex put his arm around her. "Juno, come to bed with us. We want you to."

"Yes, we really do." But Lydia's eyes said she really did not.

Juno kissed them both quickly on the lips. "No, my dears, I don't think so. I'm really tired."

Alex showed her into the little room off the kitchen. Lydia had already put clean sheets on the cot. He kissed Juno good night one more time, and headed back out to the mattress in the living room.

In the dark, Juno could hear the sound of their whispering for a few minutes. Then there was silence. She listened for noises of lovemaking, but there were none. She lay in bed thinking for a long time. Then she got up to get a glass of water from the kitchen. She peeked into the living room. Alex and Lydia were sleeping soundly on their sides, their backs to each other.

She picked up the phone and stretched the cord as far as it would go, almost back to her room. She called the overseas oper-

ator and gave him the number for a collect call. By the time a
voice came on the other end, there were tears streaming down
her cheeks.

"Hi, Daddy," she said, "I'm coming home for Christmas after
all."

Part Three

Lydia, 1972-77

Chapter Eleven

In the days following Juno's hasty departure, Alex and Lydia became increasingly moody with one another. They went to movies, saw friends, stayed up late partying, but avoided the one topic that was most on their minds: Juno.

On Christmas morning they exchanged gifts. Alex gave Lydia two antique perfume bottles from a shop on Rue St.-André-des-Arts. Lydia gave Alex a fountain pen engraved with his name and an assortment of leather-bound notebooks. Under their makeshift Christmas tree—a large branch of evergreen on which several of Lydia's necklaces hung—sat Juno's presents to them: a pair of goatskin boots from Spain for Lydia, and for Alex, a football jersey from the Inter soccer club of Milan. In order to avoid the edginess they both felt they spent the next twelve hours at the Cinémathèque, watching American classics of the forties.

In the week between Christmas and New Year's they saw as little of each other as possible without making an issue of it. Lydia hung out with friends from her workshop which was on hiatus for the holidays. Alex converted the back room to an office and tried writing at home.

On New Year's Eve, they were invited to a party at Bernard Jullien's apartment on the Quai de L'Horloge. At ten o'clock that evening, Lydia sat quietly sipping a glass of white wine in the kitchen.

"I really hate New Year's Eve parties," she said. "Everybody trying desperately to have a good time because it's expected of them."

"Oh come on, it'll be better than celebrating the new year in this place," Alex said, buttoning his shirt as he came into the kitchen.

"No. You go. I don't feel like it."

"I won't leave you here alone. You need cheering up," he said, leaning over to kiss her neck. He slipped his hand under her lace blouse.

Lydia squirmed away and stood. "No, Alex, I don't feel like it. Besides, I still have my period."

"Goddammit!" he snapped. "You've had your period for a week and a half!"

"Well, so what? It's none of your fucking business!"

"Well, I'm making it my fucking business!" He grabbed her and tried to pull her toward him. She snatched up her glass from the table and flung the wine in his face. "You bitch!" he shouted, coming after her, his face dripping.

Lydia fled into the living room. Picking up a wood stool, she held it in front of her, like a lion tamer. "Don't hit me . . . don't hit me!"

Alex stopped at the sight of petite Lydia keeping him at bay with the dilapidated stool. His anger melted into amusement, and he started to laugh.

"Jesus, look at us," he said. "George and Martha, straight out of *Virginia Woolf.*"

She lowered the stool and sat on it, smiling sheepishly. "Yeah . . . I feel better, though. Sometimes it's good to explode."

Alex sat on the mattress. "It's been so tense around here since Juno left."

"Yeah . . . Juno did bring us down. Which has made me realize that we must've been on pretty tender footing anyway."

"Look, we both feel guilty about Juno. I don't think we were on tender footing before she came, but we sure are now."

"God, listen to how dramatic we're getting. It's probably nothing more than holiday blues."

He shook his head. "It's more than that. It's more than Juno, or us. I'm going crazy . . . I'm blowing this year. I'm fucking up my chance to do something that I really want to do. Paris is great, but there are too many distractions. I've totally lost my sense of discipline."

"Oh, Alex," she said uneasily. "It's just a block, you'll get over it. I mean, you've fixed up an office. We can turn off the phone. I'll bring you meals and be really quiet. I won't let anyone or anything disturb you. You'll finish your play. After all," she laughed, "if you can't write in Paris, where can you write?"

"That's what I've been thinking about. Getting off someplace, by myself. Someplace cheap and quiet, where I don't know anyone and there's nothing else to do but write."

Lydia sat still for a moment and bit her lip. "What are you trying to say?"

"I'm going to Greece."

"Greece? You can't! Just because we had a fight?"

"It has nothing to do with our fight, or you. I made up my mind this morning. I've got to get off by myself while I still have some money and some time left. If I don't give it my best shot, I'll never know whether I could have done it or not. I'm not writing amusing school plays. I'm trying to write something that'll get produced on or off Broadway. I'm up against *real* competition."

"But I thought you loved me."

Alex came over and put his arm around her. "I do. I know I'm being a shit . . . but I've got to be selfish about this. I'm losing all respect for myself. Look, if I get a lot done down there in the next few months, I'll send for you."

"Oh thanks. That's very big of you."

"Please, Lydia. Don't make it even harder for me. Try to understand."

"I do. You don't love me and you're leaving," she said coldly.

He sighed. "There's no sense talking about this anymore, at least now." He picked up a book. "You don't want to go to the party. I don't feel like it either."

"The party? Sure, why not?" She looked in the closet, picked out some clothes, and flung them on the bed. "Happy New Year, Lydia . . . you're back in circulation again. Come on, Alex . . . we might as well celebrate."

It was not yet midnight, but the champagne corks were popping and people were kissing with great abandon. Lydia had dressed to match her mood: hair pulled back into a severe chignon, black turtleneck, black leather skirt slit up the thigh,

black-patterned stockings. Her only adornments were two un-
matching baroque earrings that she had bought from a street
vendor for a franc.

She stood in a corner smoking Gitanes and talking, in French,
to a film editor. Bernard Jullien, champagne bottle in hand,
came around to refill their glasses. He kissed Lydia on the
cheeks. "I have never heard you speak French before. Your accent is very . . . *mignonne.* You speak very well."

"Ah, you are English?" the editor said. "I knew you were not
French . . . I thought from your accent you were Swiss."

"American, actually," she said. "But my French teacher in
prep school was from Geneva."

"You look very striking in black," Bernard said. "Is this the
tradition in the United States for, how do you say, *la Saint-
Sylvestre?*"

"New Year's Eve. No, it's tradition for me. I dress to antici-
pate the year ahead."

A tall, strong-jawed woman in her late twenties approached.
Her dark hair was cut helmet-style, and she had full, sensuous
lips and a slightly flattened nose. Though Lydia had never met
her, she recognized her from her films.

"Marie Bart, this is Lydia Forrest, a friend of Alex's," Bernard
said.

Marie dipped her head at Lydia, and took Bernard's arm. *"Il
faut que je te parle,"* she said, leading him away.

Thierry, the film editor, shrugged. "She is to star in Bernard's
film."

"She's very charming."

Thierry smiled. "Which one is Alex?" She pointed him out.
"And is he your boyfriend?"

Lydia pulled on her Gitanes and stared at Alex across the
room. She exhaled, letting the smoke drift up in front of her
face. "No."

"Une minute à minuit," Bernard called out. Lydia noticed
Marie Bart across the room, pouting in the midst of a gathering
of admirers.

There was a frantic refilling of champagne glasses and the
countdown began. At the stroke of twelve, a cheer went up.

"*Bonne année,*" Bernard said, appearing at Lydia's side and kissing her.

"And happy nineteen seventy-two." Alex came over and put his arm around her.

Lydia nodded, and forced a smile. "Yeah. Happy nineteen seventy-two."

For the next few days before Alex left for the island of Spetsai, things went surprisingly well between him and Lydia. Perhaps their fight had cleared the air, perhaps they were both trying hard to renew their friendship, perhaps Lydia did not want Alex to go away thinking she was an impossible bitch.

On Alex's last night in Paris, he took her to Dominique, a Russian restaurant on Rue Bréa. Between courses, they tossed down silver thimbles of pepper vodka in toasts to everyone from Inky Clarke, the director of admissions at Yale, to Bogart, the Maltese parrot.

"To us," Lydia said finally.

"Not so fast. To you."

They drank.

"To you."

"To Juno."

Lydia tossed back more vodka. "To Juno."

"This isn't the end, you know," Alex said. "It's merely an interlude. Will you come visit me in Greece this spring?"

"Sure . . . maybe Juno can come too, on spring vacation. The Three Musketeers go to Greece."

Alex laughed. "More like the Three Stooges."

For Lydia, the weeks that followed Alex's defection to Greece were a new phase of her experience in Paris. She had been with Alex and Juno, with Noel Potter, alone and afraid, and then with Alex. Now, alone again, she was determined to overcome her fear of it.

She spent as little time as possible in the apartment. Instead she got out and explored the city, went to the theater, movies, and art galleries by herself. She sat in cafés writing letters or reading Claude Lévi-Strauss, and became expert at fending off the advances of the *dragueurs* who tried to pick her up. She threw herself into Noel Potter's workshop with more intensity than ever, and palled around with her classmates, avoiding all the people she had seen with Alex. She was not happy, nor was she unhappy. Her days and evenings were filled with activity. It was only late nights that were sometimes difficult, back at the depressing apartment.

In mid-February Lydia turned twenty. It was a mild, spring-like day, and she celebrated by hiring a horse and galloping around the Bois de Boulogne. That night, some friends from school threw her a surprise party. Even Noel Potter showed up and brought her a signed first edition of his book *Art and Essence: The Craft of Being an Actor.*

It was not quite midnight when Lydia arrived back at Rue Vergniaud. The phone was ringing as she unlocked the door and she ran to answer it.

"Mademoiselle Forrest? Un moment, s'il vous plaît." She waited through an endless clanging of coins into a pay telephone.

"Lydia? Happy birthday!" Juno said across the overseas wire. "I've been trying all day to reach you."

"Juno! Oh, it's so great to hear from you."

"How are you? How does it feel not to be a teenager any-more?"

Lydia laughed. "I haven't felt like a teenager for years. How are you? How's Yale?"

"Yale's a bit less frantic. It seems very strange without you and Alex. Listen . . . I'm sorry I made such a fool of myself. *I* still act like a teenager," she laughed. "Can you forgive me? How's Alex?"

"I got a birthday card from him. He's in Greece . . . writing his play."

"What? Since when?"

"Just after New Year's. Oh, Juno, I know this is costing you a fortune, but I just have to tell you . . . I'm really sorry about what happened. Please forgive *me.* Are we still best friends?"

"Oh shit," Juno said through the static. "I'm starting to cry. I'm the one . . ."

The operator broke in. "Your three minutes are up. Please signal when through."

"I'm out of coins," Juno said. "I'll write. I love you. Happy birthday."

After she had hung up Lydia poured herself a glass of wine and took her birthday presents out of the shopping bag in which she had carted them home. Juno's call had lifted her spirits, and she felt almost giddy. It *was* a happy birthday, and she did not feel alone anymore.

The phone rang again. She almost expected it to be Alex, but when she answered there was a French voice on the other end.

"*Allô, Lydia? Bernard Jullien à l'appareil.*" He had been trying her for weeks, he said. He was very eager to see her.

"There is a screening of Rivette's new film tomorrow afternoon. Would you like to go? We could have dinner afterward and talk."

The next day was Saturday. She had no classes, and no other plans. "All right," she said. "I'd love it."

"You know the screening room at the lab on Rue Beethoven? Meet me there at two."

The film was *L'Amour Fou.* It was about a young couple, both actors, and wove back and forth between their lives and the experimental play they were rehearsing, in and out of love and madness. It was four and a half hours long. When the lights went up Lydia sat there, stunned and exhilarated.

"I feel like I just relived my entire life."

"Me too," Bernard said. "Rivette is the true genius of the *cinéma français.*"

"I thought you were," Lydia smiled.

"I will be," he said seriously. "Come . . . we will eat at my apartment. There is something I want to show you."

Lydia leaned on the railing of the tiny balcony outside Bernard's window. A boat drifted down the Seine below her with its windows lighted up. Bernard reappeared from his office and dropped a manuscript on the table behind her. "Here. I want you to read this."

She stepped back inside and closed the window. The manuscript was thick, with a red vinyl cover on which, in gold letters, were printed the words *L'Engagement,* and below them, *Scenario de Bernard Jullien.*

"Your film . . ."

"Yes. While you read, I will be in the kitchen, cooking dinner."

For the next hour and a half she read the screenplay. She loved it. It was about an American girl who comes to Paris to study painting and becomes the mistress and then the prisoner of a middle-aged art collector. It had everything—humor, intelligent dialogue, passion, suspense. Lydia was as stimulated by it as she had been by the Rivette film. When she finished, she carried it into the kitchen.

Bernard was talking on the phone, but when he saw her face he finished his conversation and hung up.

"So . . . what do you think?"

"Bernard . . . it's fabulous. I love it. Except . . ."

"Except? You have a criticism?"

"No! No . . . it's just that . . . I'm surprised you made the girl American. Marie Bart is definitely French. And besides, she's older."

Bernard smiled. "Marie is not going to play it. I rewrote the part . . . for you."

Lydia was astonished. "For *me?* But you've never even seen me act! How do you know . . ."

Bernard shrugged. "Alex has told me again and again how much talent you have. And then, I have seen *you,* and you are always changing, always different. The first time, in that pink prom dress, you were like Scarlett O'Hara. And that afternoon at the Flore, with your jeans and wild hair, you were angry and uninhibited and *so* American. Then on New Year's Eve you were sulky . . . *très française.* As a director, I can feel what you are capable of . . . what I can bring out." Bernard filled two glasses with champagne and handed one to her. "I now have all my financing for the film. I want to go into production in three weeks' time. So—will you do it?"

"Of course!" She laughed. "Are you kidding?"

Chapter Twelve

Bernard looked around the apartment. Lydia had invited him for dinner. It was the first time he had been there since he had cast Lydia for his film. The first time, in fact, since Lydia and Alex had moved into Nelsia's apartment. The floors and windows were clean and the bare-bulbed ceiling light was covered with a colorful Chinese shade. On the walls were magazine covers, an eclectic selection that ranged from *Charlie Hebdo* to *Elle*. There were fresh-cut flowers in a vase on the table.

"This place looks better than when Nelsia was here. I used to hate it. Now it has a certain charm."

"Taking down those posters helped a lot." Lydia laughed. "Still, I'm a bit scared she'll show up one of these days and spear *me* with her bayonet."

"I had a letter from her. She will not be back for two months, I think."

"I guess you must miss her."

"No." Bernard leaned on his elbow on the counter and looked at Lydia. "Not so much anymore."

Lydia felt a thrill run through her. She forgot about stirring the hollandaise. "Are you in love with her?"

"I thought I was. For a while. She is very strong . . . very opinionated. Too opinionated. We were practically *fini* when she left."

"And now?"

"Now it is definitely *fini*," he said.

"Sit down at the table," Lydia said, a little flustered. "I think this is ready." She set down a plate in front of him and passed the curdled hollandaise for the cauliflower.

Bernard took a bite. *"Pas mal . . ."*

"Not bad? Is that all you can say after I spent all afternoon chopping and slicing and sautéeing. . . ."

He smiled at her. "It is delicious, *chérie*. What do you call it?"

"Poulet à la . . . stuffed vegetables. It's not fattening."

Bernard shook his head with amusement. "You do not have to worry about the calories."

"The camera's supposed to make you look fatter. Anyway, I always have to worry about calories. If I didn't, you'd be casting me as the plump housekeeper." She puffed out her cheeks.

Bernard laughed. "You are charming." He reached across the table and took her hand. "After dinner I want you to come back to my place."

"Oh?" she said disingenuously. "To work on that scene?"

"To make love." His eyes burned into hers. "I cannot be with you here. It brings back memories of Nelsia."

She wanted Bernard. For these past several weeks she had been waiting for him to make a move. Lydia had almost convinced herself that he had no romantic interest in her. But now, so casually, he had asked her to go to bed with him. *Damned French arrogance*, she thought. Who did he think he was, taking her for granted?

"I have memories of my own here, Bernard," she flared. "Besides, what makes you think I want to go to bed with you?"

"Only because I want you so very much," he said quietly. "I think you must feel it, too." The sincerity in his voice was so apparent that Lydia stopped being resentful.

"Yes . . . I do," she said.

Bernard came around the table to her and raised her to her feet. Lydia stepped into his arms. Their mouths fused together in a hungry kiss.

Outwardly, Bernard projected a macho Gallic cool that he had perfected as a boy by watching Belmondo in films like *Breathless*. But in the intimacy of his bedroom, Bernard's façade melted and he became a tender and considerate lover. Attracted as she had been to him, Lydia had been afraid that he would be too aggressive; she liked gentleness and romance. But Bernard seemed to understand everything she was feeling, and everything she needed. His kisses and caresses were in perfect harmony with her, and when they came together it was more than sexual. It seemed to touch and illuminate something deep and essential in Lydia.

Bernard poured two glasses of wine. They sat naked in bed and looked at each other by the city light that came through his window.

"That was wonderful," Lydia said. "*You* were wonderful."

Bernard kissed her fingers. "I have been wanting this for a long time. Since that night last summer, when you were in that marvelous prom dress. At your party for Alex."

"What took you so long?"

"At first, it was Alex. He is my friend. Then when that was over . . . when I wanted you for my film . . . well . . . I did not want you to think there was anything of the casting couch in it. This is something entirely different, Lydia, believe me."

Lydia was touched. "I believe you. Thank you, Bernard." Then she smiled mischievously. "So . . . did I pass the audition? Do I still have the part?"

He laughed. "We will not know until after take two." He pulled her to him.

Shooting for Bernard's film was to begin the next week in the country, near Fontainebleau. But first Lydia had to quit Noel Potter's workshop. There would be no time now, and besides, Noel Potter had an unshakable rule: any student who got a professional acting job had to resign.

"I've got a part in a film, Noel," she told him after class.

"Oh?" he said coolly. "What sort of part?"

"It's a good part. The lead. It's a wonderful film by a new French director."

"I see. And in French? Do you think you can handle the language."

"I think so."

Noel Potter smiled warmly and gave her a hug. "Well, then. I know you can handle the rest. I've trained you well, Lydia . . . and you've been a good student. We'll miss you."

That was harder to take than if Noel had been his usual ornery self. And it had been sad to leave her friends. They had become a close-knit group since summer, and the one constant of her life in Paris. Though she swore she would continue to see them, she knew it would never be the same again.

Lydia was on her way to becoming a film star. She felt very special. Her parents, when she had written them the news, had wired back horrified. That made her feel even better.

Bernard Jullien was twenty-four years old. He had already made seven films, each less than forty minutes long. Three of them had played together at a Parisian cinema as a feature attraction. Avant-garde critics adored him. Financial backers were leery because his work was beyond New Wave. Now at last, with his first full-length film, he felt he was ready to bridge the gap between what he wanted to do and what would succeed commercially.

It had taken him nearly a year to raise the money for this film. The bulk had come from Count Stefan de La Roche, an old friend of his brother Michel, but Bernard had been forced to do somersaults to convince the count of the film's economic potential. The Count de La Roche was extremely wealthy and put money into a number of things, but he had never backed a film before. Bernard had spent hours with him going over the elaborate charts and budgets he had drawn up that showed just how the film would be made and what audience it could be counted on to attract.

Bernard hated that part of it. After this film made a success, he would have producers and accountants to take care of all that and leave him to do what he knew and understood: directing.

Bernard believed *L'Engagement* would be the turning point in his career. He *needed* a hit. His father had been killed when he was a child, his mother died of cancer when he was eighteen. He and his two brothers had been left a reasonable-sized estate, which was split three ways. Michel had gone to England to university, and now was a vice-president of Publicis, France's largest ad agency. Bernard's younger brother was in medical school. Bernard, however, had gone through his entire inheritance, financing his films and buying the apartment with the view of the Seine. He liked to live well, enjoying great food and great wines and spur-of-the-moment trips to Morocco or Manhattan. But his flair for living well was not backed by sufficient resources to support that flair. Success and fame were what he needed and craved at this point in his life.

Deep down, Bernard was very insecure. This was his big chance, and he was scared to death that he would blow it. He could not stand the thought of living out his life on *vin ordinaire* and motor trips around France for the holidays.

Shooting on the film began. Lydia was nervous, but the dailies looked great. She kept her apartment, but often she spent the night at Bernard's after a day's filming. At breakfast one morning Lydia looked up at Bernard from her script. She had been going over her lines for that day's shoot.

"This part needs some changing. Patricia would never react like this. So accepting. She'd be much more questioning."

Bernard looked up from his notebook. "What did you say?"

"I said Patricia . . ."

"I heard," he said coldly. "Since when are you rewriting my screenplay?"

"I'm only making a suggestion. Don't forget, I *am* Patricia. I've been living inside her for quite a while now. Everything I do, I think: Would Patricia do this? Would she act this way? How would *she* brush her hair, how would *she* . . ."

"You are only an actress, playing a role," Bernard said shortly. "A role that I have written. I conceived the character of Patricia. She is exactly as I intended her to be. I do not need the insights of an actress into her."

Lydia closed the script and threw it onto the floor with a sharp thud. "Oh really? I thought filmmaking was supposed to be a collaborative art!"

"It is collaborative. I write, I direct. You act. The sound man does the sound, the cameraman does the camera, the lighting man does the lights. They all stick to their jobs."

"Bernard . . . I am an American girl. Patricia is an American girl. I *understand* her. I understand her much better than you ever could."

He turned on her in a fury. "Who are you to tell me that you understand my character better than I do? Don't forget, this is your first film and there are hundreds of actresses who would

love to take over your part. If you cannot play it as it is written
. . ."

"I can play it," she muttered, picking up the script from the
floor. "I was just trying to help."

They shot that day in an art gallery near the Champs-Elysées.
It was nearly eight o'clock when they finished. Lydia was leaving when Bernard stopped her.

"You were perfect today," he said, kissing her.

"Thank you. I felt that it really came together. It all worked."

"Wait a few minutes. I'll take you to dinner."

Bernard found a parking place on the sidewalk near the Brasserie Lipp and they dashed through the rain to the restaurant.
While they waited for a table they had a drink at the crowded
bar. Shirley MacLaine was seated with a large party near the
foot of the winding staircase.

"I'll bet *she* didn't have to wait," Lydia said.

"Shirley MacLaine, she is nothing. You will be a much bigger
star than Shirley MacLaine."

"I don't want to be Shirley MacLaine. I want to be Jeanne
Moreau. I feel so French now. These last months since Alex and
Juno left I've really come to feel at home in Paris." She put her
hand over his. "And since we've been together, I've been happy
here."

"It has been a happy time for me as well. Being with you,
working with you . . ."

"You're a wonderful director. I'm sorry about this morning—
criticizing the script. It's just that I'm so nervous about this part.
I get so wound up."

"It's only natural, *chérie.*"

"Don't you ever feel anxious?"

Bernard shrugged. "There is something Irving Thalberg once
said to F. Scott Fitzgerald . . . it is in the notes to *The Last
Tycoon.* He talked about building a railroad . . . that there can
be half a dozen choices of where to cut through a mountain, and
each one seems as good as the others. And the person in charge
has to make a decision . . . as if he knows what he is doing, as if
he had a reason. Because the people under you must never suspect you have any doubts, or it all will fall apart."

It was raining lightly as they left the restaurant. Lydia slipped her arm through Bernard's.

"I've really enjoyed this evening."

"So have I. And I have been thinking . . ."

"What?"

"Let's go back to Rue Vergniaud."

"Yes?"

"And get your clothes . . ."

She smiled. "Off?"

"No . . . packed. I want you to move in with me. Will you?"

Lydia nodded. "Yes. If you think the great star and the great director can coexist peacefully."

"Of course. As long as the great star can take direction."

The film progressed on schedule. Principal shooting was to last eight weeks. It was in the middle of the second week that Lydia moved in with Bernard. She quickly discovered that she was expected to be more than his star and his mistress. She was also his cook, his maid, and his hostess. Several times a week Bernard would troop in with as many as ten extra people for dinner, unannounced, and Lydia would have to run out for the extra wine and provisions. She would cook, be charming and entertaining at dinner, clean up afterward, and still be ready and passionate later on when they went to bed. All this plus learning lines, and getting up before dawn to be on the set in makeup and ready for the morning shoot. The shooting day often lasted thirteen or fourteen hours. And then, often as not, it was back to another meal for ten or twelve spur-of-the-moment guests at the apartment on Quai de l'Horloge.

It was exhausting, but most of the time she did not mind. She was twenty years old, and already living a life that was right out of her fantasies. She wrote Juno and Alex amusing letters about the unglamorous side of being a French movie star. But the letters made it clear that even that part was glamorous to her. And after all was said and done, she *was* still—or becoming—a French movie star. "Can you imagine the write-up in the Yale alumni magazine?" she exulted.

There were also times when Lydia and Bernard got into

screaming fights and flung things at each other before one or the other stormed out. They were both high-strung and self-centered. Both were young, both were convinced that the rest of their lives hung in the balance of this film's success. They saw their own roles enormously magnified. Lydia, in her insecurity, could not see that Bernard was just as insecure. Bernard's anxiety was manifested in his need to control every aspect of the production—and of Lydia, on screen and off. He was not quite the male chauvinist that he seemed during this period. Much of his obnoxiousness was Gallic bravado and fear.

Lydia and Bernard loved each other. But the pressure was too great for such a fragile emotion to withstand. Sooner or later it was bound to crack.

An ormolu clock hung on the wall, its ornate gilt swirls extending down toward a Louis XVI mantelpiece. Matching sofas covered in fine French silk damask bracketed a low Chinese table of teak with jade and ivory inlay. Lydia strode across the room, snatched up a bibelot from the table, and flung it in the direction of the stocky, velvet-jacketed man who was coming after her. It missed, shattering against the hard marble of the hearth in a fine spray of porcelain.

"*Coupez!*" Bernard called. As a grip hurried to sweep up the debris and place a new figurine on the table, Bernard took Lydia's arm and drew her out past the cables and light stanchions that crowded the sitting room in the duplex on Avenue Kléber. They stood on the balcony. Below in the distance were the Jardins du Trocadéro, and across the Seine the tall spidery magnificence of the Eiffel Tower.

"All right," Lydia sighed, "what did I do wrong?"

"This is a woman in a rage that has been building for months. He has imprisoned her, lied to her, toyed with her life like a wind-up doll, and now she is unleashing all that passion and fury. This is not a little girl in a snit. You must give Roger something to play against."

"*Him* something to play against?" she exploded. "What about me? The great Roger Saint-Cyr arrives on the set with a hangover and whiskey on his breath, plays as if he's looking for the

Alka-Seltzer department at Monoprix, and you tell me it's *my* fault?"

"It is always somebody else with you! The actor, the director, the hairdresser—anybody but you! Let me tell you something, Lydia, you are not a great enough actress to be such a prima donna. Roger Saint-Cyr was starring in films before you were born. He is a *professional.* You are a novice straight from the school play. At Yale, perhaps, you were something special. Here, you have a great deal to learn."

"Well, so do you, Bernard. It's your first feature. And you're so goddamn intimidated by that has-been that all you can do is put the blame on me. I'm sick of it! I'm *sick* of the way you treat me! Acting like the *enfant terrible* of the French cinema . . . well, you're an *enfant* all right, and you're sure as hell *terrible,* but you're not the fucking genius you think you are!"

"*Va te faire foutre!*" He slapped her cheek hard.

"You bastard!" Tears of pain and anger welled up in her eyes.

"Get in there! Do the fucking scene!"

She played the scene in a white heat that even sparked the hung-over Roger Saint-Cyr to act as he had not acted in ten years. When it was over the crew broke into applause and Saint-Cyr embraced her.

"Bravo!" Bernard said, coming over to her with arms outstretched.

Lydia looked at him coldly. "You're a prick, you know that?" She swept past him out of the room.

She did not know where she was going. The apartment belonged to Count Stefan de La Roche, the film's major backer. It was their first day of shooting there, and as the count was out of town she had seen nothing of it but the sitting room. She ran up the curving stairs and arrived in a thickly carpeted upper hallway lined with paintings and tapestries. She looked around. All the doors were closed. She paused, terrified of barging in on a stranger. Then she heard footsteps below approaching the stairs.

She tried a door. It opened into a small plum-colored library with rich mahogany bookcases and ornate Louis XIV chairs resting on a rose-patterned Bessarabian rug. She flung herself down onto a sofa beneath a Fragonard pastoral of bathers in a mountain stream, and clenched her fists, too angry to cry.

The door opened and a man stood there. He wore a gray business suit and carried a tweed overcoat on his arm. He was tall and slender, with pronounced aristocratic features that would have made him the perfect subject for any of the old masters whose paintings hung on these walls. He looked about forty. His brown hair swept back from a high forehead. It was cut short, with sideburns that grew into a neatly trimmed beard. His eyes were pale, between blue and a smoky gray.

"Oh, I'm sorry," she said, flustered. "I was looking for a quiet place. I didn't know where to go."

"You will find few places quieter than this," he smiled. "I use this room only to sit and read when I am alone in the evenings. I keep a fine Armagnac in that cabinet. It is very good for the nerves."

Lydia stood. "Thank you, but I don't care for any."

"Oh, excuse me. I have the advantage of you. I know of course that you are Lydia Forrest, the star of Bernard's film, but I have not introduced myself. I am Stefan de La Roche. I live here."

"How do you do?" Lydia shook his hand. "Please forgive me for barging in here like this. We were told you were away on business. Oh dear, you must think I'm terribly rude."

"Not at all. I returned in time to see the end of your scene. You were magnificent. You must not let Bernard upset you. He is young, and very talented. In time he will learn the tact and polish to go with that talent."

"I certainly hope so . . ."

"Lydia!" Bernard's voice called from the top of the stairs. "Lydia, where are you?"

Lydia gave the count a wry smile. "There he is," she said. "The diamond in the rough." She went out into the hallway.

"Lydia! If you don't mind, we have another scene to shoot. I thought I told you that *no one* is allowed up here."

"It is quite all right," said Stefan, stepping out of the room behind her. "Miss Forrest needed a place to compose herself."

"Oh, Stefan . . . you are back . . ." Caught by surprise, Bernard looked ill at ease and slightly foolish. In his jeans and worn leather jacket, with two days' stubble of beard on his chin, he made a poor contrast to the smooth and impeccably dressed Count de La Roche.

"My business was concluded earlier than I expected. And yours? Is it going well?"

"On schedule so far. We will be finished here in two more days. I hope you are not finding us too intrusive." He looked disapprovingly at Lydia.

"On the contrary, I am quite enjoying it. What I have seen of Miss Forrest's performance makes me pleased with my investment. If you need anything, my butler Charles will get it for you."

"*Merci bien,*" Bernard said. "Come on, Lydia. Back to work."

During a break in the shooting of the next scene, the butler approached Lydia with an embossed envelope on a small silver tray. Inside was a note from the count.

> *Miss Forrest,*
>   *I should very much like to invite you to dine with me this evening, if you are free.*
>   *Stefan de La Roche*

"Is there a reply?"

"Oh God . . . no. Er, tell him I'll have to let him know later."

"*Alors,*" Bernard called, "*en place!*"

The scene was wrapped after three more takes. Bernard came up to Lydia as she was removing her makeup. "I will be in the cutting room tonight." His manner was cool. "Do you want to take the car?"

"No." She made up her mind suddenly. It was a chance to get back at Bernard. He might have gotten a good performance out of her, but she did not like his method. "Count de La Roche has invited me to have dinner."

"Suit yourself." Bernard shrugged, and walked away.

Charles cleared away the leeks vinaigrette and brought fresh glasses for the wine that had been standing on the sideboard, decanted into an etched crystal pitcher.

"I hope you will like this wine," Stefan said as his butler poured. "Tell me what you think."

Lydia knew the routine from observing Alex. She lifted the glass and examined the color, then swirled the wine and sniffed its bouquet. She put the glass to her lips and took a sip, and held the wine in her mouth, feeling the taste, before she allowed it to slide down her throat.

"It's delicious," she said.

"Yes?"

"It's . . . rich and smooth . . . it's subtle . . ." She gave up helplessly. "I'm afraid I'm not much good at wine adjectives," she grinned. "What is it?"

"A Château Mordoi Bourgueil. One of the 1970s from my vineyards. Very pleasant to drink young, I think, when it is served cool."

"You own vineyards? Where?"

"In the Touraine, along the Loire."

Lydia laughed delightedly, resisting the impulse to say "far out!" "Don't tell me you've got your own château, too?"

Stefan smiled. "Only a small one. Part of it is sixteenth century. It has been in my family for ten generations. I have been restoring the vineyards since I inherited the estate. My father had rather let them go."

Lydia sat back, shaking her head. "I assumed you had some money, because you were backing Bernard's film. And of course I knew you had breeding, because you're a count. But it never occurred to me that a member of the French aristocracy would be an entrepreneur. I thought you noblemen just sat around drinking and frittering away inherited fortunes on fast cars and fast horses . . . and fast women."

Stefan laughed. "Many of them do." In the candlelight from the chandelier his eyes became a warm azure. "I adore Americans. You are so direct."

"I've been accused of being too outspoken. I hope I haven't offended you."

"You are charming. But let me be outspoken. I want to know . . . are you and Bernard involved?"

"Well, that's certainly direct. And a good question. We have been, but lately things have been strained. By the time this film is finished, we may be too."

"Ah."

Charles served the main course, bonbon-sized noisettes of venison with a purée of celeriac. Over much of the rest of the meal Stefan drew Lydia out about herself. He seemed pleased that she was from a good Park Avenue family. He spent a fair amount of time in New York on business, he told her; so much so that he was currently negotiating to buy twin town houses in the East Sixties. They had been owned by an elderly widow who kept a virtual aviary of tropical birds, and they were in deplorable condition. Her estate was offering them for sale. Fixed up, Stefan thought they would be a good investment. He would rent one and keep the other for his own use.

They talked about the New York theater. He was up to date on the current Broadway season, which Lydia had missed, and gave her a quick critique of the better offerings. He knew nothing about off- and off-off Broadway. When Lydia told him that the only exciting things that were happening in New York were at places like La Mama and the Shade Company, he jotted the names down in his notebook and promised to try them on his next visit.

With dessert, an almond-flavored charlotte, they drank a wine that was extremely sweet and full-bodied.

"Is this a Sauternes?" Lydia asked.

"It is a rather old *Trockenbeerenauslese*, a German wine from the Crusius vineyards in the Nahe region."

Lydia sighed. "There's so much to learn about wine. I know absolutely *nothing.*"

Stefan gave her a look that turned the marrow in her bones to jelly. "I know far from everything, but it would give me pleasure to teach you what I know. Perhaps when the film is over you would care to visit me at Mordoi. I will show you my vineyards, and you can begin your education."

"I'd like that very much."

"So would I. I do not wish to intrude upon you and Bernard in what must be a very painful time for both of you. But when the shooting is finished and if the circumstances are right . . ."

He took out a gold engraved card and jotted a telephone number on it. "I would very much like to hear from you."

At the end of the evening the Count de La Roche kissed Lydia's hand and sent her home in his car. He did not accompany her as he had to catch an early flight to Geneva in the morning.

En route to the Quai de l'Horloge there was some sort of a traffic disturbance. The car crept along for a block or so, and then came to a dead stop in the middle of the Pont Neuf. Lydia looked across at the lights of the Rive Gauche and thought of her early months there with Alex and Juno, and later with Alex alone. Now she was living on the Île de la Cité, right in the middle of the Seine. There was a trend there, a definite direction; and she wondered, after tonight, whether she might not be ultimately destined for the more elegant life of the Rive Droite. And of Count Stefan de La Roche.

Chapter Thirteen

Lydia's wardrobe began to undergo a change. She telephoned her mother and told her she was becoming interested in Parisian haute couture. Her mother was so thrilled she sent a money order to underwrite Lydia's new fashion look. Of course, Marjorie Forrest had no idea as to the real reason behind her daughter's sudden fascination with designer chic.

Bernard noticed the change and did suspect the reason. At first, he teased her about it. "Stefan de La Roche is a typical modern count. French aristocracy is nothing much these days. Spend a weekend with him and you will be bored out of your mind." But Lydia did not take the teasing with good grace, and after a while he dropped it. She would find out for herself.

For all their fighting in the past, Bernard and Lydia's problems had never followed them to bed. Although making love had not been a final solution, it had provided a temporary one. Now Lydia was less responsive. There were occasions, becoming more frequent, when she avoided sex with Bernard, staying up late to read or retiring early so that she was asleep when he came to bed.

It was a time of crossed signals for them. Bernard did not want to lose Lydia, though he would never tell her as much. He cared about her and he valued her as an actress. From the film's rushes it was obvious that Lydia possessed something special. Periodically, Bernard would try to make up for his causticness on the set with tenderness at home, but Lydia mistrusted his motives and responded coolly. By the time she warmed up and was ready to come around, Bernard's pride was hurt and he had withdrawn into his shell.

There were periods when Lydia thought how much she loved
Bernard and his intensity, how exciting their life together could
be. A famous director-actress team, like Claude Chabrol and
Stephane Audran. But Bernard was so erratic. There were too
many problems, being with him night and day. Their professional egos clashed constantly. At home, she bridled at his male
chauvinism; Bernard expected too much of her, and took her too
much for granted.

On the other hand Stefan de La Roche and the aura that surrounded the European aristocracy dazzled Lydia. Although she
would never admit it to herself or anyone else, deep down there
lurked her proper upbringing and a desire to please her parents.
She had been rebelling against it. Rebellion, although it was
exhilarating, was also hard work. There was something tremendously appealing and relaxing about the idea of coming home
again to such triumphant approval. Lydia knew she was project-
ing much more than had actually been established with Stefan,
but she kept replaying in her mind that evening and the pos-
sibilities that had begun to form.

Only one thing was clear to Lydia: a degree from Yale no
longer seemed important. She was living in the real world. She
wrote to Juno that she had decided not to return to school. Juno
would be upset, but Lydia knew that she was making the right
decision.

Lydia was tired. She wondered if it was anemia. It was the last
week of the long and grueling shooting of *L'Engagement*, although these last days themselves were not particularly grueling, just long and monotonous.

It was not the shooting, nor was it anemia. It was the struggle
in her head about what was going to happen to her and Bernard.
The film had brought them together and kept them together.
But by the end of the week the film would be over. She had been
trying not to think about it, to concentrate on her character of
Patricia. But now she would *have* to think about it.

She climbed the stairs, a shopping bag of groceries in each
hand, and unlocked the door. A light was on in the living room
and the sound of Pink Floyd blared from the stereo. It could not
be Bernard. He had stayed behind to shoot close-ups of Roger

Saint-Cyr. She set the shopping bags down and went into the living room to see who was there.

A woman was leaning back against the sofa. She was not pretty, but she had that French style of toughness that made her looks interesting. She was wearing fatigue pants and a Chinese peasant jacket. Her dirty-blond hair was pinned up with no particular care. She wore no makeup or accessories other than a red bandanna knotted at her neck. Around her finger, she twirled a pair of black lace bikini underpants. Lydia recognized them. She had bought them at Bloomingdale's before she left for Paris.

"Who are you . . . *Qui êtes vous?*" Lydia asked.

The young woman gave Lydia an appraising stare. "These are not my size, nor my style," she said. "But I found them in my flat. And now I am sure I know who they belong to."

"You're Nelsia."

"Yes. I am Bernard's girlfriend."

"You've been away for six months. A lot can happen in that time."

Nelsia lit a cigarette. "Yes, a lot happens, but nothing changes." She tossed the panties contemptuously toward Lydia. "But I will not discuss this with you. Tell Bernard I am home. He will want to call me."

"Tell him yourself. He'll be here soon." Lydia got the shopping bags and took them into the kitchen.

A few minutes later she heard Nelsia leave, slamming the door behind her.

Lydia put a pork roast in the oven and made a green peppercorn sauce to go with it. All the entertaining she had done for Bernard had improved her culinary skills. She was still far from haute cuisine, but she had come a long way from peanut butter sandwiches and hard-boiled eggs.

It was seven-thirty. There was time to take a hot bath before Bernard came home. She ran the water into the oversized, claw-footed tub, and with a glass of wine and a *Vogue,* she settled in for a long soak.

At nine, she removed the roast from the oven. Bernard had not shown up.

By eleven-thirty, when she heard his key in the door, the roast was cold and she was boiling.

"Where the hell have you been?"

"I'm sorry, *chérie*. I . . . I ran into a friend."

"Yes? I'll bet I can guess what her name was."

"All right. I know she was here. I ran into her downstairs. I had to talk to her."

"Oh, you did? What about talking to me? I had dinner ready three hours ago. What am I . . . some kind of fucking housewife who sits at home while you go out with your mistress?"

She raged into the bedroom. He followed her.

"Lydia . . . believe me, there is nothing anymore between me and Nelsia. I had to tell her that."

"For four hours you had to tell her? Oh please. Spare me."

"Nelsia and I were together for a long time. You don't just say 'So long, baby.'"

"Oh yeah? Just watch me. But then, we haven't been together that long, have we?"

"What do you mean?"

"So long, baby."

Lydia packed her bags and moved to the Esmeralda, a hotel that had been recommended by some of her theater friends. Her room was small and cluttered, but it looked out over the garden of St.-Jullien-le-Pauvre, and from one window she could catch a glimpse of Notre-Dame.

For the last two days of shooting, Bernard talked to Lydia only when he was giving a direction. She spoke to him only when she had a question. They behaved toward each other with such professional courtesy that everyone knew immediately that the affair between the director and the star was over.

After the final wrap there was a party on the set, with wine and bread and charcuterie, and two of the grips playing guitars. Lydia stayed only long enough to kiss the cast and crew members good-bye and pass out the little gifts she had bought for each of them. She gave Bernard his present last of all.

He smiled with surprise as he accepted the small gift-wrapped box. It contained Lydia's key to his apartment, on a chain ornamented with a little plastic pig.

Bernard handed it back to her. "Keep it," he said, looking into her eyes. "Someday you will want to use it again. Stefan de La

Roche is not a very interesting man, only very rich. It is not over between us."

Roger Saint-Cyr and several other people invited Lydia to dinner, but she said she was exhausted. She took a taxi back to the Esmeralda and it was not until she was inside her room, with her coat off, that Lydia realized the key chain was still clutched in her hand. She flung it against the wall.

"I *am* through with you, Bernard! Forever!"

Later that evening, however, she crawled around on the floor and retrieved the key, slipping it into her silk jewel case. It was over between them, she was sure. But when she tucked into bed with a copy of *L'Étranger* that Bernard had given her, she wondered where he was and what he was doing; and if, perhaps, he was doing it with Nelsia.

Lydia slept fitfully for at least forty hours that weekend. She would awake, groggy, munch on crackers, then go back to sleep some more. From time to time, she thought of calling Stefan. It was what she had imagined she would do the moment the film was over and she had broken up with Bernard, but now she did not feel up to it.

The depression was overwhelming. With the film over, there was nothing to fill her days. And no one to fill her nights. She began to wish Bernard would call—he knew where she was staying—but the phone remained silent. Anyway, there was no point in thinking about Bernard. They had no future. So she kept falling back into a heavy sleep, riddled with guilty dreams.

And then she had a dream about Stefan. He was smiling, and they were on a sailboat in a warm and sunny ocean. He told her he loved her, and in the dream she loved him back.

On Monday afternoon, Lydia forced herself to get out of bed. Bernard was not going to call and she admitted to herself that she had been wanting him to, if only for the chance to turn him down again, or perhaps to be talked into meeting for just one cup of coffee. She went into the bathroom and took a hot shower. Over the therapeutic rush of water she heard the phone ringing. *At last,* she thought, *that bastard!* Without bothering to grab a towel she rushed into the bedroom to answer the phone.

It was Alex, from Greece. The connection was full of static.

"Hey, what goes? I called Bernard and he gave me your hotel number. He said you two had broken up."

"Yes. With a clash of thunder. Oh, Alex . . . it's so good to hear your voice. I've just had a horrible weekend . . . a lost weekend."

"What? Drinking away your sorrows?"

"No. Sleeping them away . . . escaping, I guess."

"Well, I'm really sorry about you and Bernard. It's a real bummer."

"No, it isn't! It's just that . . . with the film over I'm sort of . . ."

"Falling apart?"

Lydia sighed. "Yes. Oh Alex, I wish you were here. So I could cry on your shoulder."

"I wish I were there, too."

"Hey . . . how are *you?* How's the play coming?"

"Really well. I had a great breakthrough the other day. I finally got hold of one of my characters who was eluding me. So I'm fine. But you aren't, so let's talk about you. What happened? Bernard sounded pretty down."

"Oh, it just won't work. We're not temperamentally suited for each other. Oh, Alex . . . when am I going to see you again?"

"When I'm finished the play. Hey, why don't you come to Greece?"

Lydia was tempted. She wished she could go. But she was afraid of a replay of their days together during the past fall. Besides, Alex would be working. No, they were friends still, and it was better to leave it that way. "I'd love to, Alex, but I can't. I have a few ideas of what I'm going to do."

"Oh? What?"

"I'll tell you later . . . when I've got it worked out."

"Okay." Alex's voice began to fade behind the static. "I'll call again next week and see how you're doing."

"Thanks, Alex. I appreciate it. I love you."

"I love you, too. Cheer up."

"I already feel better, just talking to you."

Lydia returned to the bathroom and shampooed her hair. As she dried it with the towel she looked hard at her face in the bathroom mirror. Her eyes were puffy from all the sleep and her skin was pale. She felt a bit weak. She had to get herself out of the hotel room before it swallowed her completely.

She threw on a pair of jeans and a sweater and went outside. She walked for a few blocks, and then stopped at a *tabac* and ordered a coffee. Drinking it in one gulp, she asked for a second, and began to feel marginally alive. Next, she ordered a *vin rouge*, to give her confidence.

Then she pulled Stefan's card out of her wallet.

Stefan was not in Paris. He was at his estate near Tours, in the Loire Valley. He seemed delighted to hear from her and insisted on sending a car to fetch her the next morning. Lydia spent the rest of the afternoon at Yves St. Laurent, in an ebullient mood. As she handed the clerk her American Express card she smiled, fantasizing that the next time she shopped here the card might read: Comtesse de La Roche.

Lydia was packed and ready hours before the chauffeur arrived at her hotel. With self-conscious elegance she stepped into the plush rear seat of the pearl-colored Bentley. As they whisked through the banlieu and south on the *autoroute*, Lydia read the *Herald Tribune* that had been placed in the side pocket for her.

When they passed Orléans and began to follow the gracefully winding Loire she put down the paper and looked out the windows. Storybook castles appeared on the high *coteaux* above the river. She remembered having read that one of the châteaux of this region was the model for the one in "Sleeping Beauty." In another, Leonardo da Vinci had spent his last days. It was an area rich in fable and history.

At Blois they abandoned the *autoroute* for a scenic road that hugged the riverbank. Lydia began to notice vineyards, the still-bare grapevines held up by stakes. They went through Tours and headed west toward Langeais. In some of the hillside vineyards men were working, and a few turned their heads as the Bentley swept past. Lydia imagined that she was the countess returning home.

They passed more châteaux. She wondered what the Château Mordoi would be like. *A little château*, Stefan had said. What was little—twenty rooms? A hundred?

The driver's voice crackled over the speaker. "*Voilà, le Château Mordoi, mademoiselle.*"

There it was, a sprawling stone edifice, dominating the lush green hillside. The car pulled through the gate and up the slope through an apple orchard. At the top they passed beneath an arch of Greco-Roman inspiration and rolled onto a wide cobble-stoned courtyard accented with small raised circular gardens of tulips.

She had expected Stefan to be waiting there to greet her, but it was a butler who came down the stone steps from the carved front doors and welcomed her in impeccable English. "The count is detained on business, Miss Forrest. He will join you for cocktails at five. I have taken the liberty of setting luncheon for you on the east terrace. Annie will show you to your rooms."

While the buxom, florid-cheeked young maid unpacked her bags, Lydia stood at the windows and looked down over a breathtaking vista of lawn and garden. There was a pond where a white sparkling Hellenic temple seemed to float on an island in the middle, and ducks cruised the smooth waters around it. Beyond that, sloping down to the river, were vineyards.

She showered and dressed and came down to the lunch that had been laid for her on the terrace: Loire salmon in champagne sauce, an endive and wild mushroom salad, and a light, refreshing Muscadet. Afterward she walked around the grounds and discovered a swimming pool with a bathhouse designed in the manner of a Chinese pagoda and constructed of painted and gilded tole. Farther on was a tennis court surrounded by palm trees, on which the only current players were a pair of peacocks.

Later she sat in a living room that was surprisingly comfortable and informal. The walls were covered in a rough-textured fiber matting and hung with an astonishing array of modern paintings: a de la Fresnaye of old men in a garden, a seated Picasso woman, a wild Fauve city scene by Dérain, a Mondrian, a Braque, an odalisque by Matisse. Lydia curled up on a chaise by the window and read a book about the region that she had found on her bedside table.

At quarter to five Stefan de La Roche walked through the door. He was dressed in a leather windbreaker and tweed trousers, with a pale blue turtleneck. His face was flushed with color, and he looked more relaxed than he had in his Paris apartment.

"Lydia! I hope you will forgive me for leaving you alone for so long. I had intended to be here to greet you, but unexpected business threw my day into a turmoil." He smiled and kissed both her cheeks. "I hope you have not been too bored."

"Not at all. I've been having fun exploring. This place is absolutely breathtaking!"

He crossed to a lacquered Oriental chest that opened into a bar. "Sherry?" he asked. "It is a custom I learned when I was at Oxford. Extremely relaxing and pleasant at the end of an afternoon."

They sipped an amontillado that was nutty and strong, and he told her the history of the château. "It was built by Henri Quatre as a hunting lodge and later given as a gift to Chlöe de Marais, a favorite mistress of his later years. A gift of love, it was —*l'amour du roi.* That is where the château gets its name, a local corruption of that phrase . . . Mordoi. It came into the hands of my family in the time of Napoléon. The major reconstruction was done by my great-grandfather in the latter part of the nineteenth century. In my father's time it fell again into some disrepair. My father disliked this area and spent most of his time in London, when he was not seeing to his mining interests in Johannesburg.

"I inherited the estate in nineteen fifty-nine, when I was twenty-seven. It had always held a special wonder for me, from the holidays I spent here as a boy with my grandparents. I restored and modernized the interiors, with the goal of making it a place where I could relax and entertain without ceremony. My ex-wife, Marie-Laure, was of a different taste. She preferred old-world grandeur. It was a constant battle between us. We compromised. Some of the rooms in her scheme of elegance still remain that way. I have not gotten around to changing them. But this room was done as I wanted. I am pleased that you chose it to read in. It is nice, is it not?"

"I love it. I must say I was surprised. I expected the château to be like your apartment . . ."

Stefan laughed. "In Paris, I have a need for more dignified surroundings. Here in the country I can be myself."

At dinner, he apologized again for neglecting her. "But to-morrow I have no appointments. I will show you the estate and the countryside. Do you ride?"

"Yes . . . but I didn't bring any riding clothes with me."

"We cannot have you riding like Lady Godiva." He smiled. "No matter. Leave it to me."

The next morning Lydia awoke feeling terrible. Her throat was swollen and sore. There was a sharp pain behind her eyes. Her body was hot and achy. She pushed the button by the bed to summon Annie, who arrived with a breakfast tray and a box containing riding clothes from a boutique in Tours. After she explained her condition, the maid left and returned with Stefan.

He sat down beside her and felt her forehead. "My God, you are burning with fever." He instructed Annie to send for the doctor. "Nothing like a few days in the country to make you healthy," he smiled.

Lydia sighed. "I'm sorry. I haven't even had a cold this year . . . and now this. I'm turning into the perfect houseguest."

The doctor arrived, diagnosed flu, and prescribed rest and antibiotics. He gave her a shot of something to make her sleep. She murmured another apology to Stefan as she drifted off.

The first thing Lydia noticed when she woke several hours later was a grand piano sitting in the middle of the room. She rang, but instead of Annie it was Stefan who appeared with a tray of soup and buttered toast. He set it down and kissed her forehead. "You're cooler. How do you feel?"

"Better, I think." She blinked, and pointed to the piano. "Is that really there?" she asked.

"I thought you might enjoy some music while you convalesce. If you like I will play for you."

"Oh please . . . I'd love it." Lydia giggled with pleasure. "I can't believe you did this."

Stefan smiled. "I am glad you are pleased. I wanted to do something to surprise you."

The next half hour passed quickly as Stefan played the twelve studies of Chopin's Opus 10. When he finished, he turned to

Lydia. "I am a bit rusty, I am afraid. I have not had much time to practice in the past months."

"It was marvelous. Where did you learn to play so well?"

"My mother was an excellent musician. All through my childhood, until her death, she insisted I study music. She wanted me to love it, as a passion. I also play the viola and a little jazz saxophone."

"Play something else . . . if you're not tired."

"I never tire of entertaining such great beauty." He smiled. "Especially when it is a captive audience. Is there something you would like to hear?"

"No . . . player's choice."

He played the march from Verdi's *Aïda*, a Polish dance by Scharwenka, and then swung into Gershwin's "Rhapsody in Blue."

Lydia clapped. "Bravo! I've never had such a nice time being sick before."

"It is Docteur de La Roche's famous music cure. Do you like Scott Joplin?" he asked, striking the first notes of "Maple Leaf Rag."

"Hmmm," she purred, settling back against the pillows. She let the music lull her and never heard the end.

The next day Lydia felt better, but Stefan would not let her get up. "These country influenzas can be stubborn. It is better to make sure."

Stefan spent most of the day with Lydia, save the time spent on business calls. He had a tray brought in for himself when she ate. He read to her from Dickens. They played Scrabble. He even brought out his saxophone and tried some Charlie Parker. His saxophone was not as accomplished as his piano, but the fact that there was something he could not do perfectly endeared him to Lydia.

She could not believe that the handsome, sophisticated Count de La Roche was devoting so much time to entertaining her. They were getting to know each other, and what she saw enchanted her. Beneath his worldliness there was a boyish quality about him, almost a shyness, which she found terribly appealing.

"This has been wonderful," Lydia said that evening. "But I don't think I can justify playing the invalid for another day. Doctor Stefan and these antibiotics have done their job. Tomorrow morning I'm going to join the rest of the world."

"Splendid. I will give you a tour of the vineyards, if you feel up to it." He took her hand and kissed each finger. "Sleep well. I have enjoyed the last few days with you more than I can say."

"So have I."

Lydia felt better in the morning, and over the next few days Stefan showed her around his estate. He said nothing about her returning to Paris, and when she raised the subject, Stefan dismissed it. "You are not strong enough yet for such a trip," he insisted. "You must stay here until we are sure there is no further danger of relapse." This was perfectly fine with Lydia. She was in no hurry.

He took her through his vineyards and the caves where the wines were aging in wooden *barriques*. On the following day and the day after they explored the château.

"These châteaux are traditionally laid out on an east-west axis," he told her. "The main rooms all open to the south."

"How many rooms are there?" Lydia asked.

"More than fifty. I confess I am not exactly sure. I used to play *cache-cache*—what you call hide-and-seek—in them with my friends when I was a boy."

"I wonder what you were like as a boy."

"I was a terror," he smiled. "If you had known me then I am sure you would not be here with me now."

"I'll bet you were cute."

"After dinner I will bring out the photo albums. You may judge for yourself."

He showed her the old chapel which had been restored very close to its original appearance with magnificent hand-carved pews and altar, and the conservatory, with splendid mirrored walls, a glazed terra-cotta floor, and a muraled ceiling that depicted the changing seasons. At Lydia's request he took her through the kitchen where she met Marcelle, the cook, and thanked her for the wonderful trays she had prepared.

On Saturday morning, she woke to the sun streaming in her windows. Annie was there fastening back the shutters. The riding habit Stefan had bought her was laid out. Lydia put it on and noted without surprise that it was a perfect fit. When she came downstairs she was informed by Desmond, the butler, that Count de La Roche was waiting for her in the front courtyard.

Stefan was mounted on a bay stallion, and there was a chestnut mare saddled for her. "Good morning," he said. "How do you feel?"

"Extremely healthy. It's amazing what a few days in the country can do."

Stefan laughed. "I thought we would work up a bit of an appetite and have breakfast out somewhere."

Lydia mounted her horse. "Sounds terrific."

They rode along the banks of the Loire. The air was warm, with breezes that carried a hint of the ocean many miles away. Lydia dug her heels into her horse's flank. "Come on!" she shouted over her shoulder, and raced ahead over a green meadow with Stefan spurring after her. She threw her head back and laughed with sheer exuberance. She was riding through a castled fairyland with a real French count with whom she was falling in love.

An hour later they stopped for breakfast at Le Cheval Rouge, a twenty-room inn near the famous gardens of Villandry. The chef greeted Stefan enthusiastically and brought them an omelette of sweetbreads and morels, freshly baked bread, and coffee.

"Monsieur Rody was an early customer when my vineyards began producing wines of the first quality. We are old friends."

After they had finished breakfast, Stefan ordered a bottle of champagne. "This is a special occasion," he said.

"Oh? What are we celebrating?"

"Us. These last days have been the happiest I think I have ever spent."

"For me, too."

"I told you that I was married once. My marriage to Marie-Laure broke up several years ago. There was no bitterness. She had no desire to have children. I wanted them very much. Mine is a very old family, and I did not want it to end with me. You understand?"

Lydia could feel her heart begin to pound. "Yes, I think so." Her mouth was almost too dry to form the words.

"Since then, I have been thinking of remarrying. But I could not find the right woman." He paused. "Now I have found her. And I have two questions."

"What are they?"

"Will you marry me? And have my children?"

Lydia squeezed his hand. "Oh yes," she said breathlessly. "And yes!"

"I've heard of whirlwind romances, but this is ridiculous," Juno laughed over the phone. "Oh, Lydia, I can't believe it! I . . . I'm stunned. How long have you known him? Where did you meet him? Tell me everything!"

"On the film. He was Bernard's backer. He invited me down here to his château for a weekend, and I got sick and stayed, just like in *Pride and Prejudice.*"

"God, how romantic! And you're really going to be a countess?"

Lydia gazed out the window of her upstairs sitting room at the vast manicured lawns of the Château Mordoi, and beyond, at the sloping vineyards that reached down to the shimmering Loire. She twisted the telephone cord around her ring finger, on which gleamed a huge emerald and diamond ring that had belonged to Stefan's great-grandmother. "It looks like it. But you're going to have to hold me up. I'm counting on you to be my maid of honor. The wedding's going to be here."

"Not in New York? How'd your parents take that?"

"Mother hit the roof. But she's going to have to get used to it. It's what Stefan wants . . . and what I want, too."

A note of concern came into Juno's voice. "Lydia, this is happening awfully fast. Are you absolutely sure about this?"

"Oh yes! Stefan is the most wonderful man I've ever met. He knows about *everything.* He's kind, he's loving, he's *so* handsome . . . I know he's older, but maybe that's what I've always needed. A man with his feet on the ground."

"He sounds fantastic." There was a short pause, and static

crackled across the transatlantic line. "But what about Bernard? Last time I talked to you . . ."

"That's over," Lydia said emphatically. "He's so immature, he's so wrapped up in himself. I'm glad I got out of that."

"Well, good," Juno said uncertainly. And then: "Does Alex know?"

"I've cabled him. It's such a bore, him not having a phone off there in Greece. If God had meant people to be incommunicado, He wouldn't have put them in the twentieth century."

For all of her elation, there was one thing that troubled Lydia. Here she was, engaged to be married, and her fiancé had not even so much as kissed her with passion yet. Aside from a few tender brushes of the lips during her convalescence, and a thrilling but semipublic embrace this morning after the proposal of marriage, their entire relationship had been virtually nonphysical. At Yale, it had been an absolute article of dogma in late-night bull sessions among her women friends that you would never marry a man you had not slept with, even lived with for a while. But so far, Stefan had not even tried anything, and it puzzled her.

Surely Stefan wanted her as much as she wanted him. Lydia wondered suddenly if perhaps, improbable as it seemed, he thought she was a virgin. Stefan was such a gentleman. He might be waiting for her to send out a signal. But, on the other hand, what if she did and it struck him as brazen? It was so hard to know how to operate at this level. Stefan was so unlike anyone she had been with.

They had cognac after dinner by a fire in the study, and talked about guest lists and wedding plans. Stefan held her close as she nestled in his arms. When he kissed her, she responded warmly and pressed up against him with purpose, but he did not take it any further.

At eleven o'clock, he suggested it was time to head upstairs. They walked up the curving mahogany staircase hand in hand, and Lydia wondered if Stefan could feel the vibrations of her anticipation.

When they got to the door of her bedroom suite, he took her

in his arms. "This has been a most extraordinary day," he said. "You have made me very happy."

He kissed her, but as the kiss ended and she felt him begin to pull away, she locked her fingers at the back of his neck in a kind of panic and kissed him urgently. She moved backward, drawing him through the doorway with her. With her foot she pushed the door until it closed with a solid click.

"Oh, Stefan . . . I'm so happy. I love you so much." They fell across the bed and continued to kiss. But Lydia could still feel a reticence in Stefan, and she worried that she should not have taken the initiative. A tremor of anxiety ran through her. Had she done the wrong thing? Had she ruined everything?

"Why, my darling," Stefan whispered with pleased surprise, "you are trembling." He pulled her closer to him. "Oh, you are so delicate . . . so very young and innocent . . ." He kissed her tenderly.

Innocent, Lydia thought. It was innocence he wanted, and he had interpreted her trembling as virginal timidity. And that had seemed to give him the initiative she had been waiting for. "Oh, Stefan," she whimpered, "I'm so . . ."

"Do not worry, my darling." He reached for the clasp at the shoulder of her white silk tunic. "It will be beautiful. You will see . . ."

It was only after they made love and Stefan had fallen asleep that Lydia admitted to herself that the experience had not been very satisfying, like a gorgeously wrapped box with a Cracker Jack prize inside. For one thing Stefan was very small. Although newspaper column wisdom had it that matters of size were irrelevant, Lydia found this not to be true. But even more surprising to her was Stefan's lack of technique. He was so overwhelming in social situations that she had built up her anticipation of his sexual prowess. But when he got beyond foreplay, Stefan was nothing but grim determination. And when it was over, he rolled off her with a sigh that seemed more like relief than passion.

But the sex would undoubtedly get better. The first time with a person was often awkward. Meanwhile, the romance of the situation was enough to keep Lydia ecstatically happy. She loved Count Stefan de La Roche, and he loved her. And she was going to marry him.

Chapter Fourteen

Lydia waited by the international arrivals gate at Orly Airport. From her high Charles Jourdan heels to her linen Dior suit she was looking every inch the countess, although she would not become one officially for another three days. But her restless, darting eyes and the incessant chain-smoking of Gitanes more suggested an actress with precurtain nerves.

Juno's flight from New York had just arrived. Alex's from Greece had landed over an hour ago. He was to meet Lydia here but she had not seen him yet. She cast her eyes impatiently toward the stream of exiting passengers, then back over her shoulder into the terminal looking for Alex.

She thought she saw Juno's dark head above the stream of tourists. At the same moment she heard a voice behind her.

"The Countess de La Roche, I presume."

"Alex!" She turned and could hardly believe what she saw. It was Alex, but with hair well below his shoulders and bleached almost white by the Aegean sun. His handsome jaw was covered by a blond, bushy beard. He was wearing a Greek peasant shirt, white cotton pants, and his bare feet were stuck in sandals. His eyes were masked by dark glasses and a thin cigar protruded jauntily from his mouth.

As Lydia was taking this in, Juno rushed toward them. Her outfit was pure Western hippie: low-heeled brown suede Navajo boots, jeans rolled to mid-calf, a long shirt belted with a wide sash of Indian beads. A three-strand Zuñi bird-fetish necklace hung down into the cleavage exposed by her open shirt.

They embraced, then stood back and looked at each other, laughing. "The Three Musketeers in disguise," Juno said.

Lydia left them to get the car while they brought their bags to the curb. She pulled up in a black Aston Martin DBS V-8 convertible with creamy leather upholstery.

"Holy shit!" Alex said. "Where did you find this?"

Lydia smiled. "An engagement gift from Stefan."

"Will he give me one, too?" Juno asked. "If I'm very nice to him?"

"If you're that nice to him I'll run you over with this one."

Alex loaded the bags and he and Juno slid into the front seat next to Lydia. With a magnificent rumble of exhaust they left the airport and headed south.

"You countesses sure know how to live," Alex said. "So how come Stefan didn't send the chauffeur?"

"He wanted to, but I insisted on coming myself. I had to get away from there. You wouldn't believe what it's been like the last few days. My family's descended on us and they're driving me crazy." She lit a cigarette from the lighter in the ebony dashboard.

"Is your mother still upset that you're not getting married in New York?"

"Oh God, she can't stand it. Real live European nobility and she can't show him off. But after a few days in the château she's beginning to come around. You should see her with her home movie camera. By the time she gets back to New York she's going to have more footage than *Gone With the Wind*. And my sisters . . . ugh!" Lydia made a face. "Jackie's divorce came through this spring and she's blatantly stalking husbands among anything she suspects has a title. Cynthia and Herbert, Mr. and Mrs. Greenwich, Connecticut, traipse around in their best Lilly Pulitzer and Jack Nicklaus greens and pinks, ordering Tom Collinses from the staff."

"What about your father?" Alex asked.

"Jesus!" she said, imitating her father's gruff voice, "this place must cost a fortune to heat!"

They lunched on a mousse of fresh pike in the garden of the Auberge de la Montespan in Orléans. Lydia barely touched her

food but lit cigarette after cigarette and sipped the '67 Château
Mordoi Chenin Blanc that she had ordered for them.

"It's still a little young."

"I think it's delicious," Juno said.

"Well, you couldn't have picked a better man as far as I'm
concerned, Lydia. I'm really looking forward to seeing the vineyards and discussing wine with Stefan."

"It's amazing how much he knows. And his friends. On weekends they sit around tasting wines and trying to place them . . .
not just the variety and the region and the vintage. But they get
into the specific vineyard, the kind of soil, and whether it grows
in the lowlands or on a hill—even what side of the hill."

"I may be a little out of my league," Alex laughed. "But I'm
always willing to learn."

"Speaking of that," Lydia said. "I don't want to sound hoity-
toity, but I hope you brought some other kind of clothes with
you. I'm sure you look perfect in Greece . . ."

Alex patted her on the arm. "Don't worry, mom. I know how
to dress for royal weddings. I'm not a diplomat's son for nothing."

"But that beard . . . it absolutely hides your gorgeous face."

"My beard? This is half a year's hard growing." But at the
look on Lydia's face, he smiled. "In fact, I was getting tired of it
anyway. I'll shave it off."

"And could we trim your hair . . . just a little?"

"God, I'm trembling," Juno said. "I have a feeling you're going to start in on me next."

"Well, as a matter of fact . . . I mean, you look absolutely
beautiful, Juno . . ."

Juno grinned sourly. "Why do I get the feeling that there's a
'but' hiding at the end of that sentence?"

"Well, it's just that Stefan's friends are older and more sophisticated."

"You don't think you're taking this countess bit a little too
seriously?" Juno protested. She was appalled at how uptight
Lydia had become. "What happened to Lydia Forrest?"

There were lines of strain around Lydia's eyes and mouth.
"Juno, please. I'm entering into a different life. You may not
think I'm a countess and I may not think I'm a countess, but by

Saturday night I'm going to be one, and I've got to look and act accordingly."

Juno felt the pressure of Alex's foot against hers. "I'm sorry, Lydia," she said, taking Lydia's hand. "I'll try to use the right fork. I'll make you proud of me."

"Oh, please don't hate me. It's so wonderful to have you both here. But look, Stefan doesn't know *anything* about the three of us . . . just that we're great friends. *Please*, don't let anything slip."

"Of course not," Juno said.

"But I thought you were taking us all on your honeymoon," Alex grinned. "Just kidding, just kidding."

Lydia smiled. "You know, I love Stefan, but it is hard sometimes. Being the way he wants me to be, being so much younger than his friends . . . and an American. Everyone's very polite and charming, but I feel a little like the baby panda in the zoo."

"Look, Stefan picked you to marry. He obviously had plenty of others to choose from. If he'd wanted a forty-year-old blue blood I'm sure he could've found one. Don't underestimate yourself."

"Alex is right," Juno said. "Just relax and be yourself. We'll stick by you."

Lydia smiled happily. "All for one, and one for all."

That evening before dinner, Juno came into Alex's room. Her hair was wound around her head in a braided chignon, and she was wearing a coral Halston crepe de chine with black high-heeled sandals. "How do I look?"

Alex whistled. "Lydia had better blindfold Stefan. I'd make you my countess any day."

"The trouble is . . . this is what I bought to wear to the wedding. How am I going to get through the rest of the weekend?"

"Just keep wearing it," he said. "They'll love you."

Juno sat on Alex's bed. "How do you feel about all this, Alex? Lydia getting married? I mean, you and she were . . ."

Alex shook his head. "I didn't exactly stake out a very permanent claim, did I? Anyway, the timing was all wrong then. Now . . . I guess I kind of have mixed feelings. I think in the back of my mind I'd always thought that the three of us would go on

and on. That somehow we *would* work it out. But that was kind
of an impossible pipe dream."

Juno swallowed and was silent for a moment. In the back of
her mind she had allowed herself to fantasize that with Lydia
married, the way might be cleared for her and Alex. But Alex
was obviously not thinking this way.

She took a breath. "I hope Lydia's doing the right thing . . .
marrying Stefan."

"How could she go wrong? Stefan seems crazy about her. And
let's face it, Lydia was cut out for this type of life."

"I guess. But I just have this feeling . . . that she's rushing
into it trying to prove something to herself. You know how
insecure Lydia can be. Besides . . . have you noticed how
much weight she's lost? And she's smoking more than ever."

"She told me she lost weight *before* she met Stefan, when she
was making the film. Look, if it'll make you feel better, I'm
concerned, too. This whole scene is a little like never-never
land, and Lydia is definitely playing the role of the enchanted
princess. But she's marrying Stefan day after tomorrow, and we
have to be supportive. She has prewedding jitters, that's all."

"I hope so. Oh, you're probably right, Alex. I guess I just have
prewedding jitters, too. I feel a bit uncomfortable."

Alex kissed her cheek. "Well, don't. Lydia needs us for comic
relief. That's our job for the weekend."

Juno laughed. "You're right. I'll change into my court jester
suit."

Alex picked up a pair of scissors off the dresser and headed
into the bathroom. "Why don't you change into your barber of
Seville outfit and render me the smooth-cheeked Alexander Sage
of yore?"

The next morning the thirty-odd houseguests rose and break-
fasted all through the morning. Some went horseback riding,
some played tennis or swam, others went off shopping. Lydia's
family were provided with chauffeured cars for a sight-seeing
trip.

Lydia had gone with her parents. Juno sat in the library and
wrote letters. Alex found her there in the late morning.

"Jesus, what a place," he said, flopping down in a chair. "I can understand Lydia falling in love here. You wouldn't even need another person."

"It's great for writing letters. I've been feeling very Madame de Sévigné this morning. No wonder they were such great letter writers in those days. You can't just toss off 'How are you, I am fine' in surroundings like this."

They went outside. Stefan was on the terrace.

"Ah, there you are. I have been looking for you. Lydia tells me that you are interested in wines, Alex. Perhaps you would enjoy a look at my vineyards?"

"I'd love it, if you're sure it's not too much trouble."

"On the contrary."

They walked out past the lawn, and down to where the sloping hillsides were combed with vines. It was a clear day, with blue sky stretched comfortably over rolling countryside, and the Loire sparkling below. On distant hilltops they could see other châteaux, and many slopes and bottomland fields covered with vineyards.

"I keep only thirty-seven acres under cultivation," Stefan told them as they walked between rows of young grapes. "It is a passion with me, not a business. We produce three thousand cases a year. None for export. I sell only to certain restaurants here and in Paris, and to a few private clients."

"What kind of grapes are these?" Juno asked.

Stefan leaned over to pluck one from its vine. He handed it to her. "This is Cabernet Franc. It is the classic grape for the *vin rouge* of the Loire Valley. We are ideally situated here. The Touraine climate is mild, with long summers." He pointed with his right hand. "If you were to draw a line due south it would run through the St. Emilion district of Bordeaux." With his left hand he gestured toward the east. "In that direction on this latitude lies the Côte de Beaune, where the finest grapes of Burgundy are grown." He formed a cross with the index fingers of both hands. "Here, where those lines come together . . . the best of both worlds."

"Are all your grapes Cabernet Franc?" Alex asked.

"No. I grow seven acres of Chenin Blanc, from which I make a rather durable and quite good white wine. It is something that

I have initiated at Mordoi since I took over. In my grandfather's day we had only the Cabernet Franc."

They climbed the *coteau* to another field, defined by a low stone wall. "The oldest vines are here, on the south slope. The Clos Marigny. My grandfather fed these vines on a special diet of seaweed and fish gut. They were nearly dead after the years of my father's neglect. I have revived my grandfather's practice." He smiled. "I do not know if it is scientific, but the grapevines seem to thrive on it."

In the vat house, Stefan introduced them to his *maître de chai*, a robust middle-aged cellar master dressed in traditional blue work clothes. "Monsieur Charbonneau is one of the few remaining masters of the old school of wine making in the Touraine," Stefan informed them. "So many *vignerons* have gone to the modern, automated methods—fermentation in vats of stainless steel, temperatures artificially controlled, testing for sugar with laboratory apparatus. Monsieur Charbonneau will tell you by pinching the grape whether it is ready. Oh, it is true that the modern methods yield a higher production and tend to eliminate or minimize human error and the caprices of nature. But efficiency is a business concept. The side effect is to eliminate also the opportunity for human excellence, and the special bouquet that only nature, unhurried, can produce. Do you know that there are over a hundred and seventy different elements that can make a wine memorable?" He ticked a few off on his fingers. "Sugar, tannin, yeast, minerals, acids, esters, polyphenols, aldehydes. . . ."

He showed them the *barriques* in which the wine aged, the wooden fermenting vats, and the large round wooden presses where the grapes were crushed at harvest time.

"What's the reason for the trend to stainless steel fermenting vats?" Juno asked.

"Easier." Stefan made clear his contempt for the word. "To control artificially the temperature of the fermentation. What was once done—what we still do here—by employing small barrels kept in cool cellars, is now being 'modernized' with refrigeration techniques." He shook his head. "Nothing is free. You pay something for all these so-called advances. In wine, the price is richness. Truth, if you will. You know the saying *In vino, veritas.* It means something slightly different, of course . . . but it is applicable. As you dilute the truth you put into a wine, so the truth that comes out of it becomes thin and meaningless."

They had reached the cellars where the wines were laid down. Stefan held the door for Juno and Alex to go in.

"Wine making is an art. It has been practiced in just such a way for two thousand years. Oh, it is a business too. But today the business aspect has become overemphasized. It is like those dreary art stores you see, especially in America nowadays. 'Original Oil Paintings!' Well, I suppose they are oil, and even paintings . . . but what have they to do with art?"

"It sounds so bleak," Juno said.

"Still, the new methods have stood up pretty well in tastings, haven't they?" Alex asked.

The count shrugged. "The taste can be acceptable, though generally it lacks the complexity one would hope for; but never mind. Taste alone is not the issue." They were walking down rows of floor-to-ceiling wine racks like the stacks in a library. Stefan reached down and extracted a dusty bottle. "This is the Château Mordoi forty-seven, the last truly great Bourgeuil produced on this estate before my grandfather's death." They walked over to a table, where he produced a corkscrew and three glasses. He opened the wine. "It needs very little time to breathe. Smell."

Juno leaned over the neck of the bottle and inhaled. A rich, fruity, slightly woodsy fragrance filled her nostrils. "Oh wow," she sighed. "That's incredible!"

"Magnificent," Alex said.

Stefan poured. "Hold it up to the light. See the color? Smell the bouquet—-slide it around in the glass, so. Now . . . taste."

It was extraordinary—a velvet richness of texture as well as of taste, a sunny, ecstatic warmth, a faint, distant hint of raspberries.

"It's like . . ." Juno struggled to find a suitable description. "It's the feeling I had writing letters in the library this morning, of the richness of another period of history."

"Ah," said Stefan, "but what if I told you that this château is not old at all—that it was built only thirty years ago with ce-

ment and reinforced steel and façades of cleverly antiqued
stone?"

"Oh," Juno said, momentarily shocked. "Well . . . I mean, it
would still be awfully beautiful, but . . ." She stopped, grinning. "Yes, I see your point."

"Even if it were a perfect reproduction, it would not have the
richness of an original. The true pleasure would be gone. And of
course, there is no such thing as a perfect reproduction."

Alex raised his wine. "Château Mordoi," he toasted. *"Vive
l'original."*

They touched glasses, and drank.

That night Stefan took over Barrier, a three-star restaurant in
Tours, for the prewedding dinner. The dinner was unforgetta-
ble, and it was not just the spectacular food. The guests were an
odd assortment of French society and New York money. "Not a
good mix," Lydia later remarked to Juno and Alex. "Like Dom
Pérignon and Gold Seal."

When dinner was over, the party returned to Mordoi, where
there was a brilliant *son et lumière* display on the lawn overlooking the Loire. ("Our wedding gift to the townspeople," Stefan
explained to the guests, "to celebrate the new Comtesse de La
Roche.") Afterward, there were cards and billiards, cognac and
liqueurs. One by one the houseguests drifted off to bed.

"Don't stay up too late, dear. I want us to have time for a nice
talk in the morning," Marjorie Forrest said.

"Oh God," Lydia said, wringing her hands in mock anguish
when her mother had left the room. "You don't suppose she
wants to tell me about the birds and the bees?"

There were just the four of them left—Stefan, Lydia, Alex,
and Juno.

"Now that we have you to ourselves," Alex said, "this might
be a good time to give you your wedding gifts."

While Juno and Alex went upstairs, Stefan put his arm
around Lydia and kissed her. "Tomorrow at this time you will
be the Comtesse de La Roche. All this ridiculous wedding business will be behind us."

"Oh, I can't wait to get off by ourselves. I wish we had just

eloped. Or told the chauffeurs to take my family someplace far
away and lose them."

Stefan laughed. "Your family is not as bad as you think. And
your friends, Alexander and Juno, are absolutely delightful. I
have enjoyed them very much."

"Oh, I'm so glad. I was afraid that you'd find them . . ."

Stefan laughed. "You worry too much, my love. I am not as
stodgy as you think."

"I don't think you're . . ."

Alex and Juno returned with their gifts and handed them one
at a time to Stefan and Lydia.

"The ones that Stefan has are for both of you. The ones for
you, Lydia, are more personal," Juno explained. "I hope you
don't mind, Stefan."

"But of course not. You three are old friends. I am not jealous."

Stefan and Lydia opened the official gifts first: an antique
Greek wine decanter from Alex, and a silver picture frame of
Navajo design from Juno.

Juno's present to Lydia was the rolled-up painting Hollis had
done of the three of them. "I'm afraid you'll have to reframe it,"
Juno said. "It was too large to bring on the plane."

Lydia kissed Juno. "This is so wonderful. I'll put it in the
little sitting room off my bedroom. It's my favorite place to cozy
in and read. I'll feel even cozier with the two of you hanging
above me."

"Now I may become jealous," Stefan laughed.

Lydia opened the package from Alex. It was a signed manuscript of his newly finished play, *Other Lovers*. "Oh, Alex, I can't
wait to read it!"

"While you're reading it, memorize the part of Linnea. I want
you to play it when it gets produced. I've already sent it to an
agent in New York who loves it."

Lydia lit a cigarette. "Well, actually, I'm afraid you'll have to
get someone else. I . . . that is, Stefan and I have talked about
it. I'm not going to try and have a career. There will be too
much to do as Stefan's wife . . . traveling, entertaining . . .
having babies." She smiled at Stefan and took his hand. "But we

will certainly be in the opening night audience, cheering louder than anyone else."

"But of course," Stefan said. "Now, my love, I know you want to stay up all night with your friends, but you must get rest. Come along to bed." He stood, and kissed Juno's cheeks and shook Alex's hand. "Thank you for the very lovely and special gifts. We will treasure them always. Good night."

Lydia hugged both her friends. "Thank you for being here. I couldn't have survived this weekend without you." She left the room with Stefan.

Alex picked up the cognac decanter. "Let's adjourn upstairs for a postmortem. This room is too big for an intimate chat."

"You look upset, Alex."

"Well, Jesus, I am upset. I wrote that fucking play for Lydia. She'd be brilliant in it. I mean, did you hear her? 'Stefan and I have decided I won't have a career.' Jesus!"

"You'd better come upstairs, you're shouting. We can't wake up the servants."

In Juno's room, Alex raged around, swilling back cognac. "You were right, Juno. It's a bad idea for Lydia to marry that guy. He's going to turn her into a fucking hostess."

"I know, Alex. But this is what she wants now, to do what Stefan wants. They'll probably mellow out after a while. Give her time."

"I haven't got time. I wanted her to star in this play."

"Well, you don't have a producer yet. By the time you do maybe Lydia will have changed her mind."

Alex shrugged. "I had the whole fucking thing worked out. Lydia was going to star in it and Stefan was going to produce it. Shit!"

Juno opened the window and looked out at the moon. "I think we're both going through a lot of changes this weekend. Somehow I thought that we'd all always be inseparable friends. I guess it was naïve. It just never occurred to me that we'd wind up going in different directions. It hurts to know that Lydia has someone else now, and I guess I'm a little jealous. I know we'll still be friends but it'll never be the same again. We'll never be as close, or as free as we were." Juno sat on the windowsill. "As much as I hate the idea of it, I guess we're growing up."

Alex came over and sat next to her. "Lydia's going in different directions, not us. We're still close *and* free. Come on, let's lie on the bed and talk."

Juno stretched out next to Alex, propped up on embroidered lace pillows. "I can't help it. I feel so sad. Like something's lost forever."

Alex finished the cognac and set it on the bedside table. "Look, maybe we have lost Lydia. But we have each other. Maybe that's what was meant to be all along."

"I've wondered that, too."

They kissed, but after a while Juno pulled herself away. "God, Alex, I can't make love to you with Lydia down the hall. I'd feel bad about it. This whole place makes me feel strange. But I do want you, you know that, don't you?" Alex did not answer. Juno looked over at him. His eyes were shut and his breathing was growing louder.

Juno leaned over and kissed his cheek gently, then took off his shoes and pulled a blanket over him. She changed into her nightgown and slipped into bed next to him, under the sheet. Alex mumbled something in his sleep and put an arm over her.

The next morning when Juno awoke, Alex was not there. She dressed and went downstairs. There was a buffet breakfast set up in the dining room. Juno ate part of a croissant but that was all her nervous stomach could handle. She went outside. The sky was overcast, and it looked as if there was a good chance of rain. Workers were putting up canvas pavilions and setting up tables and chairs for the wedding.

Alex appeared from around the corner of the terrace. He was wearing corduroy pants and a linen sports jacket, and sipping a Perrier. "Do you think if I order a new head it'll be here by this afternoon? I think I overdid it last night."

"Depends on your frame of reference," Juno said. "You're still a virgin, if that's what you're worried about."

"Ohhh, it hurts to laugh. Come on, I want to show you something."

He led her around to the east lawn. There was a crowd standing around a large heater that was blasting hot air into an enormous burgundy balloon.

"The getaway car," Alex said. "Weather permitting."

"Stefan does have a lot of style, no doubt about it. I think we should tie some shoes and tin cans to the gondola."

"Lydia was out here a while ago. She looked like Marie Antoinette staring up at the guillotine. She's absolutely terrified."

"Probably a good thing. It'll keep her from worrying about the ceremony. Who's going to fly it?"

"Stefan. He's an avid balloonist. One of his many Renaissance man hobbies. Lydia says she's going to be the first bride to wear a parachute over her wedding gown."

In the late morning, when the civil ceremony took place at the Hôtel de Ville there was a light drizzle falling. But by noon the sky had brightened and by four, as five hundred guests arrived from neighboring estates and Paris, it was clear and blue. Stefan and Lydia exchanged their vows, according to the Protestant ritual, beneath a centuries-old rose arbor. Stefan was dressed in a cutaway and dove-gray trousers. Lydia's gown was a cream-colored, many-tiered Givenchy, and around her neck she wore an emerald necklace that had belonged to Stefan's grandmother. There was a garland of grape leaves and tiny roses in her hair, and she carried a bouquet of the same. Juno stood by her as maid of honor, and Michel Jullien, Bernard's brother, was the best man. Bernard had sent his regrets.

Later, after the orchestra had played the wedding waltz, and hundreds of doves and white balloons had been released into the sky, Alex danced with Lydia.

"You are the most beautiful countess in the history of France."

"And the happiest. I can't believe it . . . me, the Comtesse de La Roche. I keep thinking I must be dreaming."

Alex pulled her a little closer. "It's all very real. I am happy for you, you know."

Tears filled Lydia's eyes. "Oh thank you. You and Juno won't desert me, will you? We'll always be friends?"

"Friends, hell. We're going to be courtiers."

After the wedding feast, Juno went with Lydia to help her change into her ballooning outfit: a burgundy jumpsuit with the

de La Roche family crest emblazoned on the back. Stefan had
designed one for each of them and had them made up in Paris.

Lydia handed Juno a small gift-wrapped box. It contained
three jagged gold bands.

"They fit together," Lydia said. "You can take them apart but
they always go together again. It's called a puzzle ring."

Juno threw her arms around her. "It's perfect. Just like us."

"There's something else . . . Alex. Whatever happens between you two, it's all right with me. I love you, and I want you
both to be as happy as I am."

"Hey, let's not worry about that now. We have to get you off
to your honeymoon, or the wizard will take off for Kansas without you."

The balloon was eight stories high, towering above the château. Like the jumpsuits it was decorated with the de La Roche
crest. The wicker gondola was festooned with grape leaves, and
provisioned with a silver bucket filled with champagne bottles.
Four men held the anchoring ropes while Lydia and Stefan
climbed in. At Stefan's signal they let go. As the huge balloon
rose into the air, Lydia tossed her bouquet toward Juno, but a
gust of wind carried it to be caught by a young cousin of
Stefan's. The guests cheered as the honeymoon couple floated
away over the countryside. A car filled with their luggage
started off in pursuit.

An hour or so later, Juno and Alex were in a chauffeured
limousine headed for Orly Airport. Juno had an Air France
flight later that night. Alex opened a bottle of the Château
Mordoi Bourgueil from a case that Lydia had given him as a
present and poured them each a glass.

"To the happy couple," he said. "Wherever they may be."

"Did you see the expression on Lydia's face as they took off?
Sheer terror. But I must say, it was about the most romantic
wedding I've ever seen. All those roses and doves. I still can't
believe that our Lydia is a countess."

"I still can't believe that you're turning right around and
heading home. At least spend a few days in Paris with me."

"I'd love to, Alex, but I can't. The Santa Fe Opera's opening
this week and I have to be there or else."

"Then change your flight to tomorrow night. We can have a day together, and you can still get back in time."

Juno shook her head. "I'm cutting it pretty close as it is. I wish I could."

"Yeah. Well."

They sipped their wine in silence. Juno thought about how nice Paris would be, alone with him. All weekend she had been waiting for some sort of signal from Alex. But now it really was too late. And it was obvious to her that Alex did not really feel about her the way she did about him. She would love to spend that night and the next day with him. But what would be the point? They would still be off in separate directions afterward. She had a summer job, and another year at Yale. Alex had to work on getting his play produced. She would get herself all churned up, and it would be for nothing.

The limousine pulled to a stop in front of Air France, and the chauffeur got her bags out of the trunk and gave them to the porter. Alex and Juno stood together on the platform.

"Look, I'm really sorry I can't stay. I'd like to, but, you know, commitments . . ."

Alex kissed her. "I know. Anyway, I'll keep you posted on what I'm up to, and where I'll be living in the fall." He started to get back in the car, but instead reached out his arms to her. They embraced for a long moment. Then he pulled away.

"Well, so long. Have a good trip." Alex got into the limousine. Juno waved, and headed into the terminal feeling totally miserable. She supposed she had made the only decision she could have made. But where was the comfort in that?

Alex watched Juno until she had disappeared inside the terminal.

"*L'Angleterre,*" he said to the driver. "*C'est à quarante-quatre Rue Jacob.*" As the limousine swung out into the airport traffic and headed for his hotel, he sat back, thinking. It was best that Juno could not stay, after all. His relationship had always been with both Lydia and Juno, and he had made a mistake before when he had tried to make a separate thing of his feelings for one of them. They were his two closest friends, and it was better to keep it that way. Lovers were easier to find than friends.

It did not occur to Alex that perhaps he had merely picked the wrong one the last time.

Chapter Fifteen

They walked along the Majorcan beach hand in hand, letting the waves rush over their bare feet. Stefan was quiet, and Lydia was content to watch the sailboats far out beyond the breakers.

"You know," Lydia said, "the only bad thing about leaving on a honeymoon is that you don't get to find out what happened to everybody after you left. I mean, I wonder if my sister went off with that Spaniard, Don Carlo de Something-or-other . . . Does he have a castle, by the way?"

"No. A very nice villa near Barcelona."

Lydia shook her head. "That won't do. She'll be wanting a castle at the very least. After all, she is the oldest sister." They walked along in silence again for a few minutes. "And Alex and Juno . . . I wonder if they spent some time in Paris together."

"Oh, I suppose we will find out all the answers soon enough. For my part, I am glad all the formalities are over."

She squeezed his hand. "But not the marriage?"

"You can be sure I will never leave you, my love. I could not marry anyone else and go through all that again."

"Hey, that doesn't sound much like a compliment. You're *supposed* to say, Lydia, I'll never leave you because I love you so much."

Stefan bent down and kissed the top of her head. *"That* goes without saying."

As the sun sank below the horizon, they turned and walked back toward the speedboat that waited to return them to Stefan's yacht. The yacht was anchored in the old harbor across the bay from Palma, the capital of Majorca in the Balearic Islands where they had been cruising the past week.

"I ordered a quiet dinner tonight. Unless you would prefer to go into town?"

"Well, it might be fun to go for a drink along the seafront. Then we can come back and relax."

"That is fine with me. Whatever you would like."

Although neither would admit it, Lydia and Stefan were beginning to feel the strain of being alone with each other. The weather and the yachting had been pleasant but, away from the Château Mordoi and Paris and his friends and business colleagues, Stefan had become increasingly restless. It was boredom, Lydia speculated out of her insecurity. She began to be anxious that she did not know how to amuse him outside of the bedroom. In fact, since their engagement they had spent very little time alone together. She had been back in New York for a month, and when she had been with Stefan their life had been a round of parties, entertaining and being entertained. It was hard for Lydia to enter into the conversations of Stefan and his friends. Either it was wine, or business, or books she had not read, resorts she had not been to, music she had not heard, or amusing anecdotes about members of the international jet set whom she had never met. During the period before the wedding, Lydia had been content to listen and be admired.

Now Lydia and Stefan were alone, except for the chef and crew, and she was forced to face the fact that they were very different from one another. But they were married, and she had to figure out how to make it work.

On Stefan's part, he did not worry about his relationship with Lydia. He wanted her to bear him an heir. Undoubtedly, she would become more sophisticated as she grew older and took on his interests. That was why he had decided on a young wife: Lydia was someone he could mold into the perfect Comtesse de La Roche. Marie-Laure had been too strong to direct; he had been young himself, and deeply in love, when he married her.

Stefan was not deeply in love with Lydia, although he was not indifferent to her vibrance and beauty. Still, he regarded her as an accessory. He was not much interested in getting to know her any better than he already did, since he planned to change her. He wanted her as she *would* be—the elegant, self-assured

Comtesse de La Roche, and most important, the mother of the future count.

They chose one of the cafés along the Paseo de Sagrera. A waiter brought their drinks, a whiskey neat for Stefan, a Campari and soda for Lydia. She was casually draped in a white gauzy ankle-length dress. Stefan had on custom-tailored white trousers and jacket, with a straw Panama that had belonged to his grandfather. If one did not know he was a count, one would certainly guess that he was of noble blood. He had a way of gazing at things down his long chiseled nose with a passive expression, without moving his head.

"You've been very quiet today, Stefan. Is anything wrong?"

"No, darling. It is not unusual for me to become lost in thought when I am alone."

"But you're not alone. You're with me," Lydia teased, although there was an edge to her voice.

"It is a compliment to you that I can relax when we are together."

"Ah, very good. You've redeemed yourself. But you're sure I haven't done anything . . ."

Stefan put his hand over hers. "Of course not. I will tell you when you do something to displease me. I believe that a man must be candid with his wife. That way, problems have no chance to grow out of proportion."

"Do you believe likewise, that a woman must be candid with her husband?"

"Oh God, Stevie . . . it *is* you! Tony spotted you from the promenade and thought it was you, and I said, no, Stevie would *never* come to Majorca . . . he finds it so boring." A tall woman with boyish black hair and enormous, heavily mascaraed brown eyes swept over to their table. She spoke with a British accent.

"You are right. We are not *in* Majorca. We are parked outside." Stefan stood, smiling, and kissed the woman's cheeks. A man came over and embraced him warmly.

"I want you to meet the new Comtesse de La Roche. Lydia, these are old friends . . . Maggie and Tony MacGraw."

Lydia shook their hands. "I know the name . . . you sent the

marvelous Malcolm Morley painting as a wedding gift, along
with your regrets."

"What fabulous memory you have, my dear. And you're even
lovelier than I had expected." Maggie MacGraw was somewhere
in her thirties, and quite attractive, with pronounced cheekbones, a wide mouth, and large white teeth.

"But this is such a coincidence," Tony MacGraw said. He was
older, with a round, balding head and perhaps forty pounds of
excess weight distributed evenly around his body. "Ricky and
Celia are here, too. Why don't you join us for dinner? There's a
smashing new bistro up the beach a ways."

Stefan looked delighted. "Sounds splendid. Unless you would
prefer to join us on the yacht?"

"Absolutely not," Maggie said. "I loathe swaying around on
the ocean. If God had meant us to be on boats, he would've put
Dramamine in our veins."

At dinner with the MacGraws and the other couple, Ricky
and Celia Wade-Eastham, Stefan was more gregarious than
Lydia had seen him in days. He and Tony MacGraw had
roomed together at Oxford. Ricky and Celia were friends of
Maggie's. Ricky, who was sleek-looking but rather void of personality, produced a popular series for the BBC, and Celia, pale
and whiny, was a theatrical costume designer.

"Are you going to Charlie's shoot this fall, Stef?" Tony asked.
"We missed you last year. I say, what a time we had. One of the
best ever."

"Except for those frightful Americans—do you remember,
Tony?"

"Hank and Rita." Tony ground the names out with a bur-
lesqued American accent. "Big construction chap from Los Angeles. Charlie—he's Lord Gresham," he explained in a smiling
aside to Lydia, "marvelous place in the Cotswolds, splendid
shoot—anyway, Charlie's going in on some condominiums with
this chap in Palm Springs. Hank puts up two thirds of the capital, Charlie invites him to the shoot . . ."

Celia trilled with laughter. "Oh, Tony, you're terrible!"

"No, excellent arrangement. Charlie makes a few pounds,
Hank and Rita go back to Los Angeles with their slides and get

to tell how they 'made the acquaintance of Lord Gresham—
damn nice fella, y'know?' Everybody gets what he wants."

"Except the poor bloody rest of us," Maggie laughed. "God, I
thought I'd die having tea with Rita. 'Who does your hair,
honey? I've been trying for years to get just that shade.' You
know what Cornelia Harrington says about Americans—they
. . ." She broke off suddenly with a grimace. "Oh, all *right*,
Tony, you needn't break my toe. Of course I didn't mean *you*,
dear," she said brightly to Lydia. "There are Americans and
Americans."

"In any case," Stefan pointed out, "Lydia is French now."

"And *très charmante* she is," said Ricky gallantly.

Fuck all of you, Lydia seethed, as she drained her glass. All she
wanted to do was go back to the boat, but she knew Stefan
would never agree this early in the evening. No, she had to force
herself to act out her role as the charming young countess.

There was a great deal of champagne, followed by wine, followed again by champagne. Everyone was in high spirits, except
Lydia. She knew it was unreasonable, but she resented seeing
Stefan so animated when for the last week with her he had
seemed so lethargic. She drank more wine and felt her irritation
growing—with Maggie, who so flamboyantly took center stage
and kept touching Stefan and calling him "Stevie"; with Celia,
who ignored her completely and seemed content with making
catty remarks and asking her husband for "ciggies"; with Ricky,
who patted her on the back so often she was beginning to feel
like a prize terrier; with Tony, whose pats were more surrepti-
tious and kept to the area below the table. But mostly with
Stefan, who never looked at her as he amused the group with
stories of his visits, in disguise, to rival vineyards in Bordeaux,
Burgundy, Italy, and California.

Maggie had written a best-selling book called *How to Say the
Right Thing at the Right Time*, "a brilliant and witty send-up of
conversational gambits," according to the *Times*. She regaled the
group with stories of her American promotional tour.

"I did a television show in Chicago, I think it was. It was one
of those breakfast shows. I met the host just before we went on
the air and the first thing he asked was if I wanted a drink.
Judging from his breath, I'd say he had already had quite a few.

Anyway, we sat down in the studio. He said to me, 'I imagine you've done a million of these interviews. Everybody always asks the same questions, right?' 'Right,' says I. Just then the little red light went on the camera. He introduced me, held up the book, and then said, 'Tell us about it, Maggie.' I started talking and the camera came in close to me. Then out of the corner of my eye I saw him get up and walk out of the studio. There I jolly well was, all by myself." She laughed. "Talk about saying the right thing at the right time. I had to interview myself for the next twenty minutes. At which point he came back, thanked me, and sent me on my way."

"Oh God, Maggie, you have the most amusing life," Stefan laughed.

Lydia laughed too, but she was getting sick of Maggie and her amusing life. The wine had gone to her head and she felt dangerous. "Tell me, Maggie," she said, her voice mocking the older woman's drawling English top-drawer accent, "what *is* the right thing to say when a man is squeezing your thigh under the table —as Tony has been doing to mine for the past half hour?"

Maggie stared at Lydia for a moment, then gave her a condescending smile. "Nothing, my dear. Absolutely nothing."

Later that night, back on the boat, Stefan showered, got in bed, where Lydia was waiting seductively for him, and turned off the light.

"Stevie," she said in a mocking of Maggie's accent, "how about a little meat for my locker?"

Stefan did not answer.

"Stevie . . ." she said again, this time in an American Southern accent, "how about a little lube job for my motor?"

Stefan turned over on his side, away from her.

"Stevie . . ." Lydia said again, but this time he sat up and turned the light back on.

"That is quite enough, Lydia! This evening you have been insufferable. Pouting during dinner, then insulting Tony and Maggie. Do you realize that Tony MacGraw is an M.P. and one of my greatest friends? I know you had too much to drink, but can you understand how rude you were?"

"Don't you care that he was feeling me up? And anyway, do

you realize how patronizing Maggie MacGraw was to me? How thick she laid it on about what a sweet young thing I was?"

"She was paying you a compliment."

"Like hell! At least she'll never be a sweet, young thing again . . . if she ever was."

"Stop it!" Stefan's eyes were blazing.

"Make me. Show me that you still like me."

Stefan kicked the sheet down to the foot of the bed. He pointed to his limp member. "You show *me!*"

Lydia went down on him, sucking him furiously into a full erection, which for Stefan was less than four inches. He began to moan as she brought him nearer and nearer to a climax, then she stopped and kissed her way up his flat stomach and sparsely haired chest. She stretched her body over his, and while her fingers frantically rubbed her clitoris, she guided Stefan inside her.

She liked being on top. The position maximized his limited penetration and stimulated her. She pushed herself deeper into him and swiveled around to face in the other direction. Stefan dug his hands into her slim hips and moved them up and down frantically. A moment later, he arched his back and spewed into her with a loud groan.

Lydia, panting, lay back on top of him. By the time her breathing had quieted, his had grown heavy with sleep. She slipped out of bed and took a hot, sobering bath. Afterward, she dried off and walked naked onto the deck outside their cabin. For a long time she stared at the twinkling reflection of the moon on the water and thought about how foolish she had been at dinner. She supposed she could not really blame Stefan. Maggie was witty and sophisticated. Tony was one of Stefan's oldest friends. And she had nothing in common with them. She loved Stefan and wished desperately that he would be proud of her. Presently, she went back to bed and masturbated until she fell asleep.

At nine-thirty the next morning she awoke with a terrible thirst and an even worse headache. She put on a Chinese kimono and her dark glasses and went out on deck. A breakfast table was set for one, and the steward poured her a large cup of espresso. Stefan was not on deck. She assumed he was in the library, reading or poring over maps. The steward put a silver tray in front of her containing a letter. It read:

> *Lydia,*
>   *I have business in Paris that must be attended to. I have instructed Enrico to take you anywhere you would like. At your convenience, I have arranged for a plane to fly you to Tours. À bientôt.*
>
>   *Stefan*

The emotions that ran through Lydia as she read the note were a mixture of fear, humiliation, and rage. For a moment she sat, staring at the note with her eyes burning. Then with a scream she kicked over the breakfast table, sending silver and china crashing onto the deck and overboard. "You bastard!" she yelled. "You bastard, Stefan!" She ran past the startled Enrico, and into her cabin.

For the next twenty minutes Lydia screamed and cursed and threw everything in sight. She hurled all of her clothes out of her closet onto the floor and stomped on them. She cried and pounded her fists on the bed. Then she got out her suitcases and stuffed the clothes into them.

There was only one thing to do: leave Stefan, have the marriage annulled, move back to New York. Not New York, she decided a moment later, she would have to deal with her parents there. And certainly not Paris where there would be too many conflicting memories. Maybe London or California—she could get a job acting in movies or TV.

Life was so ironic, she thought as she zipped the suitcases closed. Ten days ago her destiny was set. Now the life that stretched out ahead of her was shapeless. Stefan did not want her; it had all been a terrible mistake. She wondered whether she had really wanted Stefan, or if the attraction had been to the title and sophistication. And, she reminded herself, she had been on the rebound from Bernard Jullien.

Lydia went into the bathroom, showered, and put on fresh makeup. Her hangover headache was still with her, exacerbated by the tantrum. She took a couple of aspirin and decided that what she needed most was time to think.

Picking up the phone, she dialed the captain's number. "Enrico . . . I'll be going to St. Tropez."

At St. Tropez, Lydia told Enrico she would no longer be needing the yacht. Then, so Stefan could not trace her should he try, she took the train to Cannes and checked into an inexpensive hotel on the Rue d'Antibes. She had not received her new passport, so to the world she was still Lydia Forrest. She walked along the crowded Croisette across from the beach and finally settled on the Blue Bar to sit and have a drink. Presently a very attractive young man with long hair and a bushy blond beard came looking through the crowd for a vacant chair. He stopped at Lydia's tiny table.

"*Ah, pardon, est-ce-que je peux m'asseoir ici?*" he asked in halting French.

Lydia shrugged.

"*Merci,*" he said, taking off his backpack and setting it on the floor under the table. He wiped his brow. "*Il fait chaud aujourd'hui, n'est-ce-pas?*"

"Yes, it is."

The young man smiled. "Well, shit, you're an American. You sure look French." He extended his hand. "My name's John."

"I'm Lydia."

He pointed to her nearly empty glass of white wine. "Can I buy you another? I've been hitching around, speaking almost nothing but French or Italian for the last month. I try to avoid Americans in order to work on my languages, but sometimes my brain aches from all the effort. Does that ever happen to you?" He caught the waiter's eye and ordered Lydia a wine and a glass of beer for himself.

"It used to. Not anymore. But I'm getting tired of France. I'm thinking of moving somewhere else. I don't know where."

"Speaking of moving. Do you happen to know a cheap place around here to get a room?"

"The Wagram. Not far from here. That's where I'm staying."

The waiter put down their drinks and John paid him. "I'm due for a real bed and a shower. I've been camping out mostly, and getting clean in the ocean."

"*If* you can get clean in the Mediterranean."

John smiled. "Yeah, really. Well, here's to you. I heard some-where that there's going to be a fireworks display on the beach later. Wanna go?"

"Maybe. I'll see how we're getting along."

John leaned back. "If you weren't so beautiful I'd say you're in kind of a bad mood."

"No . . . I'm always like this." But she decided she enjoyed the diversion of talking to the good-looking, friendly American. She grinned.

"Hey, that's better. You over here studying, or what?"

For the next half hour, Lydia gave him a very abridged ver-sion of her life in France, leaving out the affairs with Noel Pot-ter, Alex, and Bernard, and the marriage to Stefan. She left in the part about starring in Bernard's film.

"Wow, you're a movie star. Far out."

Lydia laughed. "Well, I'm hardly a movie star after one film that hasn't even been released."

"Nevertheless, I'm impressed. And you were a Yalie . . . I just graduated from Princeton. Going to grad school at Colum-bia in the fall. Hey, are you hungry? Let's find some place cheaper than this and get something to eat."

"Okay . . . and then we can catch the fireworks."

They went to the fireworks, and afterward there were more fireworks back in room 21 at the Hotel Wagram. For three days Lydia and John made love, swam, ate pizza and bouillabaisse, talked about books and rock groups, read the *Herald Tribune*, and discussed the Nixon-McGovern presidential campaign. After all these months around the European aristocracy, John's unaf-fected Americanness was a wonderful change for Lydia. For those three days she was completely herself, and it gave her back a sense of herself.

"Why don't you come with me to Spain?" he asked. "We could work on our Spanish at all those bullfights and midnight sup-pers. Then maybe you might want to come back to New York with me."

"In another life I might have." Lydia sat up in bed and lit a cigarette. "But this one's gotten too complicated. There's some-thing I have to tell you."

The next day, at the Nice-Côte d'Azur airport John hugged Lydia by the gate for her flight to Paris. "This seems like a thirties movie. American boy meets runaway countess. Three glorious days on the Riviera . . ."

"And then they have to part, to go back to their responsibilities in the real world."

"But don't forget how those old movies always turned out. The countess runs off with Gary Cooper. Love triumphs over all."

"Not this time, I'm afraid. But I'll never forget the last few days. They've really been special."

"For me, too. Listen, when you come to New York for a visit at least call me at Columbia. We could have a drink and talk over old times."

Lydia laughed. "Okay. I promise." She kissed him again, and then ran to catch her plane before it took off.

Midway back to Paris, she realized she had never gotten John's last name.

Chapter Sixteen

She was back. But she wondered if this was where she belonged, and if she would ever fit in. Everything in the Paris apartment testified to the life she had returned to. It was grand, but claustrophobic; elegant, but rigid. It was a fairy tale, but she remembered that the princesses were often prisoners in fairy tales, and that the Brothers Grimm did not always write happy endings.

Lydia regarded herself as one of those special people who were at home in any situation, from Park Avenue drawing rooms to dope-filled garrets on the Left Bank. Becoming a countess was merely another facet of her adaptability. That was what she had thought when Stefan had asked her to marry him. But the subtle structure of European society turned out to be more difficult to crack than she had imagined. Being an American, it was something that was not in her blood. She felt it, and Stefan's friends made her feel it. There was also her youth. That was less important. She would get older; but she would always be an American.

There were two ways to deal with the situation. She could hold on to, and flaunt, her Americanness. Or she could, as an actress takes on a new role, join them in their own game, work at becoming as aristocratic as Stefan could possibly wish. She was not pleased with either prospect. There had to be something in the middle of those two options. She was not exactly sure what it was, but she knew that something in the middle was what she would be most comfortable with. This was her life. She had spent twenty years developing into one sort of person. She did not want to kill that person in order to please

Stefan. The past few days with John had strengthened and reju-
venated her, and restored some of her old self-assurance.

Stefan was out when she arrived. She had tea and read a magazine while she waited, with apprehension, for him to return. A
little before six she heard the front door open and Stefan's voice
talking to Charles, the butler, in the downstairs hall. She listened as he climbed the stairs and came toward the bedroom.
She took a deep breath and tossed the magazine down on the
bed next to her.

"Hello, darling," she smiled as he came through the door.
"I'm home."

"So I see. Do you have any idea how worried I have been the
past few days? My secretary has phoned every hotel in St.
Tropez, on the entire Riviera. I was getting ready to hire detectives. Where have you been?"

She searched his face for signs of concern but saw only controlled anger. "I needed some time by myself. To think. I had no
idea you would be so concerned. As a matter of fact, when you
left me without any notice in the middle of our honeymoon I
had just the opposite impression."

"I was called away on business," he said coldly. "I believe I
made that clear in the note I left."

"The note? I wasn't dead, Stefan, I was only asleep! You
could've waked me up to let me know about this *business* that was
so important. *If* it was business. I didn't think of hiring detectives to check up on you."

"I had no intention of checking up on you. You dropped out
of sight for the better part of a week. I was frantic. You could
have been hurt, or killed . . ."

"Hurt?" she exploded. "You're damned right I was hurt. And
humiliated. To be abandoned in the middle of my honeymoon! I
had certain naïve ideas that the bride and groom were supposed
to spend it together . . . but then this is only my first marriage.
Perhaps you learn as you go along."

"I certainly hope you will learn. If you had not behaved so
abominably that night . . ."

"Aha! It had nothing to do with business, did it? It was my
punishment for being a naughty girl. And you accuse *me* of
behaving badly!"

"Don't shout!" he said; and then more softly, "Perhaps we have both made a big mistake."

She looked at him, suddenly anxious. "You're not just talking about the last few days, are you?"

Stefan sat down on the bed. "No. Perhaps we did not fully consider the differences in our backgrounds and our ages when we fell in love."

Lydia stared into her lap for a long moment. Finally she looked back at Stefan. There were tears in her eyes. "Did you fall in love, Stefan?"

"I made you my wife. I gave you my name."

Lydia nodded. "That's not answering the question, but . . . Well, I fell in love with you. That's why I married you, and that's why I came back. I've done a lot of thinking over the last few days. About us, about our problems. I think we can work them out . . . if we try to understand each other. If we try to have realistic expectations about each other. That is, if *you* still want to try."

"Yes . . . I would like to try," he said quietly.

"I'm not Marie-Laure. Or Maggie MacGraw. I can learn a lot of those tricks. I'm a good actress. But I'm still me, and I still want to be me. I'll try hard to act the way you want me to, but I'll also need some time to myself. I think what happened back there was just that it all piled up on me. I felt suffocated . . . but it won't happen again." She took his hand. "I'll be the best little countess you ever saw."

Stefan smiled. "And what shall I do? Buy Rolling Stones records and grow my hair?"

"Hmmm . . . you might look nice in a ponytail and jeans."

As the Comtesse de La Roche, Lydia began learning a great deal about life in a château on the Loire. The first thing she learned was that with fourteen servants there was never a night when all of them were out. The second thing she learned was that there was absolutely nothing to do once she had finished her thank-you letters for the thousand or so wedding gifts, and pasted the nuptial photos into an album. She decided she wanted a pet but Stefan told her that was out of the question: he was allergic to domestic animals. Lydia requested an exotic pet.

Stefan relented and bought her a cheetah but soon discovered that he was allergic to it as well. Lydia became involved with a tankful of tropical fish. They did not make Stefan sneeze, but they did not come when they were called either.

Entertaining was high on the list of duties for a French countess. In Paris, they gave large dinner parties or small midnight suppers after the opera. At Château Mordoi, they gave small dinners or large weekend house parties. In either case there was little for Lydia to do. Stefan invited the guests, and the menus were planned and prepared by the chefs and their staffs.

In Paris, the Moroccan cook, Moustafa, held forth with the best continental and Northern African cuisine. At Mordoi, Marcelle Piccoli, who had cooked for Stefan when he was a child, provided the table with heavier-sauced, more traditional French cuisine.

One morning Lydia awoke early and decided to make breakfast in bed for Stefan. She was in the enormous tiled kitchen preparing a mushroom omelette, one of her specialties from the days with Bernard Jullien, when the venerable Marcelle appeared.

"*Ah, Madame la Comtesse, que faites-vous là?*"

"*Je fais la cuisine pour le comte . . . une omelette avec les chanterelles.*"

Marcelle put on her apron. "*Non, non. Ne vous dérangez pas, je vous en prie.*" She looked scornfully at the omelette and scraped it into the garbage.

Lydia decided to take up a musical instrument, and Stefan bought her a harp. She spent two hours a day, four days a week on lessons. After two months she gave it up.

"I'm afraid I'm terrible at it," she told Stefan. "The hopeless harpist. But if I ever make it to heaven, I'll at least have an edge on the other recruits."

"Never mind, my love. We'll find you something else. Perhaps a flute. Oh, by the way, I have a surprise. Michel and Marielle Jullien are coming for the weekend, and so is Bernard. He has finished editing *L'Engagement* and will bring a print for us to view."

"Oh . . . what fun." Lydia had forced all thoughts of Bernard and the film out of her mind. It seemed long ago, although it had been little more than six months. She felt as if she had gone through decades of experience since then. The movie was a part of a distant youth. Even when she had boasted of it to John at Cannes it had seemed a bit unreal. She was not sure whether John had even believed it, or if he had believed that she was a countess on the lam.

Lydia and Stefan stood on the front steps and watched the Mercedes pull in across the courtyard and come to a stop below them. The chauffeur came around to open the door. Marielle Jullien was the first to emerge, followed quickly by Michel. Last, almost reluctantly, Bernard got out of the car.

Marielle kissed Lydia. "You look ravishing, *chérie.*"

"And you look ravishing yourself, Stefan," Michel said. Stefan was dressed in a three-piece charcoal suit with a silk shirt and tie. "Perhaps a little overdressed for a weekend in the country."

Stefan laughed. "But not for Paris. Regrettably, something has come up which requires my presence there tonight."

"We cannot have a screening without the backer," Bernard said with a smile.

"Oh, I will be back tomorrow. We will show your film in the evening."

"But I cannot wait until then," Marielle complained. "I am so dying of curiosity. Why don't we screen it tonight . . . and again tomorrow for Stefan. All good films must be seen at least twice. Would you mind, Stefan?"

Bernard protested. "I think Stefan should be in the audience of the first showing. It is his privilege."

"*Merci bien*, Bernard. But I do not mind. I would not want to make your lovely sister-in-law wait. You can show it tonight if you like, and I will see it tomorrow." He smiled. "But do not give away the plot, Marielle. It will all be a surprise to me."

"What?" Michel asked. "Haven't you read the screenplay?"

"I told him the plot," Bernard said. "He did not have the time to read it. It has changed some since then."

Stefan kissed Lydia good-bye. "Well, *adieu, mes amis. À demain.*"

The end leader flickered across the screen. For a moment there was only the square of projected light and the snapping sound of the film spinning on the take-up reel. Then Bernard turned off the projector and flipped on the lights in the drawing room.

Marielle leapt up and threw her arms around Bernard. "Bravo! It is brilliant." There were tears in her eyes.

Michel shook his head. "Well, little brother," he said in a husky voice, "you have lived up to your promise."

Bernard hunched his shoulders under his leather jacket. "This is only the work print. There is still some tightening up to do." He looked over at Lydia, who had not moved since the lights came on. "So," he said, "you did not like it?"

"I'm in shock. I don't know what to say."

"Lydia, you were extraordinary," Marielle exclaimed. "I had no idea how talented you are." She looked mock-accusingly at Bernard. "*You* never told us. You let us go on thinking you were the clever one."

"Well, it takes a brilliant director, eh, Bernard?" Michel said, draping an arm around his brother's shoulders.

But Bernard had not taken his eyes off Lydia. "I am still waiting for your reaction," he said to her.

"I don't know . . . it gave me chills. It was like watching a dream that I'd had before. It didn't seem like me up there. It was like watching another actress."

"And she was brilliant!" Marielle said.

"Yes," Lydia laughed. "Yes, she was. But it wasn't me. It was all Bernard." She looked at him. "You are a wonderful director . . ."

Bernard stared back at her without smiling. "And you, Lydia, are a star."

Michel poured four cognacs and passed them around. "What's your plan for releasing it?"

Bernard waved a hand. "As you know I'm behind schedule."

Michel turned to Lydia. "He has been shooting some commercials for us this summer."

"To make enough money to finish this film," Bernard explained. "Anyway, I hope to have it ready to show to Gaumont next month. And then maybe a release in January, or possibly we will wait and show it first at Cannes, at the *Quinzaine.* Of course, it depends on how people like it."

"They will like it," Marielle said seriously. "I know we are family, but I think we know films as well. I admit I was dubious when you cast Roger Saint-Cyr, but his performance is quite perfect. The way his character changes from that scene in the art gallery where they meet. He is so courtly and charming . . . you *like* him so much. And then that amazing scene when he spies on Lydia as she is preparing for her bath. She is so innocent, so unsuspecting . . . but he . . . it is almost like another character emerging. Saint-Cyr has not given a performance like that since *Nuit de L'Enfance* in whatever it was . . . nineteen fifty-five, I think. Perhaps never. It was *you*, Bernard. *And* you, Lydia . . . oh, what a shame that Stefan does not want you to pursue your career."

"I think he will change his mind when he sees this." Michel came over and took Lydia's face between his hands and kissed her on both cheeks. "You were absolutely splendid, my dear."

"Stefan is very old-fashioned," Marielle said, shaking her head. "I am not so sure he will want to share Lydia with the world. He has his nineteenth-century notions of honor, of what a woman should and should not do. Not a woman, actually . . . *his* wife."

Michel grinned. "No countess of mine is going to work! Well, never mind," he said. "Perhaps this film will pull Stefan into the twentieth century."

"Unzip me, darling." Marielle slipped out of her dress and underthings and put on a robe. She was an attractive, chestnut-haired woman in her early thirties with large breasts and a slim body. She had studied for a year at the Rhode Island School of Design. Now she was a successful ceramicist. Her whimsically elegant tableware sold for high prices in the Primavera boutique at Printemps in Paris, at Harrods in London, and Bloomingdale's in New York. She was a likable woman with an infectious, exuberant manner. She had been the first of Stefan's crowd to champion Lydia, and they had become good friends. She sat at the dressing table and applied cold cream to her

face. Michel was in the bathroom brushing his teeth. They had
left Lydia and Bernard alone in the drawing room.

"Do you suppose everything's, you know, all right down
there?" Michel called out.

"Even if it were not, what could we do? You and Stefan are
not roommates at university anymore, my darling. You are not
obliged to defend his honor."

"No, I suppose not."

"In any case, it is very peculiar, don't you think—Stefan inviting us all down here and then taking off?"

Michel shrugged. "Well, he had business."

"I don't think so. Oh yes, *business*, but . . . think of it, Michel.
My old lover, Danny, who I was with before I met you, comes to
see us for the weekend. You have invited him, and then you
leave? What kind of business is that important?"

"Well . . ." Michel said, "it is a little strange. I don't know
about Lydia, but Bernard is still in love with her. Did you notice
how edgy he was in the car coming down?"

Marielle laughed. "Oh God, yes. But don't worry about
Lydia. She will pass the test, if this is a test that Stefan is putting
her through. We have had many talks. She is devoted to Stefan.
After all that trouble on their honeymoon she has made great
strides in becoming the self-assured countess that he wants. You
can see it, can't you?" She ran a brush through her thick brown
hair. "She would not jeopardize everything by cheating on Stefan, and especially not here. Now, as for Stefan . . . I'm not so
sure."

"Oh, darling, that is merely gossip. You do not know if it is
true."

She smiled at him. "I also hear some awfully racy things about
you, Michel."

"Every bit of it true," he leered. "Come here. I will show you
what I did to my secretary Françoise Prevost in my office this
morning."

After Marielle and Michel went up to bed, Bernard and Lydia
sat for a long time without speaking. A log crackled in the old
stone fireplace. The moon, nearly full, had risen over the tree-
tops and shone in through the windows.

"So . . . what is it like? Being the Comtesse de La Roche?"

"I'm very happy."

"Are you? I heard some things . . . I thought perhaps you would telephone me."

"We had problems. But we've worked them out."

"You cannot be in love with him."

Lydia smiled. "You think it's impossible for any woman to be in love with anybody but you."

"Not any woman. You."

"That's all over, Bernard."

Bernard shrugged. "I do not think so. I know you better than you think I do, Lydia. You are an actress, playing the part of a countess . . . but I have read that script. I know how it ends."

Lydia lit a cigarette but crushed it out immediately. "The film's terrific, Bernard. You are really talented."

"Yes, and you, too," he smiled. "It is a collaborative art, you remember?" She nodded. "I have an idea for my next film. I have an outline with me. I would like you to read it."

"No, Bernard."

"Just read it."

"I can't. I promised Stefan, and I plan to keep my promise. There's no point in hashing over it."

"Lydia . . . you are like the character you played in the movie. Allowing yourself to be dominated by a selfish older man."

"That's not true. I'm doing what I want to do. Look, making that movie with you was no picnic. You were pretty dominating yourself . . ."

"But you fought back. You had some spirit then." He got up and crouched on the floor in front of her and took her hands. "You saw yourself on screen. You cannot deny what you saw. You are not meant to be buried alive in a château, making silly small talk with boring, rich people. You are talented. You were meant to be an actress. You have something that comes along only every once in a while. But what good is it if you hide it from the world and yourself?"

"One picture doesn't mean much, Bernard."

"You are right. Picasso did not stop after one painting. Beethoven wrote nine symphonies. An artist has an obligation to create. You *must* work! You will only get greater and greater."

"Oh, stop it! Stop it." She tore her hands away from his. "I'm not going to change my mind. I can't . . ."

"Because you're a countess?"

"Because I'm going to have a baby."

"Oh *merde!*" He got up and went over to the sideboard to refill his glass. When he turned back he could see that Lydia was crying. "I know that I have not been on your mind that much. But I have been watching you every day in the cutting room. Your face, your body, your gestures, your intelligence. I know you better now than I did when we were living together. And I love you more than I ever did." He came back over and kissed her. "Have the child. Give Stefan an heir . . . that's all he wants. Then come back to me. It will not be the same. I have changed, too."

Lydia wiped her eyes. "No, Bernard. I like my life. Everything's changed. What happened between us is in the past."

Bernard ran his fingers through his long, dark hair and along the stubble on his jaw. His slate eyes stared at her. "But you still have the key to my place."

Stefan did not return until late Sunday. By then Bernard had left with his film. Stefan promised to see it with Lydia in Paris, but in truth, he did not seem very interested.

At the end of March, two weeks early, Lydia went into labor. The baby, a girl, was born in a private clinic in Paris. Stefan handled his disappointment graciously.

"Never mind, darling," he told Lydia when the nurse had taken the infant from the room. "We will start another one right away."

Chapter Seventeen

Lydia named her daughter Alexandra Juno Forrest de La Roche. She was a jolly blond-haired baby, and Lydia, who during her pregnancy had not been able to visualize herself as a mother, fell in love with little Alexandra from the moment she held her, the umbilical cord still attached. She had insisted on natural childbirth although Stefan wanted no part of it. As always, he was against anything that he considered trendy and refused to take an active role in the birthing. The idea of a father-to-be in the delivery room, snapping photographs of the panting mother-to-be, he considered disgusting.

A governess, Mademoiselle Jobert, had been engaged and a suite at Mordoi adjoining the nursery was redecorated for her. Lydia, however, spent a great deal more time with the baby than Stefan would have wanted. She also insisted on breast-feeding, very *déclassé* among French nobility. To Stefan's delight, Lydia had trouble providing enough milk for the baby and, after a month, was forced to resort to formula. But she was depressed for days afterward, and when she was not playing with the baby, she refused to leave her room.

Stefan began to worry and consulted the doctor, who prescribed a holiday, away from the baby. That very day, Bernard Jullien wired him that *L'Engagement* had been invited to the *Quinzaine* at the Cannes Film Festival. Ordinarily Stefan would not have considered attending. But coming on the heels of the doctor's advice, and concerned as he was about Lydia's depression, he thought perhaps it might be just the thing to lift her spirits. Shortly after receiving Bernard's wire, Marielle Jullien telephoned to say that she and Michel had rented a villa in La

Bocca for the festival and wanted Stefan and Lydia to stay with
them.

But when Stefan announced these developments to Lydia she
insisted that she did not want to leave the baby. Finally, she
agreed to go, but only for a few days. As the time drew nearer,
however, Lydia became happier and even went on a shopping
spree in Paris with Marielle, to exult in her newly restored figure.

"I am going to be a bit tense with Bernard around," she confessed to Marielle over lunch.

"Ah, do not worry. He will be so busy giving interviews and
courting American distributors. I am certain he will not have
time to sulk and tell you how much he still loves you."

Lydia put down her fork. "But . . . how did you know?"

"I am Bernard's sister-in-law, but we are also good friends. He
will get over you, sooner or later. Perhaps when he gets involved with his next film. But what about you? We have never
talked about this, but . . . are you over him?"

"Yes! Absolutely. I love Stefan. Besides, it didn't work out
between Bernard and me when we had the chance. It could *never*
work out between us. Our egos clash."

"But, *entre nous*, admit it. You are still attracted to him."

Lydia smiled. "Marielle, you're naughty. Let's talk about
something else. Do you think I should buy the Yves St. Laurent
peasant dress, or the Ungaro evening pajamas?"

They sat out in the olive garden beyond the courtyard, having
tea. La Bastide, the villa the Julliens had rented, was a quiet
haven from the madness that was what the film festival was all
about. The paparazzi had gotten wind of the fact that the star of
Bernard's film was now the Countess de La Roche. Marielle
spent most of the time answering the telephone, fending off calls
from journalists who wanted to interview Lydia. Stefan had for-
bidden her to talk with anyone from the press.

Marielle passed a plate of tea sandwiches. "Lydia and I went
down to the open market this morning. It was fine until a reporter spotted us, or spotted Lydia I should say."

Lydia giggled. "All of a sudden, within seconds, there must

have been ten of them following us, snapping photos and yelling questions."

"But Lydia was very composed about it all. She just kept picking out tomatoes as if nothing out of the ordinary were going on. Even so I thought we were going to have to hire an armored car to get out of there."

"And then someone saw Ava Gardner over by the seafood, and suddenly we were deserted. Ah, fame is so fleeting."

"It will not be fleeting after tonight," Bernard said, sipping a beer. "Look, Lydia, you cannot keep ducking the press like this. Up until now, fine, you are a curiosity. American girl, French countess, movie actress. Nobody quite knows what it all means. But tonight they are going to see you on the screen. And then it is going to be a different story. Like Grace Kelly. They will publish stories and pictures about you whether you talk to them or not."

"You know how Stefan feels about all this . . ."

"But what about you?" Marielle asked. "Aren't you excited? *I* certainly am."

Lydia hugged herself and threw back her head and laughed. "Excited? You have no idea! I don't think my feet have touched the ground since I got here."

"That's more like it," Michel said. "I was beginning to think you were too cool to be real."

"I'm real all right. And I'm not cool. I can't tell you how much I'm enjoying all this attention."

"Then talk to the press," Bernard urged. "That way, at least, they have a chance of getting it right. And think about how it will help the film. You cannot *buy* publicity like this."

Lydia pointed up to the east tower of the villa where Stefan was going over business reports. "I know. But let's be serious. I can't give any interviews."

"But it is in Stefan's own interest. If the film does well, he will make a lot of money."

"He has a lot of money," Michel said.

"Yes, Bernard," Marielle said dryly. "Haven't you heard of the tax write-off?"

"My film is not a tax write-off!" He grabbed his beer bottle and stormed off into the house.

"My little brother is a trifle oversensitive," Michel said. "Do not mind him."

"Oh, Michel, I know him pretty well. And believe me, I understand what's going on inside him. Maybe better than he understands what's going on inside me. I love making movies. I love the idea of being a star. For years it was all I dreamed about. Then this other dream came along out of nowhere, and . . . well, you just have to make choices." She paused. "It's not easy. And I know it's worse for Bernard. He has everything riding on this. I feel caught in the middle, but I've got to be loyal to Stefan."

Marielle hugged Lydia. "Of course you do, darling. Even Bernard understands that. The film will do well because it's good, and because you are good. You can be the mystery woman. That will bring its own kind of publicity."

"And remember, Stefan has never seen you act," Michel said. "Perhaps after tonight he will change his mind."

Stefan did not change his mind. When Lydia's nude scene in the bathroom came on the screen, he was outraged. He walked out, dragging Lydia with him. Bernard caught them in the lobby of the Palais des Festivals.

"You cannot do this, Stefan."

"How could you show a scene like that?" His face was mottled with fury. "Making a public spectacle of my wife!"

"She was not your wife when I shot that scene."

"It should have been cut!"

"Don't be ridiculous. It is pivotal to the whole film. Come back in, and you will see."

"I will not go back in there."

"If you don't, the press will be very interested." Bernard pointed across the lobby where some reporters were heading their way.

"Please, Stefan. Let's go back in," Lydia begged.

Faced with two evils, Stefan chose the lesser. At the film's end, the audience gave it and Bernard a standing ovation. But during the loud cheering, Stefan dragged Lydia out, shunning the press conference and well-wishers who tried to clamor around Lydia to praise her performance.

The reviews of *L'Engagement* in the morning papers were raves. Bernard was heralded as a young Truffaut, and Lydia's talent and electric screen presence predicted major stardom for her. At La Bastide, Marielle Jullien sat by the phone, fielding calls for Lydia from agents who wanted to handle her, and both French and Hollywood producers and directors who wanted her for their films.

By noon, Stefan could stand it no longer. He chartered a plane to take him and Lydia back to Tours.

They argued the entire trip.

"You're acting like a child . . . and treating me like one," Lydia snapped. "I gave up my career for you. But you could at least let me enjoy this one film. You're so selfish. Everything and everybody has to revolve around your outdated sense of honor. Why don't you join the rest of us in the twentieth century?"

"I did not think that a sense of honor was something that could become outdated. If you feel that way, then perhaps we should not be man and wife."

"Oh, come on, Stefan. Every time we have an argument you haul out that old threat."

"It is a scandal for a man in my position to have his wife exposed like that for the whole world to see. Can you imagine what people will be saying?"

"They wouldn't be saying a damned thing if you hadn't made such a big deal out of it. Christ! Go to the movies sometime, darling. Nude scenes are so common no one thinks a thing about them."

"If you are so intent on being common perhaps you should resume your career."

"Well, maybe I should! I wouldn't mind having people appreciate me for a change."

"There are brothels in Paris where men can appreciate your undeniable physical charms if that is what you want."

"Oh, Stefan, that's an ugly thing to say. Acting in a film is not the same thing as being a whore."

"I do not see much difference," he said coolly. "If you wish to be the Countess de La Roche, fine. If you wish to be an actress, fine. You cannot do both. But remember, if you leave, Alexandra will stay with me. It is my country, and I am a man of some influence."

"Are you threatening me? You don't care about Alexandra. You wanted a son. The only reason you married me was to get one."

"It was not the only reason. But it is important to me. As an American you have not yet understood. You keep harping about the twentieth century, but there are many centuries I care about. All of them infinitely richer and more attractive than the one we live in. They are all part of my heritage and my responsibility, and these are things that I must pass on to a son. Will you give me that son?"

"I don't know, Stefan. I'll have to think about it. You've said some pretty horrible things to me. I *am* an American. I *do* live in this century. If we're going to go on, you've got to let up a little. Your friends aren't all like you . . . even the ones with titles. You've got to stop being so uptight."

"It may be that I am too rigid," he admitted. "My father cared nothing about his responsibilities. He allowed his title and his estate to cheapen with neglect. It caused me great agony as a boy. Perhaps I am making you suffer for his faults. Perhaps I do not show you how much I love you. I will try to be more flexible. But I cannot be married to an actress. Will you promise me . . ."

"I've promised you that before . . . but I know now that I can't sit back and do nothing. I'm not talking about charity committees and that sort of thing. I'm going to find something that interests me, and I'm going to do it."

The Cannes Film Festival was in early May. Five weeks later Lydia and Stefan were in New York. A business trip for Stefan had coincided with Juno's graduation from Yale. While Stefan was in meetings on Wall Street, Lydia was in New Haven with Juno's parents and Alex, watching Juno receive her diploma. That evening, Stefan hosted a celebratory dinner for them all at the Four Seasons in Manhattan.

They dined in the Pool Room, at a table near the pool in the center. A bottle of Louis Roederer Cristal Rosé champagne was waiting at the table when they arrived, iced in a silver bucket.

As they were being seated, Stefan slipped a small gift-wrapped box from his breast pocket onto the silver serving plate at Juno's place. The waiter poured the champagne, and Lydia proposed the first toast.

"To New Mexico's first Yale alumna. Many called, few were chosen, and fewer still stayed the course. To Juno Johnson . . . super woman and super friend."

"Hear, hear," Alex said. They drank.

Juno noticed the box on her plate. "Where did this come from?"

"An amorous waiter, no doubt," Lydia grinned.

"According to the card it's from some count and countess. I can't read the last name. Looks foreign."

"Oh, them," Lydia said. "Well, open it anyway."

Juno carefully undid the bow and peeled away the tape. "Cartier. Oh-la-la," Juno smiled.

"Well, don't stop there. We're all dying of curiosity," Hollis said.

Juno opened the box and pulled out a gold stickpin with a small bulldog fashioned out of sapphires and diamonds. "Oh!' Juno laughed with delight. "It's beautiful . . . it's wonderful . . . I'll treasure it always . . ."

"Four years at Yale," Alex said, "and all she can manage is clichés."

"Shut up, you." She leaned over and kissed Lydia and Stefan. "It's perfect. I *will* treasure it always."

Stefan was in a good humor. That day he had closed a gold deal with the Chinese that would net him close to a million dollars. "How is your play doing, Alex? We were very impressed with the review from the . . . what was it? The *East Village* . . . something?"

"The *East Village Other*. Yes, they certainly liked it. Unfortunately, *EVO* doesn't guarantee commercial success in this town. And there aren't that many people who want to trek down to a performing loft off of Avenue B. We closed last week."

"Oh no! You mean we won't get to see it?" Lydia asked.

"Not until they make the movie," Alex joked. "But I'm working on something else now. It's going to be done off-Broadway— as opposed to off-off," he explained to Maria and Hollis. "The

New York theater is a Byzantine labyrinth of these subtle distinctions."

"Well, when you really make it big, maybe they'll put it on in Santa Fe," Hollis said. "All we hear from Juno is how talented you are."

"And you, too, Lydia," Maria added. "Are you making another film? We read some wonderful articles from the Cannes Festival about your performance."

"Oh, Mother," Juno said quickly with a nervous glance at Stefan, who glowered at his plate. "That film was made before she and Stefan were married. She's given up her career now that she's a countess."

Lydia took a sip of champagne, then smiled brightly. "Yes, actually, I'm just too busy, what with the baby and everything. Besides, I have a new creative outlet. I've taken up gourmet cooking. I'm studying in Paris three days a week, and I'm taking a course in oenology."

"What on earth is that?" Hollis said. "Sounds like medical school."

"Wines and wine making," Lydia laughed. "I'm learning to be the perfect hostess."

"But you already are, my dear," Stefan said. "She is a great success. I receive many more invitations now than I used to."

They ordered dinner and several bottles of '61 Romanée-Conti. Lydia showed baby pictures and bragged about Alexandra.

"I can't wait to see her," Juno said. "My little goddaughter."

"You'll see her tomorrow morning. And of course you've all got to come over in September for the christening."

"I hope I can," Alex said.

Juno smiled. "It'll be easy for me. Just a hop over from London."

"London?"

"Yes . . . it's my surprise. I've landed a very poor-paying job apprenticing with John Fletcher. You know, the set designer?"

"Oh, Juno, that's wonderful!" Lydia exclaimed. "We'll be practically neighbors."

"Well, at least our phone bills will be lower."

"Speak for yourself," Hollis Johnson said. "It's going to be hell on ours."

The next morning Juno came to see the baby. Lydia and Stefan were staying in one of the twin town houses on East Sixty-second Street that Stefan had purchased before their marriage. They were tall, elegant brownstones, five stories high, the façades covered with ivy and decorated with carved stone and wood trim. The easternmost of the two had been renovated for the New York residence of the Count and Countess de La Roche. From the outside it shone with polished brass and gleaming windows, through which rich wallpaper and furnishings could be seen. The other was to be fixed up and rented, but work on it had not yet been completed.

Juno rang the doorbell and a butler answered and showed her up to the nursery where Lydia was expecting her. "Well, here she is," Lydia said, holding up the baby. "The newest member of the French aristocracy."

"She's absolutely beautiful!" Juno said. "I can still hardly believe it. You . . . an adoring mother."

"I know. I surprised myself. All those latent maternal feelings popped out the moment she did." She handed the baby to Juno. "Believe me, Alexandra's the only thing that keeps me going sometimes . . ."

"What do you mean? I thought things between you and Stefan were good now."

"Hmmm, yeah. I'm more comfortable. I mean, I get along with all his friends. I don't just sit there and smile like a dummy anymore."

Juno looked quizzically at Lydia. "But how do you get along with Stefan?"

"We have our ups and downs. Very down after Cannes, but now I'm busier, so things're going okay."

"Just okay?" Juno put Alexandra into her playpen and hugged Lydia. "What's really going on?"

"Oh, Juno, I'm so confused. Sometimes I really am happy. I look at Stefan and at our life and think that it's everything anyone could ever want." Tears filled her eyes. "But then I think about Bernard and the film, and realize that's all I ever wanted to do . . . be an actress. There's no way I can change Stefan's mind about it. It's a real thing with him. He equates acting with prostitution."

"Look, I know it's nice being waited on twenty-four hours a day, and buying anything you want. But the question is, do you love Stefan? Because if not, you can divorce him. I know it would be painful, but, in the long run . . ."

Lydia wiped her eyes, shaking her head. "It's out of the question. He would never give me a divorce . . . or at least he'd never let me have Alexandra. It's not that he's so crazy about her, but he knows I am." She sighed. "The funny thing is, Juno, I really *do* love Stefan. And most of the time it's okay."

"There you go again. You can't spend the rest of your life being 'okay.' What about Stefan? Does he love you?"

"Good question. I think he does. He's considerate and attentive. But I don't know. The sex isn't great. We don't even make love that much. He didn't touch me the whole time I was pregnant. He said he didn't want to risk hurting the baby, but it was almost like . . ."

"He was only interested in sowing the crop?"

Lydia nodded. "He's a bit more active again now that I'm back in circulation. He desperately wants a son."

"But you just had a baby."

"Yes . . . and I think I'm having another one."

"Oh, Lydia, no! It's too soon. You have to give your body a chance to bounce back."

"Well, I had a really easy pregnancy with Alexandra," she smiled reassuringly. "It's going to be fine. And if it *is* a boy, then things'll be better with Stefan."

"I'm sure they will," Juno said.

But Juno had her doubts. She thought about Lydia all afternoon as she shopped with her mother. That evening, she had a farewell drink with Alex at the Algonquin.

"It seems like a risky way to patch up a marriage," Juno sighed. "Popping out babies to plug up the leaks. Of course, Alexandra is adorable . . ."

"All babies are adorable," Alex pointed out. "And you know,

this next one could be a girl, too. More than half of them are, statistically."

"Oh Jesus, Alex. What's going to happen to Lydia?"

"I worry about her, too. But she's a survivor. Look, the best thing we can do for her is give her a chance to blow off a little steam. We certainly can't live her life for her."

"No, you're right."

Alex ordered another round. He reached into his pocket and pulled out a folded sheet of paper. "I know you've probably got a million people to look up in London, but I'm going to give you a few more. Pay special attention to the name at the top of the list. Shep Wise. An old school pal of mine, and a very nice guy."

"Okay, Alex. Any chance you'll be getting to London anytime soon?"

"Gee, I wish. But I'm going to be up to my ears for the next eight months anyway, with this new play . . ."

"Yeah," she said quietly. "Well, I'm going to be pretty busy, too."

He put his arm around her and kissed her cheek, and leaned his forehead against hers. "I'm going to miss you, Juno. You and Lydia are the only two people I've ever been totally comfortable with. I just wish . . ."

Juno waited as Alex trailed off, lost in thought. "What, Alex?" she asked, exasperated. "What do you wish?"

He looked up at her and grinned wryly. "Oh . . . I don't know. Why does life have to keep changing everything all the time?"

"It's us, Alex," Juno said. "Not life. We do it."

Chapter Eighteen

December 20, 1973

Dear Juno,

    I'm sorry I couldn't talk when you called last week. I wasn't really getting ready to race out to a party with Stefan. The truth is I didn't feel up to talking, even to you. Remember when I told you what a breeze it was being pregnant with Alexandra? Well, the tables have been turned on me. I'm sick as a dog. I've been sick since August although I've tried to keep it a secret. (You never suspected when you were here for the christening, did you?) Then last month I nearly had a miscarriage and had to stop doing just about everything. I got anemic and started losing small clumps of hair. Dr. Brassard ordered me to bed where I'm supposed to spend the majority of my time until the baby comes, in early March.

    I AM GOING OUT OF MY MIND!!!!

    Stefan, as expected, hasn't touched me since we left New York. That depressed me a lot at first, although now I feel too awful and cowlike to ever be touched again.

    And now, from bedside, I have to start interviewing nannies. Mlle. Jobert gave her notice a couple of weeks ago. She told Stefan, in so many words, that I was interfering with her duties, spending too much time with Alexandra. Can you believe it? Spending TOO MUCH TIME with my own daughter? Oh, Juno, A. remains wonderful. She has almost a full set of teeth now and last week she took her first steps . . . to me! And she's getting so tall. I wish you could spend Xmas with us, but I know you can't resist the lure of that New Mexican green chile stuffing. Do give my love to your parents & call me when you get back to London.

God, if this baby's not a boy I don't know what I'll do. I couldn't go through this again . . . I've never felt this horrible in my entire life. I haven't even been able to go Xmas shopping for Alexandra's first Christmas . . . Stefan's new secretary has taken care of it all for me. S. has been in South Africa the past ten days or so. I realized this afternoon that I haven't really missed him.

Michel and Marielle Jullien are coming for the weekend with a bunch of rented films to cheer me up. I don't know what I'd do without them . . . they've really become my friends more than Stefan's this last year. They report that Bernard is shooting his new film & having an affair with the actress who's starring in it. So what else is new?

I guess you heard that Alex's play closed already. Well, it ran longer than the last one but he still sounded very down when I talked to him. Oh . . . I wish you two were here with me right now. And that I was feeling better. I wish . . . I wish . . . Oh, here comes Alexandra to kiss me good night.

Merry Christmas, my dear. I love you.

> *XXOO,*
> *Lydia*

MARCH 4, 1974
LANGES-SUR-LOIRE

MS. JUNO JOHNSON
12 ADAM AND EVE MEWS
LONDON W8 ENGLAND

GIRL BORN 6:00 A.M. TODAY. 8 POUNDS 3 OUNCES.
HELLISH LABOR. NO NAME YET. HADN'T CONSIDERED
POSSIBILITY. LETTER SOON. LOVE LYDIA.

Dr. Brassard told them that Lydia's body needed a rest. She was still young and could have more children, but the doctor advised that they wait a few years.

From the moment she was born, Stefan showed virtually no interest in the new baby. Lydia named her Stephane India in hopes of triggering her husband's affections for his second daughter, but she ended up calling her India because Stefan did not respond. And from the moment of the doctor's announcement about her childbearing, Stefan showed a similar lack of interest in Lydia as far as sex was concerned. A couple of months after the delivery Lydia got a prescription for birth control pills. A couple of months after that when her advances and then her pleas to Stefan went unheeded, she gave up the pills and had a diaphragm fitted, just in case. But the diaphragm lay unused in the back of her dresser drawer.

To the world they still appeared the perfect couple. Stefan gave her expensive gifts. They entertained, they traveled together, they were seen at openings, benefits, restaurants, and nightclubs on both sides of the Atlantic. The children and nanny often traveled with them because Lydia insisted on it. But the nanny could count on the fingers of one hand the number of times that Stefan had come to the nursery on his own to visit his daughters.

Lydia threw herself back into her study of gourmet cooking and oenology. She studied in Paris and apprenticed at the three-star restaurant in Tours. The kitchen now became her domain. She planned the menus and supervised the dinner parties with a firm hand. She installed the latest culinary equipment in the vast château kitchen. On weekends and when the spirit moved her she cooked there amidst the nineteenth-century ambiance of marble and copper pots. Marcelle took this invasion with ill grace at first, but when it became clear that it was acquiesce or leave, she acquiesced.

More than the kitchen, the whole château began to hum to Lydia's tune. She redecorated, she commanded the staff, she ruled over social events, all with an assurance that was light-years beyond the way she had been the first year of her marriage. Her strength was born out of desperation and boredom. Control, she had decided, was what it was all about. And if she had no control over her and Stefan's most intimate moments, she took control over all other aspects of their life together.

Stefan did not seem to mind relinquishing most of his former responsibilities. Lydia's principal rival, in fact, was Marc Higgins, Stefan's secretary. She had never felt comfortable with him. His attitude toward her was a mixture of obsequiousness and arrogance.

Marc Higgins was an Englishman, twenty-seven years old, with a ruddy British complexion and neatly modish blond hair. One of the maids had told Lydia that he kept a set of weights in his room. He did laps in the pool every day and was fond of displaying, Lydia suspected for her benefit, the muscular perfection of his body. But there was no question as to where his loyalties lay; he was Stefan's right arm. And though he grudgingly accepted Lydia's ascendance over Stefan's domestic and social domain, she always had the feeling that Marc was looking over her shoulder and keeping the master informed.

As for Stefan, all of his energy became focused into his business affairs; and, unbeknownst to Lydia, his sexual ones as well.

In the fall of 1976 Tony MacGraw died of a heart attack on a golfing holiday in Scotland. Stefan and Lydia went to Kent for the funeral. Afterward, Stefan stayed on at the MacGraw estate to counsel Maggie on her financial situation. Lydia stopped up in London to spend a few days with Juno.

Juno had just returned from lighting an American concert tour for the rock group Tierra, and the tiny house in Adam and Eve Mews was cluttered with the accumulation of several months on the road. She had not bothered to unpack everything, because she was moving. Juno was getting married to an English publisher named Shepherd Wise, who had been pursuing her for the past several years.

Two things had happened to finally make up Juno's mind to accept Shep's proposal. One was the Tierra tour from which she had just returned, a bizarre whirlwind of glitter, drugs, and tragedy which left her more than ready for the solid, reassuring foundation that Shep could give her. The other was something even more basic, something that had happened the year before, that had shaken Juno loose from the baggage of dreams she had trailed with her for years.

In the summer of 1975 Alex Sage had married a woman named Tory Gamble in New York.

Lydia met Juno at her place in the Mews, and they went for dinner at a favorite Thai restaurant of Juno's in St. Alban's Grove and caught up on each other's lives.

"I'm sorry Shep couldn't be here," Juno said, sipping the light crest of foam off the Singha beer the waiter had just poured. "He's dying to see you."

"I'm sorry, too. I hope he's not working too hard." Lydia squeezed Juno's hand. "Shep's a terrific person, Juno. I'm really happy for you."

"Me, too." Juno smiled. "It's about time I settled down."

"So—all three of us, you, me, and Alex, finally married off. And not to each other."

"Well, I guess it would have looked pretty odd in the *Times:* 'Miss Juno Johnson and Miss Lydia Forrest to Wed Mr. Alexander Sage.' "

Lydia laughed. "How is Alex? Did you see him when you were in New York?"

"Of course. He seems to be doing brilliantly, winning all sorts of awards . . ." Juno broke off, and shook her head sadly. "Oh, Lydia . . . he's not happy. He hates being a copywriter. He's good at it, but you know, Alex is good at everything he does. It's such a damned shame."

"He really isn't writing plays at all anymore?"

"No. He says he just doesn't have the time or the heart for it. And I don't think Tory gives him much encouragement."

"That woman," Lydia said disgustedly. "She's just like that Hope Jennings and all those others he kept wasting himself on at Yale. What's the matter with Alex, anyway? Can't he tell the difference between women like us and women like her?"

"There aren't any other women like us," Juno grinned, and quickly diverted the subject to less painful ground. "Tell me about this wine business you mentioned in your last letter."

"There's not much to tell . . . yet," Lydia said. Her voice was excited, and her eyes gleamed. "But I have big plans. It all came out of the argument Stefan and I always have about the traditional versus the modern methods of wine making. I found this couple with a wonderful vineyard just across the river. They wanted to modernize, but didn't have the capital. I'm investing my money, not Stefan's. But I'm putting in more than money. I've really made a study of this, Juno. I know a hell of a lot about it. I can make it work!"

"What does Stefan have to say about all this?"

"He doesn't know. I'm waiting till I have something concrete to show him. I really think that when he sees how it works, he'll be convinced."

"That's really fabulous. You, an entrepreneur . . . I can't believe it!" The waiter brought their food. When he had left, Juno looked seriously into her friend's eyes. "And what about the rest of it, Lydia? You and Stefan?"

"Thank God for that vibrator you sent me," Lydia quipped. "No, sometimes when he's drunk he comes to my room. But it's not great knowing that I'm so unappealing to my husband that he has to be in some altered state of consciousness to be able to put his hands on my body."

"But that's terrible! Look, there's something wrong with *him*. You're a beautiful, desirable woman. You can't live your life this way."

"Every other part of my life is fine," she shrugged. "I'm actually pretty happy most of the time. And my marriage is important to me, Juno. The children . . . Stefan, too. It's not always easy, but—well, you're getting married now. You'll see."

"Hmmm . . . but what about sex? Or doesn't that matter anymore?"

Lydia sighed. "I don't know. I mean, yes, but . . ." She leaned forward, and her tone dropped to a conspiratorial whisper. "One day when I was in Paris I went to see Bernard's new movie, *Sylvie à Neuf Heures* . . ."

"I saw it in L.A. I couldn't get over how much the actress reminded me of you."

"That struck me, too. After the film I went to the Dôme and had a glass of wine. Then I called Bernard. He was alone. I went up to see him. It was an incredible feeling, going back to his apartment. Walking up the steps, it was a time warp—as if I'd never been away. And when he opened the door I felt like my insides were going to melt and run out . . ."

Juno grinned. "Sounds like three years of frustration is finally coming to an end."

Lydia put her hand on Juno's. "You know, I haven't been able to talk to anyone about this, and I didn't want to tell you over the phone for fear of someone listening in." She lit a cigarette and giggled. "God, what an afternoon! We didn't say anything.

He took my hand and I followed him into the bedroom. He lit a joint and we passed it back and forth, and we just looked at each other. That was when I came the first time."

"Oh boy, oh boy," Juno said.

"We undressed each other very slowly. Then Bernard took a rose out of a vase and tore the petals off and sprinkled them onto the bed." Lydia sighed. "And then we fell into each other and made frantic love, and romantic love . . ."

"And semantic love?"

Lydia gave a throaty chuckle. "Oh, Juno, it was fabulous! A perfect afternoon. We made love four times. All the feeling I still had for him, he still had for me. Then, later, we lay in bed and sipped champagne. I told him I was in Paris every week, that we could meet as often as he liked. And that's when the dream burst."

"Oh no. What happened?"

"Bernard told me that he didn't want to have an affair. He wanted me to leave Stefan, so we could be together in the open. So I could act again. I told him I couldn't."

"Oh, Lydia," Juno exploded. "Why the hell not?"

"It's complicated. It's not as easy as you seem to think. I told you, I'm really working at this marriage. I don't want to just walk out on it. And even if I did . . . Stefan would never let me have the girls."

"But you're their mother! Of course, you can get custody."

"Not in France . . . not when you're married to a count who's also got political clout and enough money to buy every-body off."

"But Lydia, that's terrible!"

"You know, it's funny. As much as I wanted Bernard, as much as I still want him, I loved him even more for *not* wanting to have an affair. Does that make sense?"

Juno nodded. "Yes . . . I guess it does. But that still leaves you with no sex life."

"Well, my days and evenings are filled with Alexandra and India, and my business, and all the social activities." She lit an-other cigarette. "And with a few drinks I can get through the nights."

Outside of her children, the great enthusiasm in Lydia's life these days was the business she had started with the young couple across the river. She had been studying oenology for years, originally as a way of sharing Stefan's interest in the grapes of Château Mordoi. As she had become more knowledgeable about wine, she began to take a real interest. One year nearly all of the grapes shriveled on the vine because the summer had been too hot. The next year there had been too much rain. Stefan refused adamantly to employ more up-to-date methods for wine making. Doing it the traditional way was what was important. The vineyards were a hobby anyway; he did not care if he lost money on them.

But Lydia found his point of view annoying, and typical of his bullheadedness on the subject of the "old" versus the "new." What was the point of the scientific breakthroughs in vinification if one ignored them? She discussed this endlessly with the other wine makers of the region. Some agreed with Stefan. Many did not, especially those for whom wine making was a living.

Christophe and Natalie Boulet cultivated seventeen acres of Chinon. Lydia met them at the restaurant in Tours where she had been studying haute cuisine. Their crops had suffered badly in the year of the rain. Lydia offered to invest a substantial sum of money in modernizing their operation. She would be a silent partner. Her aim was not to compete with Stefan, but to establish a successful operation using modern methods in an area virtually identical to Mordoi. Eventually she would be able to show him and back up her arguments with a proven track record.

She enjoyed the work, and the company of Christophe and Natalie. Christophe was thirty, and Natalie was six years younger, Lydia's age. He had been a journalist for *Le Monde* in Paris. She had been studying to be a psychologist when her parents were killed in an accident and she had inherited the large stone house and vineyards in L'Île Bouchard. They decided to give up Paris and take on a new life in the country. But after two years they were nearly bankrupt. Lydia came as a gift out of the blue.

Their farm was a fifteen-minute drive from Mordoi. Lydia

went there whenever Stefan was away on business, and sometimes when he was at home too, when she could come up with a
plausible story. She took the children with her. Christophe and
Natalie had a son, Jean-Claude, who was the same age as Alexandra, and they played happily while the grown-ups talked and
worked.

One spring evening Lydia and the children returned from
L'Île Bouchard and saw Stefan's car parked in front. Marc Higgins, Stefan's secretary, was standing on the steps giving instructions to the chauffeur.

"Oh, you're back early," she said.

"For several hours, actually." Marc's eyes flickered over her
with the cool insolence that she had come to expect. "The meeting broke down in the middle of negotiations."

"Where's my husband?"

"In the drawing room. Waiting for you." There was a hint of
a smile which set her pulse racing with anxiety.

Nanny met her in the entrance hall and took the children up
for their bath. Lydia went into the drawing room. Stefan was at
the bar pouring himself a brandy. From the shine in his eye
when he turned to face her she guessed that it was not his first.

"Hello, darling." She came over and put her face up to be
kissed. But Stefan's hand cracked against it in a stinging slap.

"I know where you've been. You slut!"

She fell back a step, stunned. Tears came to her eyes. "What?
Stefan, please, I knew you wouldn't approve at first but . . ."

"Not approve?" he raged. "What kind of a man do you take
me for? I have my honor."

"Your fucking honor! Maybe I should have told you, but don't
you think you're blowing this out of proportion? It's just a business deal. You act as if I'm having an affair."

"And you expect me to believe that? Your car has been seen
many times at Christophe Boulet's house. I do not think it takes
a great deal of imagination to figure out what goes on inside.
And to drag the children with you . . . it is unforgivable."

"I don't know what you're paying for your information, Stefan, but it's not worth a franc. Jesus, if you're going to spy on
me at least get someone who can do the job. I'm in business with
the Boulets. I'm backing their wine operation. We've put in

some of the modern systems that you're so paranoid against. And they work . . . I thought if I could show you . . ."

"Liar!" He swung at her again, this time with a clenched fist. Light exploded in Lydia's eyes and she staggered back against a chair, hitting the edge of the coffee table as she slumped to the floor. There was a terrible pain on the right side of her face. Stefan glared at her in fury. She scrambled to her feet and ran out of the room.

"Lydia! Come back here," he shouted. She kept running, up the stairs. He came out into the hallway. "I'm not through with you!"

"Oh yes you are," she shrieked down the stairwell. She ran into her bedroom and locked the door. A moment later, Stefan was pounding on it. She sat on the bed, quietly trembling. The pounding stopped, and his footsteps went away.

Lydia was in the bathroom putting cold water on her cheek when she heard a key turn in her lock. "Stefan!" she yelled. "Get out of here!" She ran to him as he came into the room and slapped his face as hard as she could.

Stefan picked her up and strode over to the bed. He flung her down. "You whore!" He grabbed the neck of her silk blouse and ripped it open. "I'll show you."

He undressed her brutally. When she tried to move, he slapped her down on the bed again. He pulled down his pants and entered her, forcing his way into the dry passage. Lydia screamed. He pumped into her, rasping obscenities.

In a few moments it was over.

Lydia lay there trembling for a half hour after Stefan left her room. Every part of her body ached, and there was a searing pain in her head. Finally she roused herself to go into the bathroom. She ran a hot bath and took some aspirin. When she finished her bath she was breathing normally again and the pain had dulled. She threw some things into a small bag and went to the nursery.

"The children are asleep, madame," Nanny whispered. And then she saw the bruise that darkened one side of Lydia's face. *"Mon Dieu!* What has happened?"

"I have to go to Paris this evening. I'll be back in a day or so.

Tell the children I will bring them each a present. Nanny, stay
with them all the time . . . don't leave them alone."

"*Oui, madame.*" Nanny looked alarmed.

"You understand?"

"*Oui, je comprends, madame.*"

Three hours later, Lydia arrived in Paris and drove directly to
the Julliens' apartment on the Rue Victor Hugo. Marielle answered the door herself, wearing a robe.

"Lydia! Oh *merde*, come in . . . what happened to you?"

Michel was away on business. Marielle led her into the
kitchen and sat her down on a love seat by the fireplace. While
she made tea Lydia told her everything.

"This is terrible! I never thought Stefan could do something
like that. And your face . . . you've got to see a doctor."

"No . . . I want to see a lawyer. Do you know one who isn't
a friend of Stefan's?"

"Yes . . . an excellent one. I will call him first thing in the
morning and insist that he see you right away."

Lydia drank her tea and poured herself another cup. She sank
back against the cushions. "Oh God," she said miserably. "I
don't know. I could never give up the children."

Marielle looked surprised. "Why should you give up the children?"

Lydia told her what Stefan had explained to her, that no court
in France would give her custody. "Even when I go to New
York with the children to visit my parents he makes me sign a
contract . . . to be sure I'll bring them back. When we're in
France he keeps their passports locked up in his bank vault."

"How awful . . . how paranoid."

Lydia nodded. "But now . . . to be accused of having an affair when I'm not."

"Especially when Stefan . . ." Marielle paused.

"Stefan what?"

"Oh, I am not supposed to say. But I have to. That bastard is
having an affair with Maggie MacGraw."

"I don't believe it. Oh shit. I do believe it. She's always been
after him . . . even when Tony was alive."

"Well, she did not waste much time when he was dead. Michel tells me it started right after the funeral."

Lydia got her handbag and fished around for her cigarettes. "That means it's been six months. And he's accusing *me* . . ." She lit a cigarette and rocked back and forth, holding her knees. "I always figured he was doing something with someone. He certainly wasn't with me. Except lately . . . now that it's supposed to be safe for me to get pregnant again. He still wants a male heir. But the rest of the time I guessed it was one-night stands when he was away on business with women one didn't know. It's so awful knowing how permanent it is . . . and who it is. That bitch! I never liked her."

Marielle put her arm around her. "These things never last with Stefan. I think he is just trying to prove something. Perhaps that he is not getting older. Anyway, it is only sex. She means nothing to him, I am sure. It is you he cares about."

"Well, he picks a hell of a way to show it! I could use some sex —and some caring. But frankly, I don't think I want either of those things from him anymore." She stood. "I've got to get some rest. You'll call the lawyer for me?"

Marielle nodded. "Michel and I will stand by you, Lydia. Whatever happens, you can count on us."

Lydia came out of the lawyer's office onto Rue Rivoli. Michel Jullien was standing on the sidewalk by his car. "Lydia," he said. He took her hands sympathetically. "Marielle told me. Come, let's have a drink and talk."

They went to the nearby Bar du Meurice. Michel ordered a martini for himself and a Bloody Mary for Lydia. She settled back in the comfortable upholstered armchair and slid her dark glasses up into her curly hair.

Michel winced. "He really hit you, didn't he?"

"Oh, it's not just the hitting, it's everything. The coldness, the suspicion, the brutality. The whole thing is a sham. I've gone along with it because, in spite of everything, I've enjoyed being the Countess de La Roche." She stirred her drink. "I guess to be honest we both went into this thing under false pretenses. I was dazzled by the idea of being a countess. He wanted healthy young breeding stock to give him sons. We both called it love."

"But Stefan does love you, Lydia. And he needs you. I know it's difficult to believe right now, after the way he's treated you. Stefan is . . ." He paused, as if searching for the right way to put it. "Stefan is complicated sexually . . . he has a lot of hang-ups. There is a kind of desperation to him, you have obviously seen it. To be a certain kind of man, a certain kind of image, his clinging to traditions . . . he is terrified to be simply himself. A twentieth-century man, with modern failings in a modern world. His marriage, your marriage, is what holds him together."

"That's all well and good. But I'm twenty-five years old and I've got a husband who makes love to me twice a year. He has it all. He's got his mistress. I don't even have a lover, and this happens." She pointed to her eye.

"I have talked to him today, Lydia. He is very upset. He knows now what you have said is true."

"Oh good," she said sarcastically. "He got a new set of detectives on the case."

"You have every right to be bitter. But do not act in haste. Much of your life with him is good. Marielle and I are very close to you. We see you together often. Truthfully, Lydia, you are not miserable all the time, are you?"

She bit her lip and looked up at the mahogany-paneled ceiling. "Oh, I don't know. No . . . most of the time things are very congenial. But I try to look into the future. In ten years is it still going to be the same? Am I going to keep having children to get him a boy, and do without sex the rest of the time? And get myself knocked around every time he has a fit of paranoia? It just seems so bleak. He doesn't *want* me, Michel . . . there's no way to get around it."

Michel ordered himself another martini. "All right. But he *needs* you, more than you can possibly know. Stay with him. For your . . . needs, there are other men besides Stefan."

"Michel, you've got to be kidding. Look at me. And I didn't even *do* anything."

"But if you did do something you would be extremely discreet."

"It's impossible to be discreet with private detectives watching every move."

"Stefan has not hired detectives. He told me. It was by chance that he found out about your visits to the Boulet farm. And leaped to the wrong conclusion."

"All right. It's a small world. We know a lot of people. If I had an affair, he'd find out by chance. Michel, there's just no way . . ."

"If you will have a son, he will leave you alone. As long as you are discreet."

"What? He told you this?"

"I know Stefan."

"I know Stefan, too. And I know me. It's not the way I want to live. Monsieur Derocles says I have a pretty solid case. And I don't want anything from him. Just the children, and my freedom."

"Take some time to think about it," Michel counseled again. "Before you do anything. Talk to Stefan. Then perhaps you two can work things out together, without any bitterness."

"Well, I'll think about it, Michel. I can't promise anything."

Chapter Nineteen

Stefan apologized for accusing Lydia of having an affair with Christophe Boulet. He even forgave her business partnership with Christophe and Natalie, and was willing to allow it to continue. As for his affair with Maggie MacGraw, he admitted it was unforgivable but begged her forgiveness. Maggie had initiated it, he told Lydia, and she found that easy to believe. He swore to her that there was no other woman. His dealings with Maggie for the last few months had been strictly financial: straightening out the mess left by Tony's sudden death. He agreed not to see Maggie again.

"I know I do not show it enough," he said to Lydia, "but I love you very much, in my own way. I do not want a divorce. Do you believe that?"

He and Lydia were having lunch together on the terrace. The children played with Nanny on the lawn, out of earshot. "Oh, Stefan. I don't know what to believe anymore. Most of the time you've been kind. We have a lot of the same interests. Your friends have become my friends. But it hurts me that you don't love the girls because they can't carry on your precious name. It hurts me that you were fucking Maggie MacGraw and not me. It hurts to have you accuse me of an affair that I wasn't having . . . especially when *you* were having one yourself." She pushed away her plate of Loire salmon. "I don't see how we can go on like this."

"Do you hate me?"

"No . . . not at all. I'm even fond of you. You're the father of my children . . ."

"But you don't love me." Stefan looked deep into her eyes, and she saw that there were tears starting in his.

Lydia looked away. "No, I don't think so."

Stefan took Lydia's hand. "Let us go on a trip together . . . without Nanny and the children along. Just the two of us. Where would you like to go?"

"I don't think there's anywhere we could go that would solve the problem. The problem isn't with here . . . it's with us."

"I know. But I thought that perhaps getting away from everything else . . . we could get back in touch with each other. It is hard to do that here. There are too many intrusions."

"Wherever we go, Stefan, there's going to be a bed. What are we going to do about that?"

"We will share it."

If the Garden of Eden had had bungalows for rent it would have been very much like Île Ouen, a tiny island a short flight from Nouméa, in New Caledonia. For their second honeymoon Lydia and Stefan chose tranquility and isolation, and they found it here. Their bungalow was on the beach of an old plantation. It looked out across a peaceful lagoon to a narrow spit of sand fringed with palm trees. Beyond the lagoon lay immense and spectacular barrier reefs where exotic, fluorescent schools of fish darted about. Inland it was lush and green, with tall columnal pine trees and fragrant flowers that grew to within a few yards of the bungalow.

In the daytime they lazed on the beach, swam and snorkeled, collected shells. Stefan sketched, Lydia read. In the evening there was good food and dancing at the Turtle Club, and afterward they took long walks along the glittering, moonlit sand.

And they made love. Stefan was tender and passionate. He was no better in bed than he had ever been, but Lydia had come not to expect miracles. He convinced Lydia that he desired her, and wanted only her. For Lydia's part she tried to be as creative and alluring sexually as she possibly could.

It began to work, at least in this fantasy setting. Lydia was not sure that it would carry back to Paris and Mordoi, but she allowed herself to think that it might. Most of the time, she did not think at all. She simply gave herself over to the enchantment of this Garden of Eden.

Then the serpent arrived.

"I'm sorry to intrude like this," Marc Higgins said as they drove in from the tiny airport. "These papers simply wouldn't wait." He looked incongruous in his European business clothes in the back seat of the rented ancient Deux Cheveaux.

"Hmmm, they must be terribly important to bring you all this way," Lydia said dryly.

"Regrettably, they are."

They arrived at the club. "I've booked you a bungalow, Marc. We might as well get right to it. Darling, are you going to swim?"

"Oh, I don't know. Maybe I'll look for a game of tennis. You won't be staying more than a day, will you, Marc?"

"I don't know. It'll be easier to say after we've been over all this."

Lydia leaned back into the car and kissed Stefan. "Work hard, darling. I'll see you later."

The briefcase stood open on the table in the small bungalow. Stefan leafed through the papers. He looked up at Marc.

"What is this? There is nothing here that could not have waited."

Marc smiled. "Oh yes there is." He put his hand on the back of Stefan's neck and drew him into a kiss. Their bodies came together and pressed close. "I missed you so much," he murmured into Stefan's hair. "And I knew you must be going crazy."

Stefan turned away. "Oh God," he moaned. Then he snapped angrily at Marc. "You had no right to come here! You know what I am trying to do."

"Yes, I know. And that's why I had every right to come. I love you, Stefan. And you love me . . . you know you do."

"No! I love Lydia." Stefan sank down into a chair and put his head in his hands. "Oh, Marc, I do not know anymore."

Marc came over and knelt beside him. He slid his hands along

Stefan's thighs and kissed his stomach. "Let me help you remember," he whispered.

Stefan pushed back the chair with a violent motion and
jumped to his feet. "No . . . I want you out of here! Tomorrow."

"If you say so."

Stefan paused in the doorway. "I do say so."

Marc was still on his knees by the overturned chair. He
smiled.

Stefan and Lydia dined alone that night at the club on curried
fish in coconut milk.

"I thought Marc would be joining us," she said.

"He was too tired. Jet lag."

Lydia put her hand on Stefan's. "I'm glad. It's been so idyllic.
Marc's turning up just reminds me that the real world isn't that
far away . . . and I'm not ready for it yet."

"He is leaving tomorrow. The business between us is finished."

She smiled. "Let's not go dancing. Let's go back to the bungalow after dinner."

They took champagne with them and sat on a blanket on the
beach. The moon was a thick crescent that cast its glow on the
quiet lapping water. The music from the club reached them
faintly. They finished one bottle and opened a second.

"Could we live here?" Lydia said dreamily. The wine had
erased her annoyance at Marc's arrival and she felt as if she were
floating in the moonlight.

"Yes . . . we will give away all our worldly possessions and
build a thatched hut on the beach."

"And drink champagne."

"*Mais oui.*"

"And make love."

Stefan leaned over and slid the strap of Lydia's dress down
past her shoulder. He kissed her shoulder, and her neck. His
hands slipped under her dress and removed her panties. "And
make love," he whispered.

Afterward, they swam naked in the lagoon. When they went

to bed, Lydia fell into a contented sleep. But Stefan lay awake.
After a while he got up and dressed.

"I knew you couldn't stay away," Marc said. He lay naked in
bed, his lower body covered by a thin sheet. A cigarette dangled
from his fingers.

"I came to talk."

"You came for this," Marc said, sliding the sheet down.
"Come here."

Stefan sat in a chair, looking at Lydia asleep on the bed. Dawn
was breaking and the light turned from white to orange on her
naked skin. Her copper hair spread around her, frizzy from the
island humidity. One leg was drawn up, exposing the soft pubic
fuzz. Her breasts were tanned brown, larger now than they had
been before her children.

She was everything he wanted in a wife. Beautiful, intelligent, poised. The perfect Comtesse de La Roche. She was everything he wanted in a woman. If only he wanted a woman.

He had been struggling for years, fighting and giving in to his
homosexuality. Sometimes he wished he could be like Marc, that
he could accept what he was and enjoy it. But the idea of it
repelled him. He desperately wanted to be straight, for the
world to see him as the happily married nobleman, with his
beautiful countess and children.

It had begun when he was at Oxford. It had been the thing to
do in his crowd, a philosophical experiment in sexuality, nothing more. Except, for him, it had been more. When he had gone
down from Oxford he had tried to put it behind him. He had
slept with women, with only the occasional crossover. Then he
had met Marie-Laure at Gstaad. She was a couple of years older
than he. She had been an Olympic swimmer and had a firm,
boyishly muscular body. She wore her hair short, Apache-style.
Marie-Laure turned him on, and he fell in love with her. With
her, he discovered ways of sex that he had not known could be
done with a woman.

They were married. It had not taken long for her to guess his
secret, but she did not seem to care. She did not want children.
Eventually, they developed an arrangement that allowed them

to go their separate ways. He could have stayed with Marie-Laure happily for the rest of his life; but as he grew older he wanted an heir. Their divorce was amicable, and she kept his secret.

Stefan wished he could reach such an arrangement with Lydia. But his feelings for Lydia were different. An inexplicable jealousy took hold of him at the thought of her with another man. His frightening outburst at his suspicions over Christophe Boulet only underlined for him how impossible it would be. There was another reason as well. He could not be sure that Lydia would be as accepting of his weakness as Marie-Laure had been. She was American. She might be disgusted and leave him, then there would be scandal and divorce.

Even without the scandal, he could not bear the thought of another divorce. He needed to keep up appearances; and Lydia was his last chance for an heir to carry on his name and his title. He could not go through the courting and winning of another woman. Socially he was up to it, but not sexually. Maggie had been a disaster. She had been aggressive and had dragged him into bed. He had been unable to perform, and he had been humiliated.

Lydia was the only woman who had managed to arouse him in years. He had tried from time to time with other women, to prove himself, but more often than not he had simply proved to himself what he really was. With Lydia he could still perform, although he often had to get drunk to do it. He tried to make himself enjoy it. And he still wanted an heir.

Lydia moaned in her sleep, and turned over and stretched her body. He reached out and pulled a strand of hair away from her mouth, and stroked her cheek.

If he were going to love a woman, it would be Lydia. He wished that he could love her.

But he could not.

Part Four

Juno, 1972-82

Chapter Twenty

The hotel, on a bleak side street in a rundown edge of Belgravia, was called the Ufton Heath. Juno nicknamed it the Uriah Heep. It had been recommended by a friend at Yale as a cheap place to stay. It was cheap, and it was a place to stay; but there was nothing else in its favor. Juno's room was a dark cubicle, its only window looking into another one, shuttered, two feet across an alleyway. The shower knob had come off in her hand the first day and only cold water ran into the tub. She had complained to the desk clerk but she was not sure he had understood. He was a Portuguese who spoke what he seemed to think was English, but Juno could not make out a word of it. And she suspected that she was equally incomprehensible to him.

But none of this was enough to dampen Juno's spirits. She was in London. She had begun her apprenticeship under John Fletcher, and they had hit it off immediately. He was an elfish man of middle age, with bright eyes, an excess of energy, a droll wit, and an attractive German wife, Ursula, who was Juno's height, a good six inches taller than her husband.

On weekends, Juno went apartment hunting, but everything she found that she could afford was cramped and depressing. On the social side, her life was cheerier. Working with John Fletcher, she had met his assistants as well as a smattering of other theater people. She got together with a few people whose names she had from friends in the States but, by and large, the meetings were awkward. So she had given it up and was now content to meet people as they happened along in the normal course of her life.

One Sunday morning she received a call back from a friend of

Alex's named Shepherd Wise, whom she had telephoned weeks earlier. He apologized, explaining that he had been out of town, and invited her out to lunch with him that day. She did not especially want to go, given her experience with friends of friends; but he was an old chum of Alex's, and she had promised that she would get together with him.

Shepherd Wise called for her at the hotel. When Juno came down to the lobby she saw a tall, thin man in a three-piece herringbone suit examining one of the atrocious reproductions on the wall. An Aquascutum raincoat was draped over his right arm. Under his left arm he carried a newspaper; in his hand, a tightly rolled umbrella. She looked around but there was nobody else.

"Shepherd Wise?"

He looked around and smiled. "Juno . . . how nice to meet you."

Juno wore corduroy pants tucked into boots that laced to her knees. Over her velour sweatshirt she had thrown on a hand-painted (by her), oversized, suede shawl. She had recently cut five inches off her hair, and now it hung loosely to her waist.

They walked out to where his car was double-parked. It was a Jaguar sedan, about ten years old but well cared for.

"That's a charming place you're staying. Looks as if it were decorated by someone's blind grandmother."

Juno laughed. "The lobby's the showpiece. You should see my room. Early bomb shelter."

"Do you feel like Chinese food? There's rather a nice place in Chelsea."

"Sounds wonderful."

The entrance to Tai-Pan, at the foot of a staircase in Egerton Gardens Mews, seemed even more like a bomb shelter than Juno's hotel room. Inside, however, the restaurant was exotically elegant, divided into compartments reminiscent of the Shanghai Express. Overhead, wooden-bladed fans turned lazily, stirring the air.

Shepherd Wise (Shep to his friends) turned out not to be the stereotypical stuffy Englishman that Juno had first suspected from his clothing. He was warm and attentive and seemed interested in what she had to say, and his sense of humor appealed to her. An editor with a publishing house in Leicester Square, he was also a theater buff.

"John Fletcher's a marvelous set designer. You couldn't have a better chap to work for."

"Oh, it's a fabulous experience. And he and his wife are terrific people. I just wish it paid a little better. I've got to find a decent place to live."

"Hmmm." Shep's face brightened. "I have an idea. One of my authors has just had his novel bought by Hollywood. They want him to do the screenplay. He's leaving in a couple of weeks, and he's looking for someone to take on his place. It's just for expenses, and all furnished. Charming little house in Adam and Eve Mews. Look, I'll ring him. If he's home perhaps we can stop by after lunch."

"It sounds too good to be true. You wouldn't believe the flats I've seen these past few weeks."

The rest of lunch they amused one another with stories about Alex. Shep had roomed with him for two years at Exeter and they had remained good friends ever since.

"We did a comedy routine in the school review: Sage and Wise, the Idiot Savants. Sort of a metaphysical Laurel and Hardy."

"Oh, can you do some of it?"

"Well, it's hard without Sage. Let's see, one of our sketches was called 'The Impossible Dinner Party.' Sage was Timothy Leary, and I played Queen Elizabeth. He was teaching me to smoke grass and drop acid. You can imagine . . . I ended up giving away Australia and Ireland and going off to study with the maharishi. He ran off with Prince Phillip. Needless to say, we were both called up on the carpet for that one. Humor unbecoming to Exeter boys."

Juno laughed. "Are you a writer, too?"

"Not anymore. I've seen too much from the editor's side of the desk. I have a trunkful of rejected manuscripts. Fortunately, I didn't write them, I rejected them."

Juno got the house in Adam and Eve Mews. It was tiny but perfect. Downstairs there was a sitting room and eat-in kitchen. Upstairs, a sunny bedroom and bath. The writer, Simon Parrie,

was going to be away for at least a year. Privately, Shep predicted he would never be back.

"Simon's an awful snob," Shep told Juno. "He goes on and on
about how hideous Hollywood is. I'm sure he'll love it."

"Let's hope he wins an Academy Award right off. I couldn't
bear to give this place up."

Alex had been correct in guessing that Juno and Shep would
get along. They began to see each other regularly and soon
drifted into an affair. They dined out, went to the theater, gallery openings, and parties given by or for his literary friends.
On weekends they sometimes drove to Tadsworth, Surrey, a
short distance from London, to visit Shep's parents at their
Georgian house, Elder's Parsonage. Then they would play tennis or go horseback riding. While Shep caught up on his weekend manuscript reading, Juno would spend long afternoons
helping his mother in the greenhouse or the kitchen. David and
Estelle Wise were intelligent, humorous people. He was a retired publisher; she wrote travel books and articles, and they
traveled a great deal. They liked Juno and it was obvious that
they hoped she would become a member of the family.

In May, John Fletcher recommended Juno for a summer job
as set designer with the Okehampton Repertory Company in
Devon. Juno was ecstatic, but Shep was not.

"It's a bloody four-hour drive going like a lunatic," he complained. "I'll never see you."

"Darling, you love driving like a lunatic. You can come for
weekends. Or take the train and read your manuscripts. And it's
only for the summer."

"But what about our holiday? I thought it was all set."

"It'll have to wait. We can go to Greece in the fall."

"I'm too bloody busy in the fall to get away. You know that."

"Oh, Shep, I'm sorry. But John recommended me for this job.
It's a big opportunity for me. It's a chance to start making a
name for myself . . . on my own. I can't turn it down."

In the end, Shep had driven her down to Okehampton and got
her settled in a small guesthouse that the theater provided for
her. Before he left they took a picnic out to an isolated spot on
the banks of the Torridge and watched the water slip by below

them in the warm afternoon sunlight as they ate cold chicken
and sipped tepid beer.

"I can't bear the thought of you working around all those
brawny leading men. I don't want you to go falling in love with
someone else."

Juno looked into Shep's blue eyes and took his hand. "That
won't happen. I'm far too happy with you. And I am going to
miss you terribly. You'll come down whenever you get the
chance, won't you?"

"I suppose I'll have to." He leaned over on his elbow and
kissed her. "I can't do this by telephone, can I?"

Juno pulled Shep close and the kiss became hungrier. She lay
back. Shep stretched out on top of her. Her hands burrowed
beneath his clothing, one reaching up his back, the other slipping beneath the waistband of his trousers and down along the
cleft of his buttocks. She felt him straining against her.

"Let's go back to your house," he whispered in her ear.

"What's wrong with here?"

"Don't be daft."

"There's nobody around."

"We can't! I'd be looking over my shoulder the whole time."

"I'll look over your shoulder."

"I don't think I could even get it up."

"A palpable lie. It's already up." She slid her hands around to
his belt buckle to uncover the evidence.

"I can see it now," he groaned, but he did not resist as she
tugged away his pants. "Respectable editor arrested for public
display of equipment."

Juno grinned. "I'll show you where to hide it," she said, shedding her own clothes.

They made love on the riverbank. Perhaps the feeling of the
sun on his bare loins acted as an aphrodisiac, but Shep was
better than he had ever been with Juno. At the end she arched
her hips against him and screamed. A moment later, he lay
shuddering and panting on top of her. "Oh God, Juno . . .
Juno."

A fly buzzed around their heads and settled on Shep's shoulder. Juno brushed it away. "Hmmm," he sighed. "Scratch . . .
right there."

After a while Juno said, "Maybe we ought to get dressed."

"I'm never getting dressed," Shep replied. His face was nestled comfortably into her neck.

A beer bottle lay within the reach of Juno's hand. Slowly, she curled her hand around it. With a flick of her wrist, she tossed it. The bottle landed with a loud rustle in a clump of bushes, ten yards away. Shep leapt up as if he had been penetrated with an electric cattle prod, grabbing his pants and holding them against his penis. "Who's there?"

"This is it, Wise. You're under arrest. Your career is over . . . your reputation is ruined. That girl you're with is only fourteen . . ." Juno broke off in a peal of laughter. "Oh, Shep, if only you could have seen the look on your face just now."

"Damn you," he said, throwing his pants in her face. "You'll pay for this!" He pinned her down and started tickling her. Juno writhed and shrieked with giggles.

"Stop it!" she gasped. "I mean it!"

"Say you're sorry."

"I'm sorry."

"Say you love me."

"I love you."

He stopped tickling. "Say it again."

"I love you, Shep." She put her hands on his waist and drew him down.

That summer, the Okehampton Rep was doing productions of *As You Like It*, Tom Stoppard's *Rosencrantz and Guildenstern Are Dead*, John Osborne's *Look Back in Anger*, and Oscar Wilde's *The Importance of Being Earnest*. Juno had never worked so hard in her life, but having creative control over the sets and lighting, she wanted everything to be perfect. She put in as many as fifteen hours a day, often getting up with the sun. When she was not working on the sets or with the lighting assistant, she was sitting in on rehearsals.

The company was a good one. Even though most of the actors were young, they had had solid training at RADA or LAMDA, the two most prestigious acting schools in London. There was one actor in the company, however, who boasted of having never taken a lesson in his life. But he was probably the most talented. His name was Ian Cambourne. He was also the most attractive, in a sexy, animalistic, not-exactly-handsome sort of way.

Juno did not like him at all. He was quite full of himself. Besides considering himself God's gift to the theater, he acted as if he were the devil's gift to women. He flirted incessantly, and probably slept with most of the women in the company at one point or another during the summer. He had a habit, which Juno loathed, of whacking her on the fanny every time he passed by her.

Shep came down for part-weekends as often as he could get away. He timed his arrival for late Saturday night, just as the theater let out, and always brought a bag of goodies—Stilton or Cricket Malherbie Cheddar from Paxton and Whitfield, chocolates from Bendicks, baguettes from Dugdale and Adams, pastries from Louis, smoked Scottish salmon from John Gow, York ham from Partridges, wine from Harrods. Sundays were theirs, and they would pack a lunch and head out in the Jaguar for the wild, rocky beaches of the north coast. They would meander through tiny hamlets like Westward Ho! (one of Juno's favorites) on Bideford Bay, and Combe Martin, a sheltered little spot beneath huge cliffs on the Bristol Channel where the waters were cool but swimmable and there were meadows of geraniums and heliotropes for idyllic picnicking. Other times they would head south, to the sunnier beaches along the English Channel, or to follow the River Dart as it wound through apple orchards and sleepy ancient villages.

After the hectic pressure of her eighty-hour working week, these Sunday excursions were balm to Juno's soul. She thought that she would like someday to have a little cottage here in Devon, but she could not decide between the exhilarating ruggedness of the north or the temperate rural charm of the south. Wherever it was, more and more the daydream came to include Shep. She was not passionate about him, but she was comfortable with him. He was a lot like Alex. They could talk about anything and everything for hours, or drive in silence without feeling the need to make conversation. She had not fallen in love with Shep, because he was not Alex. But that was not Shep's fault. And she had to get on with her life.

Juno's work with the Okehampton Rep was exhausting, but though she dropped into bed dead tired at night, she awoke every morning eager to get back to it again. She had made her preliminary designs for the sets in London but, once there, the space and the company dictated a multitude of changes. She was never completely satisfied with her sets for *As You Like It* which opened the season, though they were well reviewed. *Look Back in Anger* was more an exercise in translation: she relied heavily on her recollection of her room at the Uriah Heep, and an artist friend's walk-up flat in Hampstead to create a stark setting for Osborne's bitter drama.

Rosencrantz and Guildenstern was her triumph. It freed her imagination in both sets and lighting. Her eerie, surrealistic effects even drew comment from one London critic, and John and Ursula Fletcher made a special trip down to see it.

"I'm proud of you, Juno. I taught you well," John said, as they sipped ale and bitters at the Black Swan Inn.

"Oh, John," Ursula said. "It's Juno's talent that got her here."

"I think maybe my talent got me to you, John. But it's what I learned from you that got me here. I owe you a lot."

"All I did was keep you off the streets," he joked. "Seriously, Juno, you have the eye. What's important in the theater is to keep it focused on things that will stretch you. What do you and Shep talk about, eh? Does he want to get you off to design nurseries and living room sets?"

"Now, John!" Ursula interjected. "I think that's Juno's business."

John patted her shoulder. "Juno and I are in the same business. At least for now, we are. What about it, Juno? Are you coming back to me in the fall?"

"Of course. If you give me more money," she laughed. "I don't know what's happening with me and Shep. I like things with him the way they are, but my own ambition's still the most important thing to me. I can't give it up, even for him."

"Good girl. That's what I'd hoped you'd say. As a matter of fact, there's something coming up this fall that's going to bring in a pretty penny. You know me, every once in a while I like to

take a break from the artistically rewarding flops. There should
be a little profit in it for you, if you're interested."

"How could I not be interested?"

Ian Cambourne went by with two mugs of beer. "Eh, Juno,
coming by my room again tonight?"

"Only in your dreams, Ian."

"That's the young man who played Rosencrantz, isn't it? He's
got quite a lot of talent," Ursula said.

"He's got quite a lot of cheek."

"Aha! Romance rears its ubiquitous head?"

"No, John . . . not a chance. Even if his cock were as big as
his ego."

"Let me know when you find out."

Juno laughed. "There are times when a woman's no *does* mean
no."

"Ah yes . . . so I've discovered."

That weekend Shep could not come down. A group from the
theater was going on a day's outing to Dartmoor. Juno had decided to spend the day resting up and reading, but the day was
so beautiful that she decided to go along after all. They drove to
a farm where someone had found out they could rent horses,
and then struck out for the uncharted wildness of the Dartmoor
National Park.

The sky was high and blue, flecked here and there with clouds
as fluffy white and unthreatening as the flocks of sheep they
passed on their ride through the heathered hillsides and down
along the moors. There were seven of them: Mick White, Juno's
carpenter, and his apprentice, Justin Gidleigh; Ian Cambourne;
Henry Buckland, who played Guildenstern; and two other actors from the company, Rosalie St. Ives, and Claire Reed.

After several hours they came upon an oakwood forest with a
trout stream running through it. They caught fish and cooked
them over an open fire. While the fish were cooking, Ian
Cambourne produced some organic mescaline. By the time they
finished lunch, they were beginning to experience the sharpen-
ing of colors and heightened awareness of the sounds and mood
of the ancient forest.

"Here, not far from this spot," Ian said, prying the cap off a

Whitbread ale, "is where the legendary outlaw Tom Blackthorn prowled and preyed on wealthy merchants and innocent maidens. In just such a grove as this, he laid down the bodies of the one for plunder, and of the other for pleasure."

"Which was which?" Rosalie giggled.

"Tom Blackthorn? Never heard of him," Justin said. "What was he, a sort of Robin Hood?"

"Never in your life," Ian said. "He took from the rich all right, but he kept it for himself. A very modern man for his time, actually. He was a figure of a man, he was. Strapping, six foot tall, dark hair, wild and curly . . . arms," he extended his own, "like a blacksmith's. Eyes as blue as the sea and twice as cold."

"In other words, he looked just like you, Ian."

Ian smiled. "Mothers would keep their daughters in line by threatening that Tom Blackthorn would get them. But somehow the young maidens would still wander out onto the moors, for he was rumored to be a legendary lover as well as a legendary blackguard."

"Of course . . . they go hand in hand," Claire laughed.

"Once a year, Tom Blackthorn would seize the most luscious of the daughters of the region and carry her off to his quarters, deep in the forest. They would search—fathers and brothers, neighbors and friends—but never found a trace of her or the brigand king, for these woodlands were home to him. The maiden would be returned, for ransom, six months later, always six months to the day. Old Tom would get the money without being caught and escape back into the wild, untamed forest . . ."

"What about the girl? Was she returned unharmed?"

"Oh yes. Unharmed . . . but never the same again. No man could ever make her happy after that. Many chose to die by their own hand rather than live out their life without Tom. Others grew old, waiting for him to return for them. And the young ones kept wandering out into the moor, hoping for that season to be Tom Blackthorn's bride."

"And whatever happened to him?" Juno asked.

"Legend has it he caught the clap and died," said Justin.

"Nay, lad, he still walks abroad in these moors and forests . . ."

"But it's been about fifty years since he's seen a virgin," Mick laughed.

Ian nodded his head sadly. "Tom Blackthorn's had to make certain compromises in the twentieth century."

The horses grazed in the soft grasses among the ferns. Rosalie, Claire, and Justin threw off their clothes and went wading in the cold brook. Mick and Henry disappeared hand in hand. Juno wandered off picking flowers, the colors exploding around her like fireworks. The mescaline carried her on a wave of senses, through the forest and back through time. Down that path rich merchants rode, behind every tree Tom Blackthorn lurked. She could almost hear the voices of happy, singing maidens, and the scolding tones of their mothers urging them back to the house.

And then, from behind, a rough hand covered her mouth; another gripped her breast. "You're Tom Blackthorn's bride this season," a voice growled.

She twisted, brought an elbow back into something soft. There was a sharp grunt and the hands released her. Juno dropped her bouquet of flowers and sprinted off, giggling, down a path streaked with the sunlight that filtered down through the trees. Behind her came heavy footsteps, and the same voice.

"I shall have you, I shall. You can't escape from Tom Blackthorn!"

Juno looked back, laughing. "I can run faster than you any day." But her foot caught in something and she tumbled into some ferns. In a flash, Tom Blackthorn was upon her.

"I've had my eye on you. You're the fairest of all the village girls. You're mine now. You cannot escape my spell."

"Do I have to stay till spring?"

"Nay, forever. Old Tom Blackthorn's found what he's after."

"Oh," she said, a little breathlessly, "and what's that?"

He kissed her. With tearing and fumbling, their clothes came away. For Juno it was not jeans and T-shirt that were tossed into the bushes, but a long peasant dress that laced up the bodice. Ian's clothes, too, had taken on the look and texture of garments from a century long ago. The forest was the same as it had always been.

The sex was lusty and passionate. It tapped the wild animal streak in Juno that Max Milton had first exposed in her at Yale, that she longed for and feared. It was a release to her, a throwing off of layers. The bandit king rode her roughly, and she clawed his back with her nails and bit his shoulder. She came once with a shrill cry, but he was still hard inside her.

And then the mood changed. A song of a different beat rose out of the forest's hum. Ian became gentler, a poetic troubadour, and she the lady of the castle, no longer a peasant. They reached climax together this time, and it was as pure and sweet as the song of the robin that perched in the tree above them. A medieval bird, a twentieth-century bird, there was no difference. They were simply man and woman, and could have lain like this in any century.

The sun was dipping lower and a breeze began to stir the leaves around them. Ian held Juno tight in his arms to keep her warm, and they listened to the sounds of the woods.

Presently, they heard familiar voices calling them. It was getting late. They had to return the horses before dark or, the farmer had warned them, they could get lost.

Juno sat up. "Well, Tom Blackthorn. It's been six months. Time for me to go." She searched the ferns for her clothes.

"You can leave the forest, but you can't leave the spell. It wasn't just the mescaline, it was us. You and me. Juno and Ian. It's real. We are now."

For the next week Juno teetered on the edge of reality. On the one hand, there was work, many hours of it as she fretted over the sets for *The Importance of Being Earnest*, the play that was to close the season. On the other hand, after hours, there was Ian Cambourne. He was brash, yes, and cocky, but his body was magnificent. In sex, he was pepper to Juno's salt, gin to her tonic, bread to her butter. Whatever they did in bed together *worked*.

And she began to see another side of him, the side he did not freely show. He was from a working-class Cornish family, one of eight children. His father was a fisherman, his mother took in sewing. As a child he had virtually lived in the only movie theater in town. His every action and reaction had been practiced in front of a mirror, and measured in terms of movie stars: would Steve McQueen do it this way, would Richard Burton say it that way, would Michael Caine show this or that emotion? When he was sixteen he discovered the poetry of Dylan Thomas, and read it, furtively, so that his family and his classmates would not know and think he had gone soft. He began to write poetry. With some coaxing, once she discovered this bent of Ian's, Juno got him to show her some of it. It was not very good. It tended toward the sentimental and the self-dramatizing and leaned heavily on the legacy of Dylan Thomas. But Ian's poetry was endearing. It was the fact that he wrote it at all, rather than the poetry itself, that recommended it.

But the sex, the sheer animal magnetism, was the consuming center of their relationship. Juno knew that it was a fling, that it could not be anything else. But desire for Ian dominated her waking hours, and thoughts of Shep receded. When she did think of Shep it was with guilt and reluctance. She was terribly fond of him. He was a much nicer person than Ian, a much better person. But Ian turned her on so completely that she rationalized about the situation. Ian was a summer romance, and she had been working hard: she *needed* it, she told herself. Of course, who knew how long summer would last?

Juno and Ian talked about their romantic commitments. She told him about Shep. He told her about a woman named Alice. He had met her in London two years ago when he had first come up from Cornwall to try the London stage. She owned an antique shop and lived above it. He had moved in with her. She was older; Juno was not sure how much older. Apparently she had helped him when he had needed help. But Juno gathered that the relationship was on the wane, though Ian did not say so in so many words. Alice had not come down to visit him all summer.

But Shep came down the next weekend. They went to the Black Swan after the show on Saturday night, where Juno drank a little too much. When they went home she told him she had cramps and did not feel like making love. The next day Shep suggested a drive down to Land's End. It was a long drive, and they talked very little, but it was not the comfortable silence

that they were accustomed to. By the time they got there Juno's
mood was dark. They had fish and chips in a little pub.

"What's going on, Juno? What's wrong?"

"Nothing."

"Oh come on. You haven't spoken six words since we left. You
won't even laugh at my jokes."

Juno shrugged. "I don't know . . ."

"You're not mad because I didn't come down last weekend? I
couldn't, darling. It was business. Boris Tennersley. Surely you
don't think I have a lady somewhere."

Juno bit her nail and looked away out the window. The sky
had grown dark under storm clouds coming in off the ocean.
"No, I don't think that. I wish you did."

Shep's usually pallid face drained of all color. He sat back in
his chair, cradling his mug of ale between his hands. "I see," he
said. "One of those brawny leading men."

"It's not what you think . . ."

"Ah. What do I think?"

"Shep . . . I wouldn't hurt you for anything . . ."

"No, no. Mustn't hurt Shep for anything." He tried a smile.

"Look, I don't know what's going on. It happened very suddenly. I'm confused . . . I'm sure it's nothing. But . . ." She
trailed off.

"It's certainly something. Who is it? Rosencrantz or Guildenstern? Not Guildenstern . . . he's a bit faggy. Must be that
strutting Welshman."

"He's not Welsh."

"I stand corrected. It's good to clear up the important points."
He threw some money on the table. "Let's go."

Shep drove back to Okehampton at a dangerous speed with
the radio blaring to forestall conversation. At Juno's cottage he
collected his things in silence.

"Shall I make you a cup of tea? We ought to talk. I don't want
you going off mad."

"Don't go away mad . . . just go away. Is that it?"

"Oh, Shep. Forgive me, I don't want us to end like this. It's
not that simple. I *do* still care for you . . ."

"And what's that supposed to mean? Am I supposed to wait
by like a faithful dog while you make up your mind?"

"No . . . of course not. I know that's not fair."

"Fair? Do you think it was *fair* to make me spend my bloody weekend on the bloody highway so you could drop this little bombshell into my lap? This sort of thing is traditionally handled by the mails."

"All right! I wanted to see you. You make me sound so cool and calculating. I'm all mixed up, Shep." She started to cry, leaning back against the kitchen table and bunching her fists against her eyes.

Shep sighed. "I'm the one getting dumped here. Why is it always the woman who gets the tears?" He went over and put his hand on her shoulder. "Look, don't take on so. You'll get over it. I'll get over it. Everybody gets over these things." He kissed her on the forehead and picked up his bag. "Good-bye, Juno. I'm not going to wait for you to come around."

When she heard the sound of his motor starting she wanted to run out and call him back. It was not that her feelings for Shep had changed. It was just that Ian had overwhelmed her so completely. With him in her life there was no room for anyone else.

By the time the sound of Shep's car had faded in the distance, Juno was feeling guilty and miserable. This had probably been one of the worst mistakes of her life. But she had made it, and it was done. She put on a jacket and headed to the Black Swan where she was sure Ian would be.

On stage, Lady Bracknell grilled the unfortunate Miss Prism on the disposition of a certain handbag over a quarter of a century earlier. The audience roared with laughter. It was the final week of the season, and *The Importance of Being Earnest* was their biggest crowd pleaser.

The set had been both one of the simplest and most difficult for Juno. Working with a limited budget and limited space she had used imaginative lighting to make one set do the work of three. But the result had been spectacular. The audience and the critics had loved it.

To Juno the real revelation of the production was Ian. She knew he was talented, from the other plays, but she had not thought light comedy would fit into his range so successfully. Ian had used his native cockiness to create an Algernon who was

both brash and sexually appealing, and his comic timing had
won him some of the biggest laughs of the show.

The actors took their curtain calls, and Juno brought up the
houselights. By the time she got back to his dressing room, Ian
had taken off his makeup and was buttoning up his jeans.

"Sodding old Lady Bracknell and cucumber sandwiches," he
complained.

Juno kissed him and ran her fingers over his bare chest. "I
know you don't like this play, but you're so terrific in it. You're
a born comic."

"I'm a born lover. You know that. Come on, what d'you say
. . . shall we go to the Swan or just straight to bed?"

"Hmmm . . . I vote for bed."

"Good girl." He smacked her buttocks. "We'll make tonight
special. End of the run."

"You idiot. Tonight's Friday. You've got another show to play
tomorrow, remember?"

"Yeah . . . but Alice is coming down. I told you, didn't I?"

"No." Juno felt her skin going cold.

Ian put on his shirt. "I thought I told you."

"Why is she coming down? Didn't you tell her about us?"

"She doesn't keep tabs on me. We both knew it would be a
long summer."

"Is that what it's been for you? A long summer?"

"Look, love, I thought I made it clear to you. Alice keeps me
together. But you're great, too. There's no reason we have to
end. We can see each other in London . . ."

"But you'll live with her."

"Well . . . yes. I mean, it's all set up that way." His voice was
matter-of-fact, but he could not meet her eyes. He picked up his
jacket. "Hey, come on, let's not let this bring us down. We've
still got tonight."

Suddenly, Juno was furious. "Fuck you, you bastard! So I'm
just another disposable piece of ass. How the hell could I have
let myself get involved with you? I should've listened to my own
instincts . . . hell, I didn't even *like* you."

"Come on, you're making an issue . . . nothing's really
changed."

"Boy, that's the truth! You're the same bastard you always were."

She turned to storm out. Just before the door slammed she heard his parting words.

"Does this mean you're not going home with me tonight?"

The next day was agony for Juno. Alice arrived a little past noon and took possession of Ian. The rest of the company was very sympathetic to Juno, and she hated it.

The end had come so unexpectedly. During the last three weeks Ian had been loving, attentive, and completely faithful to her. She had begun to believe that all his womanizing during the earlier part of the summer was merely because he had not found her. She thought she had reformed him, that she had turned him into a one-woman man. Now, seeing him with Alice, she realized that perhaps he had been one all along.

Somehow Juno got through the day. She did the show, even went to the end-of-the-season party where she made a point of not drinking too much. The last thing she wanted to do was lose control and create a scene. She had the feeling that Ian expected it. It was one last little satisfaction that she could deny him.

She caught the early train the next morning. It was the slow train. The express, two hours later, would have gotten her to London sooner, but she wanted to get away without seeing anybody.

In any case, Juno was in no hurry to get to London. There was no one waiting for her there.

Chapter Twenty-one

•

Simon Parrie went Hollywood, as Shep had predicted. But he did not want to get rid of the little house on Adam and Eve Mews and was very happy to let Juno remain. He had been back for the month of August, between films, and had satisfied himself that Juno was a responsible caretaker of his possessions. She had added a few of her own, from antique shops and flea markets, and they fit in wonderfully. When Parrie returned to Los Angeles, he left Juno with a two-months-notice arrangement.

Everywhere Juno went the first few months back in London, every play, every gallery, every party, she looked for Shep. Sometimes when she was alone for an evening she dialed his number, but pressed the button down before it started ringing. John and Ursula Fletcher had a large party on November fifth, Guy Fawkes Day, and unbeknownst to Juno, they invited Shep to come. But he sent a note of regret, saying he would be in Germany for a book fair.

She talked fairly often with Lydia, but Alex had dropped out of sight, and Juno and Lydia were worried about him. His most recent play had closed in October after a run of less than a month at the Theater de Lys on Christopher Street, in spite of good-to-mixed reviews. Alex had invested his own money in this one and had lost more than he could afford. Now nobody seemed to know where he had gone.

At Christmas Juno took a week off from work and made her annual visit to Santa Fe. On Christmas morning she was drinking mimosas with her parents when the telephone rang.

"You get it," Hollis said to Juno with a smile. "When you're home, it's never for us."

It was Alex.

"Alex! Merry Christmas to you too, but where have you been? Lydia and I have been frantic. You just disappeared after your play closed."

"I had to get away for a while. Sorry, I didn't mean to worry you, but I didn't feel like talking to anyone."

Juno detected a strange, depressed tone in Alex's voice. "Oh, Alex, are you all right? Where are you?"

"I'm back in New York. I just talked to Lydia, she told me you were home for Christmas. So—how are *you?*"

"Oh . . . I'm okay. I'm really working hard with John. Other than that, things are kind of quiet."

"Nothing new with you and Shep?"

"No. It seems to be pretty final. So—what are you doing? Starting a new play?"

Alex laughed wryly. "You may not believe this, but . . . I've got a job in an advertising agency."

"Oh, Alex, no . . ."

"Hey, it's not so bad. I can afford new socks, new shirts, two meals a day . . ."

"But you . . . working nine to five? I can't believe it! What's it like?"

"I don't know. I just started a week ago. Ask me in six months."

"You're still writing, though, aren't you? You're not giving that up?"

Alex was silent for a moment. "Oh, I don't know, Juno," he sighed. "I just need a change. You know how it is . . ."

"Yes. Of course."

Alex laughed. "Don't worry about it. They love me at the agency. A failed playwright is practically royalty in the ad world."

Juno laughed too. But it upset her to hear Alex talking like this.

"Any chance of you stopping off in New York on your way back? I really miss you, Juno. I'd love to be able to just sit down and talk."

"Oh, so would I, Alex. But I can't. I had to practically resort to tears to get even Christmas off from work. We have a big opening in two weeks . . ."

"Sure. Well, I'll talk to you soon. I love you, Juno. Take care of yourself."

"I love you too, Alex. Merry Christmas."

Alex's troubles made Juno realize how lucky she was to be doing what she really wanted—working in the theater and getting paid for it. That winter, John Fletcher had three important shows opening, two in the West End. Often he and Juno worked well into the night. If she had not known Juno better, Ursula said, she would have sworn that John was having an affair.

Juno did manage time for a social life. Her parents sent her care packages of green chiles and *posole* from Santa Fe, and she began having Sunday soirées featuring tacos and enchiladas and *chiles rellenos* and *huevos rancheros*. There was no one special in her life, but she had a lot of pals to do things with in her free time. She whiled away the gray rainy weeks of March and half of April in a fitful affair with a married Swiss film producer, but neither of them was very interested, and it withered under the first thin rays of spring sunlight.

Juno was invited to return to Okehampton. Before she accepted, she inquired to be sure that Ian Cambourne would not be there.

In May, Hollis and Maria Johnson came to London. They spent a week going to shows and concerts and museums, and then Juno took a holiday with them and they flew to the Loire valley to visit Lydia.

Hollis and Maria were duly impressed with the Château Mordoi, and even more so with the way Lydia had taken charge. But all three of them noticed a sadness in Lydia, or rather, an absence of the happiness that one would have expected to find in a young woman who seemed to have everything.

One night Juno and Lydia sat up late talking, after the Johnsons and Stefan had retired. Juno tried to pump Lydia about what was bothering her, but Lydia insisted she was happy.

"Oh, our sex life is back in a bit of a lull . . . but that's to be expected, after a baby . . ."

"Lydia, it's been over a year since India was born."

"Yes . . . well. It'll all work out. What about you?"

"Nothing much to tell."

Lydia giggled suddenly. "Some sexual revolutionaries we turned out to be. Quite a comedown from the glory days at Yale and in Paris."

"I wonder how Alex is." Juno looked at her watch. "What time is it in New York?"

"Seven or eight, something like that. After all these years I still haven't got it straight. Let's call him."

Lydia dialed the number. It rang six times and she was about to hang up when a woman answered the phone.

"Hello, Lydia . . . it's Tory. Alex is out buying champagne . . . to celebrate. Guess what? We're engaged."

Lydia paused. "Oh . . . that's wonderful, Tory." She made a face at Juno and mouthed *getting married*. Juno's jaw dropped. "Have you set the date?"

"Yes. August seventeenth. At my parents' place in Westchester. I certainly hope you and Stefan will be able to make it."

"Oh . . . well. Absolutely. Listen, give Alex my love, will you? And congratulations."

She hung up the receiver, shaking her head. "I can't believe it. Alex getting married. And to *her*."

"When did you meet her?"

"Oh, when we were in New York in March. She's absolutely beautiful, I'll give her that. And nice enough. Not to mention rich. Her father's Gamble of Gamble Technology. It's just that, I don't know, she doesn't have much of a sense of humor. There's no real spark to her."

Juno laughed. "Not as nifty as we are, eh?"

"Seriously . . . I can't figure out what he sees in her."

"Well, there's no accounting for love. Look at some of the people I've been involved with."

"Yes, but you didn't marry them." She lit a cigarette. "Then again, who am I to talk."

Juno could not attend Alex's wedding because she was in Okehampton. She would have gone, of course; but she was glad to have an excuse not to. When she returned to London that fall, she went back to work immediately with John Fletcher, design-

ing a play about Lady Gregory, a major force behind the found-
ing of the Irish National Theatre.

On opening night Juno and the Fletchers were in the audience. Juno had bought a new dress, a Sonia Rykiel, for the occasion. She wore her hair up and looked slinky and sophisticated.
During intermission she circulated in the lobby, eavesdropping
on people's comments and greeting friends. She saw Shepherd
Wise at the same moment he saw her.

"Juno!" he said warmly. "It's so good to see you." He was
with a pretty brunette whom he introduced as Constance Ag-
new. Constance smiled and shook hands. They chatted for a few
moments about the play and the sets. As the lights flickered for
the second act, Constance excused herself "for a quick dash to
the loo."

"So, Juno," Shep said. "How have you been?"

"Busy." She paused. "I've missed you, Shep."

"You could have called."

"I didn't think you'd want to hear from me. And then Alex
told me you were seeing somebody."

"That's over. What about you?"

She shrugged. "No one special."

"Can I ring you?"

"I'd love it. I'm still at the same old place." She laughed.
"Thanks to the Hollywoodization of Simon Parrie."

Juno and Shep took up again. It was just as it had been before.
They had a wonderful time together, enjoying the same things,
laughing at each other's jokes, making love. They seldom quar-
reled.

They went to spend Christmas weekend at Elder's Parsonage
with Shep's parents. It was a warm and happy traditional English Christmas: roast goose with chestnut stuffing, flaming
plum pudding, rich eggnog, and hot wassail. Friends of the
Wises dropped in late in the afternoon, and they sang carols and
played charades.

Shep gave Juno a beautiful antique model of a Victorian theater, in cardboard, painted paper, and velvet. She gave him a
coach bag from Dunhill's. That night, after the Wises had re-

tired to bed, Shep poured two snifters of cognac and he and
Juno cozied up together on the carpet next to the fire.

"You know, this is the first Christmas I've ever spent away
from Santa Fe. I thought I'd feel a bit sad, but it's been absolutely wonderful. Your parents are so warm and hospitable."

Shep leaned over and kissed her. "Just my parents? What
about me?"

"You're *hot* and hospitable," Juno smiled. She folded her fingers around his.

"It's been good, since we got back together. Wouldn't you
say?"

"Hmmm . . . yes, I'd say. Even great."

Shep put his arm around Juno and they gazed into the flames
for a few moments, without speaking.

"I've been thinking a lot about you these last few weeks,"
Shep said, finally. "About us. I'm ready for something permanent in my life. I've never loved anyone as much as you, Juno.
I've been thinking that perhaps we should go the whole distance
. . . and get married."

Juno looked into Shep's loving eyes. "I must admit, I've
thought about it, too. I love you, Shep."

"You love me," Shep said. "But will you marry me?"

Juno nodded. "Yes. I think I'd love to."

Juno was sure she was in love with Shep. And she wanted to
marry him. But whenever he tried to pin her down on a wedding date, she sidestepped it. There was always something.

Shep had told her that marriage need not hinder her career.
He worked hard, and long hours, and he was all for her working, too. As long as she was there for him when he came home.
And that, perhaps, was the rub. Juno worked erratic hours with
John Fletcher. When they were in the frenzy of a production
there was no way she could break to go home and fix dinner, or
take a weekend at will to drive down to the country. All that
could be worked out, Shep assured her.

But marriage to Shep and its permanency sent chills through
her when she thought about it. If she were going to marry anybody, it would be Shep. Alex was married. There was no use
keeping that flame alive any longer.

Juno and Shep spent most of their free time together, and often she slept over at his flat. Still, she liked having her own place to come home to. Somehow Juno kept putting off setting a date.

Shep and Juno shared many interests, but one they did not share was rock music. The fastest rising new group on the rock scene was one called Tierra. Juno had been following their ascendancy because her friend Garth Meacham from Scrap Metal was the lead singer-guitarist. She had not seen Garth since 1971 when she split up with Tony Silver at the end of the Scrap Metal tour.

In early May, Tierra was doing a concert at the Albert Hall. Juno bought two tickets, but Shep was not interested in going so she invited Claire Reed. They had become good friends, after two seasons together at the Okehampton Rep where Claire had acted. Claire had freckles and kinky-curly short red hair, and the sort of looks that were constantly changing, from unremarkable to almost beautiful. She was currently enjoying some success in a BBC series, *A Life in Fiction*, where she had the small but talked-about role of a blind heiress. She was also up for the lead in a West End musical, *Shamrock*, that was scheduled for fall.

Claire had turned down an offer to return to Okehampton that summer. Juno had not made up her mind whether to go back or not. Shep wanted her to stay in London, and Juno thought perhaps she had gotten as much track record as she could at the Rep. Still, she had grown to love her summers in peaceful Devon.

The Tierra concert was sold out. Juno had managed, through a friend of John Fletcher's, to get front-center seats.

"I'm very impressed," Claire said, as they sat down. "I've never sat this close at a rock concert before. All the better to see your friend Garth Meacham. He's absolutely divine."

"Hmmm, but he's not exactly my friend. I mean, not anymore. It's been five years. I doubt if he'd remember me."

"Juno? My God, it is you!"

"Well, someone remembers you," Claire said.

Tony Silver hopped down off the stage and gave Juno an exuberant hug. Tony had put on a little weight since Juno had last seen him, and his hair was thinning, but he was still dressed in vintage hippie. And still road managing rock groups. He was happy to see Juno again.

"Look," he said, "there's a party after. At Garth's. I'd really like for you to come. Both of you," Tony said, looking at Claire. He jotted down the address on the back of a book of matches, and then had to dash off.

"Oh, this is super," Claire said. "Maybe I can get myself a rock star."

The concert was fabulous. In the five years since Juno had seen Garth Meacham he had not changed physically, still tall and dark and lean. But he had gained authority on stage. Garth had always been charismatic, but now he was looser, more of a showman. He knew how to play the audience into a frenzy, and even Juno found herself leaping to her feet and dancing to the music. And she could not deny that she still found him devastatingly attractive.

The party, at Garth's town house in Kensington, was wall-to-wall people. Tony Silver told Juno that Garth had just bought the place, with royalties from Tierra's first album which had gone platinum in less than six months. It was sparsely furnished, and most of what was there looked as if it had been picked up from the street at one time or another. Juno looked around intently though, to store impressions that she might be able to call upon for a set someday.

Claire went off with Tony in search of drinks, and Juno continued to wander. She watched Garth, surrounded by people, high from the exhilaration of being on stage, and thought how odd it was that five years had passed so quickly. Suddenly Garth saw her. He disengaged himself from the group of admirers surrounding him and came over to Juno.

"It's the Wild West woman." He kissed her on the lips. "What happened? You dropped off the earth. Where've you been keeping yourself?"

"Oh, here and there. I'm living in London now."

"No shit! You still doing lights?"

"Lights. Set design. I'm working with John Fletcher."

"Say, that's great. Listen . . . ." Somebody pulled his arm, hauling him off in another direction. "I want to talk to you," he called back. "What's your number? Never mind, I'll find you."

Two days later, a side of Scottish salmon was delivered to her door at Adam and Eve Mews, with a note:

I remember you used to kill for this. How about sharing it for breakfast tomorrow morning? I'll be there at nine.
                                                                Garth.

It was presumptuous, but sweet. After all these years Garth not only remembered her but her passion for smoked salmon, too. She was seeing Shep that night and ordinarily she would have slept over, but having breakfast with Britain's top rock star was irresistible. And her curiosity was piqued as to why Garth wanted to see her. She would have to make an excuse to Shep.

Juno got up early and washed her hair. She spent half an hour agonizing over outfits before she finally got impatient with herself and put on her everyday work outfit, jeans and a T-shirt. At nine o'clock she had coffee ready and the salmon sliced on a plate. She had also laid in cream cheese and an assortment of bagels and rolls. At nine-thirty the coffee was cold. At quarter of ten she was leaving for work when a pink limousine pulled up in front of the Mews, and Garth jumped out.

"Where're you going, girl? I thought we had a breakfast date."

"I'd given up on you. I'm heading for work."

"But I'm starving. Haven't you got half an hour for an old friend? I'm sorry I'm late."

Juno smiled. "Well, there is an awful lot of salmon. Come on."

She heated up the coffee and set a cup in front of him. For ten minutes they talked about the old days with Scrap Metal. Then Juno leaned back and propped her cowboy boots on the table.

"It's great to see you, Garth. But what's this all about?"

"Isn't it enough that we're just seeing each other again?"

"It's enough, but I get the feeling it's not all. There's something on your mind."

Garth grinned. "Ah, the Wild West woman has ESP. What is it? The Indian blood or all that peyote? Anyway, yeah, there is

something. We're leaving at the end of June for a tour of the
States. How'd you like to do the lighting?"

"Oh wow." She shook her head. "I don't know . . . I have a
tentative commitment to do sets at Okehampton . . ."

"Oke bloody Hampton? Do you know how much bread you
can make on this tour?" He named a figure.

Juno whistled. "Holy shit! Are you serious? That would buy
me my Porsche."

"Well, then?"

"I'll have to think about it. There are, you know, personal
considerations."

"Three months. He'll wait for you. Look, I'll up it another
couple of grand . . . to cover your phone bills."

"I'm going to have to talk it over with him, Garth. I can't give
you an answer now."

Juno knew what Shep would say. If he did not want her going
to Okehampton, he sure as hell was not going to like the idea of
her touring the States for three months with Garth Meacham
and Tierra. Still, he should understand. If their relationship was
going to work, she had to be free to take any job she wanted to.

Then there was the money. She would be crazy to turn it
down. It was more than she could make in a dozen seasons at the
Rep. It would buy a lot of extras when she and Shep got married. And economic independence had always been a grail of
sorts to Juno.

But she knew herself. Her old attraction to Garth was still
there, and this time there would be nobody on the premises to
prevent them from coming together. Of course she was engaged
to Shep, but Shep would be thousands of miles away.

The parallels to Ian Cambourne were obvious. If she had any
sense, Juno told herself, she would turn down the job. But she
did not want to turn down the job.

And she was sure she could fend Garth off if she wanted to.

Chapter Twenty-two

The din of the crowd that ripped through Madison Square Garden was, *Rolling Stone* later reported, probably the loudest sound heard on this planet since the third eruption of Krakatoa. Tierra left the stage but the noise continued, grew, and finally settled into an insistent rhythmic demand which exploded as the group returned for their first encore.

The band members picked up their instruments, and the noise rose even louder. Garth Meacham raised his hands over his head. Juno threw a purple-orange haze over the stage and brought a spot in on Garth.

"Thanks . . . thanks . . ." He waited for several moments while the audience quieted down. "Thank you very much. Now we'd like to do a new number . . . one I just wrote. It's never been done before. And it's called 'Wild West Woman!' "

The crowd roared. Garth hit a chord, spun, and leaned into the mike. "Wild West Woman . . ." he screamed,

> "What makes your legs so long?
> I got to ask myself
> How to get you in this song.
> Brown eyes, long black hair,
> Nonstop body, every part of you is there,
> Wild West Woman,
> Nothin' that you do is wrong.
> And I want you . . . yeah . . .
> And I want you . . ."

As she manipulated the lights, Juno grinned with amazement. Not many women got propositioned like this, in front of tens of thousands of screaming rock fans. It was pretty impressive, she had to admit . . . though Shep would not be pleased when he heard about it. It could not exactly be called a love song. A lust song, maybe. Garth had not come on to her yet, and she had been waiting for his first move. So this was it. She could not help being excited and flattered. She was immortalized in song, like Judy Collins in Steve Stills's "Suite: Judy Blue Eyes" . . . if this song turned out to be a classic like that.

> ". . . What's it gonna take
> To get you in my bed?
> Reach in my mouth,
> Grab my stomach, pull me inside out,
> Wild West Woman,
> Remember everything I said,
> 'Cause I want you . . . yeah . . .
> Wild West Woman . . ."

The dressing room was bedlam. Guests, press, security men, groupies, entourage milled around, passing bottles and joints, eating shrimp and steak tartare from the lavish buffet, everybody trying to talk over everybody else.

Finally, Garth came over to Juno. He put his arm around her with a sexy smile. "Well, girl . . . what did you think?"

Juno felt her stomach leap with the thrill of anticipation. But she kept her voice casual. Whatever she ended up deciding to do, she would not blow her cool. "Pretty subtle, Garth. Will you write one for Shep, too? He's bound to feel left out."

"He's an ocean away, luv." He ran his hand slowly down her back. "And I'm right here." He paused, staring deep into her eyes. "So . . . what d'you say?"

"It's a great song, Garth. But I've got a date with an old friend."

"Don't forget, I'm an old friend, too." He kissed her. "Well, no hurry. It's going to be a long tour."

Alex and Tory Sage lived in a co-op on Fifth Avenue in the upper Eighties. It was on the twenty-second floor and commanded a magnificent view of Central Park and the buildings to the west and south. The apartment itself had been designer-decorated with red walls, black-lacquered molding, and white ceilings. The furnishings combined Oriental and Art Deco, and the art on the walls was modern.

Midnight supper had been a lobster soufflé, arugula salad, crusty peasant bread, and a chocolate-orange mousse.

"Would you like espresso, Juno? Or tea? We have normal and herbal." Tory Sage cleared away the dessert plates. She was, as Lydia had described her, a beautiful woman. Her skin was creamy and her dark brown hair was blunt cut just above her shoulders. She was about five-seven, with a trim figure, and the legs of a stocking model.

They had coffee and liqueurs outside on the terrace. A light breeze stirred the humid air through the potted palm trees.

"Alex," Tory said, sipping her Kahlúa, "tell Juno about your marvelous idea for the Voisin Motors account."

Alex wrinkled his face with disgust. "No, Tor, I don't want to talk about advertising."

"Oh, don't be ridiculous." Tory turned to Juno. "He's so modest. It's really terrific. We're going to have this silver car—it'll catch the sunlight in every direction—on a raft going up the Nile, and . . ."

"Stop, Tory! Really, let's not talk about it. It's only what I do for a living."

"Oh God. Juno, was he like this when you knew him? He never has any enthusiasm for anything."

"Not true," Alex said, annoyed. "Just no enthusiasm for the world of Madison Avenue."

"Are you working on another play?" Juno asked.

"I have five pages that have been gathering mold in the top of my closet."

"There's never time," Tory said. "We usually see people or do something after work. And most weekends we go up to my parent's place, or to the Island. We're thinking about buying a house in Springs."

A bit later, Tory stifled a yawn. Juno looked at her watch. "Oh, it's nearly two. I'd better be going."

Tory waved her hand. "No, no. I'll just slip off to bed. You two probably have loads to talk about after all this time."

"I'm afraid I have a lot to do tomorrow."

"Well, I'll put you in a cab," Alex said.

As they walked across the sumptuously understated lobby, Alex took her arm. "Let's go have a drink. There's a place over on Madison that's open late."

They found two seats at the end of the crowded bar. At a little past two on a Saturday night, the place was doing a brisk Upper East Side business.

"I can't get over you," Alex said with a smile. "Pocahontas with her British accent. Jeez, we thought you were exotic before."

"Ta. I can't get over *you*. You sound the same, but you look so straight."

"Thanks. I needed that."

"No . . . you look wonderful with short hair. Very New Wave."

"Oh, I forgot to tell you," Alex said. "Lydia called the other day. Sends her love. She was just heading off with Nanny and the kids to the Riviera for a few weeks."

Juno rolled her eyes. "Tough life."

"Well, she was bitching because Stefan's off in Japan. Hey, speaking of travel . . . how's Shep taking this wild trip of yours?"

"He was not happy. It's a sore spot, Alex. I don't know . . . I really love Shep, but it's hard getting it all worked out."

"Shep's a patient guy, but you can't expect him to be a saint. I mean, here you take off on an extended tour with the world's leading sex symbol . . . you can see Shep's point."

Juno made a face. "Of course I see his point. But I couldn't turn down the money. And it's a free trip to the States . . ." She caught Alex looking at her and gave him a guilty smile. "Yeah, I see his point."

"You and Shep love each other. You've weathered stuff before. Anyway, when's the wedding going to be?"

"I don't know. That's what Shep keeps asking. When we get

the time, I guess." Juno took a sip of her cognac and let it burn slowly down her throat. "I love being engaged . . . but the idea of being married scares me a little, I guess."

"Look, it's never going to be the right time. You just have to do it. I need some warning so I can put in for vacation. Us nine-to-fivers can't just split when we want."

"What about the nine-to-five business, Alex? When are you going to start writing plays again?"

"I never seem to find the time."

Juno smiled. "Like the man just said, you've got to *make* time."

He sighed and toyed with his drink. "I don't know, Juno. I don't seem to want to anymore. I sit there in my office and come up with lines like 'We're taking away Mrs. Harris's Mop 'n Shine,' and then I come home and sit in front of the typewriter and I just want to puke."

"But, Alex, writing plays is what you're all about. I didn't put myself through all these years of apprenticeship and poverty to design just anybody's plays." She took his hand. "Darling . . . we're talking major talent here. Don't blow it."

Alex shook his head wryly. "A human mind is a terrible thing to waste."

"But what about Tory? Doesn't she want you to write?"

"Sure . . . ads." He gave Juno a short smile. "She thinks I've got a lot of talent, too. Don't judge her, Juno. She loves the business and she's really good at what she does. She's the youngest full producer at the agency."

"I'm not judging her, Alex. I think she's terrific," Juno protested with more enthusiasm than she felt. "And she's beautiful, and a great cook . . ."

"Yeah, she's great. Everything about our life is great. Except me."

"Oh, Alex. Really. Self-pity? From you? Look, you're blocked right now. It happens to every creative artist. But you'll work through it. You've just got to make yourself do it."

"Yes, mama. Will you be my muse and sit on my shoulder?"

"Sure, but I'd better lose weight."

There were not many taxis on Madison Avenue at three-thirty in the morning. They walked north, browsing in lighted shop windows and keeping an eye open for a cab. Eventually, an

old Checker came rattling to a stop. Alex opened the door for
Juno.

"It's been great seeing you." He pulled her to him for a farewell kiss. Their lips met, and he pulled her closer. She felt something wild surge through her, and she clenched her fists in the
back of his hair and squeezed him tight. For a moment they
were lost in each other.

"Hey, you want this cab or not?"

Sheepishly they separated. "Well . . ." Juno said. "Good
night."

"Good night."

Juno climbed in. "The Plaza," she said. As the cab pulled
away, she turned back and waved. Alex saluted.

The taxi made a left on Eighty-ninth Street, and another left
on Fifth. Juno settled back against the tattered leather seat as
they flew down along the deserted avenue. She felt very sad,
suddenly, for all of them.

During the next weeks Juno covered more of America and
saw less of it than she would ever have believed possible. Cities
and towns homogenized into one another, so that Philadelphia
became indistinguishable from Buffalo, Cleveland from Detroit,
Atlanta from Birmingham. Everything was auditoriums and sta-
diums and outdoor parks, lighting grids and sound systems and
stages, limos and helicopters, security guards, trailers, dressing
rooms, hotel rooms. Every date was a sellout. At every airport
there were armies of screaming teenagers, at every hotel and
motel there were more of them trying to break through the
barricades; they stood, screamed, sobbed, and fainted, whether
the group was there or not.

Tierra traveled in several private Gulfstream jets with an entourage that included technicians, managers, accountants, record company executives, lawyers, bodyguards, press agents, reporters, photographers, drug suppliers, wives, mistresses, kids,
selected groupies, an acupuncturist, and a masseuse. Brad
Chang, the award-winning documentary filmmaker, was recording Tierra's American tour with a film crew—three ubiquitous
cameras and tape recorders that seemed to intrude everywhere,
public or private, waking or sleeping, night and day.

"Wild West Woman" had become a real showstopper. Since the night Garth had unveiled it at Madison Square Garden word had traveled ahead of them. His record company had rushed the single into release. Now everywhere they went the kids were screaming for the song, and fringed leather jackets and cowboy hats began to crop up with growing frequency in the oceans of frenzied fans that packed Tierra's concerts.

Shep kidded her about it when they talked on the phone, as they did several times a week. "I always thought you were exotic. Now you're a bloody fad. I've taken to wearing a Stetson to the office."

"Oh, Shep . . . I hope you don't mind too much."

"Not at all, darling. I hear your song everywhere. It makes me feel closer to you."

"Oh, I wish I were close to *you* right now. Next to you, in bed. Why did I ever get involved in this tour anyway?"

"For the money. Which you promised you would spend on keeping me in the manner to which I have become accustomed."

Juno laughed. "We will have fun spending it, won't we?"

"*We* won't . . . *I* will. Remember? It was a rather rash promise on your part, but I plan to hold you to it."

"Well," Juno said. "That's okay. Just as long as you plan to hold me, too."

"Don't worry about that, darling." Shep knew that the only way to keep Juno was to give her plenty of slack. He had come to realize that her affair with Ian Cambourne would have blown over if only he had kept his cool about it. He was not going to make that mistake again. What was going on in America was Juno's business.

But aside from the song, Garth had not overtly renewed his attempt to get Juno to go to bed with him. He seemed to be waiting for her to come to him, confident that she would. In the meantime Garth did not lack for sex. There were three girls in particular who satisfied his every need, singly or in combinations. Juno called them Flopsy, Mopsy, and Cottonbrain. Flopsy was a Swedish import named Fiona, a contortionist who could bend her body into extraordinary positions. Mopsy was Marianne, tall and gorgeous, with the body of a Greek statue and brains to match. Cottonbrain, a former Playboy bunny named Colette, was also known as "the Collector." She was a veteran of many tours. The Collector had a charm bracelet of tiny gold records, each engraved with the name of a different artist, one for each chart-topping single she had slept with.

Juno's best friends on the tour were Tony Silver and Tad Otis, the teenage genius who played keyboards. She spent her leisure time with them and avoided being alone with Garth. She and Garth played a game of seduction, eyeing each other, withdrawing, feigning indifference, each secure in the knowledge of the other's desire, each determined not to make the first move.

And then in Houston, it was Garth who blinked. Juno came down to the band's dressing room below the Astrodome to consult with Tony Silver on some technical matters. The Collector was oiling Garth's body with the baby oil that he applied to make his torso gleam as he coiled and sprang and strutted on stage. Garth was sprawled in the satin-covered barber's chair that traveled with him, nibbling distractedly at the mound of fresh lobster salad he always required in his dressing room before a show. Juno could feel his eyes on her as she talked to Tony.

"Hey, girl," he called to her as she turned to go. Juno sauntered over to him. The Collector stood by, polishing his chest with a proprietary caress. At his feet Fiona was doing yoga, her body jackknifed in a perfect plow.

"Hm?"

"We've hit the halfway mark. Five weeks down, five to go. I thought maybe we should get together and celebrate. Dinner, just the two of us . . ."

"And bed, just the five of us? No thanks." She patted his cheek and went out. As she left the room she was suddenly aware that one of Brad Chang's camera crew was recording the scene. They were so much a part of everything that one seldom noticed them anymore.

Well, if the movie played in London this would be documentary evidence to Shep of her fidelity.

Tierra played Tingley Coliseum in Albuquerque on a Saturday night. Her parents came down for the concert. The next date was Tuesday in Denver, so Juno took a day off and drove back up to Santa Fe with Hollis and Maria after the show.

"So what did you *really* think?" Juno asked them.

"My hearing may never be the same again," Hollis said, "but I liked it."

Her mother smiled. "Well . . . it's just not my kind of music, darling. But that boy is awfully sexy. I can see why he gets the girls screaming."

"What about that number . . . 'Wild West Woman'? Would that happen to be about anybody we know?"

Juno laughed. "Oh, you picked up on that, eh?"

"Yeah . . . parents have an obligation to pick up on everything," Hollis said.

"Don't worry. I haven't become one of Garth's groupies."

"Good girl," Maria said. "It never works to share a man with somebody else."

Juno wondered if Maria was alluding to Alex and Lydia and the summer they spent in Paris. Perhaps she was merely throwing out a general piece of motherly advice. At any rate, she was right. It never did work to share a man with anyone else.

The next morning Juno slept late and Maria brought her breakfast in bed. On the tray next to her *huevos rancheros* was a rolled-up *Pasatiempo* section from the Friday *New Mexican*.

"Look at page fifteen. There's an article about you. 'Local Girl Lights Up Tierra.' They dug up an old picture of you from high school. I don't see why they couldn't have called me for something more up to date."

Juno smiled and turned to the article. "Oh God, this is from when I won that art prize."

Her mother hugged her. "Oh, Juno . . . I'm so proud of you. You've really done something with your life. You've seen the world and made your mark on it."

"Oh, Mom. Thanks . . . but I haven't done that much yet."

"You will." Maria sighed. "Just always keep your goals in focus. Don't bury yourself the way . . . the way so many

women do. It's what I've tried to drum into you since you were
a little bitty girl."

"I know, Mom. I understand."

"And what about Shep? Does he understand?"

Juno laughed. "Shep is the most understanding man alive.
He's got to be, with me."

"Well, I'm happy for you, dear. Oh . . . I meant to tell you. I
ran into David Abeyta. He's in town for the weekend and would
love to get together with you, if you have time."

"Oh, Mom . . ."

"Oh, Mom what? You and David went together for years.
He's just as nice a boy now as he was then, though he was never
right for you. He wants to see you, that's all. Don't tell me
you've gotten too hep for your old friends."

"Hip. It isn't that. It's just . . . I don't know what we'd talk
about."

"That's easy, darling. You'll talk about you."

She had fit back into her own house easily, but driving up the
dirt road to David's parents' house on Apodaca Hill was a real
time warp. Just like the old days, there were a bunch of cars
parked out in front. She went through the heavy wooden gate,
and there was the yard, full of flowers as always, and full of
David and his friends drinking beer, as if they were still back in
high school.

"Juno!" David jumped up and came over to her. He smiled
and started to open his arms to give her a hug, then appeared to
think better of it, and extended his hand. "You look great. It's
great to see you."

The others clustered about her, calling out greetings that
were half jovial and half shy.

"Carlos, how are you? Liza . . . I love your hair. Richard
. . . Tina . . . Chris . . ."

David's parents came out and welcomed Juno with kisses and
cries of delight. She hugged them back. With them there was no
self-consciousness. It was different with her contemporaries.

She was ushered to a chair and a cold Carta Blanca was put in
her hand. It was almost like being back the way they had been in
high school, except that it was not. They were all deferring to

her. She was the one who had gotten away and swum in the waters of international celebrity. Everyone admired her clothes and laughed at her English accent. They wanted to know all about London and Tierra and especially Garth Meacham.

For the next hour Juno told them amusing stories and gave them inside gossip. She felt the strangeness of not being one of them anymore. And the relief of having escaped. Tina was a checkout girl at Albertson's. Liza was married to a realtor and pregnant with her second child. Richard owned a flower shop. Juno's life was the interesting one, and this was acknowledged by all of them.

When she left David walked her out to the car. "I didn't really get to hear about what you're doing, David."

"Oh," he shrugged. "I graduated from law school in June. Now I'm out on the Navajo Reservation. I'm working with them on a land rights case. It's pretty interesting, actually. But, I mean, not like what you're doing."

After dinner, Juno sat out on the terrace with her father and watched the sun go down behind the Jemez Mountains. Her mother was playing at the Opera. The sky stretched from the bright ball of fire on the horizon to orange, to peach, and faded into a deep and peaceful blue-black overhead. They leaned back in their chairs and sipped coffee in silence as the night darkened and the stars came out. Juno could not remember when she had last experienced such total peace and quiet.

"How was your afternoon?" Hollis asked finally.

"Oh, it was fun. It was good to see everybody . . ."

"A little tough fitting back in? You can't go home again, that sort of thing?"

"I don't know, Dad. I'm *not* the same person I was then. I'm not saying I'm better or worse, but . . . oh, everybody carried on as if I were some sort of celebrity, and I guess maybe I sort of felt that way too. I never even bothered asking David about himself until I was leaving. You know what he's doing? Working with the Navajos. Here he is doing something really worthwhile, really *helping* people, and all I can do is carry on about my glamorous life. Some glamour. Sex, drugs, booze, and airports. I felt like such a jerk!"

"Well, I suppose if you had wanted to help the Navajos you'd be doing it. Instead you're doing what you've always wanted to, since you were a little girl. It's not better or worse than any of your classmates, just different. You always had it in you to travel, to make your own mark."

Juno poured herself another cup of coffee. "I guess so. I'm sure as hell traveling. It's kind of hard sometimes to figure out if I'm going anywhere, or just away from something."

Hollis nodded. "Shep, maybe?"

"No, I don't think so. I love Shep." She looked at her father. His head was backlit in the light that spilled out from the living room window, leaving his face almost completely in the dark. She could feel his expression, though. Love, compassion, concern. "Maybe it is Shep," she sighed. "No, not Shep. Marriage, all that. Look at Lydia and Alex, what they've gotten themselves into. I just saw Alex in New York, and met his wife. She's got him pinned down like a butterfly on a board. You should hear him—he's using words like 'responsibilities.' He's not writing plays anymore."

"Well, you know, honey, a lot of people get to using words like 'responsibilities.' It's one of those things about growing up. I even catch it slipping out myself, every now and then."

"I know, but . . ."

"You're not still kids together. I know it hurts, but that's the way it is. Don't try to hang on to all that stuff too hard, Juno. I'm not saying grow up, settle down, accept getting older. Just accept the way things are. There may be some unhappy things about Lydia's marriage, but there's a lot she's happy about too, you could see that easy enough. Alex, I don't know. I haven't seen him in a long time. But he's a bright guy. If he's got himself into the wrong kind of life, he'll figure it out. And if he's got plays in him, he'll write them."

Juno reached out through the darkness and squeezed her father's arm. "You're right, Dad. Thanks."

"Do yourself a favor, honey. Don't saddle Shep and yourself with Lydia's and Alex's bad marriages. If they are bad. Every now and then you run across one that works just fine."

"Like you and Mom."

"Well, twenty-eight years . . . it's a little soon to get cocky. But so far, so good."

It was after the Labor Day concerts in San Francisco, two weeks before the end of the tour, that Juno noticed the change. Flopsy and Mopsy were gone. She was not sure just when they had decamped. Since she rejoined the group in Denver, Juno had stopped paying attention to the sensual interweavings of Garth and his harem. She had pulled back from the flirtation she and Garth had been carrying on since New York. He still turned Juno on when she thought about it, but she made herself not think about it very often.

Now Flopsy and Mopsy were gone. And Cottonbrain, the Collector, seemed to have been shunted aside, and had taken up with Tad Otis, the young keyboard player. Colette was alternately morose and hilarious. In her good moods, she told them all she was giving Tad his sexual education, and Tad acknowledged it, grinning, blushing, shyly proud. But they were also doing too many drugs, and Juno and some of the others began to worry about the kid. He was still able to hold together on stage, but he was pushing the limits.

Juno decided to talk to Garth, to see if he could convince Tad to cool it. Somewhat to her surprise, Garth was in tune with the situation and also worried.

"Look, it's my band. I could get another keyboard player, but the kid's phenomenal. I tried to pack Colette off to New York but she's not budging. She's latched onto Tad to get back at me. The lady is supremely fucked up. And the kid's in love. I bloody well don't know what to do."

"The tour'll be over soon. But that won't make any difference. Tad's planning to take her back to London. She's really bad news."

"I'm hip. But I can't stop her from jamming stuff down her throat and up her nose and into her veins. She's not my bloody responsibility."

"But Tad is. I mean, Colette knows what she's doing, but he doesn't. He's just wowed by what a great fuck she is."

"I'll talk to him. Maybe I can figure out something." He slumped back in his chair. "Fuck, I've had it. It's all I can bloody do to hang on another two weeks myself. I'm sick of all this shit that's going down. D'you hear Kenny caught the clap from some space cadet in St. Louis?"

"Hey, Garth." Tony Silver stuck his head in the door. "Sandy needs you . . . to go over the recording contract. He's waiting for you in his room."

As Garth got up to go he fixed Juno with a hard stare. "You know why I got rid of 'em, don't you?"

Garth did not have to talk to Tad Otis as it turned out. After the concert in San Diego, Tad collapsed and was rushed to the hospital. They pumped his stomach and released him the next day. He was okay but seriously shaken by the incident. The Collector disappeared shortly afterward; no one seemed to know where she had gone. Tad was a bit morose after she took off, but he was too glad to be alive to mope for long.

The night Tad was rushed to the hospital Juno stayed up keeping vigil with Garth and Tony and the other members of the group. They had been allowed to hide out in a tiny supply room, away from the hoard of reporters and hero-worshipers who had shown up as soon as word of Tad's collapse had leaked to the outside. When the word came that Tad was going to be all right, Garth insisted that everybody go back to the hotel and get some rest. But he and Juno and Tony stayed, in order to be able to see Tad when he came to. After all the craziness of the past weeks, this night they sat sipping Pepsi from a nearby vending machine and reminiscing about the Scrap Metal days.

Garth seemed stripped of all glitter. He was there, concerned, vulnerable, caring. "You know, Tad comes from the same neighborhood I do in Liverpool. It hasn't changed much since I was a kid. It's either stealing cars or playing music. I was fourteen when the Beatles came up. It's funny, Tad was the same age when Scrap Metal took off. When you're that age, rock stars are everything. There's nothin' else matters. Just the music, and the fame. You never see through the cracks at all the dirt inside. All the different ways to kill yourself. And ultimately it's all bloody ridiculous. If he'd died I'd've had to face his mum, and what the fuck do you say? He was famous, he made a lot of money, a lot of chicks balled him. So bloody what?"

Maybe Juno was not running away from anything. Maybe she was running away from everything—away from Shep, David and her childhood, Lydia and Alex, away from Garth. Maybe it was time to stop running, to turn and face something: herself.

Goddammit, she was attracted to Garth. She had been jerking herself around this whole tour. Making up her mind to sleep with him, then pulling back when she saw him surrounded by other women, or when a phone call from Shep pricked her conscience. But something had started between them years ago. An unconsummated lust.

Except now it went beyond that. She knew Garth now. He was egomaniacal and selfish, but he was a poet too, and a brilliant performer. And he did care about people. Juno had seen that in his concern over Tad.

He cared about her now. But was it because she was the only woman around him who had steered clear of his bed? He had made a gesture, gotten rid of the three bunnies. But what would happen if she were to finally end this dance of flirtation and go to bed with Garth? Would it be the real thing? A commitment, a relationship? Or would Garth lose interest once the challenge was gone? Would he get rid of her, too?

And there was Shep. Lately, they talked on the phone nearly every night. Juno knew he was being faithful to her, and she had been faithful to him. But now she felt so torn. It was beyond the horniness she felt. She had been celibate for longer than this before. It was the different life-styles, the different worlds she was straddling. On one side there was Shep . . . loving, secure, witty, presentable. Shep would fit in anywhere. He was her link to the world she knew, the world she had grown up in.

Then, Garth. A life with him would be exciting, but how much excitement could a person take, day in and day out? Garth was a superstar. Juno would always be in his shadow. How would she deal with her own ego? How would she deal with the women who would always be throwing themselves at Garth? Could she bear to share him?

There was only one answer. Juno had to get it on with Garth and go from there. She could not fully commit herself to Shep as long as she had doubts. A fling with Garth might turn into something, or it might be just that . . . a fling. And what was wrong with a fling? If she was in fact going to marry Shep, this might be the perfect good-bye to single life.

The crowds began to pile up outside the Hollywood Bowl in the early morning. They were basically good-natured—smoking dope, dancing, blowing bubbles, flipping Frisbees through the air. Some girls took off their tops and shook their breasts to the music that blared from radios and cassette players, attracting the passing interest of a few of the people in their immediate vicinity. Entrepreneurs wandered through the crowd selling Tierra T-shirts and gourmet drugs.

Juno came by mid-morning to supervise the union crews who were putting up the light grids and to set up the board. When she left around five with Tony Silver the crowd was huge and beginning to get restless. As they made their way to the limo a girl rushed over and grabbed Juno's arm. "Is he in there? Is Garth in there? I've got to see him!"

They escaped into the car. "No originality," Juno said. "It's the same everywhere."

"Yeah," Tony said. "You come to appreciate cleverness. Like that bird who got into Garth's hotel room in Chicago by climbing up the side of the building."

Juno laughed. "Where there's a will there's a way."

"Not bad," Tony said. "Talk about originality."

Garth's bungalow at the Beverly Hills Hotel was filled with the usual retinue. The TV was on, the telephone kept ringing, a buffet and bar had been set up. Tobacco and marijuana smoke mingled in the air. Clive Riggins, the drummer, was stretched out on the masseuse's table getting a rubdown. Garth was in the corner with his acoustic guitar, working on a song. Juno went over and sat on the arm of his chair.

"How about tonight?" she said.

"How about tonight what?"

"I'm tired of playing games. I'm ready for the main event."

A smile spread over Garth's face. He put his hand on her thigh and squeezed it. "Sounds good to me."

Juno got back to her room after the concert around one. Garth had had to put in an appearance at a party given by the head of the record company. He promised to be there by two.

She showered and washed her hair, and ordered a bottle of champagne from room service. She put on a large Tierra T-shirt that just covered her buttocks, and sat on the bed drying her hair and watching *Casablanca* on the late movie. When the end credits rolled on the screen, she looked at her watch. It was quarter of three.

Well, Juno, she said to herself, *you're not the irresistible piece of ass you thought you were.* Garth had obviously found someone to distract him at the party. She should have gone, she supposed. He had wanted her to. But if his attention span was no better than that, fuck him.

Juno opened the champagne and poured herself a glass. "Here's to you, Shep," she said. "It looks like I'm going to be faithful after all."

Colette had slipped into Garth's bungalow early in the evening, when the night maid was clearing up and turning down the bed. It was not difficult. She had been around this scene so long there was no trick she had not tuned to perfection.

Oh, she knew all the ropes—had woven many of them herself, from the raw hemp of anxiety. It was an anxiety to be included, a fear of missing out on something important. Colette had grown up on a frozen dirt farm in a tiny town called Palmarolle, Quebec, with nothing around her but cows and ice hockey players. As she grew older, and her body suddenly blossomed from skin and bones to something exciting and negotiable, she fled Palmarolle and made her way south, eventually coming to New York.

Colette lied about her age to get a job as a Playboy bunny. But her real love was rock music, and specifically, rock musicians. She slept with many of them and wore her charm bracelet of trophies proudly. But she had never fallen in love with any of them until Garth Meacham.

The Collector. She had begun to hate that nickname now. She had not added a Garth Meacham charm to her bracelet. It was not like that with him. But Garth could not see that. And so he had thrown her aside with the others, to make room for Juno Johnson. Well, it was not going to be that way.

The bungalow was dark, except for what pale illumination came through the windows. Colette pulled off her rhinestoned calfskin boots and peeled down her skintight jeans, then unbuttoned her soft painted chamois shirt and dropped it on the pile on the floor. Naked, she wandered around the room, touching things that were Garth's.

She began to shiver with nervousness, so she got her works out of her bag and gave herself a quick fix. After that she felt better. She knew that it was going to be all right. Garth would be back here to meet Juno by two, Colette had heard him say that. He would find her in time and save her, and then he would know how much she and only she loved him. He would realize how much he loved her, too.

At one o'clock Colette opened the bottle of pills and swallowed them.

Tuesday was her birthday. In three days she would be thirty. And this time she would get what she wanted.

The phone rang in Juno's room around three. She had just turned off the lights.

"Hello?"

It was Garth. "It's the Collector," he said. His voice was trembling. "She's dead. Can you come down here?"

Juno arrived just after the police. Colette's body was spread naked across Garth's bed. There was an empty bottle of pills on the floor beneath her dangling hand. She had scrawled "I love you, Garth" in lipstick across her body. Some of the letters were backward, as if she had done it in a mirror. A police photographer was taking pictures.

Garth came over and hugged Juno. "She was there when I came in. The cops say she's been dead about an hour. Oh Jesus, Juno."

Juno held him and rocked him until a policeman came over. "We've got to take down your statement, Mr. Meacham."

"Okay."

"Looks like she thought you'd be back a little sooner."

Juno stood mesmerized, staring at the body. There were needle tracks up both arms. A faint bluish tinge was beginning to form around the edges of her mouth. One hand cupped with bizarre modesty between her open thighs. Juno had never seen a dead person before. She kept waiting for Cottonbrain to move.

The inspector had out his notebook. "Did you know her, Mr. Meacham?"

"Yeah, she hung around the tour for a while."

"What was her name?"

"Colette . . . that's all she ever used. I never knew her last name."

After the police had removed the body, Garth came up to Juno's room. They sat and talked and drank until daylight. They fell asleep together fully clothed on Juno's bed.

The tour ended two nights later. She and Garth never did make love. Instead of waiting to take the private jet back to London, Juno booked herself on a commercial flight.

"I'm sorry it didn't work out, luv," Garth said as she was leaving. "Maybe when I get back to London."

Juno kissed him. "No, Garth, I'm sorry. It just wasn't in the cards. I'm getting married."

Chapter Twenty-three

The twelve-hour TWA flight from L.A. to London was a decompression chamber for Juno. She ordered three Bloody Marys when the stewardess came around and drank the first one down in a long swallow. After nearly three months on tour with Tierra, she was richer, thinner, strung out from too much wine and cocaine and too little sleep, and still shaky from Colette's suicide. She thought a lot about Garth and what had and had not happened between them, and after the third Bloody Mary, as the 747 sped ahead through time zones, she finally slept. When she woke up the sun was streaming through the window. It was one-thirty in the morning Los Angeles time, but midmorning in London. They would be landing in a few hours.

Juno went to the bathroom and splashed water on her face. She brushed her hair, changed her shirt, and put on fresh makeup. Her face looked tired to her, and slightly unfamiliar, and she wondered if Shep would still look the same. So much had happened, she wondered too how it would be with Shep. Would they fall back into their easy relationship, or would they be estranged?

The plane landed on schedule at Heathrow, and Juno went through passport and customs feeling apprehensive about seeing Shep. If he was there at all. She had wired him, but being the middle of the day he may have had a business luncheon he could not get out of.

When she came out with her bags, she saw Shep and waved. Instead of coming to her he turned away, raising his arms. Before Juno could figure out what was going on, he brought them down in a conductor's gesture and she heard the first strains of a

Mozart divertimento. Beyond him, she saw a woodwind quintet, in evening dress, seated on folding chairs.

Juno broke into a smile. "I don't believe this!" She ran to Shep and embraced him as the crowd in the airport broke into delighted applause.

"Welcome home, darling," he said after he kissed her. "After all those weeks of total hipness, I decided you needed a complete change."

At that moment a butler appeared, rolling a tea cart containing tea, sherry, cucumber sandwiches, and Cornish pasties.

Juno laughed, locking her arm in Shep's. "You're crazy . . . this is wonderful!"

"Will you have tea, Miss Johnson?" the butler asked.

"Of course."

The quintet moved into a mazurka by Tchaikovsky and Juno sat sipping her tea, chuckling and shaking her head. "Oh, Shep, I can't tell you how wonderful it is to see you."

Shep smiled and sat down next to her with his glass of sherry. "I'm awfully glad. This would have been a hell of a letdown if you hadn't."

Juno took his hand and squeezed it. "I love you so much. I think I had to get away in order to realize it."

"Then I haven't lost you to the glitter of the rock world?"

"Oh, Shep, never again. Not even for the money."

As the quintet went into an Irish chanty, Juno finished her tea. Shep went over and gave some instructions to the butler.

"All right, darling. Are you ready for Phase Two of your welcome home?"

"My God, Shep . . . here?"

"No," he said, smiling. "Not here."

The suite at the Hyde Park Hotel in Knightsbridge was filled with assorted flowers. On the table by the brass bed was a bottle of wine in an ornamental silver *drageoir*, and next to it was a tray of hors d'oeuvres.

Shep tipped the bellboy and closed the door behind him. He turned to Juno and smiled. "Now," he said. "Phase Two?"

"If it can start with a bath."

"It does. Run moments before we arrived. It's piping hot, full of bubbles, and waiting for the same thing I'm waiting for. Your gorgeous naked body."

Juno soaked in a seascape of bubbles in the majestic bathtub, melting away the weariness of the trip. From the bedroom came the sounds of Paul Desmond's saxophone playing "My Funny Valentine" from *Desmond Blue*, her favorite tape. She got out of the bath, toweled off, and rubbed her body with Fracas body lotion.

Shep was lying naked in bed, on top of the covers. Rising in perpendicular magnificence from the center of his body was a large erection, tied with a bow and garnished on top with a smoked oyster from the hors d'oeuvres tray. "Phase Two, part two."

Juno laughed and flung herself upon him to devour the smoked oyster.

For a while they played, spreading nipples with cream cheese and nibbling it off, drinking the wine and dribbling it over each other's bodies, sucking toes and fingertips. For both of them it was the end of a three-month fast, and they drew it out, making it last as long as possible. But finally Juno felt a tremor building up inside her that could not be put off any longer.

"I want you now," she whispered, and kissed Shep with savage intensity. He pulled her down on top of him and she cried aloud with pleasure as he entered her. She rode him, screaming with exhilaration, until they crescendoed and came together, almost at the same time. They lay there, panting and sweating and sticky, and in love.

After a while Shep raised himself up on an elbow and poured the rest of the wine into their glasses. "Welcome home," he said.

Juno smiled contentedly. "I've never felt so welcome."

He ran his fingertips over her long tanned body. "You've lost weight."

Juno pinched his waist. "You haven't."

"What do you mean?" Shep protested indignantly. "I've been jogging ever since you left."

"My God, you must be exhausted," Juno giggled. "Oh, Shep, you do look wonderful. I've missed you so much."

"Don't ever go away again. No, cancel that. I didn't mean it. Do whatever you want, as long as you come back to me."

"You know what I want, Shep?"

"No." He kissed her breasts. "What?"

"I want to get married. Soon. As soon as possible."

A wide grin spread across his face. "Have you got the chap picked out?"

"No. But I'm interviewing . . ."

They were married a week before Christmas at Elder's Parsonage, Shep's parents' home. Hollis and Maria Johnson flew over several weeks before to help Juno get ready. They helped her move out of the tiny place on Adam and Eve Mews, to the profound regret of Simon Parrie, and into a considerably larger town house that she and Shep had bought on Egerton Crescent. Juno had taken off the fall to recuperate from the Tierra tour and to work on decorating the town house. She and Shep were keeping three floors and renting out the ground floor to a writer friend of Shep's.

It was a small ceremony. Lydia was matron of honor, and Alex was Shep's best man. Lydia's daughters, Alexandra and India, were flower girls. John and Ursula Fletcher were there, and Claire Reed, and several of Shep's and Juno's closest friends from theater and publishing. At the reception afterward, Alex and Shep entertained with vintage Sage and Wise routines, from their prep school days. John Fletcher sang an old music hall number called "They're Moving Father's Grave to Build a Sewer," Hollis Johnson responded with a recitation of "The Gobbuluns'll Getcha," Maria played the piano while Juno and Lydia did a duet on "She's More to Be Pitied Than Censured."

Late in the evening, after all the guests had gone, the Johnsons left for the little inn up the road where they were staying, and the elder Wises retired to bed. The three couples sat up by the fire, sipping brandy and talking.

"Come on, Juno, tell," Lydia wheedled. "Where are you two going on your honeymoon?"

Juno shook her head. "Uh-uh. You wouldn't tell, remember? I'll tell you this . . . we're not going by balloon."

Lydia suddenly burst into a fit of giggles. "Oh, Alex—remember the time at Yale when you were trying to impress that girl from Vassar? That time with the plane?"

"Oh yeah! One of my great moments," Alex reminisced. "Candy, her name was. I asked her out for a cup of coffee. I picked her up at her dorm in a chauffeured limo. I was in black tie. We drove to the local airfield, where I had a private plane standing by. We flew to Boston, while a uniformed steward, who was my faithful roomie Bruce Hopkins, mixed martinis and served us canapés. In Boston another limo met us and took us to the Ritz. We walk in. The maître d', primed beforehand with ten bucks and the kick of being in on a college prank, greets us, 'Ah, Mister Sage, what a pleasure to have you with us again! The usual table, sir? In the corner?' 'Quite right, Frank,' I say. We're seated. A waiter appears bearing a silver tray with a silver coffee service, and two cups. He pours. We drink. We leave. Back to the limo, back to the plane, back to Poughkeepsie. Back to her dorm. I kiss her good night."

"And you never even called her again," Juno remembered, laughing. "God, you can imagine what she thought . . . that she had blown it by having bad breath or smelly armpits or something."

Alex grinned. "It was too perfect. Nothing I could have ever done would have lived up to that. I couldn't see her again. Besides, it turned out she was a little boring."

"Gosh, Alex," Tory Sage said, a little plaintively, "you never told me that story."

"Oh well . . ." he smiled apologetically at his wife, and then suddenly turned to Juno and Lydia. "Oh, remember that roommate you had . . . the one who was never there?"

Juno's face lit up. "Kippy O'Connor!"

"The girl with the reputation for giving the best blow jobs in New England," Lydia giggled. Stefan made a disapproving face.

"Right. That's the one. I saw her on the subway about a month ago. She's a nun."

"A nun?"

"I swear to God. Black robes, white collar, and rosary beads all over the place. *She* recognized me."

"I can't believe it," Juno said. "Oh, I wonder whatever happened to Tommy Hoadley . . ."

Tory yawned pointedly. "This is fascinating," she said. "I *love* other people's 'remember when' conversations."

"I'm sorry, honey," Alex said. "We'll be going in a few minutes. As a matter of fact, Tommy Hoadley is a vice-president of a chain of dry cleaning stores. But Whit Zimmerman told me Tommy's running a poker game in the back of one of them . . ."

Shep leaned over and tapped Tory's arm. "Can you come with me and help me whip up some savouries?"

"Don't they make you mad?" Tory fumed as they went into the kitchen, past Stefan who was sitting perfectly upright in his chair, sound asleep.

Shep smiled and shook his head consolingly. "Don't worry about it," he said. "They haven't all been together in a long time. Let them have their memories tonight. We'll have them back tomorrow."

The next morning Juno and Shep flew to Morocco on their honeymoon.

"I don't know why I was so nervous about getting married," Juno said, as she fed Shep ripe figs in their room at the Hotel Mamounia.

"Many virgins feel that way before their wedding," Shep assured her solemnly, and then he laughed. "I don't know why you did."

"You mean . . . that stuff we did before . . . that was *it?*"

"No, not really. You're still a virgin until you've been tied up." He smiled angelically. "Shall I ring for room service to bring up some rope?"

For the next two weeks they tanned themselves by day and made love in the warm and magical Moroccan nights. Juno was glad that she had finally taken the step of commitment to Shep. She was relaxed and contented, and so was he.

Back in London, Juno returned to work with John Fletcher, concentrating mainly on lighting design. Shep changed jobs and became senior editor of a small but prestigious publishing house. They kept up a busy social schedule, and their dinner parties were sought-after invitations, bringing together witty theater and literary people and Juno's old Yale friends who passed through London. Twice a year Juno and Shep coordinated their schedules and took a holiday. Sometimes it was a relaxing fortnight in Devon or Santa Fe, other times it was a photographic safari in Africa or a trek through Bhutan.

The passion disappeared rather quickly from their marriage, but their sexual life was perfectly adequate. Sometimes they made love every night for a week; other times weeks would go by. It seemed to Juno that this was probably normal enough for married life; and after a conversation with Lydia, who had finally produced a son for Stefan and had not had sex with him since, Juno decided that she was damned lucky. Once when Shep was away Juno slept with an actor she had been attracted to, but she felt too guilty to enjoy it. She was not interested in getting involved in an affair.

Juno and Shep got along very well, although as years passed and their professions consumed more time, they were together less and less. Book fairs and business trips took Shep away for the occasional week, and although Juno's work was in London there were hectic binges that kept her up late and got her out early, so that even though they were sharing the same quarters, she and Shep went for days without running into each other.

There was a more serious flaw in their basically congenial life, and it became increasingly a bone of contention between Shep and Juno. Shep wanted children. Juno was not ready. Her career was going well; *it* fulfilled her. Children now might throw it off course. She did not close the door, but the moment was never right to go through it either. It bothered Shep, Juno knew that, but there was plenty of time. She was still young. And Shep could wait; he had waited before.

Shortly before their fifth anniversary, Juno was offered a job to do the lighting for a new private nightclub, Mollie's. It was to be located on Kensington High Street and would cater to an exclusive British and international clientele. It was a new direction for Juno and she was very excited about it.

Five years was the vague timetable that Juno had set in her promises to Shep for getting pregnant. Back in the winter of 1976 it had seemed comfortably off in the future. Now, all of a sudden, it was here.

On their anniversary they dined at Langan's Brasserie with Claire Reed and the man she was currently seeing, a director named Sean O'Fegan. Claire had just returned from a six-month stint on Broadway in *What the Dickens,* which had been transported from its successful West End run. Sean had directed the London production.

"To the happy couple," Sean toasted. "Five years of marriage. A new record in this blighted second half of the twentieth century. My longest marriage only lasted three years. And that was when I was *really* in love. How do you do it?"

"We never see each other," Juno laughed.

"Well, if anything happened to your marriage it would absolutely destroy everybody's faith in the whole lousy institution," Claire said.

"Oh please." Shep held up his hands. "We can't stand this sort of pressure."

"Yes, Claire, if we don't make it till our next anniversary we'll know who to blame."

"I'm as blameless as the Blessed Virgin. Can't a body simply worship at the shrine?"

"By next anniversary, we'll be an entire Holy Family for you to worship. This is the year we throw out the Pill and start fornicating in earnest," Shep announced.

"Oh, Juno! That's marvelous."

Juno smiled and took a sip of her champagne.

Later that night, as they were getting ready for bed, Shep picked up Juno's plastic disk of birth control pills from her dresser and tossed them into the wastepaper basket.

"In an informal ceremony this evening in the home of Mr. and Mrs. Shepherd Wise of Fifty-three Egerton Crescent, contraception was banned until further notice. When asked what his plans were for the immediate future, Mr. Wise answered, 'I'm going to fuck my bloody brains out.' "

Juno laughed as Shep dove into bed next to her. But after they had made love and Shep had fallen asleep, Juno retrieved the pills from the wastepaper basket, took one, and concealed the disk in the back of her lingerie drawer.

Shep's parents were spending the winter in Cuernavaca and had left the house in Tadsworth open for Shep and Juno to use on weekends. But they had used it seldom. Juno's work on the club, Mollie's, took most of her time, and she was also working with John Fletcher on two big-budgeted West End productions. One week in March, Shep insisted that he and Juno get away for a quiet weekend at Elder's Parsonage. Juno relented, feeling a bit guilty about leaving Shep alone so many evenings.

They left London midafternoon on Friday, to avoid the weekend traffic. Shep drove and Juno dozed as they passed through the gray outlying areas of the city. When she woke they were on the highway. The sky which had been promising rain all day had opened into a light drizzle.

"I must've dropped off," she said. "How long did I sleep?"

"About half an hour. I'm glad. You really need the rest."

"Yes . . . you were right to insist we get away this weekend. I don't even care if it rains. Then we can stay inside and be cozy without the pressure of *doing* things."

Shep laughed. "We can do inside things. Like work on the baby. I'm sure the reason you haven't gotten pregnant is because you're overworked." He glanced over at her. "Still, I've been thinking. Maybe you should see a doctor. You know, have the equipment checked out to make sure everything's in the right place."

"I've had checkups before. Everything's fine."

"You don't think it's me, do you?"

"Darling, not everybody gets knocked up right away. There's *nothing* to worry about."

Shep smiled and rubbed his hand along her thigh. "I love you."

"I love you, too." She hated deceiving him about the Pill. She felt rotten. But it would not be for much longer.

The next morning Juno slept in. Shep decided to do the weekend marketing by himself but remembered he was short of cash. He found Juno's handbag on the hall table and took fifteen pounds from her wallet. As he was putting it back he saw the pink birth control disk. He picked it up and looked at it. Friday's pill had been taken. He felt hurt and betrayed. Then an uncontrollable rage rose through him.

He took the stairs two at a time and flung open the bedroom door. "Wake up!" he shouted.

Juno's eyes opened with alarm, and she sat up in bed. "What's wrong?"

"What the goddamn fucking hell is this?" He threw the pills at her.

"Oh . . ."

"Is that all you can fucking say? *Oh?*"

"Shep . . . I'm sorry . . ."

"What sort of a game do you think you're playing? Jerking me around like this . . . lying to me!" He came at her and Juno shrank back. For the first time since she had known him she was truly terrified that he was going to hit her. Instead he grabbed up the plastic disk and hurled it against the wall. When it landed on the floor he picked up a boot and, using it as a hammer, smashed the disk again and again until the plastic was shattered and the pills were ground to powder. Then he turned back to Juno, breathing heavily. His eyes were still full of fury.

"Do you have a lover? Is that why you're never home nights? Is that why you couldn't give up your bloody precious pills? Because you were afraid it might be his kid and not mine?"

"No, Shep." Juno's face was as pale as the sheets. "It's not that! It's nothing like that. It's just . . ." She broke off and began to cry.

"Oh, Christ! Spare me. Come on, stop it! I want to hear what you have to say. I'm dying of curiosity to hear what you have to say." Shep sat down in the armchair by the window and glared at her.

Juno reached for a tissue and dabbed her eyes. Tears continued to roll out of them. She began to hiccup. Shep kept looking at her unsympathetically. "Shep . . ." She hiccuped again. "It isn't at all what you think. There's no one else. Just you. I . . . I've kept taking the pills because . . . I'm not ready to have a baby." She hiccuped again. "I mean, it's very easy for you to sit back and announce that you're going to have a family. But *you* don't have to get pregnant. *You* don't have to give up your career . . ."

"Hey, wait a minute! I thought you were the bloody liberated one. How many times have I heard you hold forth to your women friends about the importance of working after you have children? I'm not Mr. Male Chauvinist. I'm willing to change nappies and babysit while you work late. I'll interview nannies. I'll even make baby food in the bloody blender. It's true, though, you will have to have the baby. Biologically there's no way we can get around it."

"I do want to have a child, Shep. Just not now. Give me six months. I'll be finished with the club, and I'll take some time off. Then we'll do it."

"How many times have I heard this before? I'll be finished with the play . . . I'll be finished with the club. You know, Juno, we could start now. You could have your six months and still have three to spare. If you were serious."

"I am serious, Shep. But what if I had one of those lousy pregnancies like Lydia had with India? I've got a contract with Mollie. I can't risk getting sick and not being able to finish the job. Surely you understand that."

"All right, Lydia had a tough time with India. But we saw her before she had Forrest, and she was glowing. Even playing tennis in her ninth month." Shep sighed. "I'm thirty-four years old. I want to have children while I'm still young enough to do things with them. I don't want them calling me Gramps."

"Don't worry, darling. You still have many childbearing years ahead of you." She got out of bed and knelt beside him and put her arms around him. "Six months. I absolutely promise."

Mollie's Club opened in September with a splash of publicity second only to the Royal Wedding the year before. The invited guests at the opening included members of the royal family, the aristocracy, and untitled wealthy who ranged from barristers to rock stars.

The design of the club was high-tech space station, swirling white molded-plastic levels joined by ramps, automatic sliding doors, and moving stairs. It was Juno's lighting that lifted it off the ground. The club was crisscrossed with laser shafts and ee-rily moving balls of colored light. Each area was bathed in a different color to establish its mood. Periodically sections of the floor lit up. Around the walls were large porthole windows through which could be seen a galaxy of stars and planets that Juno had created.

Juno and Shep arrived with Ursula and John Fletcher, and

Claire Reed, who was with the co-star of her first film, a hand-some American actor named Perry Bennett. The television cameras followed them as they walked through the glare of lights and disappeared inside.

Mollie Spencer rushed over to them and gave Juno a kiss. "Everything's going splendidly. Darling, it's absolutely stunning. Everybody's talking about the lighting. And Shep . . . you look stunning tonight, too. Claire . . . what a ravishing dress . . ."

Mollie took them to their table and rushed off to greet Prince Andrew. They drank champagne and Juno accepted the congratulations of friends who stopped by. Finally, when there was a break in the action, Juno lured Shep onto the dance floor.

"You've done an extraordinary job, darling," Shep told her.

"You see," she teased, "I wasn't having an affair. All those nights I was working late I was really working."

"So you were. I can see why you were so excited about all this."

Shep was a good dancer, all arms and legs and energy. He was happy for her tonight, she could tell that, and yet she had the feeling that there was something bothering him, too.

On the way back to their table, Juno took his arm. "Are you all right, darling? A penny for your thoughts."

Shep patted her hand. "Oh . . . everything's fine . . . a bit tired. But this is your night. You've earned it. I won't drag you home until you're ready to go."

Mollie came over. "Shep, darling, you won't mind if I steal Juno for a few minutes?"

"Of course not." He kissed Juno's cheek.

"There are some Italians who are dying to meet you, Juno. Let's see, ah, here they are. Gianni Corelli and Mario Trapani . . . this is Juno Johnson-Wise, the lady you've been asking about. Juno, darling, I'm sure your ears were burning. These gentlemen have been saying some marvelous things about your lighting. They are opening a club on the Costa Smeralda, and they're absolutely mad to . . ."

Corelli interrupted, laughing. "Mollie, do not tell her everything. I have carefully rehearsed my little speech."

"You're right, darling. I'm sorry. I'll leave you three alone."
With a fluttering of her white hands she was gone.

Gianni Corelli smiled. "We would very much like you to visit
Sardinia with your husband, as our guests. And while you are
there, you can look at the location of the club we propose to
build."

"From what we have seen here," Signor Trapani added,
"there is no question in our minds that you are the one person
who can truly do justice to Evviva!"

"I'm very flattered. And very tempted. But I'm afraid I'm
going to be tied up for the next year or so."

Corelli smiled. "We will not be put off as easily as that. But
perhaps this is not the right place to conduct this discussion.
Here is my card. I will be at the Dorchester until the middle of
next week."

Juno accepted the card. "Thanks a lot. But I really don't think
there's much chance . . ."

"Even so. You know where to reach us."

Juno rose the next day around noon. Her head ached a bit
from all the drinks of the night before. But otherwise she felt
marvelous. She showered and went downstairs in her robe to
make coffee. To her surprise, Shep was sitting in the window
seat. Several morning papers were on the table in front of him.

"Hello, darling, I thought you had a tennis date."

"Oh no. I canceled it. I've been reading about you in the papers. Mollie's is a rave, and you, darling, are the woman of the
hour."

Juno grinned. "Really? Where? Let me see!" She scanned the
reviews that Shep had set out for her. "I can't believe it. You'd
think I'd designed the Statue of Liberty. It's all so exciting!" She
poured herself a cup of coffee. "Have you had breakfast? Are
you hungry?"

"No, and no. Coffee's all I feel up to. Look, after your coffee
do you want to get dressed and take a walk with me?"

"Hmmm. That's a lovely idea. It looks like a beautiful day."
Then she looked at Shep's face. There were dark, bruised shadows around his eyes, as if he had not slept, or slept only a little.

There was the slight twitch in his cheek that he got when he was tense. "Shep . . . what's the matter?"

"That job you did on the club . . . all these critics are right, you know. It really is sensational. You are an extremely talented woman. This is what you were meant to do."

Juno brought her coffee over and sat next to him. She looked at him uneasily. "Only one of the things. I'm keeping my promise to you, you know. I'm throwing my pills out. Any seed you plant from now on . . ."

"Stop, Juno." His face had no color. He took her hands. "Oh, Juno, I'm so sorry . . ."

"Shep, darling . . . what is it?"

"Oh God, I don't know where to even start." He took a breath. "I feel so terrible." He stood up and crossed the kitchen and leaned on the counter by the toaster. His next words were spoken with his back to Juno. "We haven't seen much of each other these last months. Oh, I'm not blaming you. What happened just happened." He turned around to face her. "One day last spring I was picking out a tie in Harrods after work. It was a night I knew you wouldn't be home till late. Anyway, I ran into Claire. She was free, too, so we had dinner. Honestly, darling, all we did was talk about you and how wonderful you are. I dropped her off in a cab that night, and that was all there was to it."

Juno looked at him apprehensively. "That night . . . but there were others, right?"

"God knows there was plenty of opportunity," he said resentfully. "You were busy so often, working late so many nights. About a week later, Josh at the office gave me a pair of tickets to the ballet. I called you, you remember? But you couldn't get away. So I tried Claire, on the off-chance that she might be free. And she was. That night was the beginning. Neither of us set out to have an affair. I mean, we've known each other for years. She adores you . . ."

"Yeah . . . I can see that. What are friends for?"

"Oh please, don't hate Claire. She feels as bad as I."

"Okay . . . you're having an affair, and I was too busy to notice. So. Where do we go from here?"

Shep closed his eyes. "Oh, Juno, I hate this. I wish it could be

undone . . . but it can't. No, I don't know, maybe it's all the
way it was meant to be." When he opened his eyes there were
tears in them. "Juno . . . Claire's having a baby. Our baby. I
care about you so much, Juno . . . I always will. But I love
Claire, and I want this baby. She wants it, too . . ."

Juno looked at him, in shock. A choking feeling rose in her
throat. "And you want a divorce?"

"I don't want to hurt you."

"But you want a divorce."

"Yes," Shep said.

The house on Egerton Crescent was put up for sale. Juno and
Shep used the same lawyer, and he was handling everything. It
was all to be split down the middle. There was no quarrel.

Juno fluctuated between numbness and overwhelming sadness. She hated Claire, who had been her close friend and had
betrayed her. She wanted to hate Shep, too, but she could not.
He had always made it clear what he wanted. It was she who
had tried to have it her own way, on her own terms. She had
been totally engrossed with her career. No, it was not Shep's
fault; it was hers.

But the sense of loss engulfed her. She had finally been ready
to settle down and have a baby with Shep. Shep, who had been
her closest friend for a long time. Now there was no Shep. And
there would be no baby.

Two weeks later, after a tearful parting with John and Ursula
Fletcher, Juno headed for Sardinia. Her life, as she had lived it
for the past seven years, was simply over.

Part Five

Alex, 1974-83

Chapter Twenty-four

The New York *Times*, September 16, 1974

THEATER: 'A HERO'S DEATH'; AN IRONIC FIST IN A VELVET GLOVE

By Walker Monk

Near the end of the first act of Alexander Sage's *"A Hero's Death,"* which opened last night at the Theater de Lys, Harvey Latham (Christopher McClellan), the so-called hero of the ironic title, says bitterly *"bravery is an accident. Only a creep would want to be a hero."* This is the message that Sage delivers in his interesting but desultory drama of a man whose mask is torn off by fear of death in the rice paddies of Vietnam.

Harvey's one act of bravery was instinct. During high school he saved three children from a burning house and became a small-town hero. He accepts his heroism with the same credulity as he accepts his patriotism. When he is drafted he reports without question. But on the eve of his company's departure for Vietnam he comes face-to-face with both of those isms and finds that neither can stand up to his fear of death.

The play takes place in the forty-eight hours between Harvey Latham's desertion and his suicide. He hides out in the Brooklyn apartment of Kerry Masters (Donald Standing), a college acquaintance whose crippled leg has kept him from testing his own courage as a conscientious objector. The two are not close friends, but Kerry is the only person Harvey can think of who will not judge him. And he is right. His parents hang up on him and his girlfriend Kate (Ellen Brill) agrees to see him only to change his mind.

This is a drama of dialogue and ideas; and if the ideas are not partic-

ularly original, the dialogue is nimble. Sage is a facile writer who polishes the surface of his subject to a brilliant shine; but like Turtle Wax, he has no concern for what lies beneath the hard shell finish. As in last season's flimsy but witty "Other Lovers" he still has the power to make us laugh, but the laughter here is an ironic safety net, as deceptive as Harvey's heroism.

Christopher McClelland gives a compelling performance as Harvey. As the crippled idealist, Donald Standing is eloquently pathetic, if perhaps too controlled. Miss Brill takes Kate as far as the script will allow, and perhaps a bit further. Michael Girard's direction of the actors is neat, although his pacing is uneven. Jack Tilden's set is appropriately depressing. The lighting by Mioshi is of the too-dark school. One has the feeling the actors may be doing things we know not of.

"A Hero's Death" is ultimately a glibly depressing indictment of the prefabricated shells within which we lead our lives. Sage has an interesting voice; someday perhaps he will have something important to say with it.

Alex stood at the back of the theater and counted the house. There were thirty-seven people in the audience. At the final curtain the applause was enthusiastic but seventy-four hands were not enough to make much noise.

He picked up his coat and went backstage. Chris McClelland was talking to some friends. Alex recognized them as the occupants of row C. "You were great tonight," he said, patting Chris on the back as he walked by. *Friends,* he thought to himself. *Not even the general public. How much longer can we go on like this?*

"Alex," Donald Standing called out. "How did it look from out front?"

"Terrific. You were hot tonight."

"The house was better," the actor said, a little anxiously.

"Yeah . . . I think it's picking up. Word of mouth."

Ellen Brill appeared, turning up the collar on her crocheted sweater. Her brown hair was still back in the ponytail that Kate wore in the play. She had naturally pretty looks—dark eyes, clear skin, no makeup when she was not on stage. She kissed Alex. "Ready?"

"Sure. You want to go for a drink?"

Ellen shook her head. "Too tired. Let's just go back to my place." She slipped her arm through his. "Good night everybody."

While Ellen put a Billie Holiday record on the stereo, Alex helped himself to a beer. "Want one?"

"Why not. You hungry? There's cold chicken and half of a Hershey bar."

"Where's the other half?"

"I gave it to Tyger." She picked up the cat and sat on the sofa. Alex handed her a beer.

"Were you out front tonight for the whole show?" Ellen asked.

"Yeah. It was a good night. You've really got that business with the telephone working beautifully."

"How many people did we have?"

"Oh, I don't know. It's definitely picking up."

"Come on, Alex. How many?"

"Thirty-seven."

"Well, that is better than last night. Of course most of them were Chris's cousin and her friends from Fairleigh Dickinson. Look, Alex, you can be straight with me. What's the prognosis?"

"Word of mouth's building. We're been open only three weeks. These things take time."

"And money. Thirty-seven tickets, Alex. That doesn't even pay the janitor."

"Give me a break, for Christ's sake! What, have you got something better to do?"

"I might. I'm sorry, Alex, but I've got to know. Irving wants me to go out to Hollywood. They're testing for a new series and he thinks I'm perfect. Not that I'm so gung-ho for television, but the money would be incredible."

"So you want to leave the play?"

She came over and sat on the arm of his chair. "It's not that I want to leave the play. I love it, you know that. It's just that . . . if it's going to close . . . I mean, they're casting this series now. I'd have to get out there by next week."

"And what about me? What about us?"

"Why don't you come out, too? You could find plenty of work
. . ."

"TV, shit." He got up and grabbed his coat.

"Oh, Alex, come on. You've got to understand. I'm not going
to leave the play . . . but if it's going to close anyway, I just
want to know."

"Okay. I'll let you know in a day or so."

"Thanks. That's all I'm asking." She leaned her body up
against his and put her arms around his neck. "Come on to bed,
why don't you? I'll give you a wonderful back rub."

Alex kissed her lightly, without feeling. "No. I think I'll head
home." He slipped out of her arms and left, closing the door
sharply behind him.

John Kinsolving poured coffee from the Mr. Coffee on his file
cabinet. He sat a mug down on the desk where Alex was looking
at the figures John had laid out for him.

"Look, old buddy," John said. "There's no way you're going
to make those numbers turn black, no matter how long you
stare at them." John Kinsolving was Alex's age, an investment
banker whose father had made a fortune manufacturing indus-
trial fans. He and Alex had met playing squash at the New York
Athletic Club and had become good friends. John was rangy and
athletic, with pale blond hair and brown eyes. He had put up
half the money for *A Hero's Death*. Alex himself had put up the
other half.

"How much would it take to keep it going . . . say, another
two weeks?" Alex asked, tossing the balance sheet on John's
desk. "Give the momentum a little more chance to build."

"More than you've got, Alex. More than I can afford. There's
a technical term for this in the financial market . . . it's called
up shit creek without a paddle." He put his hand on Alex's
shoulder. "I'm sorry. It's a great play. We got some good reviews
. . ."

"Yeah . . . the *Soho News* and the Bergen *Daily Record*."

"And the *Voice* and *The Daily News* . . . hell, even the *Times*
wasn't a pan."

" 'Sage has a voice . . . someday he'll learn to talk.' "

John grinned. "You should read what they said about Eugene

O'Neill when he started out. Look, Alex, I don't regret my investment. Everybody knows when you put money into the theater you're gambling your ass off. If I'd wanted a guaranteed profit I'd have backed Neil Simon. I believed in *A Hero's Death.* I still do. I consider it money well spent."

"Thanks, John. I appreciate it."

"Hey, look, it's not the end of the world. It's the end of this run . . . but there'll be more plays. What did the *Voice* call you? One of our most promising young playwrights? The next one'll do it for you, Alex."

Alex finished his coffee. "There won't be a next one. I'm written out."

"Bullshit. That's what you said after the last one."

"Yeah. But this time it was my money. I've got to get a job. I'm sick of all this."

"Don't take it so hard. You'll write another play. And I'll invest in it. Just don't get it done before the next fiscal year." He poured himself another cup of coffee. "By the way, Rosemary wanted me to invite you and Ellen to come for brunch on Sunday."

"Tell her I'd love to, but she'll have to fix me up with one of her beautiful friends. Ellen's heading for the coast as soon as the show closes."

"Oh? For a vacation?"

"Probably for good." He stood and smiled. "You know how some weeks things just don't go your way."

"Hey, I'm sorry. I thought you two were good together."

Alex shrugged. "Turns out it was a run-of-the-play contract. Well, I'll let you get back to your wheeling and dealing."

John walked him to the elevator. "I know you're feeling down, Alex. But you have no reason to. You're damned talented, and you're going to make it big." The elevator door opened. "Okay. See you Sunday at high noon."

Alex took a cab uptown. He was meeting Bruce Hopkins and a couple of other Yale friends at Orsini's for lunch.

Closing notices. That should be the title of his next play, or his autobiography. Or his suicide note. Today was Thursday. He and John had agreed to close the play after Saturday's performance. He had never posted the closing notices himself before. He had never been the producer before.

He had never been broke before.

And suddenly he could not face the idea of an extravagant lunch with his successful classmates. Bruce was a young executive with Occidental Petroleum. They were all young executives, and he was a failed playwright.

"Hey . . . let me off here," Alex instructed the cabbie as they passed Thirty-fourth Street.

Alex strolled up the Avenue of the Americas amid the lunch-hour crush of bodies. Secretaries on their way to Chock Full O' Nuts, guys pushing racks of cheap clothes. People scrambling for a living, and he was going to be one of them now. He bought a hot dog from a Sabrett's stand and turned into Bryant Park. A mime was performing in whiteface and a Marcel Marceau hat. A crowd of about fifty people had gathered around. More, he reflected, than had been in the Theater de Lys last night. He took a bite of the hot dog. It tasted terrible and he threw the rest into a trash can.

Actually, he thought to himself, things were not as bad as all that. He had twenty thousand dollars' worth of IBM stock his grandmother had left him. Back in the spring he had given it to Daniel Meisner, another Yale friend who was a stockbroker. Daniel had figured he could double it by taking Alex out of IBM and into some "more active issues." He had seen Daniel for lunch a few weeks ago, and his friend reported that his investments were "doing great" in spite of the lull in the current market. "I've got you in auto parts and Caravan Mobile Homes," Daniel told him. "With money the way it is, nobody can afford to build anymore. Nobody puts down roots. America's on the move."

Alex found a pay phone and reached Daniel on his way out to lunch.

"Hey, Alex. How's the play doing? I haven't caught it yet, but I'm planning to go next week."

"Better plan to go by Saturday. We're closing."

"Hey, that's a shame."

"Look, Daniel, what's happening with my portfolio? I need to get liquid."

"I'd hang on a couple of months, man. Market's going to go up."

"I haven't got a couple of months. I need the cash now."

"Whew . . . bad timing, Alex. The fact of the matter is Caravan's filed a Chapter Eleven. To be perfectly frank, they don't know what the fuck's going on down there right now. Their management team's huddling with the SEC next week and . . ."

Alex felt a cold anxiety strike his stomach. "Come on, Daniel. What's the bottom line? What have I got left?"

"Well . . . with the auto parts and that frozen chili company, and looking down the road, if Caravan gets this thing turned around . . ."

"How much?" Alex yelled into the phone, making no attempt to conceal his anger.

"Jesus, man." Daniel's voice was cool. "Let me figure it out a second." He came back on. "Well . . . let's say about three thou, give or take a few hundred."

"Oh shit." Three thousand. That would not last long. His apartment was five hundred a month.

"Alex? You still there?"

"Yeah," Alex sighed. "Sell it. Sell everything."

"You're making a big mistake . . ."

"Yeah, tell me about it." Alex slammed down the phone.

John Kinsolving threw a closing night party at the Coach House. The mood was forced gaiety in the best theatrical survival tradition. The ship had sunk. Another ship would come along.

The champagne flowed. A great deal of it flowed into Alex. He was sitting next to John's wife, a pretty, tense-looking brunette. Rosemary Kinsolving was a junior editor at *Mademoiselle* and was working on a novel. She was a little tipsy herself and she buttonholed Alex flirtatiously.

"Well, *I* thought it was a *marvelous* play. I mean, I was the one who talked John into backing it. He has no sense about that sort of thing."

"No sense?" John said, looking up from a conversation with Ellen Brill. "What do you mean?"

"I mean that you're not creative. You are analytical, not abstract . . ."

"Oh God," John laughed. "We're about to get the 'Why can't you be more like Alex?' speech."

"Well, darling . . . look at the way you dress. Alex *looks* like an artist. You look like an investment banker."

"Rosemary," Alex said, "he *is* an investment banker."

"That's what I mean," she said.

Alex excused himself and went to the men's room. He was feeling a little drunk. He splashed some water on his face and looked at himself in the mirror. Alexander Sage, failed playwright. Alexander Sage, junior executive at Welton Oil. That was what his mother had lined up for him. He had talked to Cassie in Dallas this afternoon. She had not even tried to hide her smugness over the play's closing. She wanted him to come down next week. She would throw a party, kill the fatted calf for the prodigal son. Sid Welton would be there. "He's always liked you, Alex. And you are a Yale man, after all. It's about time that education started paying off." Sid Welton, Alex recalled, had a plump, bovine daughter of marriageable age.

He went back out. Ellen was talking to Donald Standing. She shot him a questioning look. They had not been alone together since their confrontation Wednesday night. She was leaving the next morning for California. He knew she was wondering about tonight, but he was not in the mood to give her an answer.

Alex poured himself another glass of champagne, took one sip, and set the glass firmly on the table. He had lost his taste for it. He was suddenly very tired.

"Well, *mes amis*. I want to thank you all . . ." Alex turned to John. ". . . for backing the play . . ." He looked at Chris and Donald and Ellen, and Michael Girard, the director. ". . . and for bringing it to life so brilliantly. Maybe we'll all be together again under happier circumstances. Alas, I must go into the night."

"Wait," Rosemary said. "We'll give you a ride . . ."

John put his hand on her arm. "Let him go. I think he needs to be alone."

Ellen watched Alex as he said good night to the maître d'. She grabbed her coat, said a hasty good-bye to the others, and rushed

out of the restaurant. Alex had just hailed a cab on Sixth Avenue
when she caught up to him.

"Wait! Alex, please. Let's not end it this way."

Alex turned to look at her. "How would you like to end it?"

"You know what I mean. Can't we go somewhere and talk?"

"I'm going home."

"Then I'll come with you."

When they got to Alex's apartment he poured them each a
brandy.

"Not for me, Alex. I've had enough."

"I haven't." He took off his jacket, tossed it on the floor, and
turned on the TV.

Ellen switched it off. "Alex, I want to talk to you. I don't
understand why you're so mad at me."

"I'm not mad at you," Alex said sullenly. He only vaguely
understood why himself. It had been her questioning that had
brought it home to him that *A Hero's Death* was not going to
make it. In ancient Greece they executed messengers who
brought bad news.

Ellen unbuttoned her blouse. "Make love to me."

"I don't feel like it tonight."

"Ohhh . . ." she pouted, lightly mocking. She unzipped her
skirt, and the red silk settled around her ankles. "Snap out of
your funk, Alex. Play the moment."

Alex looked up at her, distracted. "Ellen, I told you, I'm not in
the mood."

"Mood, mood." She slipped off her black bikini panties, and
trailed them across Alex's face. He brushed them aside. "Oh,
you're a hard case tonight." Leaning forward, she massaged his
cheeks with her breasts, and then sat down astride one of his
thighs, rubbing herself against him.

"Okay, goddammit!" He shoved her down savagely onto the
rug. "You want to get fucked? I'll fuck you." And in that instant
he hated her. Selfish, insensitive bitch! She looked up at him
expectantly, half-smiling, smug. God, how he wanted to hurt
her. He wanted to fuck her until she screamed with pain. His
erection pressed against his fly. He tore open his pants and flung
himself down on top of her.

"My goodness," Ellen smirked, "the mood certainly changed."

He slapped her. There was no thought behind it. It was a motor impulse, ignited by anger and drunkenness. Her face snapped to one side and a red mark stood out on her cheek.

"God, Alex! Take it easy."

He hit her with the other hand and shoved himself brutally up into her. She was wet. She moaned and arched her pelvis up against him.

"You like this, don't you, you bitch? It turns you on." He slapped her face again, and this time she put her arms up to ward off the blow. Furious, he pulled them aside and continued hitting as he pumped into her.

"No, stop!" She was crying and trying to protect her face, but at the same time her hips were responding to his onslaught below. "Not my face, Alex. Please! Don't mess up my face!"

The audition. The fucking Hollywood audition. That was all she could think about.

What was he doing? What kind of craziness had she triggered? His hands dropped to his sides, and he stared down at her, panting. He had never done this before, never hit a woman before. Ellen was twisting beneath him with her arms crossed over her face. She was wildly aroused, and suddenly it sickened him. She sickened him, and he sickened himself. He pulled out of her, and stood up with his erect penis wet and glistening.

"Get out. Get your clothes on and get out."

When she was gone Alex took a shower. As punishment he made it as hot as he could stand, turning the handle farther and farther until it burned his skin. He began sobbing as he stood under the spray, overcome by guilt and self-pity.

Finally, when he had pulled himself together, he got out of the shower and fixed a cup of coffee. By the time he finished drinking it he felt completely sober, and he was thinking clearly.

He was not ready for Welton Oil, but he could not live long on three thousand dollars. Not in New York anyway. But Greece. He had lived for practically nothing in Greece, and he had done good work there. Then he remembered the ticket to Dallas his mother had arranged for him to pick up at the airport.

He would pick it up. He would fly to Dallas, but then he would
keep on going, south to Mexico. Mexico was cheap. There were
huts on the beach down along the Yucatán that you could rent
for ten cents a day. Three thousand dollars would last forever
there, and he could write.

He took down a suitcase from the closet shelf and began to
pack.

Chapter Twenty-five

The VW van bumped along the coast on a rutty road that was hardly more than a path. They were in no great hurry. The cooler was full of beer, and a fat joint was making the rounds.

The driver was a twenty-seven-year-old American hippie named Charlie Goebel. He was stocky with a large paunch, and he wore a straw hat to keep the sun off the balding head that had earned him the nickname "Huevo." His girlfriend Mindy was short and scrawny with pockmarked skin that was tanned a dark brown. There was also an Italian couple, Enzo and Franca, who had been hitchhiking from Colombia. They had been on the road for eighteen months and estimated that they would reach their final destination, Alaska, in about five years.

Alex sat in the front seat, wedged in between Huevo and Mindy. He had met them in Veracruz two nights before. They were making for Chichén Itzá, more or less, but they did not particularly care when they got there. Last night they had camped inland along a stream where the vegetation was thick and so were the mosquitoes. Today they were back on the Gulf of Mexico, heading out along the Yucatán. It had been several hours since the last gas station, and nearly that long since they had seen another car. They had passed a tiny village a couple of miles back, where they had bought bananas and jicama and brown paper cones of steamed garbanzos, soaked in lime juice and sprinkled with chili powder. The afternoon was fading, and they were trying to settle on a place to camp.

"What about down there?" Franca suggested, pointing to a wide stretch of empty white beach below them.

"Looks good," Huevo agreed and swung the wheel sharply off

the road before Mindy could protest that "just a little bit farther" they would find the perfect spot.

They parked the van on the side of the road, gathered their
gear, and ran down to the beach. The sun was low behind them,
but the day was still hot and the sand burned beneath their feet.

"Anybody for a swim?" Mindy looked up and down the
beach, and then crossed her arms and skinned her long Indian
cotton shirt over her head. "Looks safe enough," she said, and
ran naked down into the water.

"She's crazy," Huevo observed. "She got busted for swimming naked back in Oaxaca. Deserted beach just like this one,
you'd've sworn there wasn't a fucking human being for a hundred miles. But shit, they can smell naked female flesh just about
that far. First thing you knew, a carload of fucking *chotas* peels
up with siren howling. Must've been half the local precinct
crammed into that cop car, like the circus. I had my jeans back
on, making the fire. They took Mindy in, and it cost me fifty
bucks and a promise to leave the area to get her sprung."

"I am not taking chances," Franca said, stripping off her shirt
and jeans to reveal an extremely skimpy bikini.

"I don't know if they'll be able to tell the difference," Alex
laughed.

But no sirens or police cars appeared. After they had swum
they built a campfire and cooked a dinner of freshly caught fish
and beans. Huevo rolled a couple of joints and then took his
stash box about thirty yards from the fire and buried it in the
sand near a heavy piece of driftwood.

"You never know when they're gonna come down on you," he
said to Alex. "You don't want to have any shit where they can
find it. And if they're lookin', they'll find it anyplace. If they
find it in your car, they'll take your fuckin' wheels, man. That's
how you can tell *federales*. You see a Mexican driving an American car with American plates and a submachine gun in back,
that's a *federal*."

The fish was flaky and delicious, grilled over the open fire.
They ate it and the beans with their fingers, and washed it down
with beer while the sky grew dark and stars filled the sky.
Huevo passed around a joint.

"This is good *mota*," he said. "From the West Coast. I got it from a guy who flies it up to Arizona. He makes two trips a year, pulls down a hundred grand . . . profit."

"Yeah, you can make a lot of money. If you live to spend it," Enzo said. "A Dutch guy named Pieter I met in Sinaloa wanted me to go in with him on running some opium to California. A week's work, I would have made a quarter of a million. That's what this guy Pieter said. I thought about it . . . who wouldn't? But Franca talked me out of it. I went to meet the guy at some bar to tell him I wouldn't do it. When I got there, there was police cars out front and an ambulance. They were carrying Pieter out . . . all shot to pieces. Man, he was a mess. The police had come to arrest him and he'd tried to shoot it out with them. Well, you can't blame him. If they'd taken him he'd rot in jail. And man, these Mexican jails, they are the worst."

"If Enzo had gotten there five minutes sooner, he would be dead, too," Franca said, and shuddered.

"Stay away from heavy dope, that's a good rule of thumb for getting along in Mexico," Huevo advised. "Stay away from anything that's gonna bring you into formal contact with the police. Jails down here are full of dumb Americans who are gonna grow old while their parents try to pull strings to get 'em out."

Mindy yawned. "I'm wasted. I'm going to sleep."

"Yeah, good idea," Huevo said.

While the others laid out their bedrolls, Alex wandered off to urinate in the bushes that lined the edge of the beach. He had consumed a hell of a lot of beer. As he relieved himself his mind dipped back over the last few days. Yes, he had made the right decision, to get away from New York. He had his typewriter and a new idea for a play was beginning to edge into his brain. Tomorrow, he decided, he would split from the others and go off by himself. He had spotted some abandoned huts on the beach about a half mile outside the village they had passed. That would be a good place to stay for a while.

He was distracted from his thinking by a rustle in the bushes about ten yards to his left. Then suddenly, to his right, a double-barreled shotgun appeared from behind a clump of tall brush. It was aimed directly at his cock. And the stream that flowed from it stopped abruptly.

"*Acabe lo que esta haciendo,*" a voice said. Alex understood enough Spanish to know that he was being given permission to finish peeing, but his body would not comply. He quickly covered himself and zipped up his fly. Nearby, a half dozen roughly dressed men stood up from their concealment, all with guns pointed in his direction. Several of them carried machetes as well.

"Holy shit!" Alex said under his breath. A shotgun poked into his ribs and they herded him across the beach to the campsite.

"Arriba todos! Arriba!" The big man who seemed to be in charge strode into the center of the group. The others scrambled to their feet. Mindy edged close to Huevo.

"What's going on?" she demanded in a shrill voice.

The big man stared at them menacingly, without speaking.

Oh God, I'm going to die here, on this beach, was all Alex could think. He glanced at the others. They looked as scared as he felt.

The big man barked an order in Spanish, and two of his henchmen fell to their knees and began rooting through the packs. The man in charge lowered the barrel of his shotgun. *"Capitán de policía federal!"*

"Federales," Huevo muttered with audible relief. "At least they're not fucking bandits." But his eyes were still wary.

"Tienen drogas?" the captain asked.

Alex started to answer and felt Huevo's foot dig sharply into his.

"Sorry. *No comprende,* " Huevo said. "No speak Spanish."

The captain looked around at the group disgustedly. *"Marijuana?"*

Huevo shook his head. "No, thank you."

The Captain glared suspiciously. *"Americanos?"*

Huevo nodded, smiling. "Yes. *Sí.*"

The men on the ground stood up. *"Nada, Capitán."* At the same time two more men appeared from the road in the direction of the parked van. They, too, indicated to the captain that they had found nothing.

Alex was still trembling as they conferred in Spanish too rapid for him to comprehend. Then the captain turned back to Heuvo, and a big smile spread across his face. "So," he said in English, "you are clean."

Huevo bobbed his head respectfully. "Yes, sir. Clean as a whistle."

The captain squinted. "You have *pomos?*" He pantomimed a drinking motion with his hand.

"Beer . . . *cerveza,*" Huevo said.

The captain looked at his men. Then he nodded. "*Cerveza,* okay."

They emptied their cooler and gave all their beer to the *federales,* but the captain took only eight bottles, one for him and each of his men. "You keep," he said, patting Huevo kindly on the shoulder. He grunted an order to his men, and they went off into the darkness. "Hang loose!" the captain called back, and there was a burst of laughter from the men.

From the distance they heard the closing of car doors, and more laughter as the *federales* drove off.

Huevo opened the remaining beers and passed them around. "What did I tell you?" He smiled at Alex. "Piece of cake."

Alex grinned. "Yeah, I saw that look on your face . . . total fear."

"Well, I'm not a fucking idiot, man. If they take you in, you're in one piss pot of trouble. They can hold you as long as they feel like without booking you. Then you're tried by a judge . . . no such thing as a jury. Then it's the slammer till your nose hairs turn white."

"If they'd been bandits they'd have probably been so pissed off that we didn't have anything they'd have killed us," Mindy said, taking a long swig of beer. "That sure knocked the sleep out of me."

"It's always better to pretend you don't speak Spanish, even if you do," Enzo said. "Sometimes it pisses them off and makes them madder, but usually it works, they don't want to bother with you."

"That's good to know," Alex said. "How often does this sort of thing happen?"

Huevo shrugged. "As often as you don't want it to. The mood strikes 'em, and there they are, doing searches on busses, trains, isolated spots like this. Especially us *jipis.* You never know."

The next morning Alex said good-bye to Huevo and the others, gathered his typewriter and suitcase, and walked back up the beach to where he had seen some palm frond huts. He found a fisherman mending his boat and discovered that the huts belonged to the man who owned the *tienda,* the little grocery store in the nearby village.

When he emerged from the store, he had rented the best hut for four dollars a month and stocked up on beer, nonperishable staples, some vegetables, a kerosene lamp, a blanket, and a secondhand frying pan.

A parade of children trailed him back to the beach. They offered to carry things for him, to help him get settled, to gather firewood. Alex felt a bit like the Pied Piper. The children hung around all afternoon, and some older people joined them later in the day. Everyone was very friendly. Alex glowed with acceptance. He should have done this years ago. This was going to be a writer's paradise.

It was past dark by the time Alex was alone again, and he lit the kerosene lamp. He sat on the overturned packing crate that was his chair, by the larger one that was his desk, and rolled a sheet of paper into his typewriter. He had an idea for a black comedy involving two people who meet through a classified ad in the back of *The New York Review of Books.*

Alex typed in the words "Classified Romance" on the title page. He sat back and looked at it, then x-ed out "Romance." He smiled with satisfaction. Below it he wrote, "by Alexander Sage." *A good start,* he thought. He turned down the lamp, got himself a beer, and took a walk along the beach in the moonlight before bed.

The next morning, he got up early and made something that resembled coffee in his frying pan. After a wake-up swim he came back to the hut and ate a box of raisins for breakfast. He sat down at the typewriter and began making character notes. After a few minutes he was aware that there was somebody standing in the doorway. He looked up.

"Buenos dias!" It was the fisherman he had spoken to the day before, smiling his sparse-toothed smile and holding up a fish. *"Para usted,"* he said, thrusting the fish at Alex.

"Gracias," Alex said, and tried to think of the Spanish for "You

shouldn't have." He took the fish and put it in his cooler. *"Gracias,"* he said again. The fisherman stood there smiling. *Christ,* Alex thought, *maybe it's not a gift. Maybe he wants me to buy it.*

"Cuánto?"

"No, no," the man said, wagging a finger at Alex. *"Regalo."* He made no move to leave. Alex offered him a box of raisins, but he shook his head.

"Well," Alex said, "I have to get back to work. *Trabajo."* He pointed to the typewriter. "Thanks again."

The man nodded and smiled and backed out of the hut. Alex waved good-bye and sat back down to work on his characters. Minutes later, he heard what sounded like giggling coming from under his window. He looked out to discover about ten of the village children squatting on the ground next to the hut. He grinned, put his finger to his mouth, and told them that he was working. For the rest of the morning the giggles continued and the number of children doubled.

Alex cooked the fish for lunch, along with rice and *salsa,* and ended up sharing it with all the children. Afterward he was hungrier than he had been when he started. He explained to the children that he *had* to work and told them to run along. To his relief, they did . . . only to return less than an hour later with an offering of slightly mushy bananas. He thanked them, but this time they would not leave. They sat outside his hut, trying to be quiet but mostly whispering and giggling. Alex had a hard time holding on to his concentration.

In the late afternoon, more villagers wandered by, and Alex was forced to knock off for the day. He smiled and chatted with them in his limited Spanish, then decided to try to get away by taking a long walk down the beach. When he returned to the hut, to his relief, they were all gone.

For the next few weeks Alex got much less writing and reading done than he had planned. Here he was, living on a deserted beach in the far reaches of Mexico, and he was being plagued by the friendliness and generosity of the locals. They simply would not let him alone, no matter how often he explained that he needed solitude to work. They were quite content to sit in his hut, or right outside, and wait for him to finish. They would not dream of bothering him, they said as they sat down to silently observe the handsome *Americano* with hair bleached nearly white from the sun.

By the end of a month, Alex had had it. There was no way he could concentrate. The villagers never tired of coming around. There were more visitors now than at the beginning.

There was a bit of a dilemma, however. How was Alex going to get out of paradise? No bus came anywhere near the village, and tourists were few and far between. The more he realized how isolated he was, the greater Alex's cabin fever became.

One morning Alex was sitting glumly on the beach, looking out over the water. Curro, the fisherman who sometimes brought him fish, came by. As usual he stopped to talk.

"*Qué hay, Americano? Problemas?*"

"*Sí.*" His Spanish had improved in the month he had been there, but it was still far short of conversational. "*Quiero andar a Ticul.*"

"*Ah, Ticul!*" Curro grinned and bobbed his head.

"*Sabe dónde puedo encontrar el autobús?*"

"*Autobús? Sí.*" He named a village that Alex recognized. It was about twenty miles up the coast.

"Oh boy." A long walk, but he could not hang around here anymore. "*Gracias,*" he said.

That day, Alex packed up his typewriter and rolled his clothes into the blanket. He gave his suitcase and the rest of his gear to the villagers. They were sorry to see him go and tried to load him down with presents in return, everything from mangoes to live chickens and a pig. With sign language and Pidgin Spanish he declined, explaining that he had to travel light.

Around noon he set out, trailing village children behind him in a comical procession. He had not gone a quarter of a mile before Curro appeared, waving to him enthusiastically and calling "*Americano!*"

"*Hasta luego!*" Alex called out.

But Curro plucked him by the sleeve, grinning, and tugged him toward the beach. "*Venga.*"

Alex shook his head. "Sorry . . . I've got to go."

"*Mi barco . . . yo te llevaré.*"

The children cheered and followed as Curro pulled Alex
down to the beach where his tiny boat was pulled up on the
sand.

"*Venga . . . a bordo.*"

Alex looked dubiously at the dilapidated fishing boat.

"*A bordo . . . a bordo!*" Curro urged. He took Alex's blanket
roll and tossed it on board. Behind him, on the sand, the children giggled and danced.

Alex took a deep breath. This boat, he knew, would never
make it as far as the next town. But to decline would be rude,
and make him look ridiculous. Alex had two choices, he realized:
to get in the boat and face certain death, or to refuse and make a
fool of himself.

Alex put his typewriter over the bow and climbed into the
boat.

But Curro's boat made it to Frontera by midafternoon, and
even more improbably, Alex managed to catch a bus within an
hour. It was headed in the opposite direction from Ticul, but he
did not care. Going with whatever turned up was part of the
magic of traveling in a foreign place. Around midnight, hungry
and sweaty and wishing he had taken Curro's boat all the way to
New York, Alex rolled out of the rattling tin vehicle into the
city of Oaxaca. All he wanted in the world was something to eat,
a shower, and a real bed to sleep in for the next few days.

Near the second-class bus station was a small cantina that was
still open. Alex sat down and ordered a cold beer. It was a place
that served free snacks, but Alex noticed that he was being
passed over as the plates of what looked like tacos went around.

"*Por favor,*" he said, signaling to the *cantinero.* "*Botanas?*"

The bartender squinted dubiously at Alex, then shrugged and
motioned to the waiter to set a plate in front of the blond,
bearded *gringo.*

"*Gracias.*" He took a bite. Something like liquid fire ripped
through his mouth and throat. He was used to spicy food, but
this was a different level. With tears in his eyes he drained his
beer and ordered another.

Smirking, the bartender set a beer in front of him and stood
there watching.

"*Muy bueno,*" Alex said, and took another bite. He was aware that the waiter and the other patrons were watching him, too. The second bite burned, but his tastebuds were becoming anesthetized. He washed it down with a moderate gulp of beer. He noticed a strange aftertaste. He could not place the flavor of the filling.

"*Muy bueno,*" he said again, smiling at the bartender. "*Qué es?*" The bartender informed him that the filling was what Alex understood to be cooked blood. The entire cantina watched to see how the *gringo* would react. Alex knew he had to finish the plate. He hoped he would live to tell the story.

"*Muy bueno,*" he said again. "*El sabor es interesante.*" Keeping a firm hold on his stomach, he ate. When he finished, he paid, gathered his stuff, walked two blocks, and threw up in an alley.

The next noon, after ten hours' sleep and a couple of Lomotils, Alex was feeling decent again. He strolled around the plaza and sat in a sidewalk café. He ordered a Coke and a hamburger, and sat back to look at the bustle of activity in the square.

He decided he would stick around Oaxaca for a few days, then head down to the Gulf of Tehuantepec to try writing again. Huevo had mentioned an inexpensive hotel in Puerto Angel. He would be less of a novelty there than he had been in his hut on the beach. And there would be hot and cold running water. He should be able to work well down there; after all, he was not trying to write *Robinson Crusoe*.

As the waiter set down his hamburger, Alex noticed a pretty girl watching him. She was very tan, wearing a white cotton skirt and a multicolored Indian shirt. She looked American and about twenty. Her hair was blond and clean, and there was a Nikon with a photo lens swinging from her shoulder, along with a leather handbag.

When Alex met her gaze, she smiled and walked purposefully over to his table. "Mind if I join you?" she asked.

"Not at all."

"Oh, you're American. Thank God, I thought you were Swedish or something. My name's Sally Avery."

They shook hands. "Alex Sage. From New York."

"I hope you don't mind. I'm not this forward in Shaker

Heights, but it's a real hassle for a girl traveling alone in Mexico. All these macho men. They won't leave you alone."

Sally ordered a Coke and a hamburger, too, and Alex learned that she had been in Mexico for six months. She had come down with her boyfriend for summer vacation from Northwestern. But they had broken up in Cuernavaca, and she had decided to stay on. She enjoyed being on her own, but wherever she went she tried to latch on to a male companion for protection. That way, she could see the sights without constantly having to ward off unwanted attentions.

"It's not a pickup," she laughed. "Just for company. I'll pay for my own lunch. But if you're alone, let's hang around together."

"Sounds good to me. What do you want to do?"

After lunch they walked through the large open street market where Sally bought several heavy Indian blankets to send to friends. They stopped at a stall where an Indian was selling amulets and herbs. She picked up an amulet made of feathers and carved wood. The vendor said it would ward off evil.

"I'll buy it for you," she said to Alex. "In this country you need all the help you can get."

"Thanks," he said, "but you should have one, too."

"Oh no, I don't need one."

"Well, maybe something to ward off macho." He selected one and gave it to her.

They took a taxi out to the Zapotec ruins at Monte Alban and spent the rest of the afternoon wandering through the Great Plaza of the ancient "city of the gods," which dated back to 1500 B.C. Alex was enjoying himself, and Sally certainly seemed to be. She took his picture and had him take hers, and she asked another tourist to take one of them together. She laughed a lot and hugged him.

"Having fun?"

"Oh, Alex, this is the best time I've had in I don't know how long."

"Me, too."

"There's a drink stand over there. I need to take a malaria pill. Could you get me a fruit juice?"

When Alex came back with two fruit punches, Sally was star-

ing out over the beautiful Oaxacan valley with a look of unutter-
able sadness on her face.

"Hey, what's the matter?"

"Oh!" She looked at him distractedly for a moment. Then she
smiled. "I was thinking about all the people who've lived here,
and how transient life is . . . how whole civilizations can just
disappear." Sally took her drink from Alex. She took a pill out
of a prescription bottle in her purse and swallowed it with the
fruit juice. "This is too nice a day to get down. Let's go have a
look at that pyramid over there."

It was after seven in the evening by the time they got back to
Oaxaca.

"Want to get some dinner?" Alex asked.

"I want to wrap those blankets and get them down to the mail
desk. And I've got about fifty postcards to write."

"Oh, you can do that tomorrow."

"No, I'd like to get it taken care of. Anyway, I want to take a
shower and change."

"Then why don't I come by and pick you up here at your
hotel in an hour or so?"

"Okay. Hey, I've got some peyote up in my room. It's supposed to be fantastic. This guy laid it on me in Puerta Vallarta.
He didn't want to take it back to the States with him on the
plane. I've been saving it for the right time. Are you interested?"

"Peyote? I haven't done any since college. Sounds great."

"Okay. I'll see you around eight. Room four twenty-four.
We'll take the stuff, and then while we're waiting for it to work
we can go over to the zócalo. They have free band concerts
there."

Sally's hotel was one of the most expensive in town, done in
colonial style and situated near the main square. From the way
she had spent money at the market and insisted on their taking a
taxi to Monte Alban instead of a bus, Alex gathered that she was
from a wealthy family and had no problem getting money from
home. He was surprised that rich, indulgent parents would con-
done their daughter's solo travel through Mexico.

"Hi, Alex," Sally said, letting him into her room. "I bought
some yogurt to help the peyote go down easier." She divided the

buttons into the yogurt and gave Alex his portion. After they had taken it she produced a bottle of gold tequila and poured them each a drink. Overhead the ceiling fan whirred, noisily in need of oil.

"This really has been a wonderful day," Sally said. "I'm glad I met you."

"Me, too." Alex downed his drink and poured another. "Where are you headed after this?"

"Oh, I don't know. I'm pretty much taking it one day at a time."

"What about college? Aren't you going back?"

She shrugged. "I don't think there's much college can do for me at this point." She flopped down on the bed, tucking her knees up under her, and leaned against the pillow.

"Don't your parents mind?"

"My parents are dead. I have a trust fund. I'm sure as hell not planning to go back to Shaker Heights."

Alex laughed. "That's the way I feel about Dallas. My mother and stepfather want me to come home and get a quote decent job, unquote."

"And give up New York City, and writing plays? Oh, Alex, don't do it!" She held out her glass in the air. "Here, more tequila, please."

The evening was warm, and the liquor and peyote were making them both warmer. They exchanged travel anecdotes. Sally had not had the problems Huevo had had in Mexico about drug searches, perhaps because she stayed in the better hotels and did not hitchhike or take buses down back roads. Still, she avoided taking chances. She had picked up Alex, she told him, because she knew instinctively that he was "a good person."

"God, Sally," Alex warned her. "Look at the front pages of the newspapers . . . some of the worst mass-murderers look like the boy next door."

Sally grinned. "Well, nobody lives forever."

"It's not safe for you to keep this up. You've got to find somebody to travel with."

"Are you offering your services?"

Alex smiled at her. "I might be. Except I have to write. I need a lot of peace and quiet."

"I could promise you plenty of that." Sally paused, and looked at him with her round blue eyes. "Why don't you bring yourself and the tequila over here next to me? I'm beginning to feel like I'm shouting across the room."

The tequila was already working; the peyote was starting to. Alex looked down at the rug as he crossed it. His feet appeared to sink down much farther than the pile would normally allow.

"What about the *zócalo?* Do you want to get some air?"

"I'm beginning to think I'd rather stay here. I don't know, when I'm tripping sometimes crowds make me feel a little crazy."

"That's fine with me. We've had enough local color for one day." Bang! Alex felt the peyote starting to race through him. He began thinking about the movie with Raquel Welch, *Fantastic Voyage,* when somehow a bunch of scientists find themselves traveling in a boat down the veins and arteries of the human body. Alex lay down next to Sally, and all he wanted to do was get inside *her* body. He had been celibate for over a month. Suddenly he wanted her more than anything in the world. He was beginning to think he was in love with her. Her skin was so brown, her hair so blond, her breasts were so . . .

But her breasts were shielded by the lilac Mexican embroidered dress she wore. "Turn over," he whispered.

Sally turned over, setting her glass on the table next to the bed.

Alex unzipped her dress, pulling the zipper down slowly, feeling each metal tooth yield. Centimeter by centimeter, the smooth brown skin of her back came into view until finally the zipper reached the end of its trail above a stripe of pink bikini underpants.

"Ooooh," Sally moaned, slipping her arms out of the cotton sleeves. She sat up and slithered out of the rest of the dress, like a snake shedding its skin. "Mmm, this peyote is incredible. I can see the molecules in the air."

"I'm concentrating on the molecules in your skin. It's amazing—tiny little Roman candles going off."

"Let's see if you have any." She reached up and began unbuttoning his shirt, while he gazed down in fascination at her body. She had large breasts that lolled slightly to the side as she lay on her back. Alex became absorbed by her nipples, and the aureoles that surrounded them. He saw them as sand castles on a beach, then as Chinese coolie hats, then as loaves of round Italian peasant bread, rising in their yeast. He bent his lips down and took one nipple into his mouth, as Sally pulled his shirt away and began working on his belt.

The drug redefined the sexual landscape. A nipple became something new and completely unexperienced. He tasted it, sucked at it, ran his tongue around it and felt its texture. Sally undid his belt and fly and pulled his jeans off. Alex hardly noticed. He was lost in his rediscovery of the nipple.

When Sally began to moan, he looked up and smiled at her. He kneaded the flesh of her breasts and sides and belly with his hands. It amazed him how alive it felt. "You're beautiful," he told her. "You're really beautiful."

"So are you!" Sally had begun conducting her own exploration of Alex's penis with her fingers. Now she pushed him gently back against the pillow and moved to examine it at closer range. "Ooh," she sighed. "It looks like a giant mushroom. It's like *Alice in Wonderland*. There's a sign hanging around it . . . it says, 'Eat Me.' "

"Always obey signs," Alex counseled.

She moved her lips around the head and drew him into her mouth. "Like rubber," she said, pulling up to let her smiling lips rest on the tip. "Like hard rubber." She moved down again for another sample. "Or calamari . . ." And then, down lower, running her tongue over the scrotum, "Ohhh . . . eggs. Warm, just-peeled hard-boiled eggs, in a satin bag . . ."

They moved around each other with eyes and lips and fingers, squeezing, licking, prodding, and penetrating. When he came into her it was like being absorbed, as if they were both in the same body together.

For hours they made love and talked. They showered and made love there, and then came back to the bed.

"Let's take some more peyote," Sally said. "It's starting to slip. I don't want it to end."

"It's pretty strong. Stronger than you realize."

"Oh come on, I *want* to," she pleaded, almost desperately. "I want to stay up there. Hey, I've got some opium. Let's do that.

It'll bring us down easy. We'll make love some more . . . then we can sleep in each other's arms. Oh please?"

Finally, against his better judgment, Alex allowed her to fill a pipe full of opium from a vitamin jar and share it with him. Soon he could feel the new drug drifting through his body, coiling around the other high. He and Sally made love—he did not know how many times more, or for how long—and at some point after dawn they fell asleep.

When Alex awoke it was dark outside. The bedside lamp was lit; they had never turned it off. Every part of his head ached dully, as if the pain were wrapped in cotton. He looked over at Sally. She was still asleep. He got up slowly, careful not to disturb his head, and made his way to the bathroom. After he relieved his bladder, he brushed his teeth with Sally's toothbrush, and spent the next twenty minutes under a tepid shower.

When he got out he felt a bit better and began to realize he was hungry. He came back into the bedroom and picked up his watch. It was eight-thirty. It had been over thirty-two hours since he had eaten anything but the yogurt and peyote. He put on his clothes, not trying to be particularly quiet, hoping that Sally would wake up and want to go out for something to eat.

After he dressed he went over and sat on the bed next to her. She was lying on her stomach with her head cradled in the crook of her arm. He hated to wake her, but he was starving. He did not want to just slip out and leave her.

"Sally," he said softly. "Hey . . . time to wake up." He put his hand on her buttock and shook her gently.

The moment his hand touched her flesh he knew there was something very wrong. Her skin felt cold.

"Sally!" he said sharply. "Wake up!"

With dread, Alex took her by the shoulders and turned her over. She looked asleep, but there was a whitish tinge beneath her tan, like brown tissue paper stretched over white marble. He looked at her chest for signs of life: there were none. She was not breathing.

"Sally!" Alex slapped her cheeks, and then put his mouth over hers and blew air into her lungs. She did not respond. He took another deep breath and tried again. For ten minutes he worked over her, trying every first-aid technique he could remember. But it was no good, and he knew it. Sally Avery was dead.

Alex shivered. He suddenly felt very cold, and his head was pounding again. The police. He had better call the police. He went to the telephone, but a wave of nausea came over him, and he went to the bathroom where he retched dryly. As he crouched there over the toilet, with his guts in involuntary spasm, Huevo's voice sounded somewhere in his inner consciousness. *Stay away from heavy drugs . . . What you want to avoid in Mexico is any formal contact with the cops . . . Americans rotting in Mexican jails while their parents try to pull strings . . . It's not your country, man, things can get pretty weird down here . . .*

Alex stood up finally and splashed water on his face at the sink. He was trembling.

He had to call the police, but what would he say to them? How could he explain? It would be hard enough to explain to American cops, in English. But to the Mexicans, in halting Spanish—it would be impossible. Look at the facts. There were drugs . . . and a girl was dead.

Americans rotting in Mexican jails . . .

Finally he could not pick up the phone. He dressed Sally in a nightgown so that she would not be found nude and pulled the covers gently up over her chest. Then he took the remaining peyote and opium and flushed them down the toilet. He searched her baggage and found some marijuana and flushed that away, too. Alex checked Sally's handbag. He found the prescription bottle. To his surpise, it was phenobarbital, not malaria pills. He put it back. There were tissues, sunglasses, traveler's checks, a wallet, cosmetics, and her passport. He opened it. Sarah Kincaid Avery. Born September 15, 1954. He looked at her photograph. As he replaced it, his hand still shaking, he saw the amulet he had bought Sally at the market. He was not sure why he did it, but he took the amulet and stuck it in his pocket. A hell of a lot of good it had done her.

Why did she die? They had spent the day together. Alex had eaten and drunk the same things she had, taken the same drugs. If the stuff was bad, why was *he* still alive? He should be dead too. But he was larger, his body could absorb more than hers. Even so, it had knocked him out for fourteen hours. Then he remembered that she had taken phenobarbital too. Maybe that had made the difference. ·

He stared down at Sally. She looked so beautiful . . . as if she were merely sleeping. Why did she die? Was it an accident, or did she know what she was doing? Perhaps she had tried to rouse him, realizing she was in trouble. He stood there looking down at her, sick with grief, and more terrified than he had ever been in his life.

There was a quick knock at the door, and the sound of a key turning in the lock. "*Criada,*" said a perfunctory voice.

"Hey—no!" Alex blurted as the night maid poked her head through the door. "*Occupado* . . . busy . . . go away. *Vaya!*"

The maid backed out into the hall. "*Perdóneme, señor,*" she said, hastily closing the door.

Oh shit! Had she had a good look at him? Had she picked up on the fear in his eyes? Or had she only seen another strange *gringo?*

He had to think, as rationally as possible. He could not leave anything here that could possibly identify him. The maid would tell the police that Sally was not alone . . . that she was with a blond, bearded *gringo.*

His fingerprints! They were on everything. He got a towel and went through the room, rubbing away his prints from the passport, the glass, the tequila bottle, Sally's toothbrush, the shower, toilet handle, doorknob, wherever they might be. Her camera was sitting on the bureau. *Christ,* those pictures at Monte Alban! He rewound the roll of film and removed it and put it in his pocket. Then he wiped the camera with the towel.

Alex walked over to the bed and sat next to Sally, tears streaming down his cheeks. They had talked about traveling together. They might have fallen in love. Now she was dead. It did not seem real.

Making sure that no one saw him leave Sally's room, he walked down the stairs and through the lobby as unobtrusively as possible. In his own hotel he packed his things quickly and called the airport. There was a plane for Mexico City at eleven-thirty that connected with a flight to New York.

He paid his bill and took a taxi to the airport. In the men's room, before boarding the plane, he shaved off his month's growth of beard and trimmed his hair with the scissors of his Swiss army knife.

As Alex stood in line to board the plane he felt more conspicuous than he had ever felt in his life. Tall and fair, the top half of his face tanner than the bottom . . . every passenger seemed to be staring at him, everyone in a uniform seemed to be scrutinizing him . . .

In the Mexico City airport a squad of *federales* walked through the waiting room, and he froze where he was sitting. But they walked by and took no notice of him. When his plane was announced he stood up with relief and headed for the gate.

From behind him a gruff voice barked, "*Señor . . . espere un momento!*"

Alex turned in a panic, the color draining from his face. A security guard was pointing at him. Alex swallowed. "*Sí?*"

"*La máquina de escribir.*" The guard pointed to the floor where Alex had been sitting.

His typewriter! Sweating, he came back and picked it up. "*Gracias,*" he said. "*Muchas gracias!*"

On the airplane he slept fitfully, dreading the arrival in New York. Would they have wired ahead his description? Would the police be waiting for him there?

Chapter Twenty-six

It did not look like an office. The desk was an oval oak table. There was a maroon chaise longue with a scrolled back support, and a lamp made of an antique butter churn stood next to an easy chair upholstered in a calico print. A patchwork crazy quilt decorated one wall, a bright American Primitive scene of a rural New England village hung on another. One might have expected a stone fireplace, and the smell of bread baking.

The intercom buzzed. "Mr. Sage? Don't forget your lunch date at twelve-thirty."

Alex pressed the talk button. "Thanks, Jane. I'm leaving right now." He looked out the window. It was still snowing. He put on his overcoat and Australian bush hat and headed out for a lunch date at the Oyster Bar in Grand Central.

It was late January. Alex had been back in New York for nearly three months. For two of them he had been working as a copywriter at Lattimore-Dover, a trendy middle-sized advertising agency on Madison Avenue at Fifty-sixth Street. Tim Corcoran, a friend from his Yale days, was an account executive there. Alex had run into him in Doubleday's at Fifty-third Street a few weeks after his return from Mexico. They had gone for a drink and Tim had talked him into coming around to Lattimore-Dover for an interview. The personnel director had been delighted to get Alexander Sage, Yale man and playwright. "I saw *Other Lovers*," she had said. "It was *so* clever. Are you working on anything now?" "Got something on the back burner," Alex had told her, "but from now on I'm going to combine playwriting with a normal life."

That was all Alex really wanted after Mexico. A normal life.

He was desperate for ordinariness. He was desperate to forget Sally Avery. But of course he could not forget her, never for longer than an hour or so. The memory of her haunted him as he went about establishing a new routine to fill his days, a routine in which as many minutes of the day and night as possible were filled with obligations to keep him occupied.

And although Alex did not especially like writing television commercials, he discovered he had a knack for it, or so Milt Marsh, the creative director, kept telling him. Alex got to the office early and stayed well past six every night. It kept his mind busy, and his bank account full. He was pulling down a respectable thirty grand. Not a bad starting salary, and Milt had already indicated that Alex would be getting a "substantial" raise by summer.

None of his life seemed real to Alex anymore. All the old happy patterns were gone. When he was writing plays he used to get up around eleven, have lunch with a friend, write until six, go out until one or so, then come back (if he returned alone) and write until daybreak. He made his own schedule. No one dictated that he be anywhere at any time. Now he wished someone would lay out every moment for him, so that he would not have time alone in his apartment to think and remember.

Alex had nightmares about Sally. Not that her death was his fault. But he *could* have stopped her from smoking the opium, from drinking so much tequila. And he *should* not have run away. It had been a cowardly thing to do. He had been innocent; surely he could have made the authorities believe it.

On the other hand, he told himself often, jails are full of innocent people. Foreign jails, especially.

Alex had had the roll of film he took from Sally's camera developed when he got back to New York. After he had forced himself to go through the slides, he selected one he had taken of Sally at Mount Alban and had an eight-by-ten print made of it. The photograph now sat in a carved wooden frame on a bookshelf in his living room, flanked by the two amulets he and Sally Avery had bought for each other on that fateful day back in November. This served as his shrine, and his penance. Someday he would write a play about her, as penance, too. For now, though, his typewriter lived in a closet, gathering dust. And if anyone who came to his apartment noticed the photograph and inquired about it, Alex told them merely that she was a friend, in a tone of voice that made them change the subject quickly.

The Oyster Bar was crowded and as always, noisier than most New York restaurants. John Kinsolving was waiting at their table, sipping a Chivas on the rocks.

"So," Alex said after shaking John's hand warmly, "what brings you to midtown at this time of day?"

"Nothing," John said. "Once every few weeks I give myself a treat, a journey from Wall Street."

Alex laughed. "That's a great title for a play . . . *Journey from Wall Street*. I can see it on the marquee."

"By Alexander Sage?"

"No . . . Alexander Sage is into making money these days. No time for playwriting. How's Rosemary?"

"Fine. Disappointed that you haven't been around much since you got back from Mexico."

"You know how it is. Getting a job has disoriented my life considerably. I'll come out of the coma soon."

The waitress appeared and Alex ordered a beer and fried oysters. John ordered the Lake Winnipeg goldeye.

"Rosemary's having another one of her famous brunches this Sunday. Very arty crowd, but I'm sure you'd be welcome anyway. I'm invited."

Alex laughed. "And she wouldn't by any chance have an attractive, arty friend she wants me to meet, would she?"

"I'm only empowered to let that slip if absolutely necessary," John said. "Are you seeing anyone, by the way?"

"No."

"Well, then . . ."

"Actually, John, I'd rather not. Why don't you and Rosemary and I get together for dinner some night, just the three of us?"

"Boy, you're a changed man," John said flippantly, but he looked serious. "What happened to you in Mexico anyway?"

"Nothing!" Alex flared. He shook his head and tried to smile. "Sorry, John. It's just this job. It's a tough adjustment, working for a living."

"I've never gotten used to it myself," John grinned. "But, hey, don't let it make you give up sex. Things are tough enough without that, believe me."

"Not the voice of experience, I hope."

"Oh no, all I have to do is put on jeans and get out a sketch pad and Rosemary can't keep her hands off me. But seriously, when are you going to get back to normal? This monkishness doesn't suit you."

"Oh, I'll snap out of it. Give me a little time."

Madison Square Garden was packed and crackling with the excitement that attends a New York Knicks–Boston Celtics basketball game. At five minutes before tip-off crowds were still surging past the turnstiles.

Tim Corcoran handed Alex his ticket. "In case we get separated," he said. "These are terrific seats. Two rows behind the Knicks bench. They're the Corning Communications seats. One of the main reasons for keeping their account."

The game had started by the time Tim and Alex made their way from the refreshment stand to court level with beer and popcorn. The usher dusted off their seats, and Alex tipped him.

"Jesus, these *are* great seats." A few feet away, almost at arm's reach and larger than life, were the towering figures of Earl Monroe, Walt Frazier, Spencer Haywood, and all the others Alex had only seen from much farther back, or on television.

At the half, Tim went for more beer. When he came back, he nudged Alex. "Hey, look who's sitting over there."

Alex looked. Two rows back and half a section over was Tory Gamble, one of the producers at Lattimore-Dover. Alex knew her only slightly. She had a reputation for aloofness and did not socialize much within the agency. Not that men at the agency had not tried. She had a striking natural beauty, with clear blue eyes and skin that glowed as if she had just come in from a long walk down the beach or a canter through the countryside. Her hair was dark, medium-length, and thick.

"You know, I took her out a couple of times, but we didn't connect," Tim said. "I had visions of easy street."

"Oh? Is there a lot of money there?"

"Money? Are you kidding? She could afford seats on the free-throw line. Her old man's Joe Gamble, noted polo player and zillionaire. You don't play polo, by any chance, do you, Alex? It'd give you a good leg up on that one."

"I was never very good, he said modestly." Alex laughed. "But as a matter of fact I have played a little. My father played when he was abroad in the diplomatic service. I never really took to it in a big way. I was okay."

Tim looked at him, a grin spreading over his face. "Hey, polo is polo. Make your move, man."

"The chemistry isn't there. I've talked to her a couple of times. Going over story boards. There was never any come-hither."

A tall good-looking man came back to the seat next to Tory and handed her a box of Cracker Jacks. He said something to her, and she laughed and kissed his cheek.

"Looks like it's all academic, anyway. She seems pretty involved with that guy," Tim said.

The second half started. Before long the Knicks were down by fifteen points. Alex's mind started to wander, and he found himself turning to look up at Tory Gamble. Something about her intrigued him tonight. Perhaps it was seeing her here, out of the business context. Or perhaps it was her obvious passion for the game. She was not someone he would have thought of as a basketball fan. In fact, she was not what he would normally have considered his type. He had dated girls like Tory when he was at Yale and they were at Smith or Wellesley or Briarcliff. Rich, well-bred, mohair inside and out. There were few surprises to girls like that. Perhaps this was what appealed to Alex about Tory Gamble in his post-Mexico state of mind.

In any case, she was the first woman who had aroused his interest since Sally Avery's death. He turned to look at her again and caught her eyes on him.

"Way to go, Pearl!" Tim shouted. Earl Monroe had just stolen a pass and raced the length of the court for a lay-up, and the Boston lead was down to eight. The Garden crowd was in a frenzy. For the remaining minutes the Knicks continued to whittle away at the Celtics' lead. Alex and Tim were on their feet, screaming. So, a quick glance backward told him, was Tory Gamble. With six seconds on the clock and Boston leading by one, Spencer Haywood pulled down a rebound and flung an outlet pass to Monroe for a fast break. Monroe took it down the floor and at the last second dished off to Frazier. The buzzer sounded with the ball in the air. It hit the rim, circled for an eternity, and dropped through for the winning basket.

Tory Gamble and her date were thirty yards closer to the exit, but somehow Alex and Tim found themselves next to them in the exuberant crowd that funneled down the ramp.

"Jesus, hell of a game!" Tim said.

"It sure was," Tory said. She introduced the man with her. "Bill, this is Tim Corcoran, and Alexander Sage. We all work together. This is my brother, Bill Gamble. Bill's in from Detroit, home of the hapless Pistons."

"Good to meet you, Bill," Tim said, shaking hands. "Glad you got to see a real team. Hey, you two want to join us for a drink?"

Tory Gamble looked at Alex. "Sorry, I'd better pass. I've got a seven o'clock flight tomorrow morning for Hilton Head. We're shooting that Jimmy Connors spot."

"Well, next time, then," Tim said. As they rode down the escalator he grinned at Alex. "Her brother. Okay, Alex, time to get out the old polo mallet."

"What about this?" Alex said to Milt Marsh. "We've got a penthouse terrace and beyond that a nonstop shot of the Manhattan skyline. On the cocktail table in the foreground we have a bottle of Don Diego and two drinks and the caption says . . . 'A Rum with a View.'"

Milt chuckled. "I love it. Maybe we can do a whole series. Rum puns. That's good, Alex." He looked at his watch. "Oops, gotta go see the guys from Johnson and Johnson. I'll catch you later."

Alex sat back down at his typewriter. *Rum puns,* he thought to himself. *It's amazing what people will do for a living.* And yet a certain part of him was pleased. At the ripe old age of twenty-six he had started a new career, and he was doing well at it. "Rum at the Top," he typed . . . "A Rum for Your Money" . . . "Don Diego . . . the Rum that Wasn't Built in a Day . . ."

There was a quick knock on Alex's open door, and he looked up to see Tory Gamble.

"Ah, you're back from your week with Jimmy Connors. How's your backhand?"

"Better than ever," she said, unsmiling. "Listen, Alex, I've got to talk to you about that Kellerco commercial you wrote. It needs something. I'm getting ready to make up the budget for it . . ."

"Look," he said, "I can't discuss business during business hours. I've got to work up this whole campaign for Milt by five. Anyway, anything that involves criticism, I need a drink. What about the King Cole Bar at the St. Regis at five-thirty?"

"Sorry, I can't," she said automatically. Then she shrugged and softened a bit. "Well, I guess I can."

Alex ordered a second drink but Tory had barely touched her first. She was all business, so Alex was too.

"It's got to be scaled down. The budget on this will scare them right back to Colorado."

"I don't think it has to be so expensive."

"Alex, you're a good writer, but you don't know much about production costs."

"Don't I?" He thought about *A Hero's Death*, and the money he had lost. He smiled sourly. "You could be right."

Tory did some calculations on a legal pad, and together over the next fifteen minutes they worked out a compromise.

"Good," she said, gathering her papers back into her brief-case. "Well, I've got to run."

"I was hoping you'd have dinner with me."

"Sorry, I really can't."

"That's the trouble with women like you. No spontaneity."

Tory bridled. "What do you mean, women like me?"

Alex grinned. "Unspontaneous women."

"I'm too busy to be spontaneous."

"I, on the other hand, am too spontaneous to be busy."

Tory smiled. "So that's your secret." She closed the clasp on her briefcase. "Look, I'm due at a dinner party in Westchester at eight. Why don't you come with me?"

For a moment Alex was speechless. "Won't that make thirteen at the dinner table or something?" he said, finally.

"An extra man is always welcome at these things. And it's my parents who're giving the party. Besides, I thought you were so damned spontaneous."

"Compared to you, I'm an amateur."

Her father's chauffeur met them at the Ardsley-on-Hudson train station. It was beginning to snow. Big flakes whirled through the beam of the Mercedes' lights. The snow was already beginning to cover the ground as they turned in past massive stone pillars and started up a long driveway lined with Douglas firs.

Lindsay Gamble greeted them in the entrance hall. "Nice to meet you, Alexander. I was delighted when Tory called. This is such wretched weather. I wouldn't have blamed you a bit if you'd phoned in sick, Tory."

"Oh, Mother, I promised you I'd be here."

Mrs. Gamble smiled. "How sweet of you, dear. And how nice to have an extra man." She took Alex's arm and led him toward the living room. "And such a handsome one."

Halfway through dinner Alex realized he could just as easily be in Dallas at one of Cassie's soirées. The group was the same: an oil baron and his elegant third wife; a bejeweled, anorexic heiress and her fiancé, an art dealer; the Somebodys who owned the adjoining "farm" and appeared to both be in an advanced state of alcoholism; and Gabriel Lewis, a novelist who had recently won the National Book Award, with his much-publicized lover, a beautiful English actress in her late forties. Tory's nominal date for the evening was Porter Brooks, a slight young man with a receding hairline and glasses. Tory took Alex aside and explained that she and Porter had "known each other forever."

"He's just here to balance the table," she told Alex; but Porter did not seem pleased by Alex's unexpected inclusion.

"Victoria tells me you're a marvelous copywriter," Lindsay Gamble said, as the maid cleared away the Brie and oyster soup.

"I used to be a playwright," Alex said. "But . . . a man has to eat."

"Sage," she said thoughtfully. "You aren't by any chance related to the Sewell Sages of Princeton?"

"No. Actually, my father just retired to Old Lyme. He was a diplomat."

"Not Elliot Sage! Why how marvelous. Joe and I knew him in Portugal. He plays polo. So does Joe. Do you?"

"Not recently."

"Well, this summer you absolutely *must* come out. Joe! We have a polo player here. He's Elliot Sage's son."

After dinner Joe Gamble showed Alex his study. Trophies and framed photographs lined the walls. There was Joe Gamble in polo regalia. There was Joe Gamble with Jack Kennedy, Joe Gamble with Armand Hammer, Joe Gamble with Lamar Hunt, Joe Gamble with Charlton Heston, Joe Gamble with Bill Paley, with Giscard d'Estaing, with Ronald Reagan, with Edward Bennett Williams, with Clare Boothe Luce.

"Here's your father. Back in fifty-eight, I think it was. I was setting up a trade deal with the Portuguese government. A helluva polo player, your father. I expect I must have met you then, too."

"No, sir. My parents were divorced. I spent every other year with my father. I was in New York in fifty-eight."

"But you play polo." Joe Gamble clapped him on the back. "That's just fine. Cigar?"

When they emerged from the study with brandy and cigars a short while later, Alex had a feeling that he had just passed some sort of a test. Lindsay Gamble looked over at her husband and smiled.

By the time polo season rolled around, Alex and Tory were engaged. Alex did not consciously remember falling in love with Tory. They had begun dating after the night at her parents' dinner. Alex was tentative at first, wary of heavy involvement, but as time went on the relationship was easy and there seemed no reason to pull back. His father was delighted, his mother approved, Tory's parents welcomed him as one of the family. His friends envied him and were happy to see him snapping out of the moodiness that had enveloped him since his return from Mexico.

The only person who seemed reserved in her acceptance of Tory was Lydia. She had been in New York and he and Tory had met her and Stefan for dinner. On the surface it had been pleasant and convivial, but Alex was aware of a coolness be-

tween the two women. He put it down to jealousy. Alex had
given Tory an abridged version of his friendship with Lydia and
Juno at Yale and in Paris. But he could tell that Tory guessed at
more than he told her.

So, Tory did not like Lydia, and Lydia did not like Tory. Alex
was not surprised. They were very particular for each other, the
three of them—Lydia, Juno, and himself. Alex and Juno were no
less judgmental about Stefan. Stefan was not good enough for
Lydia, for all his charm and wealth and title. He was not making
Lydia happy. Alex and Lydia both approved of Shep for Juno,
but that romance had gone by the boards over Juno's tempestuous fling with the Cornish actor.

So Juno was free, Lydia was married. And now Alex was
engaged. Why, he asked himself sometimes, was he not marrying Juno? But he knew the answer to that one. The answer
had been there since Paris, when he had broken the balance of
the special thing that existed between the three of them by pair-
ing off with Lydia. It did not work, and the misery it had produced, between him and Lydia, him and Juno, and Juno and
Lydia, had taken a long time to heal.

But Lydia was married now. Still she had played by the rules.
She had married someone else, someone on the outside. She had
not upset the balance. Neither could Juno; neither could he.

It was a very complicated relationship.

With her parents approval established, Tory's reserve evaporated. She became almost kittenish when she was alone with
him. She fixed him gourmet meals, including breakfast in bed
whenever he slept over at her Fifth Avenue co-op. This occurred often since Tory did not particularly care for Alex's
place in SoHo.

Sex with Tory was not predictable, and it was spontaneous.
They slept together after their third date, a basketball game.
Alex had never been to Tory's apartment before, and it was
everything he expected it would be—great view of Central Park
and the surrounding skyline, rooms decorated in impeccable
taste.

What he did not expect was the passion that she unleashed
when they went to bed. They had begun with champagne and a

little polite nuzzling on the sofa of her enclosed greenhouse terrace. Later they moved into the bedroom. She put Dvořák on the stereo and closed the curtains, although only someone on Central Park West with a telescope could have seen them.

Then she walked slowly across the room to Alex and entwined her hands at the back of his neck. "I've been waiting for this since the first time I saw you."

Alex smiled, disbelieving. "You didn't even look at me the first time you saw me."

"Every woman at the agency was throwing herself at you. I had to be different. I pretended not to look."

"It worked. You sure had me fooled."

"Oh, Alex!" Tory pressed her lips to his in a long, eager kiss. Her body ground into his. Little whimpering, chirping sounds rose up from her throat. "Undress me!" she panted.

Alex slowly undid the buttons down the front of her Diane Von Furstenberg shirtwaist, as Tory stood with her eyes closed and her hands at her sides, breathing deeply. When he reached the last button he pulled the dress open.

He almost laughed. She was wearing a lace-trimmed diaphanous red bra with the centers cut out, exposing nipples which appeared to have been reddened with rouge. As the dress slipped to the floor he saw that her panties were of the same style; dark pubic hair curled from a slit in the middle. A black lace garter belt encircled Tory's waist with long satin straps extending down to her stocking tops.

"I bought this at one of those tacky shops on Seventh Avenue . . . with you in mind," she whispered. She looked up into his eyes and he could detect a glint of insecurity. "I hope you like it."

"I love it." Alex leaned down and kissed a nipple that protruded through the opening in the bra. "You're amazing, Tory."

Strangely, Alex did find it exciting. With another woman he would have been amused by the outfit, but not particularly turned on by it. But Tory Gamble always looked so proper. Frederick's of Hollywood was the last thing he expected to see under her successful-young-career-woman exterior. He found it endearing of her to want to appear in something cheap and sexy for him. And the cheap sexiness on her was overpoweringly erotic.

The intensity of Tory's sexual hunger was astonishing. While Alex undressed she stretched out on the bed and writhed like a fifties movie star, fingering herself through the open crotch of her panties. When he stretched out next to her she offered her fingers for him to lick. And when he touched her she went wild, bucking as if his hands were charged with a thousand volts. She responded to everything he did as if it were the most arousing thing that had ever happened to her.

Alex felt a momentary panic. This was the first time he had been with a woman since that awful night in Mexico. A cold sweat broke out on his skin. For a moment he thought of fleeing the apartment, back to his monk's cell in SoHo with its icon of Sally's picture and the amulets.

But Tory's frenzy began to transmit itself to Alex. He plunged into her through the slit in the gauzy underpants, forcing himself to blot out everything but the moment. As her fingernails raked his back he slapped her ass hard and felt an answering surge of current from her body. They made love frantically, noisily, and when they had finished Tory lay on her back staring up at the ceiling with glazed eyes.

After five minutes, when her breathing had returned to normal, she sat up and smiled at Alex brightly. "Would you like coffee?"

Victoria Winslow Gamble became Mrs. Alexander Tyson Sage at a lavish ceremony at her parents' estate. Lydia and Stefan were there; Juno was not, as her duties at the Okehampton Rep prevented her from getting away. She sent a telegram of congratulations and an Art Deco clock from Galerie 1900 on Grovesnor Street.

Joe Gamble, as *his* wedding present, provided the newlyweds with a rented Lear jet to take them to Painted Falls, the one-hundred-thousand-acre ranch in southern Colorado he deeded over to them.

Chapter Twenty-seven

That fall, Alex won his first Cleo Award for a soft drink campaign and was promoted to senior copywriter, along with a nice raise. Tory was terribly proud of him.

"Oh, for God's sake, it doesn't mean anything," he shrugged. "They love to give out awards in this business."

"Now, Alex," Tory chided, "don't be so modest. I think you're wonderful. And this is just the beginning, darling. There are going to be plenty more in the future. You're absolutely brilliant." She smiled with satisfaction. *"This'll* show everybody."

Alex knew what she meant. It had worried Tory that people would whisper behind her back that Alex was marrying her for her money. Even though he came from a "good family," he had run through most of his own money in his playwriting days. At the time of their marriage he was only a junior copywriter with a fairly small salary. Even at the agency, she was senior to him. But now things were changing, getting in their proper perspective.

And Tory proved an excellent prophet. Over the next few years the awards piled up. Alex's salary leapfrogged to an impressive level, and he moved to a corner office on the prestigious twelfth floor.

On the day that he was named a vice-president of the agency, Tory breezed into his office, pausing to polish with her sleeve the already gleaming brass plaque newly set into his door. "We're going to celebrate tonight, Mr. Vice-President," she announced, leaning over to kiss him. "I've made reservations at Elaine's. I'm going to show you off."

"Oh no, Tory, we can't. We're going to Ken's play tonight, remember?"

She made a face. "Oh, I forgot." She ran her fingers up the back of his neck and caressed his hair. "Honey, do we *have* to go tonight? It's just a dinky little off-Broadway thing. I'm sure we can get tickets later on in the week. I wanted tonight to be special."

"Tonight's special for Ken," Alex said patiently. "It's opening night, and it's the first show he's directed in New York. Besides, we're invited to the party afterward."

Tory kissed him again, on the neck. "All right, darling. We'll put on a good face. But tomorrow night, it's Elaine's, and then Studio 54 after that, to make up for it."

The play, a bittersweet reminiscence of a family during the Depression, was thin, but well-acted and brilliantly directed by Alex's old friend Ken Jordan. Tory remained mostly silent during intermission while Alex mingled with friends from his playwriting days. At the party, in the Village town house of the producer, Tory became more vocal and made it quite clear that she looked down on the assembled group. Fairly early, Alex made his excuses, collected their coats, and left.

As they walked along Waverly Place looking for a cab Alex was quiet as Tory chattered on. "I mean, really, Alex. What a bunch of cheek-kissing phonies and fags. And that dippy little what's-his-name . . . the guy who wrote it. He was absolutely drooling over me all evening. It was kind of amusing, actually. I flirted like mad. But I mean, can you imagine me with a playwright?"

"It *is* hard to imagine, isn't it?" Alex said sarcastically.

"Oh, Alex . . . don't be silly. I didn't mean you. Besides, you don't write plays anymore." She slipped her arm through his and squeezed. "You've got an important job now, darling. You're a vice-president."

"Yeah," Alex said. A cab with its light on stopped at the corner. Alex stuck out his hand.

In the spring of 1980, Lydia took over Vivarois in Paris, to introduce her wines. They were bottled under the labels of Clos

de la Forêt and Domaine Boulet. Alex flew over from New York.
Tory did not come. She was in Puerto Rico shooting a commercial, but Alex knew that she would not have come anyway, even
for Paris.

Alex arrived on the Concorde in the early afternoon at
Charles de Gaulle. He grabbed a taxi into the city and checked
into his room at the Abbaye St.-Germain on Rue Cassette. His
room was on the ground floor next to the garden. He showered
and changed, and then walked over to the Deux Magots. It was a
warm spring day, and the outside tables were crowded, but he
found an empty one and sat down, and ordered a *demi* of beer.

He glanced around him. It was incredible that the place
should look exactly the same, when so much had changed for
him and Juno and Lydia since that summer when they had lived
together nearby, in Jean's apartment on the Rue Bonaparte. He
had sat here, day after day, working on his play, while Lydia
studied with Noel Potter, and Juno took French classes and
sketched at the Opéra and the Comédie Française. Now Lydia
was a countess-entrepreneur, Juno was an important set designer, and he was . . . an adman in New York. What had happened to him? What had happened to all those plans and
dreams?

He finished his beer and signaled the waiter for another. He
shook his head a little wryly. Thirty years old, and here he was,
sitting in a Paris café and pining for the good old days. He half
expected Juno to come around the corner with her sketch pad
under her arm, or . . .

"Alex! I don't believe it."

Alex looked up, and there was Juno, but not with a sketch pad
under her arm. Instead she was tall and sleek in a golden
bomber jacket and black velvet knee pants. Her hair was permed
and frizzed around her shoulders. She looked fabulous.

"My God, Juno, I was just sitting here thinking about you."
He jumped up and embraced her. "This is incredible."

"I was taking one of my nostalgic walks. I do it every time I'm
in Paris and have a couple of free hours. I was thinking about
you . . . with your schoolboy notebook, sitting here writing.
And then I looked over, and there you were."

"But not writing." Still holding her hands, he stepped back

and studied her. "I like the new look . . . it's sensational. But then you always were sensational. Sit down. What'll you have to drink?"

"*Vin rouge,* to get in the mood for Lydia's wine thing. Where's Tory?"

"In Puerto Rico, shooting an airline commercial. How about Shep?"

"Holed up with a drunken writer, trying to eke the last chapter out of him. He sends his love."

"How's the new show coming?" Alex asked.

"Pretty well. The usual headaches. Except they're much higher-priced headaches than they used to be. God, when I think of those spit and cardboard jobs we did at Yale . . . the sets for this show are going to go over a hundred thousand pounds."

"Whew," Alex whistled. "But just to put it all into ridiculous perspective, I spend more than that for a thirty-second TV spot."

"Congratulations on your new title, by the way. That's marvelous." She took a sip of her wine. "Speaking of titles, are you getting the itch to write plays again? You know I'm just waiting to design one for you. I'd do it for nothing."

He looked at her seriously. "I know you would, Juno. Oh hell, I don't know, maybe it's just gone. I come back at night, and I just don't feel like beating my head against the typewriter. I really don't have anything original to say. I don't know . . . maybe I'm not hungry enough."

"Well," she smiled. "Don't throw away your typewriter. Just tell yourself your muse is on a sabbatical. You'll get hungry again, I know it. Oh . . . speaking of hungry, what time is it? Shouldn't we be heading over to Lydia's shindig?"

Vivarois, one of Paris's great three-star restaurants, was on Avenue Victor-Hugo. By the time Juno and Alex arrived, the gray and white and burgundy dining room was filled with Lydia's invited guests. She saw them as they came through the doorway and broke away from the group where she was standing to greet them. Her face was tense, and there was a glint of fire in her eye which Alex recognized as disapproval.

"Well . . . you got here," she said. "And only forty-five minutes late."

"Oh, don't scold, Lydia. We're sorry. But you'll never believe what happened. We ran into each other at the Deux Magots . . . just like old times."

"Just like old times," Lydia repeated grumpily. "Well, you'd better come in. We're just about ready to sit down."

It had been Lydia's inspiration to introduce her wines as part of a dinner, instead of the usual wine-tasting format. She and the Boulets had invited Parisian and international wine and food critics, and a judicious sampling of important people and restaurateurs. And, of course, some good friends, like Juno, Alex, and Michel and Marielle Jullien, for moral support.

"I'm putting you at different tables. To spy. Juno, the big critic at your table is Miles Sutherland. Alex, you have Auguste Duterre and Amy Sinclair. I want candid reports of what they say."

"Juno . . . Alex. So good to see you." Stefan came over to kiss Juno's cheek and shake Alex by the hand. "It was good of you to come such a long way for Lydia's big night."

"Stefan's hoping I'll fall on my face," Lydia smiled brittlely. "Aren't you, darling?"

"How can you say such a thing?" Stefan looked hurt, and perhaps a little guilty. "I am very proud of you."

"Well, I'm all nerves." She put a cigarette to her lips, and Stefan lit it. "I wish I'd never gotten involved in this whole thing."

"No, you don't," Stefan said.

"No, you're right . . . I don't. All right, here goes. Let's be seated."

Lydia and Natalie Boulet had spent days choosing the menu, but their diligence was rewarded. Their red Chinon wines were a perfect accompaniment to the dinner—*feuilleté* of truffles, lamb with a tent of eggplant, *bavaroise* in a sauce of fresh tomato *coulis* with a dollop of spinach, and black currant mousse.

Alex felt a knot of anticipation in his stomach as he watched Auguste Duterre lift his glass of the Clos de la Forêt. The portly Frenchman pursed his lips, squinting through the claret red liquid.

"The color is not bad," he said, almost reluctantly. "Perhaps a little pale, but . . . not bad."

Amy Sinclair, the birdlike American food critic whose anorexic figure gave the impression that she found more to criticize than enjoy in the course of her work, agreed. "The nose is agreeable, Auguste," she pointed out. "A little fresh, but it has the basic qualities you'd want in a young Chinon."

So far so good, Alex thought. He found that his fingers were literally crossed beneath the table. *Now taste it.*

Duterre lifted the glass to his full lips, gave it a slight swirl, and took a sip. He held it in his mouth, closed his eyes, and swallowed. The whole table, including Amy Sinclair, seemed to be holding its collective breath.

Duterre smiled. *"Distingué,"* he pronounced. "It has charm. Very pleasing."

Alex let out the breath he had been holding with a sigh of relief.

"You know, Auguste," Amy Sinclair said, "it really climbs a bit above the Chinon level. It has great promise. A wine to keep a close eye on."

Alex caught Lydia's eye and gave her a discreet thumbs-up sign. She beamed back at him and winked. Juno was seated behind him, unfortunately, so he could not easily look at her or glean how her table was reacting to the Clos de la Forêt.

He could see Lydia beginning to relax as the evening wore on, although she was barely touching her own food and wine. The wines were very good, Alex thought, as good as any Loire wine he had ever tasted, including Stefan's. Not as full-bodied as a Bordeaux or Burgundy, but lightly fruity, full of vitality, and extremely drinkable. Lydia and the Boulets had done well. They had a lot to be proud of.

Alex regretted that he, Juno, and Lydia could not be at the same table, but it was one of the inconveniences one suffered for friends. He was sorry that the three of them could not be alone together *after* the dinner but, like Paris and playwriting, that too was part of the past. He remembered one of the books that they had read together sitting around his room in Branford, *Be Here Now.* That was his problem. He had extreme difficulty in being here now. It was something he was going to have to work on.

There was no point in morbidly wallowing in memories of the two beautiful women who were no longer his.

When the party had ended he, Juno, and the Boulets and the Julliens went back to Lydia and Stefan's apartment on Avenue Kléber. Everyone's spirits were up. The consensus was that the evening had been a success. Lydia was glowing, but tactfully trying not to gloat in front of Stefan. Stefan, although perhaps a bit subdued, was all charm and affability. However, he did make his excuses and retired soon after they arrived. The Boulets left soon after that, and a bit later, Michel and Marielle Jullien.

"Well, I suppose we should take the hint, too," Alex said.

"No, please. Stay for another drink," Lydia urged. "I've been building up to this evening for so long I don't want it to end yet." She took Alex's hand and then Juno's. "Thank you both so much for being here. It helped enormously. Stefan's been quite decent about the business, but it's still a bone of contention. And I still can't convince him that all of my modern equipment is better than his traditional methods."

"He'll come around," Alex said.

"And even if he doesn't, you've proved yourself to be a wonderful businesswoman," Juno said. "And you've done it yourself. Who'd have ever thought our actress would turn out to have a good head on those pretty little shoulders," Juno teased. "What do they say . . . money begets money?"

"I'll drink to that," Alex said. And then, suddenly: "Remember that time we drove to Deauville for breakfast? Why don't we do it now. Hang convention," he said with a sweep of his arms.

"Hear, hear," Juno said. "Except I don't think any of us are sober enough to drive. Why don't we take a cab to Les Halles?"

"What do people have chauffeurs for?" Alex said. "Besides, I want to make love to both of you on the beach."

"At this time of year?" Lydia laughed. "We'd freeze our asses off."

"On the other hand, it's nice and cozy here." Alex's tone was bantering but his eyes were sharp with challenge.

Juno glanced apprehensively at the stairs. "Stefan's up there."

"But sound asleep." Alex came over and sat beside Lydia, who was sprawled on the sofa. With his eyes on hers he put his hand on the inside of her thigh, just above the knee, and slowly eased it upward.

Lydia held his stare and did not move. She reached out her hand toward where Juno was sitting. "Come here," she said softly.

"You're both absolutely bonkers," Juno protested. But she slipped out of her chair and came to kneel next to Alex.

He kissed Juno. Lydia was beginning to moan beneath the fondling of his hand. He could feel a pressure releasing from his head, a relieving of the tension that was always with them whenever they were together. His other hand slipped beneath the line of Juno's velvet shirt, and found her breast and the nipple that was hardening there. Lydia raised her hips for him to pull her panties off, and moaned deeply.

A door opened upstairs and the light from Stefan's room spilled out into the hallway. All three of them froze. For a long moment their breathing stopped and there was no sound but the loud pounding of their heartbeats. Then they heard Stefan's footsteps coming down the hall.

"Oh my God," Juno breathed. Quickly she scrambled back to the chair where she had been sitting and buttoned her shirt. Alex pulled the skirt of Lydia's dress back over her thighs and leaned back, as casually as he could manage.

They heard another door open. A few moments later it closed again, and Stefan's footsteps returned to his bedroom.

Lydia breathed a sigh of relief. "He went to get a book."

"Something exciting, I hope," Juno said. And they all burst out into giggles.

"For a few minutes there, I felt like I was sixteen again." Alex shook his head. "An experience I had hoped never to repeat."

Lydia, still laughing, wiped her eyes. "Well," she said. "I guess that takes care of that. Damn it all."

"I'm afraid you're right," Juno sighed. "If ever there was the hand of God reaching down with a sign, that was it."

"Well . . . anybody up for breakfast at Les Halles?" Alex suggested. "We can't get in any trouble there."

Milt Marsh put his legs up on the polished black conference table and leaned back. "Okay . . . the problem, as I see it, is to turn around the image *without* changing the name of the product. Bring Yancy Root Beer into the eighties. They missed the sixties and seventies."

"Why don't they sponsor rock concerts in the park?" Mary Preston, junior copywriter, said. She was a very bright new member of the team, only a year out of Bennington.

"Negative. Old man Yancy won't go *that* far." Milt glanced around the table. "You're being very silent, Alex. Got anything cooking?"

Alex Sage looked up from the notepad where he was making drawings of the new kitchen Tory wanted to build at the ranch. Next to him, Dave Lattimore was twitching his pencil in the way that meant they had better come up with something in another minute. Mary Preston looked pert and alert, cloyingly obnoxious in her desire to climb the corporate ladder three rungs at a time. The others, Jim Kerr and Bryan MacDougall, were veterans of forty years, if you added up both their terms in this agency. They looked both eager and sad. Graying admen were not in style these days.

Alex knew the problem at hand but he had not been listening for the past twenty minutes. He tuned out more and more often. He did not care anymore, not that he ever really had, although when he was courting Tory and early in their marriage he had been into playing the game. Milt Marsh was still waiting for Alex's answer. So Alex did what he had always been able to do when put on the spot. He flipped out an answer.

"Why don't we claim it's natural. That it comes from an underground spring. Like Perrier."

The others continued to look at him, Dave Lattimore impatiently, and the others quizzically.

"Oh . . . I get it!" Mary Preston let out a brittle twill, intended to pass as a laugh. "That's funny, Alex. Kind of a spoof on those natural drinks."

"Yeah." Bryan MacDougall spoke, for the first time all afternoon. "That's what we need. Humor."

"Forget it," Jim Kerr said. "Even if you're going for humor you can't claim Yancy Root Beer comes from an underground spring. Truth in advertising and all that shit."

"You can get around that," Alex said. "Do it animated. Throw in a slogan at the end . . . the next best thing to being natural, or something like that. Look, see, you have these old Western geezers crawling through the desert. They see an oasis up ahead and they keep crawling and then it turns out to be a mirage. Then a beautiful woman appears and hands them two frosty Yancy Root Beers. They gulp it down . . ." Alex was going now. Even Dave Lattimore was beginning to pick up. Alex had the ability to muster enthusiasm and generate it, even when he could care less.

In half an hour they had pinned down the Yancy Root Beer presentation. As they left the conference room, Dave Lattimore came over and patted Alex on the shoulder. "You did it again, Alex. I thought you were off the wall for a while, but you pulled it all together. How about a drink?"

"Have to take a rain check, Dave. I have a date."

"With your wife, I hope."

"Who else?" Alex said. "See you tomorrow."

Tory was out on location today, and Alex was supposed to do the shopping for dinner. She had invited Carter and Penny Jennings over that evening. Penny had roomed with Tory at Pine Manor. Carter had inherited some money, but not nearly enough, and had recently begun working for a living, for Penny's father in his construction business. Because of this, Carter had become very bitter, though he did little more than occupy an office. Tory was afraid her friend Penny's marriage was teetering. These little dinners were her way of helping out.

"I'm up in the clouds," Carter was saying. "Penny's down in the mud. I'm visionary. I'm afraid I'm not very practical."

"Oh yes," Penny laughed, looking adoringly at her husband. She was a sturdy plain girl who clearly could not believe her luck in landing Carter Jennings. To her, Carter was handsome and poetic. To Alex, he was a drip and a bore. "I handle everything from fixing the gutters to paying the bills. I don't want Carter bothered with things like that."

"Sounds very nice," Tory said, smiling at Alex. "But don't you go getting any ideas, Alex."

"Carter's working on a book!" Penny announced rapturously. "Darling, tell them about it."

"Well," Carter began pompously, "it's not a popular work. Not one of your Broadway smashes, Alex." He smiled to indicate that this was a witticism. "Actually it's a biography of a rather obscure nineteenth-century American poet named Arthur Thornton."

Alex burst out laughing. *"The Hawthorne Cycle,"* Alex said, and noted with great satisfaction the stunned disappointment on Carter's face.

"Yes . . . that's his best-known work," Carter said lamely.

"God, Arthur Thornton, the Asshole of Pleasantville. We worked up an evening at Yale: 'The Worst American Poets Read Their Worst Poems.' I played Thornton. Let's see . . . 'Bring me fresh manure, let me spread it on my fields./Anon the tender shoots shall sprout, and all that Nature yields . . .' Am I right, Carter?"

"Alex," Tory said sharply. "Would you get the apples and Brie?"

"In a minute," Alex said. "I'm truly fascinated to know why Carter has exhumed old Arthur Thornton."

"He's quite an important voice," Carter said with brittle control. "No one has ever done a biography of him."

"I can't imagine why," Alex laughed. He was aware of Tory and Penny glaring daggers at him. He knew he would have to pay for this but he was enjoying himself too much to stop. He had suffered through too many excruciating evenings with Carter and Penny over the past years. "Carter, you've gone off the deep end this time."

"Alex means you have a tremendous amount of work ahead of you," Tory said quickly.

"The hell I do." Alex was suddenly annoyed. "I meant what I said. Arthur Thornton's a joke."

"I'm afraid I can't agree with you, Alex," Carter said stiffly.

"Carter, it's getting late," Penny said. She smiled at Tory. "The babysitter . . ."

"Alex, I just don't know what got into you," Tory fumed as she cleared the table. "You were terribly rude to poor Carter. They didn't have to get home to the babysitter. It's only nine-thirty."

"It's later than he thinks," Alex said darkly, and poured himself a brandy. "Want one?"

"You know the trouble Penny's having. It's up to us to encourage Carter . . ."

"I refuse to be responsible for encouraging Carter."

"You know what I mean. I agree he's a bit overbearing, but Penny's crazy about him, and she's my best friend. You know that's why I have them over here. To show them what a happy marriage is like."

"Oh? What is it like?" Alex muttered under his breath, but Tory heard him.

"Alex!" She put down the dishes with a clatter. "What the hell do you mean by that?"

"I mean, are you *happy*, Tory?"

"Well, of course I am. What a question." She paused. "Aren't you?"

Alex stared out the window over Central Park. "I don't know. It's not something I think about much." He sipped his brandy and turned to look at her. "I'm a playwright. I haven't written an intelligent line of dialogue in over seven years."

"Come on, darling. You're the best writer at the agency."

"Oh, wonderful. You know what I mean."

Tory rolled her eyes impatiently. "I don't believe you. You and your plays. You're as bad as the college football hero who spends the rest of his life reminiscing about the Big Game. Face it, darling. You're in the real world now."

"This is the real world? 'I've found something better than Clean-O . . . *new* Clean-O.'"

"Yes! And it's a job that pays you good money. It's the world I work in too, and I don't care to hear your supercilious putdowns of it all the time. Alex, I love you, but you were not exactly Shakespeare in the playwriting department, now were you? What, three plays, none of them on Broadway . . . combined running time four weeks?"

"Four months."

"At Yale you were the wonderful, clever dramatist. But look outside, darling. There's no ivy. There's no quad."

"So you think I live in the past?"

"Yes!" Tory shouted. "All I ever hear is how happy you were

before you met me. Your plays . . . Lydia . . . Juno . . .
those idyllic days in Paris. I saw that play you started working
on a couple of years ago. Your life with those two . . . fucking
women!"

"You read it?"

"Of course . . . you didn't keep it locked up. How do you
think I feel? Always having to compete with the two beautiful
ghosts of your past. And your present. I mean, they never let
you alone, do they? Juno writing you soul-searching letters
about the breakup of her marriage with Shep . . . Lydia calling
up drunk in the middle of the night to pour out her troubles
. . ."

"For Christ's sake. They're my *friends* . . ."

"They're more than your friends! You've got to work it out,
Alex. You *are* living in the past. And I'm here now . . . in nineteen eighty-two."

"Tory," Alex sighed. "I'm not unhappy with you. It's everything else in my life. I feel empty inside. I've been thinking
about it a lot recently. I'm thirty-two. It's time to shit or get off
the pot. I'm quitting my job and going back to writing plays."

"Oh, darling," Tory said, exasperated. "Look, if you have to,
do it in your spare time."

"What spare time? You plan something for every night of the
week, and we're away weekends. We went through this, remember? I can't write part-time."

" 'Can't' or 'won't'?"

"Won't, then. I've got to change my life before it changes me."

"Oh, very good, Alex. Jot that one down. You can use it in a
play sometime."

"Be fair, Tory." Alex poured another brandy. "I've got to give
it one more shot, and I can't do that halfway. I'm leaving the
agency. What about it? Are you with me or against me?"

Her eyes became teary. "Why do you have to put it like that?
Of course I'm not against you . . . I *love* you. I . . . I just wonder whether you love *me*. Do you, Alex?"

"Yes."

But he wondered if he did. Perhaps it was not a question to
examine too closely. Tory loved him. She did her best. But when

he got right down to it, Tory was unyielding. She wanted everything in her life, including him, to be the way *she* wanted it.

He had never seen anyone more afraid of the unfamiliar. Tory wanted Alex to stay in advertising because it was a world she understood, in which she felt comfortable. But Alex the playwright would inject her life with all sorts of unknowns that she would not be able to control. Tory desperately needed to have control.

Alex had never realized before tonight how jealous she was of Juno and Lydia. Now he admitted to himself she had reason to be. He had never truly felt about Tory the way he did about those two. It was like a political race where two liberal candidates split the vote and the conservative slips in.

Sally Avery figured into the picture, too. Her death had frightened him into the world that Tory held out to him. It was the world he had grown up in, and it had been easy to fall back into it. He understood Tory. When you are scared of life, the familiar is the best refuge.

He heard the starting hum of the dishwasher, and Tory came out of the kitchen. "I'm going to bed," she said. "Are you coming?"

"In a little while."

"You're not going to brood, are you?"

"No. I'm going to read for a bit."

Alex took a joint from a brass box on the coffee table and went out to the terrace. A warm Indian summer breeze blew out the first match and he lit a second. He inhaled deeply, kept the smoke in his lungs as long as he could hold it, and then let it drift out.

Juno and Lydia. He had tried to exorcise those spirits in the play that Tory had found. He had started it soon after Juno's visit to town with the rock group. But the play had not worked out because he had never worked out his feelings about its subjects.

Alex wanted his marriage to work. His own parents had been divorced when he was very young; he had never considered divorce an option for himself. But it was common enough, especially among his friends. Tim Corcoran was on his third wife. Juno and Shep had split up. Lydia and Stefan certainly ought to.

John and Rosemary Kinsolving had recently separated. What was so special about him?

It was time for him to have his own way. If Tory could accept that then their marriage would survive. If not . . .

Alex flicked the roach away and watched two cars drag race up the park drive. He turned and went inside.

A week before Thanksgiving, Alex quit his job and moved out. There had been a big scene with Tory. She wept and argued and begged him to stay. But when it came down to it she would not compromise. Tory could not accept his decision to give up the life she had wanted for him, for them.

So Alex took a loft space on Greenwich Street in TriBeCa, and Tory filed for divorce, to the horror of their parents and most of their friends. Alex wanted nothing out of the marriage. The apartment, the furniture and paintings, the ranch in Colorado, the summer cottage in the Hamptons—all of these things he was content to let Tory keep, uncontested.

Alex set up his typewriter and began writing again. For the first few weeks it went miserably. He began to wonder if he had made a terrible mistake, romanticizing his talent and throwing away the "perfect" marriage and job.

And then one day it all clicked back. Alex began a new play, *Plants*. It had to do with relationships, and it was very funny. Alex found himself chuckling over his typewriter.

His social life picked up. He began seeing old friends and making new ones. Although he was happy, the breakup with Tory had left him feeling guilty. He did not miss being married to her, but he missed her friendship. One evening about four months after they had split, he called her to see if she wanted to get together for a drink. She hung up on him.

A week later Alex was working late on his third draft of Act One. The telephone rang. He reached across the cluttered desk, knocking over a box of Stoned Wheat Thins as he picked up the receiver.

"Alex? It's Juno." Her voice crackled urgently over the transatlantic line. "Something terrible's happened!"

Part Six

1983-Present

Chapter Twenty-eight

Limousines crowded the cobblestone courtyard and stretched down the long drive that wound through the apple orchard. Chauffeurs stood in clusters, talking quietly among themselves, or leaned against polished fenders reading newspapers in the bright spring sunlight.

Their employers gathered on the south lawn of Château Mordoi. They were nobility, princes of finance and industry, priestesses of society, even royalty. Their clothing was somber and their tones were hushed as they greeted one another.

"Sebastien . . . how good to see you," Michel Jullien said, shaking the hand of a man who still claimed succession to a monarchy that no longer existed, and had not for generations.

"Michel . . . Marielle . . . how delightful. But what terrible circumstances. I saw Stefan only last month at Regine's. He looked well. How old was he?"

"Fifty-one."

The two men shook their heads with the grim relief of contemporaries shaken by the departure of one of their own.

"And how awful for poor Lydia," Marielle said. "She was with Stefan when he had his heart attack. One minute he was sitting up in bed, the next minute . . ."

Sebastien sighed. "Terrible . . ."

"She is holding up well," Michel said.

Juno and Alex stood together during the graveside service. It was held in the de La Roche family burial ground, on a hill overlooking the Loire. Lydia, red hair flaming under a black-veiled hat, was by the flower-covered casket with her three children. Alexandra and India, ten and nine, held their heads high like their mother. Five-year-old Forrest, the new Count de La Roche, looked curiously around at the throng of assembled mourners. While the service droned on in French, Juno watched Lydia closely. She noticed that her old friend appeared tense in a way that seemed separate from her grief.

When it was over and the casket had been lowered into the ground they walked back to the south lawn where a lavish buffet luncheon had been laid out in silver dishes on white lace cloths. Lydia, subdued but gracious, greeted the guests and accepted their condolences.

As the afternoon wore on the mourners trickled away. By evening only the Julliens, Lydia's parents, and Alex and Juno remained.

After dinner Lydia put the children to bed herself and stayed with them a long time. When she returned downstairs the others were gathered by the fire in Stefan's study, sipping cognac.

Lydia's mother stood up and hugged her. "We're awfully tired, darling. Jet lag, and then all of this. Your father and I are going to bed. You ought to get some sleep, too."

"I will, Mother. Good night. Thank you for everything." She kissed her parents.

"Can I pour you a cognac, Lydia?" Michel Jullien asked. "Or something else?"

"Cognac would be fine," she sighed, sinking into the down-cushioned sofa.

"You look exhausted," Marielle said. "Wouldn't you rather go to bed?"

"I'll sleep again sometime. Right now I'm still working on adrenaline. I feel like part of me is sitting back watching the other part of me rush around and cope with everything. I guess that's normal." She looked at her friends. "Thank God, you're all here. Juno . . . Alex . . . I haven't even *seen* you yet."

"Oh, Lydia, this is all so awful. *Are* you all right, really? Jesus, what a shock for you . . . being right there with Stefan when he . . ."

Lydia shook her head, and Juno saw again that sharp tension around her eyes. She glanced at the Julliens, and then looked back at Juno and Alex. "That's not what really happened . . . it's just what we told the papers. The real story has to be a secret . . . for the children's sake . . . for Stefan's sake too." She put a cigarette in her mouth and Alex lit it for her. "It mustn't go beyond this room."

Lydia sat back and took a long drag on her cigarette. "You remember when Stefan and I nearly broke up, then we got back together again and went on a second honeymoon in New Caledonia? That was when I got pregnant with Forrest. For the next few months after we came home everything was great. Stefan was really trying.

"Then he seemed to lose interest in me sexually, but I didn't think much about it since he was never interested while I was pregnant. He had a lot of business deals going on and spent a great deal of time with the man who was his secretary then, Marc Higgins.

"Anyway, one day I decided to go for a swim. When I got down to the pool I heard sounds coming from the pool house. Unmistakable sexual sounds. One of the maids had been flirting with the gardener, and I assumed it was them. I didn't mind what they did, but you can't allow that sort of thing to go on in your pool house. I went over and tapped on the door but they didn't seem to hear. So I opened it.

"It was Stefan. And Marc Higgins." Lydia paused and shuddered, remembering. "I suppose I should have guessed. When I thought back, it was all so obvious. And I think Marc wanted it to be obvious. When I walked in on them he lay there and looked up at me with a little smile on his face . . . triumph. As if he were saying, 'Okay, you've found us. Now you know. What're you going to do about it?' "

"Oh Jesus," Alex said. "What did you do?"

"Amazingly enough, I held on to my cool. I told Stefan I wanted to see him when he was through. Then I closed the door and went back to my room. In no time at all, Stefan was there, white and shaking. I'd never seen him like that . . . he was scared, really scared. He begged me to try to understand. I was furious, disgusted. I'm sure I would have left him right then if I hadn't been pregnant. I told him I wouldn't even talk to him until he'd gotten rid of Marc. Within an hour I saw Marc leaving. He looked stunned. I think he truly thought he was going to win.

"The whole thing really shook me. I still didn't know what I was going to do. And then I realized I felt a tremendous sense of relief. It wasn't *me,* it was *women.* I'd gone through so many years of doubting my sexuality. Now I saw that he had really tried with me . . . Stefan told me I was the only woman who could arouse him at all anymore. His life with me and the children was the only thing that meant anything to him. He felt his homosexuality was a curse. He desperately wanted to shake it off. He had tried before, he told me. This time he began to see a therapist.

"When Forrest was born, Stefan was ecstatic. He finally had his son. For the next year or so while he continued to see the therapist we did have some sex life. Not much, but he tried. We both tried. It's funny, after all the years of feeling trapped I knew I could leave him anytime I wanted. He had no hold over me anymore. But I cared about him, more maybe because of this vulnerability. He was wonderful with the children, even the girls who had been such a disappointment to him before Forrest was born.

"Finally, we just stopped having sex at all. On the surface we were still the social, happy Count and Countess de La Roche. And though he swore to me that he hadn't fallen back into his old habits I was pretty sure he was having the occasional fling. I thought about having him followed so I would have proof when I confronted him. But . . . Stefan really couldn't help what he was, and in every other way he was generous and attentive. I had to come to terms with it. I didn't want to leave him, and leave all this. So from time to time, with great discretion, I began having the odd one-nighter too . . . just to reassure myself."

Lydia picked up the cognac decanter and refilled her snifter. "And then three nights ago . . . we were in Paris. We had been to a cocktail party. Stefan said he had a business meeting. I went on to dinner with some friends and got home around eleven-thirty. Stefan wasn't back yet. I got in bed to read and must've drifted off. The next thing I knew the phone was ringing. It was close to three.

"There's a place in Paris called Johnny's. It's a private gay club. It was Johnny himself on the phone. Stefan was dead. He'd had a heart attack, brought on by too many amyl nitrites, Johnny thought. Johnny didn't want any scandal . . . he was sure I wouldn't either. He arranged for Stefan to be brought back to the apartment. Nobody saw anything. We put Stefan in bed, and then I called the doctor."

Lydia took a sip of cognac. The tension was gone from her face, replaced by utter exhaustion.

The next morning the Julliens left after breakfast, and Alex drove Lydia's parents, along with the children and Nanny, to the airport in Tours. The Forrests were taking their grandchildren to Spain for a short holiday, to get them away from the sadness that clung to Château Mordoi.

Lydia spent the morning with Stefan's lawyer, beginning the tedious process of resolving Stefan's estate and sorting out the morass of business deals that were pending or unfinished at the time of his death.

Juno went riding with Christophe and Natalie Boulet. When she returned, Alex was back from Tours and lunch was being set out on the patio. Lydia had not yet come down.

"God," Juno said. "I've been thinking about it all morning. About what Lydia told us." She paused. "Did you ever suspect he was gay? I mean, did he ever give off any signals to you?"

"No . . . you've got to hand it to him. Stefan was the most perfect gentleman I've ever met."

"He really was. I never got any sexual vibrations from him at all, but I just put it down to his good breeding. You know, even from men who are happily married you usually get some kind of sexual awareness."

"As you did from me, darling."

"That's different," she said fondly. "Anyway, this thing is devastating for Lydia now. But when she gets over all this it should do a lot to restore her sexual self-confidence. She's been so down on herself . . ."

Alex nodded, smiling. "Getting three children out of a man who was basically a homosexual is no mean accomplishment."

"That's true. You know, I'm just beginning to realize what a hard time Stefan must have had all these years . . . being gay, trying so hard to be something he wasn't. Like his affair with Maggie, that Englishwoman." She poured herself a glass of wine from the decanter on the table. "I guess it *did* cross my mind from time to time, that he might be gay. But it wasn't so much anything *he* did, it was out of loyalty to Lydia."

"Any man who couldn't be turned on by a woman like Lydia . . ."

For a long while they were silent. Then Alex shook his head. "It's so ironic," he said. "The three of us . . . all single again. Things happen fast."

"I'll say," Juno sighed. "It's hard to believe."

"Six months ago we all knew where our lives were going. And now look."

"At least you made a choice, Alex. You're doing what you *want* to do. Me, I'm just drifting."

"Oh, come on, Juno," Alex said. "From what I hear, you're the toast of international café society. Lydia wrote me after she and Stefan went to Sardinia for the opening of Evviva! She said it's a smashing success and you're the reason."

"Well, even if that were true . . . I sort of feel like I'm living in exile. I can't really go back to London . . . at least I don't want to. Not with Shep and Claire and the baby."

"London's a big city," Alex said.

"Not that big."

"I guess none of us made such a great success of our marriages." He looked up toward Stefan's study where Lydia was still closeted with the lawyer. "Well, I don't know. Maybe Lydia did better than any of us."

"Yeah . . . she's a lot more shaken up than she realizes."

Twenty minutes later Lydia emerged from the house and joined them. She had on a black sweater and trousers and no makeup. There were dark circles under her eyes and she looked small and frail as she took her seat at the table. "Sorry I'm late. Business. It's going to take forever to get Stefan's affairs straightened out. Well . . . it's good, I suppose. It'll keep me occupied . . ." Her voice trembled. She shook her head and waved her hand as if brushing away a bothersome insect. She tried to smile. And then, suddenly, everything gave way.

Juno came over and knelt beside Lydia's chair, cradling Lydia in her arms while she sobbed uncontrollably. Alex looked on helplessly, not quite knowing what to do.

"It's okay, Lydia," Juno said. "Cry. You need to." Juno was crying herself.

After a while Lydia accepted Alex's handkerchief and dabbed at her eyes and blew her nose. "Oh God. You must think I'm crazy, but in spite of everything I really did care for Stefan. We were married for ten years . . . Christ, almost eleven!" Her face distorted again into miserable weeping. "Oh, Juno . . . Alex . . . *what am I going to do?*"

Chapter Twenty-nine

Count Nicolo di Rodolfo stepped from his eighty-five-foot Benetti, the sleek white *Pegaso*, into a courtesy *lancia* dispatched from the club Evviva! and extended his hand to assist the Princess Marta Lampeggio. They were joined by their guest, Gustav Pallenberg, a Swedish architect who was the husband of American heiress Nina Carruthers.

The motor launch hummed smoothly toward the grotto entrance.

"Oh, Gus, I think you will love this club," Princess Marta enthused. "It is the newest place. Simply fabulous. The lighting, the atmosphere, it is always changing."

"You know," the count said, "this is Gianni Corelli's place. But the real genius is an American Indian girl he imported from London. You will enjoy meeting her."

The *lancia* slipped beneath a low outcropping of jagged rock and into a grotto lit from unseen sources in pink and peach and violet, like an underground sunset. Rock music reverberated from the walls of the cavern. The *lancia* pulled up to an alabaster berth. A handsome young man wearing white pants and a jacket with Evviva! emblazoned across the breast assisted them onto the dock. *"Benvenuti all'Evviva!,"* he said with a dazzling smile.

They climbed wide stone steps cut into the grotto walls, past waterfalls and tiny lily ponds, to a marble doorway with Evviva! in neon script arched above it. The door opened automatically into an entrance hall lit entirely by hundreds of white candles. From there they passed into the main section, a cavernous three-tiered environment that encompassed a dance floor, two bars,

and a restaurant nestled behind a waterfall. The domed ceiling
was rolled back, open to the stars.

A tall slim woman wearing a shimmering Valentino mini-
dress came over to them smiling. "Count di Rodolfo . . . Princess Marta . . . this *is* becoming your favorite place! Four
nights this week."

"After Evviva! there is no other club worth visiting," Princess
Marta smiled.

"Allow me to introduce our good friend, Gustav Pallenberg,"
Count di Rodolfo said. "Gus, this is the young woman who has
brought new flair to the Costa Smeralda . . . Juno Johnson."

"I am pleased to meet you, Miss Johnson," Pallenberg said,
with a low bow and a brush of his lips to the back of her hand.

"Welcome to Evviva!, Mr. Pallenberg. After all this buildup I
hope you won't be disappointed." Juno smiled, then turned back
to the count. "Your table is ready in the bar."

"*Grazie*," said the count. "Perhaps you will join us later for a
drink?"

"Thank you. I'd love it."

Juno had originally come to Sardinia to design the club for
Gianni Corelli and his partner, Mario Trapani. It had been
Corelli's inspiration to have a new club in Porto Cervo, one that
could be entered from both land and sea. Aside from that, he
had few concrete ideas of exactly what he wanted. But when he
saw Mollie's in London he knew that Juno was the person to
create Evviva!. And later, before the club opened, Corelli decided that Juno was who he wanted to be hostess. He was certain that her exotic looks and anglicized Americanness would be
perfect for the club, which would cater primarily to a wealthy
European clientele.

Having no other focus to her life currently, Juno had agreed
to stay for the season, till the end of September. After that, she
would see. Corelli was already trying to sign her to a contract
for the following year. He was aware that she was receiving
offers to design and manage other new clubs around the world.

Gianni Corelli and his wife Florinda had become good friends
to Juno since her arrival in Sardinia. Florinda, who had been
married twice before, had given Juno comfort and advice in

dealing with the misery over her breakup with Shep. Gianni had found her a wonderful cottage nestled among the massive boulders that punctuated the coastal hillsides, perched above the pink beach and azure water and only a short walk to Evviva!.

Juno loved the Costa Smeralda, the little pocket of elegance on the northeast coast of the wild and rugged island of Sardinia. It had been developed in the sixties by the Aga Khan as a playground for an exclusive international set, and Juno was still amazed at the way they had taken her up and made her a celebrity. During her leisure hours she was besieged with invitations to wine and dine on their yachts and in their villas. She assumed that she was a novelty to them, this season's discovery, and for that reason she was not sure that she should stay on for another. But for now it was wonderful.

Juno checked the reservations list and made a quick sweep through the club to make certain everything was running smoothly. As she stopped at the top of the stairs by the waterfall, a busboy told her that Dominick wanted to see her. Dominick Charpentier was the doorman, a husky black West Indian who had grown up in New York. He had been hired for the kitchen but Juno had promoted him to take advantage of his size and unflappable cool.

Dominick was holding a loud party of Germans at bay. He turned to Juno with a wry smile. "These dudes say they know you, Juno. No reservations."

Juno looked at them. She had never seen them before. A stout man waved hopefully. "Juno . . . hello! Hans Kummel."

"Hans . . . good to see you," Juno said diplomatically. "But there's just no room tonight without a reservation."

"That was nice," Dominick said, as the German party left. "You saved that guy's face."

"It's a knack," she grinned. "See you later, Dominick."

Juno made her way to the Nuraghi Bar, greeting people as she went. She joined Count Nicolo and his party at their table by the railing next to the dance floor.

"Well, Mr. Pallenberg . . . are we living up to your expectations?"

"Indeed you are," he smiled. "And the club is extraordinary, too."

Princess Marta laughed. "You've made a conquest, Juno. Gus is not easily stirred to gallantry. In fact, most of the time he is an absolute recluse."

"That is not exactly true, my dear Marta. I am a selective extrovert." His melancholy blue eyes lit up with pleasure as Juno grinned. "Would you care to dance, Miss Johnson?"

"Juno. I'd love to, but we'll have to make it a short one. I have to get back to work."

Gus Pallenberg was not a fluid disco dancer. Like an actor in an amateur theatrical he moved self-consciously, apparently unsure of what he was doing there. But he seemed to be enjoying himself. He was tall, with a sensitive, handsome face, and thinning blond hair flecked with silver. From the smoothness of his features Gus Pallenberg could have been in his late thirties but there was a weariness in his eyes that suggested that he might be older. And yet he smiled easily and seemed down to earth in a way that set him apart from many of Evviva!'s patrons. Juno decided she liked him.

"Juno . . . I'd like to see you again. Are you free tomorrow?" he said as they left the dance floor. "We're going to Tahiti Bay on Caprera. Will you join us?"

"I'd have to be back by six. Otherwise I'd love to."

"All right, Cinderella, we'll have you back by the last stroke of six. I promise."

Count di Rodolfo's yacht, *Pegaso*, cruised smoothly through the translucent waters to the nearby island of Caprera. Besides Juno there were other guests: Enrico Baldonelli, a Milanese pasta magnate, and his wife, Sofia, and their twin teenaged daughters; Olga di Carpa, the film director, with Pietro Ricci, her latest young discovery; and Baron and Baroness Von Austerlitz, a beautiful young couple who had recently started a line of designer swimwear.

In Tahiti Bay, the *Pegaso* dropped anchor. The company donned scuba gear to explore the colorful underwater terrain, or swam, or windsurfed. Eventually they returned to the boat for lunch: a mixed antipasto of sardines, eggplant and zucchini, pasta with mussels and tomatoes, salad, *carasau*—a crisp Sardinian bread sprinkled with salt, oil, and rosemary—and Argiano wine.

After lunch, while the others sunned themselves on the boat, Gus and Juno took the launch and went ashore. They visited the house where Garibaldi lived and died, then walked through the olive groves into town where they sat and had a glass of beer at a plain street bar.

"I've enjoyed today," Gus said.

"Me, too. Especially getting away like this. Too much luxury can be trying on a small-town girl from New Mexico."

"New Mexico? Ah, so you *are* an Indian."

Juno laughed. "Not exactly. A few genes sprinkled here and there. My grandmother on my father's side was a Zuñi."

"How fascinating. Tell me about yourself."

Juno began with the abridged version of her biography that she had polished for casual conversation. But as Gus Pallenberg drew her out she found herself telling him more and more details of her life, up through her recent divorce.

"Well, there you have it," Juno said. "But what about you? It's your turn."

Gus looked at his watch. "That will have to wait. We'd better get back to the boat."

When the *Pegaso* had weighed anchor and turned back toward the Costa Smeralda, Juno put her hand on Gus's arm. "You were going to tell me the story of your life."

Gus sighed. "Yes . . . but not here. Let's go inside."

They made their way through naked and half-naked bodies sunning on the deck, nut-brown and gleaming with oil. He led her into the salon, an ornate room with pearwood paneling, a tigereye marble floor, fourteen-carat gold fixtures, and Louis XV furnishings.

"Would you like a drink?"

"No, thanks."

Gus seemed to hesitate a moment, then he took Juno by the shoulders and kissed her. She responded, and a current of excitement ran through them both. When they separated he looked at her tenderly, and painfully. "I wanted to do that first," he said.

"I've been wanting to since last night. After what I have to tell you, well, things may be different."

Juno smiled. "Now you're going to admit that you're a famous cat burglar."

He went to the bar and poured himself a San Pellegrino mineral water. "I wish that were it. No, as a matter of fact, I'm married."

"Oh."

"I should have told you sooner. The moment when it becomes relevant is so hard to determine, and then this afternoon I found things moving much faster than I had thought they would."

"Where is your wife?"

"In Switzerland. She goes to a clinic there every so often. At the risk of sounding self-serving I have been very faithful to her. I was not looking for a casual affair. I had no intention of misleading you . . . or myself."

"I understand."

"No . . . you see, I'm falling in love with you." He came and stood in front of Juno again, but did not touch her. "If you don't want to continue to see me, of course I understand . . ."

"Well, I don't know. I have to digest this."

"Yes, yes, I know. Please, I'm not trying to rush you into anything. Think about it. Let me know."

Gus came to Evviva! again that night with Count di Rodolfo and Princess Marta. Although Juno greeted them warmly and was aware of Gus's eyes on her as she circulated about the club performing her duties as hostess, she did not respond to the question on his face.

Gus Pallenberg was the first man to whom she had been truly attracted since the breakup of her marriage, nearly ten months before. She had been feeling dead inside, and she was glad to discover those emotions stirring again. Gus's kiss had really turned her on. But he was married. And that was something she did not need.

She was in the office going over the order list when Gianni Corelli arrived. "Oh, here you are. Florinda wants to talk to you. Woman to woman, I think. I'll finish doing this. You take a break."

Florinda Corelli, a middle-aged beauty with wide-set dark eyes and a classical Roman nose, kissed Juno on both cheeks. "Hello, darling."

"How was Rome? I've missed you."

"Oh, it was fine. Hectic, you know. I am glad to be home." She paused. "I have only been back five hours, but I have already heard the rumor."

"*What* rumor?"

"You and Gus Pallenberg."

"Oh God, I can't believe it! I went out on Nicolo's yacht today. Gus was there. That's all."

"Good." Florinda nodded. "There is just no point in getting mixed up with him. He is married . . ."

"I know that. In fact, he told me."

"But how much did he tell you? His wife is Nina Carruthers. You know, rich, rich American. She is at least ten years older than he. *Very* jealous . . . possessive. He gave up his career for her."

"What do you mean?"

"He was a promising young architect. They fell in love, and then she . . ." Florinda paused, searching for the right word, "she *absorbed* him. Now he builds only for her . . . wings and buildings on her estate. She wants him all to herself."

Juno took a sip of Florinda's champagne. She did not allow herself to drink during working hours. "Then why is he here alone? I'm surprised she let him come."

Florinda shrugged. "She goes to a clinic in Switzerland. Very controversial. They claim they can reverse the aging process. You know, injections of strange chemicals." She shuddered. "I am perfectly content with my face-lift."

Juno smiled. "Thank you, Florinda, for telling me all this, but it doesn't matter. I'm not going to get involved with Gus Pallenberg."

"Good. Juno . . . I do not mean to be a busybody, but you have been hurt so badly by your husband. I do not want to see you hurt again."

Juno squeezed Florinda's hand. "I know. Anyway, why don't we have lunch tomorrow? You can show me all your new clothes."

When Juno left Florinda's table she spotted Gus again. He looked at her and smiled. She smiled back. But at the same time she shook her head.

After Juno lunched with Florinda at the Pevero Golf Club, she ran some errands, then went back to her house to sun herself on her secluded beach. In the late afternoon she fixed herself a Campari and soda and sat out on her porch with one of the books from a package her parents had recently sent her. She looked out over the water and thought about how ideal it was there. And she thought about Gus, and their kiss, and how she wanted to be in love again. It seemed as if it had been a long, long time.

The phone rang, and Juno rushed into the house to get it. "Juno! It's Lydia. Are you still serious about my coming to Sardinia?"

"Of course! You need to get away. I'm busy at night but my days are free. We can have a wonderful time."

"All right. I just wanted to make sure, because I've gone and rented a villa near Liscia di Vacca. I'm bringing Nanny and the kids."

"Terrific! When?"

"In a couple of weeks. I'll let you know exactly. I've been so busy here I don't know whether I'm coming or going. What about you?"

"Same. But I like it."

"What about men? Are you seeing anybody?"

Juno sighed. "No. Not really."

"Hmmm, do I detect something that isn't being said?"

"No. It's just that there's someone . . . but he's married. I'm not going to get involved."

"Why not? Do you like him?"

"Yes," Juno said. "That's the problem. He's the first man who's turned me on in a long time."

"Well, then, go with it. Affairs are very good for the soul . . . and the skin . . . and the cellulite," Lydia giggled.

"But, Lydia, there's no future in it."

"Juno, if there's one thing I've learned the last ten years it's take your fun when you can get it. Life's too short to sit around waiting for Prince Charming."

That evening Gus Pallenberg was not at the club. Count di Rodolfo told Juno that he had stayed back on the yacht to read. Until the club closed Juno found herself walking through her duties, distracted. She could not shake Gus Pallenberg from her mind, and the opposite advice of her two friends kept replaying in her head. Of course, Florinda was right. Absolutely no good could come out of an involvement with a married man with a jealous and possessive wife. On the other hand, Gus made her *feel* again and, as Lydia said, how often did that happen? She needed to have someone care about her. Finally, Juno decided to leave it to fate. She would not seek Gus out, but if they found each other again . . .

For the next couple of days Juno went about her usual routine, except that she found herself looking for Gus Pallenberg everywhere she went, markets, boutiques, restaurants, even golfing with Florinda at the Hotel Cala di Volpe. But he was never around. Nor did he show up at Evviva! again. Juno did not ask Count di Rodolfo about Gus because she did not want to start the rumor mills going. Finally, just when she decided that Gus had probably departed for Switzerland and his wife, he reappeared in her life.

It was midafternoon and Juno had just returned from lunching with friends in Olbia. The day was hot and the ever-present Sardinian wind stirred up only an occasional breeze. Juno ran down to her little cove, tore off her clothes, and went for a long swim. She gathered her clothes and walked back up the hill to her cottage, barefoot and naked.

Gus Pallenberg was standing on her patio.

"Juno . . . I'm sorry to barge in like this . . ."

"Gus!" Juno held her bundle of clothes in front of her. "This *is* a surprise." It was not unusual on the Costa Smeralda for a woman to be topless and even bottomless at the beach, but she was not, strictly speaking, on the beach. This was her house, and this was the man she was enormously attracted to. She hoped she was not blushing; she felt very uncomposed. "I'm, er . . . let me just throw on something." She went into her bedroom, quickly combed her hair, put on fresh mascara, a blue-and-white Greek caftan, and went back out.

"Okay, let's start all over again. Gus, this *is* a surprise."

"I know. I shouldn't have come without calling, but I was afraid you'd refuse to see me." He came over to her and gently took her hands in his. "And I desperately wanted to see you."

"I wanted to see you, too."

"When you shook your head the other night at the club I thought . . ."

"I thought so, too. But I've done a lot of thinking since then. Sit down. Let me get you a drink."

"No. Nothing for me. I just want to talk."

Juno sat next to him on the patio sofa. "Gus, I know there's no future in this. I don't expect anything from you. But I haven't felt the way you make me feel since . . . well, not for a long time."

"I have never felt this way," he said simply. His blue eyes were riveted on hers.

Gus's body was long and lean. His rib cage was very pronounced. He lit a Camel filter, missing the ashtray with the extinguished match.

Juno was lying next to him, on her side. Her legs were a bit shorter than his, her feet the same length, only narrower. "The only reason I'm sorry I don't smoke is because people seem to enjoy the postcoital cigarette so much. Tell me," she giggled, "is it better after sex or after dinner, with coffee?"

"When you've been smoking as long as I have, it becomes part of everything. I'll put it out if the smoke bothers you."

Juno shook her head and rubbed Gus's chest lightly with her fingertips. "Nothing you could ever do would bother me. You're incredible. This whole afternoon has been. I wish we could just stay like this."

"Like this . . ." The words came out softly, with the smoke. He caressed her hip and the roundness of her buttock. "Yes, I wish that too. I wish we could go away together somewhere, for a few days. I have told Nicolo that I'm leaving tomorrow. Can you get away with me?"

"No . . . the club. I can't." She kissed his chest, brushing the sparse curls with her lips. "Besides, how would that look? This is a gossipy little community, darling. You'd be amazed how people are talking about us already, after that day on the *Pegaso*. I've heard lots about you, you've probably heard lots about me. If we were both to take off on the same day, everybody would hear plenty about both of us, and you can be sure your wife would hear it too."

"To hell with other people! I just want to be with you."

"I want to be with you, too. But I don't want you charging off being rash and gallant and messing up your life for me, not after one afternoon. We hardly know each other yet, Gus."

"I know you," he said. He kissed her.

They made love again. The first time it had been explosive and passionate. For Juno it was the end of a ten-month celibacy; for Gus it was the first infidelity outside of a marriage which was, she was to learn in the coming months, much more bizarre than she had imagined.

This time their lovemaking was gentle. Gus explored her body slowly, looking for the places that gave her special pleasure. He found them in the hollows of her throat and her groin, in the dimples of her buttocks, in the little plunge at the base of her spine. He came into her with his eyes open, moving inside her with different rhythms, holding himself above her with his arms as he watched her face lovingly, enjoying her pleasure as much as his own.

"Oh God," Juno said, smiling up at him. "You're going to spoil me."

"Let me spoil you. Then we'll both be spoiled."

"Ah!"

"You're the most beautiful woman I've ever seen."

"No . . . you haven't been looking. This place is full of beautiful women."

"Yes . . . but not like you. I love you."

He moved in a way that made her cry out and twist her pelvis up hard against him. A moment later both their bodies stiffened in a series of tremors.

"You must come away with me. You can't send me off alone."

"Gus, I can't. But you could stay here."

"What about the danger to our reputations?"

"Nobody needs to know. I'll hide you. We'll make love all day, and you sleep while I go to work at night."

He kissed the bridge of her nose, and the blue-veined swell of her eyelid. "I'll be your prisoner. A prisoner of love."

"Oh good. I like that."

"I'll cook for you. I'm a good cook. I'll fix wonderful meals while you're out, and when you come home we'll feast and make love."

"I don't know if we can keep this a secret. People will see that I look too happy. And too satisfied. How long can you stay?"

He sat up, resting his hand on her thigh. He shook his head. "Only a few days. I must be in Berne on Friday."

"Oh." She covered his hand with hers. "Well . . . maybe I won't look *too* happy, then."

On Friday morning Juno drove Gus to the Alghero airport, several hours away, instead of the closer one in Olbia where he might have been recognized.

During the drive back Juno thought about Gus and their four days together. Lydia had been right, it had been wonderful. The affair with Gus had brought her out of a ten-month funk. For that she was glad. But it was over.

"It is not over between us," he had insisted in the car. "I will write you. I will call you. I must see you again." He had told her that he loved her.

But Gus had told her about Nina, too. And from what he said, and did not say, Juno could tell that he was as obsessed with his wife as she was with him. It was not love exactly . . . not love as Juno knew it, in any case. Gus seemed almost to loathe Nina sometimes, when he talked about her. Nina dominated his life; she possessed him both emotionally and economically. In the beginning, Juno gathered, it had been romantic, but now Nina's trips to the Swiss clinic for rejuvenation had generated strange psychological side effects as well. What they were precisely, Juno could not tell.

Gus had told Juno he loved her, but as they got closer and

closer to the airport she could sense his withdrawal. He was already on his way to Nina before he even left.

Florinda had been right, after all. She should never have become involved with Gus Pallenberg.

Chapter Thirty

The wind blasted across the rugged landscape, shaking the Fiat as it drove up the coast from Olbia to Liscia di Vacca.

"My Lord, Juno . . . is the wind always like this?" Lydia put up her window. "I should have brought kites for the children."

"It comes for a few days, then it goes again. It should be over soon."

"*Maman . . . Maman. Regardes les arbres . . .*"

"Alexandra . . . speak English." Lydia turned back to Juno. "We're going to New York to see my parents in a few weeks."

"But look at the trees, Mummy. They're all bent over."

Juno laughed. "The wind doesn't give them a chance to stand up straight."

"Well, so much for my hair," Lydia sighed.

As they pulled into the driveway of the villa that Lydia had rented at Liscia di Vacca the wind was dying down. The house was set into a green landscaped hillside overlooking a small sandy cove.

"Oh, it's beautiful," Lydia said. They got out of the car and the three children scampered down to the shore, followed by Nanny.

The door opened and an elderly man hurried down to greet them. "*Buon giorno, signore. Benvenute.*" He gathered the bags from the trunk and escorted them inside the house.

Lydia turned to Juno. "Oh, give me a hug. It's so good to be here!"

They embraced and then walked out onto the terrace. The children were already building a sand castle, under Nanny's supervision. Lydia and Juno perched on the low stone wall in the shade of the thatched roof of the terrace.

"Bring me up to date," Lydia said. "What happened with the married man? Did you take my advice?"

Juno nodded wryly. "Remind me never to listen to you again."

"Oh, darling . . . I'm sorry. Is it bad?"

"No, you were probably right. I'm not depressed like I was before. Now I'm depressed in a different way. But at least there was that nice little sandwich of bliss in between." Juno told Lydia all about Gus, and Nina.

"Well, at least you got your rocks off," Lydia giggled. "Now you'll be receptive to the next man who comes along. You'll get over Gus."

"What about you? I feel ridiculous harping over my problems after what you've been through the past few months."

Lydia got a tube of sun block from her handbag and rubbed it over the bridge of her nose and on her arms. "I'm hanging in there. We all miss Stefan so much. He left a mess of unfinished business deals, but it's all getting sorted out. Pretty soon I'll be free to get on with my life. Until now, I've been in some sort of limbo."

"Have you decided what you're going to do? Stay in France . . . go back to New York?"

"Oh, I don't know. I can't leave France for good. Forrest inherited Château Mordoi. I have to keep it up for him until he comes of age. So much of my life has been in France . . . but I keep thinking it's time for a change."

"There's something I've been meaning to ask you. Last time, at Stefan's funeral, it was hardly appropriate . . . but whatever happened to Bernard Jullien?"

Lydia opened her cigarette case and pulled out a Marlboro. "He got married . . . to one of his actresses. I haven't seen him for quite a while." She smiled. "I guess he got tired of waiting around for me. It's funny . . . I still have the key to his apartment in my jewel box. I've started to toss it out dozens of times. But that was puppy love. I don't know what I want now."

"Neither do I."

Lydia's vacation in Sardinia was good for both her and Juno. This was the first concentrated time they had spent together in years, and it reestablished a closeness that had been slipping away. They felt as if they were finishing sentences they had started at Yale.

And Lydia loved Evviva!. "When Stefan and I came for the opening I was so impressed with how the club looked. But now I'm impressed with how it *feels*. It's marvelous, Juno. And it all seems to revolve around you."

Lydia came to the club every night. Many of the patrons were old friends, and in this elegant, intimate atmosphere she was comfortable. Lydia began to sparkle again. She would arrive in the evening, after the children were in bed, and usually stay until closing. Sometimes Juno would come back to the villa with her for breakfast.

"Oh, Juno," Lydia said, pouring coffee as they sat one morning on the terrace watching the sun come up. "I can't believe what a fabulous job you're doing. You know absolutely *everybody!* You know more people than I do, and this is supposed to be my crowd."

"I never used to be much for nightclubs. But I must say when you're at the center of the action it *is* a lot of fun."

"Gianni wants me to talk you into staying another year. Are you thinking of leaving?"

"Oh, I don't know. I love it here, but in a way I feel I'd just be treading water. What I really loved was designing the place and getting it going. I don't know what point there is to staying on."

"Point? You're the reason people flock to Evviva!. *L'Indienne fabuleuse.*"

Juno laughed. "You remember that Arab who was in the other night with Cara Cook? He wants to open a club in Dallas, and he wants me to do it."

"Dallas? You'd give this up for Dallas?"

"I don't know. I'm toying with it. I've been in Europe a long time. I'm sort of ready to go back to the States."

"Well, you really can't go wrong. You've carved yourself out a fabulous career that you can do anywhere." Lydia stretched. "I'm ready to turn in. Why don't you stay? We can go out for lunch later."

"*Bonjour, Maman. Bonjour, Tante Juno.*" The children bounded
onto the terrace. They were going to the beach and then Nanny
was taking them to Sassari, to a circus. Juno and Lydia kissed
them. Lydia stayed behind to visit with them for a few minutes,
and Juno went off to the guest room.

Juno woke sometime around noon. Through the open windows she could hear birds singing and the sound of the water
lapping in the cove. Then she heard something else, and realized
that it was Lydia crying.

Lydia's bedroom was just across the terrace from the guest
room. Juno slipped on a kimono that was hanging behind the
door and hurried to her friend's room.

The French doors were open. Lydia lay in bed, with her arm
flung across her face, weeping heavily. Juno came and sat on the
edge of the bed.

"Lydia . . . what's wrong?"

Lydia looked up, red-faced and red-eyed. "Oh, Juno . . . I'm
so unhappy! What am I going to do? What am I going to do with
my life?"

Juno took Lydia in her arms and stroked her consolingly.
"You can do anything you want to. You don't have to rush into
anything. Things will sort themselves out . . . it just takes
time."

"Time?" Lydia sobbed. "I'm over thirty . . . I've had three
children. I'm losing my looks, and I'm getting old. I don't know
what I'm going to do . . ."

Juno took Lydia's face in her hands. "You're no older than I
am. And as far as looks you know damned well you've had the
women in Evviva! green with envy ever since you got here.
Look at you . . . three children or not, you don't look a minute
older than you did at Yale." Juno took a tissue from the night
table and gently wiped the tears from Lydia's eyes.

"Oh, Juno . . . what would I ever do without you? You're
the only constant in my life . . . you and Alex. Oh, I wish he
were here, too."

"I know. Hey, stop crying . . . everything will turn out fine.
I promise."

Tears were still running down Lydia's cheeks. She looked into

Juno's eyes. "Oh, I love you, Juno . . . I do." She kissed Juno
on the lips and ran her fingers through her long dark hair.

"Lydia . . ." The passion in the kiss took Juno by surprise.

"Oh, Juno, I'm not gay or anything. I've never done this with
another woman. We used to have Alex with us back then . . .
but, oh God, I need you. I need you to make love to me. It's been
so long since I've had love . . ."

Juno hugged Lydia against her and kissed her forehead.
"Lydia, you know I love you." She slipped her hands beneath
Lydia's silk nightgown and lifted it over her head. Then she
untied her kimono and shrugged it from her shoulders.

Lydia leaned forward and kissed Juno's breasts, and then lay
back and pulled Juno's long tan body down on top of her. "You
feel so smooth," she whispered. "This is different, isn't it? Different from with Alex . . ."

"Yes . . ." Juno moved her hand down Lydia's torso. "Look
at you . . . so tiny, so feminine," she murmured. "So . . . so
wet!" She giggled as her fingers explored the territory between
Lydia's thighs, and then dipped beneath to cup her buttocks.
She raised Lydia's middle off the bed and lowered her lips to it.
Lydia moaned and shivered.

They made love as two friends who have let down all barriers
between each other. It was total caring, total giving, an outpour-
ing of love to fit a special moment of need. Without inhibition or
misgiving, they abandoned themselves to passion and sensation.
When the climax came they felt it in both their bodies, like a
tremor from the earth itself.

Afterward they lay in each other's arms. They were friends
who had been lovers, and were friends again.

"Oh, Juno . . . I feel so much better. Like I've been lifted out
of myself . . . and totally refreshed."

"Me, too. Aren't women wonderful?" Juno laughed.

"Yes . . . it's a shame men can't be that way. Stefan *couldn't*
love both men and women."

"Well, a lot of women can't love men. I guess we're lucky."

After they had showered and dressed they drove to the Hotel
Cervo for lunch. They sat out by the pool under a bower of
grapevines.

"So." Lydia lit a cigarette and exhaled deeply. "We still haven't solved the problem of what I'm going to do with my life."

"Problem? What problem? Look at who you are. The *Comtesse de La Roche* . . . God, you know everybody. You could do anything."

"Yes . . . but *what?*"

"Well . . . you have your wine business."

"Christophe and Natalie run that. There's nothing for me to do there."

"What about a restaurant? You're a fabulous cook . . ."

"I've thought about that . . . but it's too much work. And there're too many great restaurants already."

"What about acting?"

Lydia sighed. "I'd be terrified . . . I've been away too long. I doubt if I could do it anymore."

"All right . . . let's look at your assets. Beauty, brains, money, connections. And you're clever."

"Thank you," Lydia laughed her husky laugh. "But where does that get me? You're so damned lucky. You've got it all worked out. People are clamoring to have you design clubs."

"Sure, I can always get work. But everything I do belongs to somebody else." Juno took a bite of her melon and prosciutto. "I guess I'd like to settle down in one place. With what I know now I could do my *own* club. You wouldn't believe how many mistakes are made in . . ."

"Wait a minute! Hold everything . . . *I've got it!*" Lydia broke into an ecstatic smile. "*We'll* start a club. My money and connections . . . your expertise and connections . . ."

Juno clapped her hands. "Fabulous!"

"What about New York? Those town houses . . . we could redo them." Lydia became more excited. "God, my vineyards could provide the wine . . . I could supervise the food. You'd design something incredible. I mean, it *would* be fabulous!"

"But aren't there a million clubs in New York?"

"Stefan and I have been to them all . . . I know what's there. New Yorkers are always desperate for a new place. And they've never seen anything like the place we'd do. Oh, Juno, think about it! It's the absolute perfect solution to *both* our problems."

"It'd cost a fortune . . ."

"I've got a fortune! What do you say?" Lydia was so excited
she could hardly sit still.

Juno grinned. "Okay . . . let's do it!"

But later, after Lydia had headed to New York with Nanny
and the children, Juno began to have second thoughts. The club
was a great idea, and Lydia's town houses in New York would
be perfect. But with Lydia financing the whole operation Juno
would be back where she started—designing a club for someone
else.

She sat down and figured out her finances. She had saved
quite a lot of money, from her share of the sale of the London
town house, and what she had made designing and running Evviva!. She spent very little in Sardinia; her house was inexpensive. But she would need a lot of money to live in New York,
rentals and co-ops being what they were. No, she would not
have nearly enough money left over to invest in the club.

She talked to Alex about it at length over the phone.

"It's got to be half yours," he advised her. "Otherwise it'll
never work. You two are equal friends . . . you've got to be
equal partners."

"You're right . . . now all I've got to do is rob a bank. That
should be easy."

"I wish I could invest, but that's a little out of my league these
days."

Alex made inquiries for her with his friend John Kinsolving,
who advised him that Juno would have trouble raising that kind
of money from a bank unless someone like the Countess de La
Roche guaranteed the loan. That put Juno back where she
started.

Gianni Corelli was willing to put money into the club, and he
knew others who would, too, but for a hefty percentage. No
matter how she tried to figure it out, Juno always came up short.

Meanwhile she could not stop herself from sketching designs.
It was that exhilarating time when ideas kept bursting, one after
another, faster than she could put them down. She alternated
between euphoria at the idea of the club, and despair over the
impossibility of putting it all together.

One morning, a month after she had put Gus Pallenberg on the plane to Switzerland, he telephoned.

"Juno? Can you forgive me?"

"Gus . . . I was beginning to think I'd never hear from you again."

"Juno, I've missed you."

"Have you? Not one word since you left. Where've you been? Don't they have phones or stamps?"

"I'm sorry. You have every right to be angry, but you can't imagine how difficult it's been."

Juno relented. "Are you all right, Gus? Where are you?"

"I'm in New York. And I've been doing a lot of thinking. I love you, Juno. I want you here . . . I want to work it out so we can be together. What do you think? After the season, in September, will you come?"

"Oh, Gus," Juno groaned, "if only you knew how hard I've been trying to figure out how to get to New York." She explained to him about the club that she and Lydia were planning.

"But that's marvelous, darling. Your club will be a sensation. Everybody will come."

"There's a catch," Juno said. "Money. Lydia has plenty, but I won't do it unless I can put up my share. From what I've been able to find out, that's going to be about as easy as flying to the moon."

"For you that should be no problem. I've been there with you. You've taken me there. But tell me, do you still feel the same way about me?"

"I'd talked myself out of it, but . . ."

"But?"

"Yes . . . I do."

Juno walked out to her patio and gazed at the sea. New York. Now she had two reasons for wanting to be there. And neither one of them had a chance.

Chapter Thirty-one

Marylou Freeman sat on the edge of her desk, engrossed in a phone call to the Coast. Alex Sage stood over by the window of her office. The producer's picture window gave a magnificent view down Broadway from the Paramount Building, and he could just see the top of the marquee of the Broadhurst Theater where in three weeks his new play, *Plants,* would be opening.

The office was decorated with framed posters of Marylou Freeman's hits. It was a comforting sight to Alex. Not only was he being produced for the first time on Broadway, but by one of the commercial theater's top producers. Marylou Freeman was a plump woman in her middle thirties, with brown hair and a large pretty face. She dressed conservatively and looked more like a kindly schoolteacher than a shrewd woman in a cutthroat business. But shrewd she was, as the posters on her wall showed. Alex was slightly terrified of her.

She hung up the phone. "Sorry, Alex. Where were we? Oh yes. Publicity. I want you to meet Camy Pratt. She's super . . . first-rate. She wants to set up a blitz of interviews for you . . . print, TV, radio." She scribbled an address on a piece of paper. "Stop around and see her this afternoon. She's expecting you."

"I hope you're not going to be one of those difficult authors who refuse to give interviews," Camy Pratt said as she greeted Alex.

"No . . . I'm greedy for fame."

Alex was pleasantly surprised by his publicist. She was delicate and pretty, with porcelain skin and honey-blond hair. Her enormous green eyes slanted down at the corners, giving her a brooding quality that was offset by her wide smile.

"Well, that's refreshing." She handed him a typewritten list. "Here's what we've got so far. The ones in parentheses aren't firm yet. But they will be. Have you done TV before?"

"Most of my interviews have been confined to the *Yale Daily News*," Alex said. "And that was a while back."

"Yes, I remember you had a couple of shows back in the mid-seventies. Then you dropped out of sight. What happened to you?"

"It's a long and boring story."

She grinned. "Well, I'd better hear it if we're going to pitch you to the press. Come on, let me buy you a drink. Maybe we can turn it into a long and interesting story."

The next two weeks made Alex almost regret his decision to do everything he could to publicize the play. He got to a point where he could turn off his mind and still find his mouth talking away to interviewers who asked the same questions over and over again. What made it bearable was Camy Pratt, who often came along with him. And they started seeing each other in between interviews.

"Who *listens* to that show?" Alex asked as he waved a hand at the oncoming headlights of a taxi. " 'Babs on Broadway.' Jesus, I've never heard of her."

"Maybe you haven't," Camy chided, "but she's syndicated. She's why people in Tucumcari will head for your show when they come to New York."

"People from Tucumcari don't come to New York."

At Greenwich Street they got out and Alex bought a bottle of wine at the local liquor shop.

"How many flights up to your loft, Alex?" Camy asked as they entered the small gray entryway of his building.

"What makes you think there's no elevator?"

"Even if there is I won't take it. Rickety old warehouse elevators terrify me."

On the third landing he produced a key and opened his door. "I think you'll love it," he said. "Maybe you can set something up with *Architectural Digest*."

"Oh God," Camy said, looking around. The bookcases were converted packing crates, with extra books stacked in piles along the walls and on a rolltop desk, somewhere in the middle of which was Alex's typewriter. There was an ill-matched arrangement of once-good furniture, and a well-worn Persian carpet. A Baldwin baby grand occupied a space by the rear windows. The king-sized bed, foam rubber on a plywood platform, was unmade.

"No plants? I thought this place would look like a greenhouse —inspiration for your play."

Alex opened the bottle of Château Margaux. "I had some, but I threw them all out when I finished. They were dead . . . I forgot to water them. I did talk to them, though."

Camy laughed. "Well, at least there's not much to be jealous about here. This place certainly lacks the woman's touch." She accepted a glass of wine from Alex. "Oh . . . I spoke too soon," she said, eyeing a large bulletin board crammed with photographs. "Look at all those women!"

"Friends," he said grinning. "And past loves. Nobody current."

Camy walked over to take a closer look. "You don't go in much for plain girls with glasses, do you? Hmmm . . . who's this? She looks familiar."

Alex came over. "You remember the friends of mine who want to open a nightclub? This is one of them, the countess . . . Lydia de La Roche. She used to be . . ."

"Lydia Forrest! I went to Brearley with her. She was a couple of years ahead of me. How amazing!"

"Well, you should talk to her. I think she'd be interested in your doing PR for the club. She's just moved back to New York."

"I'd love to see her again," Camy said. "Have her call me when she has a chance."

They sat on the balding sofa with the bottle of wine. "You know," Alex said, "I've told you absolutely everything about me. Now it's your turn. How did you get into the publicity business?"

"Rebellion, I guess. And I had to make a living. My mother's rich as hell, but we don't get along and I won't take anything

from her." Camy laughed bitterly. "She wouldn't give me anything anyway. I did the whole bit . . . the right schools, deb of
the year, Junior League, all that sort of thing. After that, all I
was fit for was marriage or trading on my connections. I tried
both. The marriage was no good, but the connections have
worked out nicely."

"Marylou Freeman says you're the best publicist in the business." Alex leaned forward. "You're certainly the most beautiful." He kissed her. "Can you stay over?"

"Will you put my picture on the board?"

"I'll put *you* on the board."

She laughed and reached for the buttons on her blouse.

They were in the middle of making love when the phone
rang.

"Don't answer it," Camy moaned.

"I won't."

It kept ringing.

"Oh God," Camy whispered. "Shut up!"

"Just ignore it," Alex rasped.

It rang some more.

"I can't ignore it . . . I'm a publicist! Answer it!"

Alex picked up the phone. "Hello," he said, with marvelous
control as Camy squeezed him between her thighs. "Juno . . .
gosh, how are you?"

"Juno . . . gosh, how are you?" Camy mimicked silently.

Alex pinched her nipple. "You have? That's terrific . . . how
. . . when?"

"Who . . . what . . . where," Camy whispered. She moved
her hips insistently.

"Yeah . . . it opens the thirtieth. . . . You will? Great . . .
I can't believe it. Hey, listen, Juno, I'm in the middle of something . . ."

"Somebody . . ."

"Okay . . . I can't wait either . . ."

"Neither can I." Camy squeezed his ass.

"See you soon. Bye." He hung up and leaned over and kissed
Camy's throat. "Thank you for being so patient."

"Old girlfriend?"

"Old friend."

"And she's coming to opening night? Oh goody. I'm dying to meet her."

Juno's plane landed at Kennedy at four-thirty, two hours late. By the time she had retrieved her baggage, gone through customs, waited in line for a taxi, and made it through the rush hour traffic to Lydia's new Park Avenue penthouse it was well past six.

Lydia and the children greeted Juno at the door. Lydia was dressed and ready to go. "My God, where've you been? How are you? Never mind . . . tell me later. Curtain's at seven-thirty."

Juno showered and changed quickly, emerging in a white silk crepe André Laug evening dress.

"Fabulous," Lydia said. "You certainly don't look like someone who's spent most of the last day traveling."

"Oh, it's wonderful to be here. I'm so excited. I've never lived in New York before."

"*Madame* . . ." the housekeeper appeared in the doorway. "They just called from downstairs. The car is here."

"Thank you, Henriette. Make sure the children are in bed by eight. It's a school night."

In the limo they settled back as the driver headed downtown.

"I'm so nervous," Juno said. "How's Alex?"

Lydia laughed. "We had lunch today. I ate, and he didn't. God, I hope *Plants* is a success. Camy says it's absolutely terrific. Oh . . . you don't know her yet . . . Camy Pratt. She's doing publicity for the play, and I want her to do it for our club . . . she's just fantastic. It turns out we were at prep school together. She and Alex are seeing each other, too. You'll meet her tonight."

The last of the evening-clad crowd was ebbing from the line of limousines to the inside of the Broadhurst Theater when Juno and Lydia arrived. Lydia spotted Camy peering impatiently from one of the doors, and waved.

"*There* you are!" Camy exclaimed. "I was panicked. Curtain's going up."

"Camy . . . this is Juno Johnson."

Camy shook Juno's hand. "Hello. Nice to meet you," she said

automatically. She took Lydia's arm and they swept ahead of
Juno into the theater. "Absolutely *everybody's* here. Alex is a
wreck, the poor darling."

Plants was a comedy-fantasy set in a Greenwich Village nursery. The main characters were the gardener-philosopher who
owned the store and his girlfriend, a sex therapist with a night-
time radio show. The other characters were the plants, played
by actors.

During intermission Juno, Lydia, and Camy fanned out
through the lobby, eavesdropping on conversations.

"Looks good so far," Camy said as they headed back to their
seats.

"From what I heard, they love it," Juno agreed.

And when the closing curtain fell, the audience rose to its
feet, turning Alexander Sage into an "overnight" Broadway sensation.

Afterward the party at Sardi's had that upbeat exhilaration
that a hit generates, and when the television reviews came on
the air the jubilant optimism was confirmed. Shortly after that
Camy Pratt received a call. When she returned to the table she
clinked her glass with a spoon.

"Hush, everybody. I've just heard from a friend at the *Times.*
It's a rave! We're a hit!" She looked at the note she had scribbled
on her napkin. " 'The first unqualified hit of the season.' Oh,
Alex!" She threw her arms around him and kissed him.

On the surface, Juno appeared gregarious, chatting it up with
the actors and Alex's family. She was thrilled for Alex; but,
underneath, her happiness was tempered by a feeling of not
belonging. She remembered how she had felt the day she had
arrived at Yale, the day she had first met Lydia. Everybody else
knew each other and she was the kid from the sticks. Well, the
Costa Smeralda was not exactly the sticks, but as far as New
York was concerned it might as well be. At Evviva! she had been
the center of attention. Here, nobody knew who she was.

And she had taken an instant dislike to Camy Pratt. Perhaps it
was jealousy; perhaps she still felt possessive about Alex—she
had not liked Tory either. But Camy was not being exactly

friendly. She seemed to be going out of her way to make it clear that Alex and Lydia were her domain now, and she had been pointedly snubbing Juno all evening.

So Juno was delighted when just after midnight Camy retrieved a suitcase from the cloakroom and took her leave. She was catching the red-eye to the Coast to see a European director who was planning to shoot a film in New York that fall. Juno's spirits improved remarkably after Camy's departure.

When the party began to break up, Alex took Juno and Lydia aside. "Don't leave me in my hour of triumph. I'm too high to come down. Back at my place I have a magnum of Perrier-Jouet and a bottle of cyanide . . . I was going to drink one of them tonight. The cyanide I would have taken alone, but since it's the champagne . . . join me?"

Lydia kicked off her heels and flopped down on the sofa. "It's an omen. A new era for all of us. The Three Musketeers back on top again. Alex is a smash, and our club's going to be a smash."

The cork exploded off the magnum and ricocheted off the ceiling. Alex guided the spurting champagne into three glasses. "Have you come up with a name for the club yet?"

Lydia looked at Juno and laughed. "I've got a list in my desk half a mile long."

"Oh, I know. Me, too. But nothing's right. Alex, you're the playwright . . . and you're hot. Give us something snappy."

"It'll cost you," Alex grinned. "Let's see . . . what about Gemini? You've got those twin town houses . . ."

"That's one on my list that I've already rejected. You'll have to do better than that."

Alex sat back with his glass of champagne. "What about Ménage à Trois . . . ?"

"Are you suggesting a name for the club . . . or something else?" Lydia asked.

"Why not both?"

"Come on, Alex," Juno said. "One thing at a time. First things first."

"All right. Inspiration." He drained his glass. "How about something simple, like Night Club . . . or . . . Night Life . . . ?"

"Night Life! I like it!"

"Alex, you're a genius," Lydia cheered.

He refilled the glasses. "Night Life," he toasted. They touched glasses and drank.

"Now . . . that other suggestion." Lydia stood up and reached for the zipper of her dress. "Or was that just talk?"

"You know me . . . all talk and all action. What about you, Juno?"

Juno hesitated. She was tired; the time difference was catching up with her. And it had been years since all three had made love together . . . twelve years. Then they had been young, and it had been Paris. She had fantasized about it since, but she had thought it would never happen again and that perhaps it was something best left to youth and memory.

Then Juno's eye fell on Camy's photograph on the picture board. Camy Pratt, who was trying to take her place in the triumvirate.

"I think I'm ready for a little action." Juno smiled and held out her arms to them.

Their lovemaking was different now. They were older and more sexually expert, but emotionally they were more bruised and vulnerable than they had been. Then their lives had been unknown adventures spread out before them. Now they had lived the adventures, and some had not been good ones.

Their passion took them back, and it did not seem like a dozen years. There was still that first exuberant lust for each other's bodies, and an uninhibited enjoyment of one another. But there was something bittersweet about it, too, because they all needed to be in love again and emotionally fulfilled.

The next morning over coffee they chatted and laughed easily and talked about what a good time they had had. But the night had made something clear. Alex wanted both of them, and Juno and Lydia each wanted Alex. The two women began to understand that it could not go on like this forever, and a sliver of a wedge was driven between them.

Chapter Thirty-two

An army of workmen moved into the twin town houses on East Sixty-second Street and began tearing down walls and re-shaping rooms according to Juno's design.

"It's going to take six months, and that's working overtime. But it's really going to be fabulous," Lydia said over a drink with Alex at the Carlyle. "If our money holds out," she added with a laugh.

"If anybody's money is going to hold out, yours will," he assured her. "Anyway John'll probably have some ideas for you. He's a financial genius." They were waiting for John Kinsolving to join them. He had been in London on a business trip and had missed the opening of Alex's play.

"Oh . . . and did I tell you the news? I've managed to lure Jean Raphael away from Tintin in Lyons. He's the one who got them their three-star rating and they're absolutely fit to be tied. Night Life is going to have *the* best food in New York."

"Where's the best food in New York?" John Kinsolving joined them at the bar.

"John," Alex said, standing. "Welcome back. I'd like you to meet Lydia de La Róche, my old companion in crime from the Yale theater days."

"Glad to meet you," John said.

"I've heard a lot about you from Alex," Lydia said, extending her hand. "I understand this was the first opening night of his that you've missed."

John laughed. "I don't think he'll ever let me come to another one. Hey, Alex, what raves! We're going to clean up on this one. About time you made me some money."

John ordered a vodka on the rocks. As they talked Lydia was aware that he kept stealing glances at her. He began to seem familiar to her, but she was sure she had never met him. Perhaps it was just the type; he was quite attractive, blond with brown eyes behind rimless glasses, a little shorter than Alex, with a muscular, square-shouldered build.

". . . anyway, Lydia wants someone on this side of the Atlantic to advise her on her financial affairs," Alex said. "Somebody she's in tune with. The count's people in Paris are a pretty reactionary lot."

John nodded. "Well, the first thing would be to get together in my office and let me have a look at your financial picture and . . . did you say the *count?*"

"Yes," Lydia said, "my late husband was the Count de La Roche."

John broke into a smile. "And were you, by any chance, slumming in Cannes . . . about a dozen years ago . . . with a bearded, scraggly hippie from Princeton?"

"Oh my God! *John?*" Lydia broke into an astonished smile. "I never knew your last name. This is incredible!"

"I take it you two know each other?" Alex said.

"And you really are a countess? You know, I never believed that story for a minute . . . French movie star, countess. It was a bit farfetched."

Lydia laughed. "I still don't quite believe it myself. So . . . what have you been doing all these years?"

"Columbia grad school . . . investment banking . . . and losing money on Alex's plays."

"If I use this plot line for my next one you can lose some more. Tell me . . . what is this all about?"

"You remember when I was on the lam from my honeymoon?" Lydia began.

An hour later Alex had to leave to go to the theater. John turned to Lydia. "Can I buy you dinner?"

"Wonderful," Lydia said. "Someplace French."

"Afterward maybe we can catch the fireworks."

"Fireworks? Where?"

John grinned. "My place."

Juno found a terraced apartment in a wonderful old building off Central Park West in the low Seventies. It had a sunken living room, and two bedrooms, one of which she turned into a studio. She had had her antiques and miscellaneous eclectic treasures shipped over from London and they gave the place an instant familiarity, though there was still a lot of space to fill.

Her favorite room was the large eat-in country kitchen that reminded her of her grandmother's in Taos when she was a child. Four days after she moved in she had stocked it with pots and pans and utensils from Zabar's and was preparing a Moroccan dinner for Gus Pallenberg.

The doorbell rang. Juno wiped her hands and hurried to the door, but when she opened it there was no one there.

"Gus?" she said. Then she heard a little whine and looked down to see a white puppy sniffing on her mat. "Oh, look at you!" She picked up the gangly, pointy-faced little thing. "Where did you come from?"

Gus stepped into the doorway. "From the championship kennels of Gustav Pallenberg. Happy housewarming."

"Oh, Gus! I've been wanting a dog. It's adorable . . . what is it?"

"A borzoi. I breed them. They are my great passion . . . next to you, of course," he said with a smile.

She kissed him. "Oh, thank you."

They went inside and sat the puppy in the middle of the kitchen floor. "She's paper-trained. She will be easy to housebreak," Gus said. "And she will protect you and keep you company."

Juno looked at him. "Instead of you?" she asked. "You haven't been keeping me very much company since I moved to New York."

"That will change," he promised. "Nina leaves again for Switzerland at the end of the week. She will be gone for a month this time. When she comes back she is always stronger. Then I will be able to ask her for a divorce."

"Will you, Gus? You're not just stringing me along?"

"Oh no, Juno. I love you."

Gus looked thin and tired. Since Nina's return from her last visit to the Swiss clinic he had developed an ulcer from his

agony over being torn between her and Juno. He did truly love
Juno, and he desperately wanted the normal life he knew he
could have with her. But his relationship with Nina was something strange and powerful that he did not completely understand himself.

Juno named the puppy Larushka. They put her in a cardboard box cushioned with towels while they had dinner. For
two minutes she yelped and whined, and then she was fast
asleep.

"How is the club coming along?" Gus asked.

"Oh, there's so much to do. But it'll all happen . . . thanks to
you. I met with your banker on Monday and signed the papers.
I still don't understand how you managed it. No other banker in
New York was willing to take a chance on me."

"I didn't do anything, really. Just opened the right doors."

Juno cleared the dishes and brought Gus some decaffeinated
coffee. "Can you stay tonight?" she asked.

"Not tonight, darling. But we can spend the weekend together. If you like."

Juno sighed. "I don't like being in this position . . . being
the other woman. But yes, I'd like to spend the weekend with
you."

Alex walked in past the workmen who were putting the finishing touches on the construction stage of Night Life. December sunlight filtered through the dust that hung in the air.

"Where's Miss Johnson?" he asked a workman.

"Up in the office."

Alex climbed the stairs to the second floor. He found Juno on
the phone negotiating the delivery of chrome pipes. He poured
himself a cup of coffee and waited while she finished.

Juno put down the phone and came over and kissed him. "Hi
. . . what brings you here? I didn't think you Broadway types
came out in daylight."

"I'm here with a major piece of news."

"Good or bad?" Juno smiled.

Alex shrugged. "Maybe you better sit down."

"Not good." She sat down. "Okay, I'm ready."

"I just found out who Camy's mother is. You know, the one she's not speaking to."

"Who?"

"Nina Pallenberg."

"Oh shit!"

"That's right . . . your friend Gus is Camy's stepfather."

"Oh, I need some coffee. I need something stronger than coffee, but it's too early in the day. God, does Lydia know?"

"I don't think so."

"I'd better tell her. If this gets back to Camy . . ." She picked up the phone. "Just when I thought there were only a few *minor* complications in my life."

In the months since her return to New York, Lydia had been much in demand, and she was enjoying every minute of it. After years of sexual starvation, she reveled in the smorgasbord that was now spread before her. Old friends were constantly inviting her to dinner parties to introduce her to eligible men. She had been seeing a lot of John Kinsolving and, for the past few weeks, Seth Pratt, Camy's handsome twenty-year-old brother.

Seth Pratt was theoretically a junior at Brown University, though he spent little time in Providence. He put a classmate on payroll to take notes and write papers for him. As Nina Pallenberg's spoiled and favored child he was given a large allowance, but with his dedication to gambling, alcohol, and cocaine, he managed to consistently live above it. He had met Lydia at a party at Camy's in early March and had been dazzled by the beauty and sophistication of the Countess de La Roche.

Lydia could not take Seth seriously, but she was enormously flattered that someone so much younger could find her so attractive. And Seth was totally infatuated. Lydia, thus far, had resisted the temptation to go to bed with Seth. He had a great deal of sex appeal, but there were too many complications: he was young and cocky, he was Camy's brother, and he was the stepson of Juno's lover. And there was a sinister quality about Seth that unnerved her a little, although in a way it perversely added to his appeal. So although Lydia had not slept with him yet, she was not at all sure that she was not going to.

If there was anyone she might be serious about, it was Alex.

But after all these years it was difficult for Lydia to sort out her feelings for him. He was still going out with Camy, who had become her close friend, but she knew from Camy that the affair was not catching fire. He was spending a lot of time with Juno, and this concerned Lydia more. Alex and Juno were not dating, exactly. They went to galleries and scoured antique shops and flea markets for things to fill Juno's apartment. Juno was still involved with Gus Pallenberg, although she had confessed to Lydia that things were not going the way she had hoped: Gus had yet to say anything to Nina about a divorce.

Nevertheless, Lydia was concerned. After the night of Alex's opening, when they had all made love together at his apartment, she had begun to understand that romantic coexistence between the three of them was no longer possible. Lydia was sure that Juno was in love with Alex; she was not sure whether Juno realized it. But Lydia knew that if she wanted Alex she would have to make up her mind, and make her move.

There were other tensions between Lydia and Juno. They were business partners now, and that inevitably caused problems. They had had minor clashes over many of the details and decisions to be made. Night Life was nearing completion, and Lydia sensed that Juno felt that she was working harder than Lydia. It was true that Juno was putting in more hours at the club, overseeing the lighting and special effects and decoration; but Juno did not appreciate the work that Lydia was doing with Camy, whipping anticipation up to a frenzy for the opening that was now only weeks away. The fact that Juno and Camy did not like each other was no help either. And the secrecy over Juno's affair with Gus Pallenberg only added to the strain.

One Saturday night, Seth Pratt took Lydia out to dinner and then down to a jazz club in the Village. He gave her hits of coke from a silver dispenser and did a great deal more himself. He was very glib and funny that evening. She decided to sleep with Seth, for the first time, that night.

But before midnight the combination of the drug and the drinks he had been downing turned his charm sharp and aggressive. He began needling a couple of homosexuals at the bar, and

Lydia became disgusted and embarrassed by his behavior. They fought about it, and she walked out and took a taxi uptown.

Bill, the night doorman, opened the taxi door for her. "Sunday *Times* is in, Countess. Do you want to take it now, or shall I have it sent up in the morning?"

"Oh, I'll take it with me. Thanks, Bill."

Before bed, she took a shower and made herself a cup of chamomile tea. She got into bed with the tea and the paper. After glancing at the headlines, she pulled out the Arts and Leisure section.

Her eyes ran down the front page, over a Hirschfeld caricature of Mandy Patinkin and Bernadette Peters in Sondheim's upcoming musical *Sunday in the Park with George,* and came to a dead stop at a headline in the lower right-hand corner of the page: MOMA RETROSPECTIVE OF JULLIEN FILMS.

The Museum of Modern Art was beginning a week-long festival of Bernard's films on Thursday. Bernard would be there on the opening night. She quickly scanned the article and turned to its continuation on page 14.

And there she was. A still of her and Roger Saint-Cyr from *L'Engagement.* ". . . Jullien's classic psychological thriller," the caption said, "which will open the MOMA retrospective."

Lydia had not seen *L'Engagement* since the Cannes Film Festival. The film played in Paris and New York at revival theaters from time to time, but she had never gone. Seeing it with Stefan was out of the question, and she even felt guilty about going behind his back. But that was not entirely it.

She had been afraid. If her performance was as good as she remembered, she would regret that she had allowed herself to be seduced away so easily from acting. If it were not, she did not want to know. It would shatter her confidence and destroy her belief that she had been truly talented. That belief in herself had kept her going during some of the most difficult times with Stefan.

But now Lydia wanted to see the picture. She *had* to know, once and for all, whether she was good or not. She had told Juno that she was no longer interested in acting, but that was not quite true. She was very interested but, again, she was afraid.

Lydia was also curious to see Bernard. It had been years since

that passionate afternoon in Paris, at the end of which he told
her he did not want to see her if she would not leave Stefan.
After that, Bernard had gotten married to an actress from whom
he had been divorced last summer, a few months after Stefan's
death. She had thought about calling him but had not. Call it
pride or cool; but after all, he knew that she was available. He
could have called her. And now he was in New York. If she
went to the screening she would certainly see him. She leaned
back against her pillows and smiled. Well . . . why not?

The theater downstairs at the Museum of Modern Art was
packed when Lydia arrived, late. She slipped in and stood at the
back. The director of the film department was already introducing Bernard.

Success had agreed with Bernard. He still wore his old trade-
mark, a leather motorcycle jacket and faded jeans. But the uniform looked more distinguished now than in the days when he
and Lydia had been living together. It had acquired the patina of
success. His dark hair was shorter now, and his face was clean-
shaven. And even from this distance Lydia could feel the attitude of authority that he carried.

She was aware of a bearded young man who kept looking at
her. Could he possibly recognize her? It had been over a dozen
years since she had made *L'Engagement.* Then she saw him nudge
the girl he was with, and she heard him whisper, "That's Lydia
Forrest!" Heads nearby turned, and others took up the litany—
"Lydia Forrest . . . Lydia Forrest . . ."

On the stage the director had just handed over the micro-
phone to Bernard. There was a huge wave of applause. Lydia
felt a shiver of anticipation run through her. Bernard began to
speak. His voice . . . it was so good to hear it again.

"Thank you, thank you. It gives me great pleasure to be here.
The film you are going to see here tonight means a great deal to
me. It was . . ." He paused, aware of the commotion in the rear
of the auditorium. He squinted out across the audience. Suddenly, his eyes fell on her and stopped. Through the speakers
she could hear him catch his breath.

"Ladies and gentlemen," he said, and Lydia could hear the
controlled excitement in his tone. "We have an unexpected plea-

sure here tonight. I was starting to tell you that this film has a special place in my heart. The reason for that is here in the hall with us. If she will come up here . . ." He gestured toward where she was standing. ". . . Lydia Forrest!"

Faces near her turned, then others all the way to the front of the hall, in rippling waves. Then the applause started. Lydia felt chills run up and down her. She felt tears come to her eyes, but she blinked them back. Then she took a deep breath and headed toward the podium, toward Bernard.

Afterward they went to dinner at the Café Luxembourg. Lydia was jubilant. The film had been as much a revelation to her as that first time at Château Mordoi.

"I was good, Bernard, wasn't I?"

Bernard smiled. "No, not good . . . brilliant. What a waste all these years have been."

"It hasn't been a waste," Lydia protested. "I have my children. I've been busy."

He flicked his hand. "Many women have children. Many women are busy. Very few of them, hardly any, have your talent and your magnetism. You saw tonight. You saw how the audience responded to you."

"Oh, Bernard," she said. She leaned back in her chair, and her eyes were shining. "It's so good to see you again. More than once, I've wanted to call you, but . . ."

"But you were waiting for me to call you," he grinned.

She nodded. "Yes . . . why didn't you?"

"I don't know . . . perhaps I was afraid. So much has changed."

"But now?"

He smiled. "Now I think perhaps nothing has changed. Or perhaps we have come full circle, to the beginning again."

"To a new beginning." Lydia touched his hand. "I still have the key, you know. You were right. I never could throw it away."

"It might not fit my hotel room here, but . . ."

They made love slowly and passionately, two people making up for lost time, with all the time in the world. Afterward, they shared a cigarette and lay in each other's arms.

"You know that I still love you, Lydia."

"Oh, Bernard . . ."

"I am not asking you for a declaration right now. I just want you to know."

When morning came, they ordered a huge breakfast from room service.

"I am on my way to California to negotiate for my first American film. It is called *Borrowed Time.* There is a perfect part in it for you . . . the lead, of course."

"I couldn't act again. It's been too long."

"Not when it is in the blood, as it is with you. And now you are free to do what you want."

She laughed. "Don't forget Night Life. It opens next week. You will be there, won't you?"

"Of course. I can delay California for a few days. But think about it, Lydia. Nightclubs are not what you are all about. They are what you have become, perhaps, but not what you ought to be."

"I don't know, Bernard. I'm not sure what I want anymore. Right now, Night Life being a success is the most important thing in my life."

Chapter Thirty-three

Night Life opened on the third of May, one of the first warm evenings in a generally miserable spring. The beautiful people were ready. Items and articles about the club had been saturating columns and magazines for months. The work that Juno had done on the inside, and Lydia and Camy on the outside, finally came together.

The opening was a stunning success. Critics used phrases like "apocalyptic brilliance of design," "elegance nouveau," and "disco redefined for the mid-eighties" in lavishing praise on the new club. By dawn the word of mouth had spread all over town, wherever night creatures were: Night Life was the new place to be.

Early the next evening, Gus Pallenberg came to Juno's apartment.

"Larushka!" he said, as the puppy bounced over to greet him, wagging her tail. "You're getting very big."

"Yes," Juno said. "Isn't it amazing. When weeks go by without seeing them they just seem to shoot up, don't they?"

"Juno, darling," he said, kissing her. "You know I would be with you every minute, if I could."

She looked at Gus sympathetically. It was shocking how much he had aged in the time she had known him. This was no line he was handing her, Juno knew that. He really did love her and it was tearing him apart. But for some reason which she could not understand he was unable to break away from Nina. For a while, she had deluded herself that he would. She knew now that it was Gus who was deluding himself.

"I know, Gus. But there's no point, is there?"

"Yes, there is. I love you, isn't that the point? I'd go crazy if I didn't have you."

Juno shook her head sadly. "I don't have you, Gus. And it's driving *me* crazy."

"You have me now." He put his hand on her breast. "And for the next ten days. Nina is back at the clinic, and I . . ."

Juno brushed his hand away angrily. "No, Gus. I'm thirty-two, and that's too old to be a weekend bimbo. It's over. I've had it!"

He pulled her to him and kissed her desperately. "You can't throw me away like that. I love you . . . I need you."

"No, Gus," Juno said. "You love me, I believe that. But it's Nina you *need.*"

Gus dropped his arms and look at her beseechingly. "Please, Juno. Just a little while longer."

"No, Gus. I told you," she said, softly but firmly. "This isn't the way I want to live my life. I should never have gotten involved. It wasn't fair to either of us." She stepped back. "And now I think the best thing to do is make a clean break of it. I'm sorry."

Gus sighed, and all the air seemed to go out of him. He seemed to deflate before her eyes. He started to say something, then shook his head. He turned and left.

A month after the opening of Night Life, Lydia was in her limousine heading home from the club. At four in the morning the Manhattan streets were almost empty of traffic. The black limousine sped uptown, made the turn at Seventy-seventh Street to the downtown side of Park Avenue, and glided to a stop at the curb. The doorman hurried out and opened the door.

"Thank you, Bill."

Lydia took the elevator to the penthouse. There was a large manila envelope for her on the hall table. She saw that it was from Bernard, in Hollywood. She took it back with her to her room and tossed it on the bed.

When she was in her nightgown, she opened the envelope. Inside was a screenplay in a black paper folder. The title on it

was *Borrowed Time.* There was a note from Bernard pinned to
the cover.

> *Chérie,*
>   *Now you know that you cannot hide from your talent. Now*
> *that the club is a success, you are free to return to your true destiny.*
> *I want you to make this film with me next year. It will be a new*
> *beginning for both of us.*
>   *Je t'embrasse très tendrement.*
>
>   *Bernard*

After she and Bernard had been reunited at the MOMA
screening, she had seen him almost every night until he had left
for the Coast. In the weeks since then he had called her often,
always with the same theme: that they must get back together,
that she must resume her career. But Lydia was not ready to
make up her mind yet. Night Life was exciting, and acting and
Bernard seemed dreams from a long time ago.

She got into bed and began reading the screenplay.

An hour later Lydia put it down and walked out onto the
terrace. Dawn was breaking over the city. She lit a cigarette and
sat for a long time, thinking.

She remembered the first time she had read a screenplay of
Bernard's, back in his apartment on the Quai de l'Horloge.
Then it had sent shivers through her. She was going to be a
movie star! Now she felt those shivers again. Bernard's story
was gripping, and the part was an actress's part. That was what
excited her now, not the stardom. She had been a celebrity for a
long time. Now what she wanted was to be an actress.

She thought about the argument that she and Juno used to
have at Yale. Juno would proselytize about career and self-fulfill-
ment, and Lydia saw her life in terms of the man she would
marry. Juno's point of view had seemed stubbornly trendy to
Lydia in those early days of women's liberation. But a lot had
happened since then and Lydia realized that she had to deal
with her life on its own terms, through herself, not someone
else. It was not that she had done nothing; on the contrary, with
her wine business and the nightclub and the various responsibilities involved with being the Countess de La Roche, she had

accomplished a great deal more than most women. But Bernard was right. None of it was essentially her, Lydia Forrest, nor was it what she wanted to be doing.

Lydia thought about Juno. She had changed, too. She had been so busy with her career in London that she had not noticed that her husband was having an affair with another woman. Lydia knew that Juno regretted the breakup of her marriage to Shep. Juno blamed herself entirely, for being too self-involved to see what was happening before her eyes.

But Juno did have her career, and that was what carried her through bad times. Even now, with her split from Gus, Juno had thrown herself into the running of Night Life. And she had the satisfaction of walking through the club every night and *knowing* that it was her creation. The design that had been praised and touted by so many people and publications had sprung from *her* mind, her talent.

Lydia put out her cigarette and went to bed. She wanted to call Bernard, but it was three hours earlier in California. He would be asleep. She looked at the pillow next to hers and touched it. Bernard had slept there, with her, when he was in New York. They had had nearly two weeks together, after the night of the screening.

It was not a rekindling of her old affair with Bernard. They had both changed. What had unfolded in their two weeks together was a new relationship, between two people who were older and more secure within themselves. Of course, nothing permanent was settled. Lydia, still wary from her marriage, was afraid of commitment now.

She closed her eyes, exhausted. As she drifted off, she composed her Academy Award acceptance speech for *Borrowed Time*.

Juno awoke with a start and looked at the alarm clock. Ten o'clock. *Damn*, she had overslept. Larushka usually pounced on her around nine, but even the dog was still dozing comfortably on the foot of her bed.

The intercom buzzed, and Juno realized that was what had awakened her in the first place. He was here already. Her head cleared as she rushed into the hall to press the buzzer, and then went into the kitchen to turn the heat on under the remains of yesterday's coffee. She dashed back into the bedroom and threw on a pair of jeans and a T-shirt. The elevator in her apartment building was appallingly slow. She managed to get her teeth and hair brushed before her doorbell rang.

"Good morning," she said perkily as she opened the door. "I'm almost ready. Check the coffee while I get on my boots."

"Okay," Alex said. "But we've got to get a move on it. The auction's starting right now."

"I'm ready," she reappeared. She kissed his cheek.

"Here." Alex handed her a cup of coffee and poured one for himself. He took a sip and made a face. "Jesus . . . one-thousand-year-old coffee. This is terrible."

"Oh, Alex, you say the sweetest things." She grabbed her handbag and dark glasses. "Okay, *allons-y.*"

The auction was across the George Washington Bridge and just up the Palisades, at the estate of a theatrical producer who had died the previous winter. Juno had read about it in the paper and was eager to get a look at his collection of original set drawings by such greats as David Belasco, Max Reinhardt, and Robert Edmond Jones. Alex wanted to bid on some manuscripts of plays.

Alex followed the auction signs and drove through the stone gates of the two-hundred-acre estate. Green lawns rolled endlessly up to a Tudor-style mansion that overlooked the Hudson.

"Wow," Alex said. "This is the way to live. Forget the drawings and the manuscripts, let's buy the whole place."

"Suits me. God, I wonder what it'd be like to live in a place like this."

"Lydia knows. Hey, we'll get her to buy it for us and we'll all three live here together."

Juno laughed. "You never give up, do you, Alex?"

He grinned. "Boyhood ideals die hard." There were hundreds of cars parked on a lawn near the house. A boy with a baseball cap waved them to a space. "What are all these people doing parked on our lawn?" Alex grumbled.

They wandered through the house, viewing the items for auction. When the things they were interested in came up several hours later, they were in the ballroom for the bidding. The manuscripts soon went out of Alex's range, but there was less active

competition for the set designs. Juno wound up with three: a
Belasco, and two by Robert Edmond Jones. On impulse, Alex
bought a quill pen, set in an Art Deco inkwell.

"Well, a satisfying day," Alex said as they drove back down
the Palisades. "Nothing to pick you up like spending a lot of
money."

"Too much," Juno moaned, cradling the precious drawings in
her lap to keep them from being destroyed by Larushka, as the
huge puppy tramped from side to side in the backseat, changing
windows. "But I don't care. What's the point of being a success
if you can't spend money? Anyway, I've already started paying
off my bank loan. And these are so beautiful."

Alex came up for a drink when they got back to Juno's apartment. He sipped his vodka and tonic as she went from wall to
wall, holding up the drawings to see where they would go best.

"There's something I've been waiting to tell you," he said
finally. "I didn't bring it up earlier because we were having so
much fun. But I've got to leave town for a while."

Juno turned around, holding the Belasco against her chest.
"Oh no, Alex. Why?"

"The screenplay." He had sold the screen rights to *Plants* to
Brad Blackwell, the movie star who had his own production
company and now acted in only one well-chosen film every few
years. Blackwell wanted Alex to do the screen adaptation, and
Alex had been working on it in New York. "But they get nervous, having the writer so far away. They want me out there in
Hollywood so they can look over my shoulder."

"Oh boy. I'm going to miss you. How long is it for?"

"I don't know. A couple of months, anyway. Depends on
what they see over my shoulder."

Juno came over and sat beside him. "How am I ever going to
get my apartment finished without you?"

Alex kissed her. "Leave it just the way it is till I get back," he
said. They kissed again, and then both pulled back at the same
time, as if the kiss had threatened to take them beyond the un-
written boundary that was always there. A little while later
Alex finished his drink, kissed Juno safely good-bye, and left.

She missed him even more than she had expected to. They
had spent a lot of time together in the past few months, more

than at any time since Paris. It had been time as friends, not as lovers. The standing joke between them was that they were dating stepfather and stepdaughter, and trying to figure out what relationship that would give them if the respective marriages ever took place.

The only positive aspect of Alex's absence was that it more or less marked the termination of his affair with Camy Pratt. He had not broken up with her exactly, but Juno knew from Lydia that Camy was secretly afraid that it was over.

"Ah, here you are, Juno," Dominick Charpentier said as he came into her office one day in midsummer. Juno had brought him over from Evviva! to manage the club. Larushka, now an extremely large puppy, looked up from the banquette on which she was stretched out in the sunlight. "I still say a dog that big belongs in the country."

"Yeah, well, we all have to make adjustments. Did you get the union problem sorted out?"

"It's coming along. Don't worry about it. Everything's fine. What you need is a vacation. You're up all night, then you waltz in here at ten and make work for yourself."

"What do you mean?" Juno snapped. "I don't *make* work for myself . . . there's plenty to do."

Dominick shrugged. "And you don't think the lack of sleep is getting to you?"

"No!" She made an effort to smile. "Listen, Dom, I appreciate your concern, but everything's cool. In another month or so this place'll run itself."

"Yeah . . . well, don't forget you have a lot of people who are paid to work here. Let 'em do their jobs. Make 'em do *more*. You're edgy these days." Dominick picked up the string of order sheets he had come in for. "Think about a vacation."

"Yes, Dominick," Juno said brittlely. "Is there anything else you need?"

"No . . . oh, that dude Seth Pratt was around looking for Lydia. She comin' in?"

"Who knows."

Dominick left. Juno went over and hugged Larushka. It annoyed her the way Seth Pratt kept hanging around. She was the one who ended up having to deal with him since Lydia was so seldom there. That annoyed her, too. Oh, Lydia showed up every night to play the gracious hostess, but since the club had opened she had not lifted a finger to help with the day-to-day running of the place. You could not even call her before one o'clock in the afternoon. And she was so involved with her love life that it was hard to get her to concentrate on club business.

Juno looked at her watch. It was past one, so she put in a call to Lydia.

"Hello," Lydia's sleepy voice croaked.

"Are we still on for lunch today? We have to talk about this surprise party that Kerry wants to throw at the club for Diane Keaton."

"Oh, Juno . . . I forgot. I'm having lunch with John today. He says it's terribly important."

"All right," Juno said icily. "Perhaps you could come to the club early tonight and we could talk about it then?"

"Sure . . . oh no. Camy's giving a dinner party."

"Okay . . . then I'll take care of it myself!" Juno slammed down the phone.

The phone rang again a moment later.

"Juno . . ." Lydia said. "I'll be over around three-thirty, if that's convenient."

"That's convenient. See you then." Juno took a deep breath. "Come on, Larushka. Let's go to the park." She picked up the leash and Larushka jumped to the floor and began dancing around in anticipation. "Yes . . . a walk! And maybe a hot dog . . ."

She had her hand on the knob when the door opened from the other side. It was Gus.

"Hello, Juno," he said. He closed the door and took her in his arms and kissed her before she could say a word. At first she resisted. She was in no mood for surprise romance. But he held the kiss and its warmth got to her. She began to respond as the puppy frisked and whined around them.

"Wow," she said when they finally broke apart. "What's that all about? Oh, Gus . . . have you told her?"

He shook his head. "Not yet, but I had to see you. I can't tell you how awful it's been without you, Juno." He rubbed his eyes and sat on the edge of her desk. "It's getting worse with Nina. She's only been back a few weeks and I can see the signs already. It used to be six months between her visits to the damned clinic. Now . . ."

"Goddammit, Gus, I don't want to hear about Nina! I don't give a damn about her."

"But, darling, I'm only trying to explain . . ."

"I don't want to hear it. You've been explaining to me for a year now."

He came over and put his arms around her. "I know . . . I've been a coward about this. It hasn't been fair to you, but I love you. Please believe me."

Juno sighed. "I believe you, Gus. But it's over. Unless you get rid of Nina."

As she said this the door swung open, and Seth Pratt stood there, looking at them. "Excuse me," he said finally. "I seem to be interrupting something." He turned and slammed the door behind him.

Nina Carruthers Pratt Pallenberg sat at her dressing table with a towel wrapped around her. In her raised hand was a cotton puff with some clarifying lotion on it. She became aware suddenly that the lotion had dried. She did not know how long she had been sitting like that.

It frightened her, these lapses of memory. A lot was frightening her these days. Since childhood she had been afflicted with a mild agoraphobia, but lately she was terrified to even leave the house. Sometimes now she had trouble talking. Her tongue seemed to thicken and she would stumble over words.

And her body, the beautiful body she had worked so hard and spent so much to maintain, was beginning to betray her. Nina stood and let the towel fall to the floor. She looked at herself from every angle in the myriad mirrors that lined the walls and ceiling of her dressing room. What the eyes could see was still extraordinary. Her breasts and buttocks did not sag, her skin was taut. There were no wrinkles or stretch marks. Her throat was smooth and her chin firm. At fifty, she looked thirty. Even her hands, creamy and unveined, did not give her away.

But something was happening on the inside. When she

walked now sometimes her left leg would drag and she would lose her balance. Her bowels no longer functioned properly. Unexpected tremors ran through her, and she would be seized by piercing headaches which would disappear as abruptly as they began.

Worst of all was the terror. She could not name it, but sometimes it was so intense she could not get her breath. She would break out in cold sweats and bury her face in a pillow to scream.

She was dying.

Dr. Gundhardt at the Swiss clinic would not say so. But he had not wanted to take her this last time, and it had taken bullying and begging and bribery to make him relent. He had told her from the first that the injections of his serum, Sirusol RX23, were experimental and potentially dangerous. There was the possibility of addiction, and as the body built up tolerance, a lessening of effectiveness. What he had not told her, and what he was now denying, was that in the long run the drug could produce a degeneration of the vital organs and the nervous system.

Nina could not bear the idea of getting old. Still more dreadful was the prospect of becoming an invalid. She could not hope to keep Gus if she were bedridden or wheelchair-bound. He was ten years younger than she. How could she hope to keep him if her aging process, deprived of Dr. Gundhardt's wonder drug, began to accelerate? Dr. Gundhardt had refused absolutely to accept her into the clinic again, and no threats of lawsuit or blackmail would move him.

But she could not get old. She could not lose Gus.

The crunching of gravel in the driveway brought Nina to the window. Gus's silver Mercedes came to a stop by the front steps, and he got out. He spoke for a moment with Hennings, the butler; then, instead of coming inside, Gus headed across the lawn to his kennels. Those damned dogs, Nina thought, as she went back into her dressing room. It seemed as if he spent more time with them than her these days.

Nina put on an apricot satin hostess gown. It was her best color, and the cut was low to show off the youthful swell of her breasts. She fastened an emerald and diamond choker around her neck, swept her hair up into a perfect chignon, and applied

her makeup carefully and expertly, despite the slight tremor in
her hands. A small white envelope was leaning against an Art
Deco atomizer of Pherômone. She slipped the envelope into the
pocket of her gown, and misted the perfume into her hair and
cleavage. She stood up and stepped into a pair of black sandals
with diamond clips. The dressing room mirrors on every side
told her that she looked beautiful. Nina smiled.

Gus Pallenberg said good night to his dogs and spoke to his
handler about their grooming. Then he strode back to the house.
Nina would be upstairs, asleep. He headed into the library to fix
himself a drink and read the paper.

As he dropped ice with silver tongs into a glass, Hennings
appeared in the doorway. "Excuse me, sir. Mrs. Pallenberg is
expecting you in her suite."

"Thank you, Hennings." Gus poured some scotch over the ice
and drank it in a swallow. Seth. That little bastard had not
wasted any time reporting in to Mummy. And now she was
pacing around up there waiting to confront him. Perhaps it was
just as well. Juno thought that he was afraid to speak to Nina
about a divorce and would never do it, but that was not true. He
was just waiting for the right time. And this might be it.

Gus opened the door to Nina's suite. Nina was standing by
the marble fireplace. The setting sun that streamed in through
the doors of her veranda added coppery highlights to her chestnut hair, and a healthy flush to her cheeks. She smiled at him
and held out her arms.

"Darling, you look wonderful." He went over and kissed her.

"I feel wonderful. I've missed you today. Did your meeting go
well?"

"Oh . . . yes. As well as can be expected."

She curled a lock of his hair around her finger. "Gus," she
purred, "tonight is going to be very special. I feel . . . romantic. Why don't you order up some caviar and champagne from
the kitchen. And . . ." She kissed his neck. "Dismiss the servants." She kissed his neck again. "*All* the servants."

Gus showered and shaved. He was stunned at the turn things
had taken. He had been prepared for hysterics. Instead, it was

Nina almost as she used to be. It had been a long time since he
had seen her like this. In the past year, even after her visits to
the clinic, she had become increasingly reclusive and agitated.
She looked wonderful when she pulled herself together, but she
spent a lot of time sleeping, or closeted in her suite alone.

Nina's first visit to Switzerland had been five years ago. The
results were marvelous, and it was nearly a year before she
needed to go again. She was a tigress in bed, more uninhibited
and passionate than she had ever been. Her energy was bound-
less. But the trips to the clinic became more frequent, and each
time the euphoria that followed was of shorter duration. Nina
continued to look wonderful, but there were signs, which Gus
pretended not to notice, that her mental and physical health was
failing. He had tried many times to talk her out of going to Dr.
Gundhardt. He could not blame himself. But if things continued the way they seemed to be going, he might not have to speak
to Nina about a divorce after all.

But then tonight she looked so much better. Almost the way
she had when he met her, a dozen years ago in Rome. She had
been wearing a peach chiffon evening dress and she was the
most extraordinary woman he had ever seen. He had fallen in
love with her. She had won him with her beauty, consumed him
with her passion, and dazzled him with her enormous wealth.
He had given up his career as an architect for her, because she
was overwhelmingly jealous and could not bear to have him
spend time away from her. Despite that aspect of her personality, Gus had been happy with Nina, until the visits to Dr.
Gundhardt had begun their subtle deterioration. For the last
three years, his life had grown increasingly hellish. Nina's jealousy had become obsessive, and her moods fluctuated insanely.

And yet, when she was the way she was tonight, they were
almost able to step back to the way they had been.

When he returned to Nina's room the champagne was sitting
in a silver ice bucket, and Nina was spreading caviar on toast
points. It was white caviar from the roe of albino sturgeon. Gus
opened the champagne and poured it into two crystal flutes.

"To you, darling." Nina smiled. "To our everlasting love."

They drank. Nina kissed him. "We'll always be together, just

like this. I couldn't be without you." She took a bite of toast
spread with caviar and slid the rest of the piece into Gus's
mouth. "I ordered this up from Balducci's this morning. Remember when we first had it?"

He smiled. "Our first anniversary. What gluttons we were
. . . that's all we ate."

"And it's all you're having tonight. Except for me." She
spooned a dollop of caviar onto her tongue and stuck it out
toward Gus. He leaned forward, surrounded it with his lips, and
swallowed it.

"Let's have more champagne, darling," Nina said gaily. She
drained her glass and held it out to be filled. "And more caviar.
Eat! Eat it up. Eat, drink, and be merry . . ."

Soon the bottle was empty and the caviar was gone. Nina
slipped a cassette of Ella Fitzgerald singing Gershwin into the
player.

"Embrace me, you sweet embraceable you," Nina sang along
with the tape, whirling around the room. "Oh, Gus . . . do you
remember that dress, the one I bought in Capri? Of course you
do . . . it was melon silk with . . . Whatever happened to it,
do you know?" She flew to her dressing room and began tossing
things out of her closet. Hundreds of thousands of dollars in
designer originals piled up in a heap on the floor behind her.
"Oh . . . it's not here." Her voice trembled, on the brink of
tears. Then, just as suddenly, her spirits swung upward again.
"Gustav Nils Pallenberg, you are the most wonderful architect
in the world. I love this house, what you've done to it. Why
don't we build a conservatory?"

"We did, my darling," he called out. He wondered if she was
joking. "Summer before last."

Nina danced back into the bedroom with her full-length
fisher coat over her gown. "Don't you think it's cold? I love this
coat."

"Cold? No . . ."

"No, no, they can't take that away from me . . ." Nina sang.
She staggered slightly, falling against Gus where he sat on the
love seat, and pressed her breasts against his face. "Oh, Gus . . .
Gus . . . I want you to make love to me."

Gus felt a shudder run through his body.

"Don't you want to?" She giggled suddenly. "Remember that time on Richard's plane? You were so terrified the pilot would look back. Oh, I had to stifle my moans . . . but I won't have to tonight." She clutched his hand. "You did get rid of the servants, didn't you, darling?"

"Yes . . . all of them." His nerves were on edge. Nina's erratic behavior was getting to him, and yet at the same time he was caught up in her mad enthusiasm.

"Now! I want you now." She flung the fur coat down on the floor and sank down on top of it. "Here. Come to me."

Gus stood. He felt a tick in his arm, a muscle jumping from the strain. "Yes, just a moment, darling. I'll be right back."

"Hurry!"

Gus went down the hall to his bathroom. He rummaged through his medicine cabinet for the Valium, knocking several other bottles into the sink where they shattered. He found the tranquilizer and swallowed three pills. He took a deep breath.

Nina was still on the floor, clutching herself, writhing and moaning. "You were so long, darling . . . so long. I need you now! Undress me quick."

Gus knelt down and undid the zipper. He slid her gown off. After more than a dozen years the perfection of her body never ceased to excite and amaze him. As he took off his own clothes he felt his chest tightening. His breath was coming in short gasps. He lay down on the fisher coat next to Nina.

When he touched her breast her whole body stiffened, and she cried out in a scream that startled him. But her face was flushed with pleasure, and she threw her arms around him and squeezed his body tightly to hers. "Get in me now! Quick!" she panted. She screamed again as he entered her, and locked her legs about his waist like a vice. Her breath was ragged and desperate as he pumped into her.

"Oh yes . . . oh yes . . . ohhh!" Nina's voice went up in a rising wail until it was a shrill ululating screech.

Gus felt her climax building and sucking him down like a whirlpool. He thrust faster. It was painful, even terrifying. Suddenly Nina's body went rigid with orgasm, and her throat erupted with a dry, rattling sob. He looked at her face and saw that her eyes were bulging and her pupils were great yawning wells of blackness. A tiny trickle of saliva flecked the corner of her mouth, and the veins stood out at her temples.

"Nina! What's wrong?" Gus could tell she was in convulsion. He slapped her face. He did not know much about first aid, but he knew he needed something to keep her from swallowing her tongue. He jumped up and got the silver spoon from the caviar. His legs twitched and buckled and he crashed heavily to the floor.

"Ohhh," Nina's eyes blinked, as she came out of the convulsion. Her breathing was shallow. "Hold me, Gus. I don't want to be alone."

"I'm going to call the doctor . . ."

Nina laughed. He looked at her and her eyes were shining and there was a strange triumphant grin on her face. "You can't. You can't call the doctor. You can't even call your little friend."

Gus pulled himself across to the night table and picked up the phone. It was dead. The receiver cord was severed. Horrified, he turned back to Nina. "My God . . . what have you done?"

"We're going away together, Gus. A second honeymoon. Just the two of us. We'll be together forever . . ."

"What was it, Nina? What have we taken?"

"Strychnine," she sang. "From your kennel supplies. No more nasty little rodents . . . no more nasty little girlfriends. What's she like, Gus? What's your little Indian girl like?"

"Christ! We've got to get to the hospital." He forced himself to stand and tried to lift Nina from the floor, but the effort was too much for him. He sank to his knees beside her. A huge tremor shook his entire body.

"Oh, Gus . . ." Nina went into another convulsion.

He tried to keep from panicking. The nearest phone was at the end of the hall in his bedroom. He could get to it. But the spoon . . . he had to hold it down against her tongue. He attempted to do this and drag Nina along the floor, but it was impossible. She twitched violently again and moaned. Her body slumped back in exhaustion. Gus looked at her, not knowing what to do.

So Seth had told his mother after all. She knew about Juno. Perhaps Nina had had him followed, too. She had become so paranoid these last few months. He felt an involuntary jerk and looked down to see her hand clasp his. She opened her eyes.

"On my night table," she whispered between gasps for breath. "A pad . . . paper. Write something, darling. Something beautiful . . . so the world will know . . ." She looked at him, blinking. ". . . how much you love *me* . . ."

"We've got to get the doctor. It's not too late." A surge of panic overtook Gus again. His muscles went rigid, and the room turned very bright.

When Gus came to, he was lying with his head in Nina's lap. She was stroking his forehead. "Soon," she cooed. "It will be over soon. You see, darling . . . it is too late. But not for us." She put the notepad in his hand. "I know you always loved me. She was nothing to you. Write it . . . write something nice . . . something . . ." Another fit seized Nina.

Gus realized that it *was* over. And in a way he felt relieved. It was only going on living with Nina that was impossible. It had never occurred to him that he could die with her. But then, Nina had always made the important decisions for both of them.

He picked up the pen and began to write.

Chapter Thirty-four

Seth Pratt stood on the front porch of Leighdale, his mother's estate on the Hudson, near Tarrytown. Far in the distance he could still hear the throbbing wail of the ambulance that was carrying his mother's and stepfather's bodies to the hospital. It would be a pointless trip for Nina; she had been pronounced dead on the scene, though the technicians would continue to try to resuscitate her during the race to the emergency room. Two hundred million dollars bought certain privileges, even after death.

For Gus, it was a different story. There were vital signs, though they were weak. The ambulance technicians had promised Seth they would do everything to pull him through.

Pull him through! That was the last thing Seth wanted. If Gus died, Seth figured he would inherit everything. There might be a pittance for Camy, but she and Nina had been estranged for years. Even if Gus lived, Seth would certainly do very well. But why should Gus live? Why should Gus get anything?

The police detectives came downstairs. Lieutenant Caputo stopped to speak to Seth.

"We're through here, Mr. Pratt. We've got the suicide note. We've got your statement. There're still some questions, but there's nothing more we can do tonight." He looked at his notebook. "We can reach you at one of these numbers if we need you later, can't we?"

"Yes."

"Sorry about your mother."

After the police left Seth walked back inside and fixed himself a drink. He was still shaking from what had happened. He had arrived at Leighdale a little after nine, to see his mother. He had some very interesting news for her, about Gus and Juno Johnson, and he was hoping to hit her up for five thousand dollars to settle his account with Duncan, his drug dealer. Duncan was becoming impatient with the tab Seth had run up. More than impatient.

He was surprised to find the house apparently deserted when he got there. Hennings and the other servants seemed to be gone. He had called out and, receiving no answer, had gone up to his mother's suite. That was where he had found them—his mother, naked on the floor, and Gus, naked also, slumped across her.

Seth had panicked and called the police. Then he had cursed himself for not having searched for money first. What if they sealed the place off? Fortunately, they had not. Seth drained his drink and poured another. He did a little coke, and then climbed the stairs to his mother's suite.

It did not seem possible that Nina was dead. The rooms were still full of her presence, the smell of her perfume. He picked up an evening gown from a pile of clothes on the floor in her dressing room. She had worn it last Christmas. Suddenly the loss welled up in him, and Seth buried his face in the gown and cried. She was the one person he had been able to count on, and now she was gone.

Presently, he pulled himself together. There was a wall safe behind a portrait of him as a child, but he did not know the combination. His mother must have kept it written down somewhere, she had become so forgetful. He searched her dressing table and found nothing. In her desk he found a couple of hundred-dollar bills tucked into a glasses case. It was not nearly enough. He looked around. There was an address book by the telephone on her night table, and there he found it, under the *S*s: safe—R3L10R6.

He raced to the safe and opened it. There was a diamond bracelet he could hock, and a few rings and earrings; all large stones, all salable. No cash, but more than enough to pay Duncan and keep himself subsidized until the estate was settled. Except that Duncan wanted cash . . . by midnight. Duncan had suggested that Seth's arms might be broken if he did not meet the deadline. Or his legs. Duncan had lived in Thailand after the Vietnam War and had taken up martial arts there. He was now a seventh-degree black belt. His threats were not meaningless.

Seth put the jewels into his jacket pocket, quickly closed the safe, and replaced the portrait. He searched the dresser and bathroom drawers and all of Nina's handbags, but only came up with a hundred and thirty dollars, some Swiss francs, and a ton of change.

Seth looked at his watch. It was nearly eleven. He bolted out of Nina's suite and down the hall to Gus's. A search of his step-father's bedroom and bathroom netted nearly five hundred dollars more. In Gus's study was an antique mahogany desk. There was nothing but stationery in the side drawers but the center one was locked. Seth looked for the key but could not find it. He grabbed a letter opener and easily jimmied open the timeworn lock. There was Gus's checkbook. The balance was over twelve thousand. Seth wrote a five-thousand-dollar check to cash, for Duncan, and another one for seven. He dated them two days earlier and forged Gus's signature. He sighed and smiled. The immediate crisis was over.

As he put the checkbook back in the drawer, Seth noticed an envelope. The letterhead was the First Guaranty Savings Bank. It was addressed to Gustav Pallenberg and scrawled across it in Gus's handwriting was the name Juno.

"This is unbelievable," Lydia ranted. She was in a foul mood. It had been a bad week. Forrest had broken his arm. John Kinsolving had told her that he was getting back together with his wife, Rosemary. Bernard had been delayed another week in California. "These salaries are astronomical! They're only kitchen workers, for Christ's sake."

"They have a union, Lydia. We've been ironing this out for weeks now. It's all very exciting. Collective bargaining. You should drop in sometime and catch it."

"Look, Juno, I'm getting sick and tired of your snide . . ."

The phone rang. Lydia picked it up.

Impatiently, Juno riffled through the payroll file. Gradually she became aware that the conversation from Lydia's end was "Oh no's," punctuated by an ominous silence.

"Oh *merde*." Lydia put down the receiver. She looked grave.

"What's wrong?"

"That was Camy. Seth just called her. He's gone to the D.A. with evidence that it wasn't suicide . . ." She paused, "that Gus murdered Nina."

"Murdered? Oh God. What evidence?"

Lydia came around and stood across the desk from Juno. Her face was pale with shock. "He says that *you* told Gus to do it."

"What? How could he?" Juno sat there, stunned. "*Me?*"

"Camy wasn't exactly clear, but apparently Seth says he walked in on you and Gus together . . . here at the club. And that you were telling him he had to kill Nina."

"Oh no! I can't believe this. He *did* walk in on us. I was telling Gus it was no use, that we were completely through unless he divorced Nina. I said divorce . . . not kill." Juno's brow furrowed and she bit her lip. "No . . . I remember what I said. It was something like 'I don't want to see you again unless you get rid of Nina.' "

"Oh, Juno . . ." Lydia put her arms around Juno sympathetically. "Thugs on TV say 'get rid of so and so . . .' and they mean . . ."

Juno pulled away angrily. "Well, that's not what *I* meant!"

"I know. Of course you didn't."

"Ohhh . . ." Juno folded her arms in front of her and leaned into them. "What about Gus? Does he know?"

"Yes . . . he's under some sort of hospital arrest."

"Surely they can't take Seth seriously . . . I mean, walking in and hearing something out of context."

"Well . . . apparently he has other evidence." Lydia shook her head. "Oh, Juno . . . what a mess!"

Juno looked up. "Yeah . . . it certainly is."

"The press will go crazy. I can see the headlines—'Night Life Owner Orders Murder . . .' "

"Sure," Juno said defensively. "The publicity will be terrible for the club. That's all that matters to you, isn't it?"

"Of course not, Juno. Don't be ridiculous! But we can't ignore the fact that the press will have a field day with this." Lydia sighed. "Oh, if only you'd never gotten involved with Gus in the first place . . ."

"Well, it was your idea, if you remember . . . 'Live for today, let tomorrow take care of itself.' "

Lydia lit a cigarette. "That was Sardinia . . . it was supposed to be a fling. Not some sort of torrid, tawdry romance that . . ."

"*Tawdry?* Is that what you think? You know how it's been between Gus and me. How could you say something like that?"

"It's what the *papers* will say," Lydia pointed out acidly. Her temper was beginning to get the better of her compassion. "Here I've built the club to be the epitome of taste . . . of éclat . . . and . . ." Lydia snapped her fingers. "Just like that it's gone."

"*You've* built the club? What about me? I designed it . . . I'm the one who's here running it every day."

"Yes . . . oh God, this is much worse than that cocaine scandal at Studio 54." She crushed her cigarette into the ashtray and lit another.

Juno stared at Lydia. "You don't care about what I'm going through."

"Of course I care. But we can't just bury our heads in the sand. We've got to be realistic."

"Well, what do you want me to do about it? Deny I have anything to do with the club? Sell you my share?"

Lydia paused. "Seriously, Juno, it's probably not a bad idea. You know that I know you had nothing to do with this . . . but until this dies down . . . I suppose it would help . . . disassociating yourself . . ."

Tears filled Juno's eyes, but she looked away so Lydia could not see them. She swallowed and got hold of herself. "Okay, do whatever you want. Have papers drawn up. I'll sign them."

Lydia's lips were trembling. She reached out. "Juno, I . . ."

There was a sharp knock on the door. Lydia and Juno looked at each other. "Come in," Lydia called out huskily.

The door opened. Two uniformed policemen came in.

"Which one of you is Juno Johnson?" the taller, younger one asked.

Juno turned pale. "I'm Juno Johnson."

"Miss Johnson, I'm afraid you're under arrest."

Alex flew back to New York as soon as he heard the news. He telephoned Lydia from Kennedy Airport.

"Oh, Lydia . . . thank God you're home. I tried to reach you before I left L.A. And I can't get through to Juno. What's happening?"

Lydia's voice was hoarse, as though she had been crying. "It's all so terrible I can't believe it. I got her out on bail. She's home. She pulled out her phone . . . reporters keep calling. Oh, Alex . . . she's in really bad shape . . . and really big trouble. They've indicted her as an accomplice to murder. You know, aiding and abetting. There's going to be a preliminary hearing and then they decide whether she goes on trial with Gus."

"Oh shit." Alex felt a gnawing pain in his gut. He knew it well—fear and anxiety. He flashed back to the hotel room in Oaxaca, and Sally Avery.

"It's just awful! And on top of it all we've had a big fight. She's barely speaking to me."

"Why?"

"Oh, about the club. All this publicity is going to ruin it. It seems that the loan Juno got from the bank was really from Gus . . . he put up the money for her share of Night Life . . . which means it was Nina's money. Isn't that awful?" Lydia paused to light a cigarette. "Anyway, Juno offered to sell me her share of the club, and I said yes. God, Alex, I wasn't trying to hurt her. I'm just trying to save the club. After everything cools down, of course I'll sell her back her share. She's not going to lose anything . . ."

"*If* she's not in jail," Alex said. "Well . . . it's between the two of you. I'm not getting in the middle of it. But I want to see her."

"She should be home. She's trying to avoid everybody. I mean, the reporters are practically camped out around there. She walks the dog, and that's about it."

Larushka pawed at the leash which hung from a hook on the door, and whined.

Juno sighed. "All right, Larushka . . . I've got to take you out sometime." She picked up the leash and put it in her pocket.

Larushka leaped with joy. "Heel, Larushka!" Juno said, and the dog fell into step at her side. "Good girl."

They rode the elevator to the basement and went out the service entrance. Once or twice she had been able to dodge the reporters this way, but today there was a camera crew waiting at the curb in a station wagon.

"There she is!" one of them said.

Juno set off up the street at a fast pace. "Come on, Larushka . . . heel!"

"Hey, Juno . . . Miss Johnson! Wait up. Millicent Hartman, 'Eyewitness News' . . . could we have a word with you please?"

Juno did not turn around. She began walking faster. The reporter and her crew hurried after her. Juno broke into a run. Larushka let out a delighted yelp and tore away up the sidewalk.

"Larushka! Come back . . . heel!" But the sound of a garbage truck clattering around the corner drowned out her voice. Larushka darted off the curb.

"Larushka!" Juno screamed.

Alex rang the buzzer in Juno's apartment building. He rang two longs and a short, the code Lydia had given him. There was no answer. He waited a moment and tried again. He was just turning to leave when a voice crackled over the intercom. It did not sound like Juno.

"It's Alex Sage," he said.

"Alex!" Juno buzzed him in.

She was waiting for him with the door open when he got off the elevator. She was pale and thin, and her eyes and nose were red. Her cheeks were wet with tears.

"Oh, Alex." Juno fell into his arms and he hugged her until she let go of him.

Alex made some tea and finally got Juno calmed down.

"I think it's a sign," she said. "If I went to jail what would've happened to Larushka? Now I don't have to worry about it." Her voice broke again.

Alex put his arm around her. "You're not going to jail." Juno cried softly into his shoulder.

"Tell me about Gus. How is he?" Alex asked.

Juno wiped her eyes. "Yesterday I went up to see him in the hospital. He looks awful. It's not just the poison, he really looks lost."

"But what do you think? Was it suicide, or what?"

Juno shook her head. "I really don't know. And my lawyer doesn't want me to go up there anymore . . . it fans the publicity," she said. "Gus was in kind of a daze. He didn't want to talk. But I *know* he didn't kill her. I think he loved her more than . . ." A shudder shook her body and she began crying again.

Alex held her. "I'm sorry," Juno said. "It just comes over me . . . this sort of overwhelming awfulness. You can't imagine what it's like."

Alex rocked her and let her cry. "Yes I can. I know what it's like. I've lived with it for ten years."

Juno raised her head, wet-eyed, and looked at him curiously. "What do you mean?"

He told her about Sally Avery's death on that terrible night in Oaxaca, and the guilt he had carried around with him ever since. He still saw girls in crowds who reminded him of Sally. He still got chills when people talked about Mexico.

Juno sat and listened quietly. When he had finished she hugged him. "Thank you, Alex. I don't know why when you're miserable it helps to hear about someone else's bad times . . . but it does. But Alex, don't blame yourself . . . there's *nothing* you could've done."

"Maybe not. I just don't know anymore. I've been around on it for so many years . . . I've never said a word about it to anybody. It really helps to have told you. I don't think I could've told anybody else."

For the first time that afternoon, Juno smiled. "I'll help you if you'll help me," she said. "The lame leading the blind."

Chapter Thirty-five

At a preliminary hearing the case against Juno was dismissed for lack of evidence. But Gus was indicted for murder.

Lydia sent a note to Juno, telling her how happy she was that Juno would not have to stand trial, and asking her to come back to Night Life. Juno, still hurt and bitter about the way her old friend had reacted to the scandal, tore the note into small pieces, dropped them in an envelope, and sent it back to Lydia.

Juno rode up the elevator of an apartment building on Sutton Place. The elevator came to a stop and the operator opened the door on the twelfth floor.

"It's to your right, miss."

She rang the buzzer and after a few moments Gus Pallenberg opened the door.

"Juno," he said. "Thank you for coming." He took her coat and hung it in the hall closet. "Can I get you a drink?"

"Yes, please . . . vodka with anything."

Gus returned from the bar with vodka gimlets for both of them. They sat with self-conscious formality in chairs on opposite sides of the coffee table.

"The apartment is Nicolo's New York pied-à-terre. He has been very kind to me. Some of my old friends have not been so loyal."

Juno forced a smile. "I know what you mean."

"But you have been wonderful, and I have done nothing but ruin your life."

"No, Gus . . ."

"Yes. But, thank God, now at least you are out of legal danger.

I could never have forgiven myself if you'd had to face a trial for something you had no part of."

"It's all right, Gus. But how are you holding up? Have they given you any idea of when the trial's going to start?"

Gus gave a slight shrug of his shoulders. "Sometime before Christmas, or so my lawyers assure me." His tone of voice indicated that he did not really care. "Juno, you've never asked me . . . I don't know what you think. But I want you to believe me. Everything happened just as I said in my deposition. I did not kill Nina." His voice broke. "I couldn't have."

"I know, Gus. I know."

Gus blinked rapidly and Juno fought back an impulse to go and comfort him.

For the next hour they talked quietly, as the sky outside turned to twilight and the room darkened. Gus turned on a light.

"Let me order some dinner," he said.

"No . . . thank you, Gus." Juno had all the answers she had come for. Any last doubt in her mind that Gus was innocent had been erased. But, just as clearly, she now saw that nothing would start again between her and Gus. It was over, and the finality was a relief.

At the door he kissed her cheek. "I'm sorry about all this."

"I'm okay, Gus. Let's concentrate on getting you through the trial. I know the jury will believe you."

Gus smiled sadly and stood at the door until the elevator arrived.

The Gustav Pallenberg murder trial opened in a spacious, sun-filled courtroom in the Westchester County Courthouse. In his opening statement, prosecutor Andrew Schwartz laid out a case against Gus Pallenberg that was circumstantial, but damning. He spoke for two and a half hours, painting a lurid picture of lust and infidelity and greed.

"In a murder case, ladies and gentlemen, you look for motive and opportunity . . . and motive and opportunity were present in abundance for Mr. Pallenberg. We're going to show you through exhibits and the testimony of witnesses that Gustav Pallenberg was enmeshed in an illicit affair with ˈnightclub

owner Juno Johnson, that he had lavished gifts and money on
Miss Johnson . . . but that money came from the vast fortune
of Nina Carruthers Pallenberg, and the well was threatening to
dry up. Mrs. Pallenberg had become concerned about her
younger husband's waning affection and had retained a private
detective to determine the cause. Gustav Pallenberg and his
nightclub mistress knew they had to act fast, or risk losing the
money they so desperately coveted to maintain their fast and
glamorous life-style.

"On the day of the murder—and make no mistake about it,
ladies and gentlemen, this was cold-blooded, calculated murder
—on that very afternoon Seth Pratt, Nina Pallenberg's son by
her first marriage, discovered the lovers locked in an embrace in
the office of Night Life, Miss Johnson's club. And Seth Pratt
will testify that he heard Juno Johnson direct her lover to 'get
rid of Nina.' And did Gus Pallenberg comply with her wishes?
When you have heard all the facts, and sifted all the evidence, I
don't think you will have any trouble deciding.

"What did Mr. Pallenberg do? He returned that evening to his
wife's magnificent estate on the Hudson. On arriving, did he go
directly to see her? No. You will hear testimony from the butler
and the dog handler that Mr. Pallenberg first went to his kennels . . . the same kennels where he kept a supply of strychnine for pest control. Strychnine, ladies and gentlemen—the fa-
tal poison that was found in lethal quantity in the body of the
murder victim, Nina Carruthers Pallenberg!

"Only after he had made this stop did Gustav Pallenberg return to the house, where his beautiful wife was waiting for him.
He went up to her room with his deadly package in his pocket
and greeted her with a smile and a kiss. He ordered champagne
and caviar from the kitchen, and then he dismissed the staff.
That's right . . . at Mr. Pallenberg's personal direction, all the
servants left the estate that evening.

"And then, Gustav Pallenberg mixed the strychnine in the
caviar he had ordered—white caviar—and fed his wife Nina the
deadly hors d'oeuvre, bite by bite, until it was finished. But
didn't he eat some himself? Yes, of course he did. But consider
this, ladies and gentlemen, because Gustav Pallenberg certainly
considered it: Nina Pallenberg was a tiny five-foot-two and

weighed only ninety-eight pounds. The defendant in this case, Gustav Pallenberg, is a strapping six-four who weighs nearly two hundred pounds. Any poison works in proportion to body mass. But just to be on the safe side, Gustav Pallenberg took an added precaution: he took Valium, a tranquilizer, to dilute the effects of the strychnine . . . for strychnine, as you will learn, attacks the central nervous system, and a tranquilizer makes an excellent antidote.

"And then, what did Mr. Pallenberg do? He cut the cord of the telephone in his wife's bedroom, so that when Nina began to feel the effects of the deadly poison she could not summon help. The defense will try to make you believe that this was a double-suicide attempt. When they do, remember that cut telephone cord. It is not the sort of circumstance that you would expect to find in a suicide.

"And finally, while she lay helpless and dying, he composed a suicide note, cynically declaring his undying love and affection for her. Undying, ladies and gentlemen . . . because Gustav Pallenberg had no intention of dying! He had everything to live for . . . a beautiful young mistress, and a hundred-million-dollar inheritance."

Until she was called to testify, Juno stayed away from the White Plains courthouse, on the advice of Gus's lawyer. But she followed the trial closely on the television news and in the papers. By the time Seth Pratt took the witness stand, the case against Gus seemed depressingly solid.

New York *Daily News,* January 10, 1985

SETH SPEAKS!

Seth Pratt, son of slain millionairess Nina Carruthers Pallenberg, testified today at the murder trial of his stepfather, Gustav Pallenberg. Pratt, a student at Brown University, described, in a voice choked with emotion, how he found his mother and stepfather slumped nude on the floor of her bedroom suite at the Pallenberg mansion on the Hudson.

He had come to the Tarrytown estate on the evening of July 12, 1984, Pratt testified, to warn his mother of a conversation he had overheard that afternoon between the defendant and his girl-friend, nightclub owner Juno Johnson. Miss Johnson, according to Pratt, had instructed Pallenberg to "get rid of Nina."

New York *Post*, January 11, 1985

STEPSON TELLS OF LOVE LOAN

In his second day of testimony at the murder trial of Gustav Pallenberg, Seth Pratt, son of late mega-heiress Nina Carruthers Pallenberg, told the jury of how he discovered a document that showed that his stepfather, Gus Pallenberg, had loaned his lover, beautiful Night Life cofounder Juno Johnson, half a million dollars. The document, a letter from a banker to Mr. Pallenberg, was introduced into evidence.

New York *Times*, January 12, 1985

PRATT ADMITS FORGERY, DRUG USE

Seth Pratt, son of the late heiress Nina Pallenberg, admitted today under withering defense cross-examination that he was a heavy user of cocaine and that on the night of his mother's death he had forged the signature of his stepfather, Gustav Pallenberg, the defendant in the Pallenberg murder case, on two checks totaling twelve thousand dollars. Mr. Pratt at first denied that the signatures on the checks submitted into evidence by defense attorney Edmund Carter were his, but when Mr. Carter offered to bring in handwriting experts, Mr. Pratt reversed his position.

Document Illegally Obtained

In a day of sensational testimony, Mr. Pratt further revealed that a key piece of prosecution evidence, a letter disclosing a loan by Mr. Pallenberg to nightclub owner Juno Johnson, was obtained when Mr. Pratt broke into a locked drawer in Mr. Pallenberg's desk. Speaking in a voice so subdued that he several times had to be instructed by the court to speak up, Mr. Pratt described how he had searched his mother's and stepfather's rooms for money to pay his drug supplier.

Inheritance At Issue

Mr. Pratt, who is the younger of the late Mrs. Pallenberg's two children by her marriage to tennis pro Rick Pratt, is one of the principal heirs to the Carruthers fortune. Under the terms of Mrs. Pallenberg's will the bulk of the estate, amounting to in excess of two hundred million dollars, is to be evenly divided between Mr. Pratt and Mr. Pallenberg, with the daughter, Camilla Pratt, from whom the late heiress had been estranged, receiving a bequest of one million dollars.

If, however, Mr. Pallenberg is convicted in this case, his share of the inheritance would almost certainly be challenged.

Moves For Dismissal

Following Mr. Pratt's electrifying testimony, Mr. Carter moved that the case against his client be dismissed. Judge Leo P. McCarthy rejected the motion.

Alex rented a car and drove Juno to White Plains the morning she had been called to testify.

"How're you feeling?" he asked.

"Terrible . . . scared to death. And I'm really worried about Gus. I'm so afraid I'm going to say the wrong thing . . ."

"Just tell the truth. Everything'll be okay."

"That's easy for you to say. Those lawyers are pros at twisting things around."

"Look, don't worry about Gus. The jury sure as hell won't believe Seth after what's come out about him. And that was the guts of the prosecution's case." As he pulled into a parking space at the courthouse, he turned and looked at Juno. "But what about after? If Gus gets off, are you going to . . . you know . . ."

"Marry him?" Juno shook her head. "No . . . it really was over a long time ago between me and Gus. Gus . . . Shep . . . and Lydia. I'm really hell on relationships, aren't I, Alex?"

Lydia and Juno were still not speaking. They both regretted what had happened, but each felt wronged by the other. And Alex, who cared enormously about both of them, did not want to choose sides. It had been a difficult period for him since he had been back from California. This year was the first time since they had been very young that the three of them were single and available and together. His time in California gave him a chance to think about how he felt about Juno and Lydia, whether he wanted both of them, or one of them. And if he could have only one of them, whom would he choose? And would she want him?

To avoid making any decisions, Alex had thrown himself back into work on his new play. He spent his days trying to solve his characters' problems, instead of his own and Juno's and Lydia's.

Juno was sworn in and took her seat in the witness stand. She glanced over at Gus. Their eyes met for a moment, and he shook his head sadly.

Prosecutor Schwartz sauntered over to the stand. "Miss Johnson, is it true that you and the defendant, Gustav Pallenberg, were involved in an illicit affair?"

Juno swallowed. "We had been seeing each other occasionally. But it was over."

"Seeing each other? Come on, Miss Johnson. Is it not true that you and Mr. Pallenberg met and began your relationship at the glamorous nightclub where you worked in Sardinia, a *full year* before the death of Nina Pallenberg?"

"Well . . . yes. But I told you, it was over." Juno bit the inside of her mouth nervously. Her whole body felt flushed and hot.

"Over? Was it over when you received a loan of half a million dollars from the defendant?"

"I didn't know . . ."

"Did you receive such a loan, Miss Johnson?"

"Yes, but . . ."

"And was that loan Mr. Pallenberg's money, or more specifically, Nina Pallenberg's money?"

"I thought it was a bank loan. I thought . . ."

"We're not interested in what you thought, Miss Johnson. Just answer the questions and give us the facts. Do you know whose money it was that financed your interest in Night Life, the nightclub you opened?"

"I didn't know then."

"But do you know now?"

"Yes."

"And was that money Mr. Pallenberg's?"

"Yes."

"Speak up please!"

"Yes."

"I see." Schwartz went over to the prosecution table and looked at some papers. "And you had no idea that Mr. Pallenberg was behind this loan?"

"No. I had no idea."

"But is it not true, Miss Johnson, that you were turned down for loans at every other bank you contacted?"

Juno nodded slowly. "Yes."

"Then don't you think it rather odd that the bank Mr. Pallenberg recommended to you, that *that* bank, the First Guaranty Savings Bank, would lend you half a million dollars . . . when everybody else had turned you down?"

"I don't know much about that kind of financing, Mr. Schwartz. I was too happy to get the loan to think much about it."

"Yes, I'm sure you were," Schwartz said sarcastically. "But in spite of this happiness, purchased with a loan of half a million dollars, you say it was *over* between you and Mr. Pallenberg?"

"Yes . . . it was over. And it was a *business* loan. From the bank, as far as I knew. I'd already begun paying it back."

"It didn't seem to be over on the afternoon of July twelfth, the day Nina Pallenberg died. You were seen embracing Mr. Pallenberg in the office of your club, Night Life. Do you deny this?"

"It wasn't . . ."

"Were you and Mr. Pallenberg in the office of Night Life, embracing?"

"Yes, but . . ."

"And on that occasion, Miss Johnson," Schwartz interrupted, "did you not say to Mr. Pallenberg . . . 'get rid of Nina.' Did you say this, Miss Johnson? Did you say 'get *rid of* Nina'?"

"Yes . . . but I meant . . ."

"No further questions."

Juno started to get up.

"Just a moment please, Miss Johnson," Judge McCarthy said. "Mr. Carter, do you wish to cross-examine?"

Carter looked up and shook his head. "No, your honor. No questions."

Before the prosecution rested its case, Edmund Carter in cross-examination had chipped away more of the wall of damning evidence against his client. The private detective Nina had hired admitted that before the day of his wife's death, Gustav Pallenberg had not seen Juno Johnson for several months. His account with Nina, it developed, had been a long-standing one. He had been hired in 1981, and it was not until the summer of 1983 that he had discovered an infidelity to report.

Alan Merrifield, the banker who had handled Gus's loan to Juno, testified that, under Mr. Pallenberg's instructions, Miss Johnson was given to understand that the loan was from the bank, not Mr. Pallenberg. Merrifield also verified, with canceled checks, that Miss Johnson had begun repaying the loan before Mrs. Pallenberg's death.

Hennings, the butler on the Pallenberg estate, testified under cross-examination that it was common practice for Mr. Pallenberg to visit the kennels first upon arrival home, before going up to the house. He also told the court that Mrs. Pallenberg had become increasingly reclusive, her behavior more erratic. She had not thrown one of her famous balls in over two years. The last one, Hennings said, had been planned and then canceled, for seemingly no reason, on the day of the event. Hennings had had to direct a staff of temporary help to make hundreds of phone calls, extending Mr. Pallenberg's apologies. And in the months before her death it was not unusual for Mrs. Pallenberg to spend most of her time in her room, either sleeping or rearranging her drawers and closets. Gustav Pallenberg often took his meals alone in the evenings while Mrs. Pallenberg slept.

And a startling piece of evidence came out during the cross-examination of Jack Stephenson, the dog handler. It was very unusual, he told Carter, for Mrs. Pallenberg to visit the kennels. But she had made such a visit on the day she died.

The prosecution rested, and Edmund Carter took the floor to present the case for the defense. In spite of the inroads he had made during cross-examination, the case against his client was still strong: the strychnine was from Gus's kennel supplies; Gus had ordered the champagne and caviar, dismissed the servants, written the suicide note, and taken Valium which had alleviated the effects of the poison; and, of course, there was the severed telephone cord.

The first witness called by Carter was a surprise, a name that had not entered into any of the pretrial speculation.

"Call Sharon Cluny Woods," the clerk said.

Sharon Woods was an attractive middle-aged Newport social-ite with strawberry hair, bright, clear eyes, and an animated, expressive face. She and Nina Pallenberg had been roommates at Foxcroft and had remained friends ever since. She told the court of Dr. Gundhardt's clinic in Switzerland, and his sup-posed wonder drug Sirusol RX23. Sharon Woods had gone to the clinic once at Nina's urging. She had found herself dramati-cally younger-looking and more energetic after that visit, but as the months went by and the effects wore off she began to be scared of Sirusol RX23; she looked older and had less energy than before she went. Mrs. Woods testified that she had urged Nina to stop going to the clinic, and that she knew Gus Pal-lenberg had also tried to discourage his wife's visits.

"Your honor," Schwartz interrupted impatiently, "I must ob-ject. This beauty parlor digression has nothing to do with the murder case we're trying here."

"I ask the court to bear with me," Edmund Carter said. "This testimony relates directly to Mrs. Pallenberg's state of mind on the night of her suicide."

"All right," Judge McCarthy said. "Mr. Schwartz, I think we can listen to a little more of this. Objection overruled. Proceed, Mr. Carter."

"So, Mrs. Woods . . . both you and Mr. Pallenberg tried to dissuade Nina Pallenberg from continuing this treatment?"

"Yes. But Nina refused to listen to us. She insisted on going back. At first it was something like a year between visits, but eventually it got down to months. Poor thing, she was hooked on it . . . I mean, Nina couldn't stand the thought of getting old. But I noticed . . ." Sharon Woods trailed off uncertainly.

"Noticed what, Mrs. Woods? Please," Edmund Carter urged gently.

"Well . . . Nina used to be so vibrant, so effervescent. She was always up for a party, always ready to take off on a holiday at a moment's notice. Oh, she was a bit shy with people she didn't know well, but . . . oh, in the last two years, all that changed. Almost her whole personality changed. She stopped seeing people. Even me! I had to call her if I wanted to talk to her. And she seemed . . . so nervous. Sometimes she stuttered when she talked. Her moods really shifted. Some days I'd talk to her she would cry, some days she'd laugh . . . but whatever it was, it was always extreme. I'm sure it was that clinic! Nina wasn't a pill taker, except vitamins and the stuff they gave her there. But we were all worried about her. She wasn't well . . . something had happened to her . . ."

A medical expert, Dr. Orrin Scott, was Carter's next witness. He confirmed Sharon Woods's misgivings about Sirusol RX23.

"It's been turned down flat by the FDA. It's a degenerative drug, with some short-term stimulant and skin-tightening effects, but . . . well, it's like twisting a rubber band. When you let it go, it snaps back with a lot of bounce, but each time it gets a bit more slack. And eventually, it breaks."

Other witnesses, including Camy Pratt, testified to the deterioration of Nina Pallenberg's health and personality. The final witness for the defense was Gustav Pallenberg. His bearing was dignified and composed as he crossed the floor and took the oath at the witness stand.

"Well, Mr. Pallenberg," Carter said. "You're really the only person who can tell this court what happened on the day and evening of July twelfth, nineteen eighty-four. Suppose you describe for us the events leading up to that tragic evening."

When he left the house at noon on that day, Gus said, Nina was still in her room asleep. He had driven into town to have lunch with the head of the contracting firm he employed. Afterward, on impulse, he had gone to Juno's office.

"Why did you go there, Mr. Pallenberg?"

"I hadn't seen her for a couple of months. She didn't want to see me. She knew I could never give Nina up . . . and I guess I knew it, too. But it had been difficult . . . Nina had been getting worse. Juno took me away from all that. I needed the relief that she could give me. But Juno wasn't the kind of woman to keep up a relationship like that. She told me again that she didn't want to see me anymore . . ."

"Unless you were to 'get rid of Nina,' in the phrase we've heard bandied around so often in this trial," Carter said. "What did you take that to mean?"

Gus shrugged. "A divorce. I had promised her that I would talk to Nina about it. But I wasn't being honest with her . . . or myself." In a hushed voice he added, almost to himself, "I couldn't live without Nina."

Gus went on to describe his return to Leighdale, and the events of the evening that followed. Carter made no attempt to interrupt or lead him. The courtroom listened in fascinated silence as Gus, his testimony growing more emotional and rambling, told about Nina's transformation that evening. He digressed into recollections of their meeting and their life together before her discovery of Dr. Gundhardt.

"Your honor," Schwartz objected, "can't we please get the witness back onto the topic?"

"Mr. Pallenberg," Edmund Carter said, "was the caviar already there when you returned from your suite to Mrs. Pallenberg's, after you had bathed and changed?"

"Yes . . . it was white caviar, you know." He smiled and rubbed his chin. "We had it on our first anniversary. And Nina didn't look a day older that evening. When she was well she was the most beautiful, the most extraordinary woman in the world . . . that damned Gundhardt!" His voice broke. Struggling against tears, he told how they had eaten the caviar and drunk the champagne, how he had taken Valium when he began to feel himself shaking, and how Nina had finally revealed to him the truth of what was happening.

"At first I was terrified. I wanted to call for help, for both of us, but Nina had cut the telephone cord. And she was in convulsion . . . I couldn't leave her . . . I had to hold her tongue down. And then as I held Nina I began to realize that she was right. Death was the only way we could get back to what we had been. Except I didn't die." He shook his head, as if in amazement. "And here I am, fighting for my life again, without even the time to properly mourn Nina. It's funny, isn't it . . . in a way . . ."

After the closing statements Judge McCarthy delivered his charge to the jury, and the seven women and five men retired to consider their verdict.

Chapter Thirty-six

"Okay, I've rented a car for tomorrow. We'll get up there early to wait for the verdict."

"Thanks, Alex. I really appreciate it," Juno said into the phone.

"I'm tied up for dinner, but do you want me to come by later?"

"No . . . thank you, but . . . I think tonight I want to get to bed early. I guess I just feel like being alone."

"You sure? I could come up there and not talk. Just sort of be there if you needed me."

"I need you all the time, Alex." Juno laughed to make it sound like a light remark. "But, really, tonight I just want to be by myself."

"All right. Pick you up around eight. We can get some breakfast in White Plains."

Juno ate a container of yogurt and watched the TV news. A verdict was expected tomorrow in the Pallenberg murder case, according to Jim Ryan on Channel 4. She clicked off the set.

Tomorrow. One way or another it would all be over. This limbo had been going on for so long, it was hard to believe that it was finally ending. But as bad as it had been for her, it must have been a hundred times worse for Gus.

She had thought a lot about what she was going to do next. One thing she was sure of—she was finished with Night Life. The prosecution and the press had made her sound so sleazy . . . "Nightclub owner Juno Johnson." She had never been a nightclub sort of person in the first place.

She had gotten into Night Life because of Lydia. It had

seemed like such fun to do something with her closest friend. And now, look what had happened. They were not even speaking to each other anymore.

Juno realized now that it was her fault as much as Lydia's. It was her stupidity that had put Night Life into the scandal; there was a lot of money at stake and Lydia was protecting Juno's investment as well as her own. Lydia had not been as loyal as she would have liked, but to be fair it was Juno's obsessiveness that had caused the friction between her and Lydia in the first place.

One thing was certain. No matter what she did next with her life, she was never going to use work as a substitute for facing her own problems, and the problems in her relationships with other people. Ambition was never going to dominate her life again. It just was not worth it.

The most intimate private dining room at Night Life was the Roof Garden. In the winter it was glassed in with jasmine vines covering the walls, huge pots of gardenias and orchids, and hanging baskets of bougainvillea. Outside on the terrace, evergreens were strung with tiny white lights.

Lydia lit the candles in the wall sconces herself and fussed for the dozenth time with the two place settings on the table. There was a knock on the door.

"Alex." Lydia kissed him.

"Sorry I'm late."

"I'm glad you're here." She poured two glasses of wine and handed him one. "Remember this?"

Alex tasted it. "Château Mordoi Bourgueil . . . is it the forty-seven?"

Lydia grinned. "Alex, you never cease to amaze me." She stood up on tiptoe and kissed him. Alex returned the kiss warmly. But Lydia thought she detected something; his mind was not entirely there with her.

"Come on . . . sit down," she said. "I've ordered veal piccata. Shall I ring for dinner?"

Over dinner they talked about the trial. "Carter made a good case, but you can never tell with juries. It could go either way."

"Poor Juno. Oh, I feel so terrible the way things have worked out. Can you do anything, Alex? I don't want us to keep on like this."

"She doesn't either. Just be patient with her, Lydia. She's been through a hell of a lot."

"Do you think she'll come back here?"

Alex shook his head. "I just don't know."

"I don't know either. The club was both of us. I don't want it without Juno. You know, Gianni Corelli's madly interested if we ever want to sell." She fingered the stem of her wineglass and looked up at Alex almost shyly. "And I've got other things pulling at me, too. I guess that's why I wanted to see you tonight."

"What is it, Lydia?"

"Oh . . . this script of Bernard's . . . you know, *Borrowed Time*. He still wants me to do it. He's pressing me for an answer . . . he wants to start shooting in March, on the Coast."

"It's a terrific script."

"Yes, but there are considerations. I don't know if I can still act. I mean, frankly I'm terrified at the thought of getting in front of the camera. And then . . ." She searched Alex's eyes. ". . . Bernard wants to marry me."

"And what about you?"

"Well," she said softly, "what about you?"

Alex leaned back in his chair. "You know, all my life I've tried to avoid making decisions. I married Tory because she asked me. Back at Yale I managed to avoid falling in love pretty successfully for three years. Then I fell in love with two girls at the same time. Most guys in that kind of a situation have to choose, but I've put it off for fifteen years . . ."

"And now . . . have you chosen?"

He nodded. "I still love them both just as much, but . . ."

"But . . . you and Juno need each other. You belong together. That's it, isn't it?"

"Yes."

"Does she know?"

"We haven't talked about it."

Lydia broke into a smile. "I've always hated making decisions, too. I used to spend a lot of time thinking about this. I love the two of you so much, but I mean, really, a sixty-year-old ménage

à trois . . . it would never work. I used to wonder how I'd feel
if you ever chose Juno over me . . ."

Alex took her hand. "I'm sorry."

She shook her head. "I'm not . . . not at all. It's wonderful
. . . after all this time to finally have it settled. You two *do* belong together, you always did. Just like Bernard and me." Lydia
ran her finger along the rim of her wineglass, producing a low
humming sound. "I have a confession to make, Alex."

"What?"

"I had ulterior motives in inviting you here tonight. I *am* in
love with Bernard. I guess I've been in love with him almost as
long as I've been in love with you." She looked up at him and
smiled. "God, these modern relationships are so difficult to sort
out. Being in love with you was such an important part of me
for so long. But with Bernard back in my life, I had to find out
once and for all . . . And now it all seems so right all of a
sudden. This evening could have been a disaster. Instead, we've
laid a lot of ghosts to rest. Oh, Alex . . ." She flung her arms
around him exuberantly. "I can't tell you how happy I am . . .
for *all* of us."

Lydia kissed Alex on the lips, and then went over to the intercom. "Dominick, send up a bottle of our best champagne. Everybody's getting married!"

Judge McCarthy gaveled the packed courtroom to order. The
jury filed in. Gus Pallenberg sat with his head bowed and his
hands folded at the defense table.

"Ladies and gentlemen of the jury, have you reached a verdict?"

"We have, your honor."

"Will the defendant please rise?"

Gus stood slowly and stared ahead of him. In the gallery Juno
squeezed Alex's arm.

"How do you find the defendant? Guilty or not guilty?"

The foreman cleared his throat. "We find the defendant not
guilty."

In an antechamber off the courtroom, Juno said good-bye to
Gus. They had very little to say, aside from wishing each other

well. They hugged briefly, then Juno left. She had a picture in her mind of Gus wandering alone through the enormous mansion he had spent his professional life designing for Nina.

Alex was waiting for her outside. He put his arm around her and guided her through the sea of reporters.

"Wait! Miss Johnson . . . do you and Mr. Pallenberg have any plans now that he's been acquitted?"

"How do you feel? Can you tell us?"

"Are you and Gus getting married?"

Juno paused. Microphones surrounded her face. "No. I am very happy for Mr. Pallenberg. But we have no plans."

At that moment Gus came out of the courthouse. The reporters left Juno and raced up the steps.

"Fickle bastards, aren't they?" Juno said with a weak smile.

Alex squeezed her shoulder as they started down the steps. "You could've told them you had plans to marry someone else."

Juno looked at him. "I suppose so. But it's over now. What's the point in coming up with a cover story?"

"I just thought . . . maybe you'd want to marry me."

Juno broke into a perplexed grin. "Alex?"

He pulled her close and kissed her. "Juno, I love you . . . it's about time we did something about it, isn't it?"

Tears filled her eyes. "I guess it is." She kissed him again. "I've been in love with you for such a long time."

They drove back into town, making plans. They needed a larger apartment, one with working space for each of them. They would start on a baby as soon as possible. Juno was going to design the set of Alex's new play. They would get married in Santa Fe. Juno was so busy making lists that she did not notice where they were going until Alex pulled the car up in front of the twin town houses on East Sixty-second Street. When he turned off the motor she looked up.

"Oh no . . . why did you bring me here?"

"Because Lydia wants to see you. And because you want to see her."

As Juno walked through Night Life everyone greeted her warmly.

Dominick Charpentier came out of his office. "Hey, lady!" He hugged her. "It looks good to see you here again." He stepped back and looked at her. "You all right?"

Juno smiled broadly. "I'm better than I've ever been. Where's the boss?"

"She's right here. That other lady's upstairs."

Juno kissed his cheek. "Thanks, Dominick."

They walked upstairs. As she made the familiar journey that now seemed so strange to her, Juno reached out and took Alex's hand. "I'm so nervous."

When they got to the door, she hesitated. "Does Lydia know about us?"

Alex nodded. "I think she knew before I did."

The door swung open. Lydia stood there. She looked from Juno to Alex, and then back to Juno. Her eyes glistened, and her face was tight with strain. "Oh God, Juno, I've missed you so much. Please forgive me!" She opened her arms to Juno.

Juno fell into them. "Lydia . . . I'm sorry, too."

After Alex and Juno left Lydia they headed across town to Juno's apartment. As they drove through the park the sun came out, shining on the icicles that hung from the heavy stone arches across the road, and even brightening the soot-stained snow.

Juno was glowing. "God, I can't believe it! Yesterday I was ready to stick my head in the oven. Today I'm happier than I've ever been in my life."

Alex reached his arm out and pulled her over to him. She nestled contentedly against his shoulder. "Why didn't we think of this fifteen years ago?"

"I must admit, I thought of it once or twice. But you weren't ready." She smiled ironically. "Come to think of it, I wasn't, either."

Alex nodded thoughtfully. "For such a long time I was hung up on the idea of being in love with you and Lydia. God, that day the two of you walked into the audition at Branford. You . . . tall and dark-eyed and exotic. Lydia . . . small and intense, with that husky voice. And both of you so beautiful. It was a double whammy." He laughed. "I can still feel the jolt when I think about it. I never thought either of you could fall in love with me, but when both of you did, I was ecstatic . . . I didn't want to mess with the perfection of it." He turned the car up Central Park West and stopped for a light. "But it was murder, too. All that tension in Paris . . . living together, but afraid to really go all the way with it. That's why I ran off with Lorraine Gilbert. It was something I could handle. I didn't have to be afraid of it. Then when I came back to Paris, and you were gone . . . well, that was a terrible mistake. But it's taken all these years for me to realize that the mistake wasn't choosing . . . it was choosing the wrong one."

"Oh, Alex." She kissed the hollow beneath his ear. "We all did a lot of running off in those days. A lot of mistakes. I don't think we ever had any idea of how complicated love was."

Alex grinned. "And now it turns out the secret is it's really simple. I wonder if it was all along?"

"I hope not. That would make us look pretty foolish, wouldn't it?"

"Well, us Yalies like to do things the hard way."

Juno laughed. "Does being this happy make you hungry? I feel like I haven't eaten in months."

"You haven't." He double-parked in front of Juno's building. "You go on in. I'll zip over to Zabar's and get something."

Juno showered and then spent some time straightening up her apartment, which she had let go during the trial. What she ate and how she lived had seemed frivolous indulgences while Gus was on trial. Her life was in disorder, with no focus and no future; what was the point of imposing order on her surroundings? Now she hummed as she opened the shades and dusted and changed the sheets on the bed.

After a while she realized that Alex had been gone for even longer than crowds at Zabar's ought to take. She began to worry that he had been in an accident. She would not let herself think that it had all been a mistake and he had changed his mind.

And then she heard the elevator open, and she ran to the door. There was Alex. In his right hand was a Zabar's shopping bag. Under his left arm was a gift-wrapped box, and he was holding an enormous bouquet of flowers.

He kissed her. "One thing led to another. I hope I didn't take too long."

"Just long enough for me to be worried sick. I was beginning to think you'd gotten cold feet."

"Cold feet, warm heart." He came in and set his bundles down on the sofa. "Here," he said, handing her the flowers. "I wanted to do things right. To make up for all the time when I wasn't doing things right. So, first . . . flowers."

"Oh, Alex." She kissed him. "They're beautiful."

"Next . . ." He handed her the gold-wrapped box.

"Chocolates?" She giggled. "You are ridiculous. This must be a fifteen-pound box."

"To fatten you up."

She began pulling things out of the Zabar's bag. "By the time we finish all this I'll be fat as a blimp. Hmmm . . . spring salami, pâté, Moroccan olives, baguettes . . . oh my God, beluga . . . and champagne. I'll go get some plates."

"Wait." He caught her hand. "There's something else. Come over here and sit down."

"What is it?" Juno asked as she sat on the sofa. His face looked so serious.

"Well, I said I wanted to do things right. Proposing to you on the steps of the Westchester County Courthouse wasn't exactly what I'd planned. So . . ." He reached in his pocket and pulled out a small black velvet case.

Juno opened it. Inside was a square-cut emerald ring. "Oh, Alex . . . it's beautiful." She burst into tears.

Alex held her. "I love you so much, Juno. Will you marry me?"

The few rays of sun that found their way into Juno's apartment at twilight fell across the bed where they lay, embracing. Juno kissed Alex's nose and his lips and his chin and each cheek. "Well?" she asked.

"Very well, thank you."

"No . . . you know what I mean."

He brushed a strand of hair out of her face. "It was perfect. No phantom presences."

"No yearning for anyone else to make it complete?"

"It *was* complete. How about you?"

"I don't know." Her eyes twinkled mischievously. "I'd kind of like to try adding Robert Redford . . ."

"Over my dead body." Alex laughed and rolled on top of her.

Lydia stood by the arrivals gate and watched the passengers emerging from American Airlines flight 209 from Los Angeles. Then she saw him, tanned and bearded, with a garment bag slung over the shoulder of his familiar leather jacket.

"Darling!" she called out.

Bernard kissed her. "So after all these weeks you have finally made up your mind," he said. "You are not going to change it again, are you?"

"Never. Oh Bernard, I'm so happy. I love you."

"I have not been able to think of anything else since you called last night."

She took his hand. "I've told the children. They're ecstatic. They want little brothers and sisters right away."

Bernard smiled. "Not right away. You have to do the film first. But we can practice."

"I haven't seen you in almost a month. I *need* a little practice." She stroked his cheek, teasingly. "Have you been practicing? There're a lot of beautiful women in Hollywood. . . ."

"When you arrive, there will be only one."

"You didn't answer my question."

Bernard kissed the palm of her hand. "There *is* only one," he said tenderly.

Late that evening Juno and Lydia, flanked by Alex and Bernard, made a sweeping entrance down the ramp to the main dance floor of Night Life. Old friends applauded, and champagne was on the house.

Camy Pratt was in the Mirror Bar. She jumped up and ran over to kiss Juno. "I'm so glad," she said. "I knew Gus was innocent. Thank God it's over, for all of us." Camy gave a quick ironic smile, and hugged Alex. "Aren't I a gracious loser?" she whispered in his ear.

In the early hours of the morning the four of them found themselves in the Mirror Bar again. Alex and Bernard sat at the

piano and improvised some jazz. Juno and Lydia draped themselves against the piano, smiling at each other and listening.

There was something brilliant in the air that night, something
that made colors brighter and words more musical, and the music strike more deeply. These were things that they would all
remember years later, when other memories had evaporated.
They had been through bitterness and jealousy, but they had
survived.

Gianni Corelli negotiated to buy 80 percent of Night Life,
with the stipulation that Juno and Lydia continue to be visibly
identified with the club.

Alex and Juno were flying to Santa Fe to get married, then
rushing back to New York to begin production on Alex's play,
which was set to open on Broadway in late spring. Lydia and
Bernard were going to stop at the wedding en route to California, where Lydia would be starring in Bernard's movie. They
were planning a spectacular wedding at Night Life later in the
summer, after the shooting on *Borrowed Time* was finished.

On only their second day of apartment hunting, Alex and
Juno lucked into a co-op in a magnificent old building on River-
side Drive. They moved in the contents of both their apart-
ments and agonized over what to do with it all.

"I don't know, Alex," Juno said, examining an oversized, rag-
gedly upholstered chair. "Where'd you get this monstrosity anyway?"

"On the street. It may be ugly, but it's comfortable. I won't
part with it."

Juno kissed him. "Okay . . . then it goes in your office." The
buzzer rang. "Oh, that'll be the living room rug. Macy's said
they were delivering this morning."

It was not Macy's, but Lydia who arrived at the door. She had
on jeans and her copper hair frizzed around her shoulders. Instead of a rug, she was carrying a large flat package in her arms.

"They made me come up on the service elevator with this."
She set it down in front of them. "For the two of you. The
official wedding present."

A look of delight broke over Juno's face. "I don't believe it.
The portrait!"

Alex carried the package down the steps into the sunken living room. They leaned it carefully against the wall, and with much ceremony removed the brown paper in which it was wrapped.

"*Et voilà,*" Alex said, stepping back.

There they were, Juno, Alex, and Lydia, as Juno's father had painted them fifteen years before. Seated on a sofa, against a background of Navajo rugs, arms around each other. In their eyes Hollis had captured a youthful anticipation and bravado.

"God, we look so cocky," Lydia said.

"We *were* cocky," Alex smiled.

"We still are," said Juno, hugging Lydia. "Oh, thank you!"

"Happy wedding!" Lydia kissed them both. "To my two best, dearest, and oldest friends."

"Oh gosh," Juno sniffed, "I think I'm going to cry."

Alex put his arms around them, and they looked back at the portrait. "This'll make a wonderful story to tell our children."

"Oh, mine love it," Lydia said.

Juno gasped in horror. "They don't really know, do they?"

"Of course not. I'm waiting till they come of age."

Juno laughed and gazed around the room. "Where shall we hang it?"

"It could go there over the sofa," Alex suggested.

"Or in the study . . ."

Lydia grinned suddenly. "There's really only one place . . ."

Juno looked at Alex. "Of course!"

"Where else," Alex agreed. "Over the bed."

"I hope you're getting a big one," Lydia said, taking each of their hands in hers. "You never know when the occasional houseguest might drop in."

Juno smiled. "You never know."

"Just for old times' sake," Alex said.

Lydia nodded. "And *only* occasionally."

Little Sins